I've travelled the world twice over,
Met the famous: saints and sinners,
Poets and artists, kings and queens,
Old stars and hopeful beginners,
I've been where no-one's been before,
Learned secrets from writers and cooks
All with one library ticket
To the wonderful world of books.

© JANICE JAMES.

# REQUIEM FOR A PATRIOT

January 1840. In Monmouth Court House, the leaders of the Chartist Rebellion stand accused of High Treason: Zephaniah Williams, William Jones — and John Frost, leader of the South Wales Chartists. It is through Frost's words that the author tells the story of the Rebellion and what became of its heroes. A portrait of a great humanitarian whose beliefs in right and justice lead him to the degradation of transportation, and whose principles of non-violence are betrayed by the force of the very men he is leading.

# ALEXANDER CORDELL

◆

# REQUIEM FOR A PATRIOT

*Complete and Unabridged*

ULVERSCROFT *Leicester*

First published in Great Britain in 1988 by
George Weidenfeld and Nicolson Limited
London


First Large Print Edition
published March 1991
by arrangement with
George Weidenfeld and Nicolson Limited
London

British Library CIP Data

Cordell, Alexander *1914 –*
   Requiem for a patriot. – Large print ed. –
Ulverscroft large print series: general fiction
I. Title
823.914 [F]


ISBN 0–7089–2388–7

Published by
F. A. Thorpe (Publishing) Ltd.
Anstey, Leicestershire
Set by Words & Graphics Ltd.
Anstey, Leicestershire
Printed and bound in Great Britain by
T. J. Press (Padstow) Ltd., Padstow, Cornwall

For Robert Edwards of
Coedpoeth

# Acknowledgements

I am indebted for help in research, as usual, to many librarians; they have proved an unending source of information; also to Mr Richard Frame and Dr David Osborn M.D. both of Newport, Gwent, and to Mrs H. B. Strong of Central Library (Research), Newport, Gwent; Mr M. E. Ling of S. Glamorgan HQ Central Library (Research), and Mr J. Graham Jones, Assistant Archivist of the Department of Manuscripts and Records, National Library of Wales. To all these, my thanks.

To my old friend Gordon, Lord Parry, I am indebted both for his encouragement during the writing of this work and his practical help in providing 'on site' documents concerning the history of Port Arthur, Tasmania, following his recent visit to the old convict colony.

The research of historians — too many to name here — has proved of assistance to me; none more that the chronology of events of the late Professor David Williams of Aberystwyth, whose lectures of Chartism (in the old Museum in Dock Street, Newport) I was privileged to hear. I am further grateful for extracts from *The Extraordinary Black Book of Wade*;also to Mrs Jacquilene Stewart of Perth, Australia, and her friends, for documentation from the State Library Service of Western Australia.

Finally, my gratitude to my wife and all my friends, who provided the discussion and debate necessary for me to write this evocation of men and women long passed into the mists of time.

To John Frost Esq., Mayor of Newport, ever beside me during this past year of writing, I offer my respect.

# The Chartist Rebellion

British historians have consistently relegated the chartist Rebellion into minor importance, presumably in service to an anxious Establishment eager to allay public apprehension. Ask the average student what he knows about Chartism and the answer will be lacking. Indeed, the role of most contemporary historians (save D. J. V. Jones — *The Last Rising*) has been that of 'follow my leader' ever since one early eminent among them stated that the attack upon Newport was little more than a march of a few malcontents who didn't know where they were going and what they were going to do when they got there. In contrast, lesser public disturbances have been elevated in historical importance.

For example, the Merthyr Riots of 1831, while but a curtain-raiser to the drama of nationwide Chartism, have been promoted to the stature of a Rising: of this event I have written extensively, and know that its significance was the hanging of its leader the innocent Dic Penderyn, and the raising of the Red Flag for the first time in Britain: it was never more than a local disturbance.

Rarely is history provided with such clear documentary proof of Chartist intentions as on that tragic day of November 1839. Zephaniah Williams, John Frost's lieutenant, has left behind signed documentary proof of an insurrection — 'to occupy Newport as a preliminary to an attempt to remove the Queen from the throne and form a republican government'. According to trial prosecution witnesses, Frost himself, while on the march, stated the same. Finally, the death sentence of Lord Justice Tindal upon the accused leaders was positive:

It has been proved that you combined to take possession of the town and supersede the lawful authority of the Queen, as a preliminary step to a more general insurrection throughout the kingdom.

It is no part of the historian's role to make judgement based upon supposition, and this is what has happened in Chartism's case. While it may not be in the public interest to learn how narrowly Britain came to losing a queen and getting a republic, it is inexcusable — even as an attempt to discourage future revolutionaries — to dilute historical facts.

And so, whatever one's opinion of armed insurrection by the people to gain their ends, let it today be accepted that the statue about to be erected in Westgate Square, Newport, is dedicated not to a discontented rabble, but to forbears who were prepared to die for the Utopia in which they believed. Out of their sacrifice came the Six Points People's Charter, five of which we enjoy today ... despite the denial of one of these same laws by successive Governments — they who insist that we, the governed, should keep the laws they violate. The abandonment of Equal Electoral districts, in itself, and the subsequent 'rigging' of electoral boundaries, is perverting the success of democracy in our country.

Alexander Cordell
*Rhosddu, Wales*
*March 1988*

# Van Dieman's Land

## (The Convict Colony)

The name of Macquarie Harbour is associated exclusively with remembrance of inexpressible depravity, degredation and woe. Sacred to the genius of torture, Nature concurred with the objects of its separation from the rest of the worlds, to exhibit some notion of a perfect misery. There, man lost the aspect and the heart of a man . . . This region is lashed with tempests: the sky is cloudy and the rain falls more frequently than elsewhere. In its chill and humid climate, animal life is preserved with difficulty: half the goats die in one season, and sheep perish: vegetation, except in its coarsest and most massive forms is stunted and precarious . . . The passage to this dreary dwelling place is tedious, and often dangerous. The prisoners, confined in a narrow space, were tossed for weeks on an agitated sea. As they approached they beheld a narrow opening choked with a bar of sand and crossed with peril. This they called 'Hell's Gates' — not less appropriate to the place that to the character and torment of its inhabitants: beyond, they saw impenetrable forests, skirted with an impervious thicket; and beyond still, enormous mountains covered with snow, which rose to the clouds like walls of adamant: every object wore the air of rigour, ferocity and sadness.

Rev. John West
*History of Tasmania, 1852*

# Requiem For A Patriot

Ye see me only in my chains,
ye see me only in my grave.
But behind each forehead, in
each heart, is not my place
reserved for me? Am I not
mankind's ardent breath that
endless thirsts for liberty?
So, I will rise again, before
the people stride. Deliverer,
judge, I wait to take the streets;
upon your heads, upon your necks,
upon your regal crowns I'll stamp.
For this is history's iron law;
conceit it is not, threats are
none. The day grows hot, how
cool your shade, O willow leaves
of Babylon . . .

Ferdinand Freiligrath
1810–1876

# THE
# TRIAL
# OF
# JOHN FROST
# FOR
# HIGH TREASON

*Under a special commission*

*held at*

# MONMOUTH

*In December 1839, and*

*January 1840*

# The Verdict

SPECIAL ASSIZE, MONMOUTH
THE COURT HOUSE.
*Thursday, 16 January 1840*

The prisoners, *John Frost, Zephaniah Williams* and *William Jones* were placed at the bar.

*The trial of John Frost, Zephaniah Williams and William Jones.*

The sentence by Lord Chief Justice Tindal. He saying;

"John Frost, Zephaniah Williams, William Jones, after the most anxious and careful investigation of your respective cases, before juries of great intelligence and almost un-exampled patience, you stand at the bar of this court to receive the last sentence of the law for the commission of a crime, which, beyond all others, is the most pernicious in example, and the most injurious in its consequences, to the peace and happiness of human society — the crime of High Treason against your Sovereign. You can have no just ground of complaint that your several cases have not met with the most full consideration, both from the jury and from the court. But as the jury have, in each of these cases, pronounced you guilty of the crime for which you have been charged, I should be wanting in justice to them if I did not openly declare, that the verdicts which they have found meet with the entire concurrence of my learned brethren and myself . . .

"It has been proved in your case, that you combined together to lead from the hills, at the dead hour of night, into the town of Newport many thousands of men, armed, in many instances, with weapons of a dangerous description, in order that they might take possession of the town, and supersede the lawful authority of the Queen, as a preliminary step to a more general insurrection throughout the kingdom.

"It is owing to the interposition of

Providence alone that your wicked designs were frustrated. Your followers arrive by daylight, and, after firing upon the civil power, and upon the Queen's troops, are, by the firmness of the magistrates, and the cool and determined bravery of a small number of soldiers, defeated and dispersed. What would have been the fate of the peaceful inhabitants of that town, if success had attended your rebellious designs, it is impossible to say. The invasion of a foreign foe would, in all probability, have been less destructive to property and life. It is for the crime of High Treason, committed under these circumstances, that you are now called upon yourselves to answer; and by the penalty which you are about to suffer, you hold out a warning to all your fellow subjects, that the law of your country is strong enough to repress and punish all attempts to alter the established order of things by insurrection and armed force; and that those who are found guilty of such treasonable attempts must expiate their crime by an ignominious death.

"I therefore most earnestly exhort you to employ the little time that remains to you in preparing for the great change that awaits you, by sincere penitence and fervent prayer. For although we do not fail to forward to the proper quarter that recommendation which the jury have entrusted to us, we cannot hold out to you any hope of mercy this side of the grave.

"And now, nothing more remains than the duty imposed upon the court — to all of us a most painful duty — to declare the last sentence of the law, which is that you, John Frost, and you, Zephaniah Williams, and you, William Jones, be taken hence to the place from whence you came, and be thence drawn on a hurdle to the place of execution, and that there each of you be hanged by the neck until you be dead, and that afterwards the head of each of you shall be severed from his body, and the body of each, divided into four quarters, shall be disposed of as Her Majesty shall think fit, and may Almighty God have mercy upon your souls."

# Book One

Book One

# 1

Monmouth Gaol. Condemned cell.
Thursday 16 January, 1840

I COULD not sleep.
"You are awake, Frost?" asked
Zephaniah.
I said, sitting up, "How many more times
will you ask that? Of course I'm awake. The
prospect of being hanged does nothing to
induce sleep."

"You are also worried about your
stepson?"

"Scarcely, at a time like this."

Zephaniah said with sincerity, "Your
stepson, William Geach, is an astonishing
young man. Were he my own, I would be
worried."

"Astonishing," said William Jones from
his corner, "but a fool. If I had managed to
salt away twenty thousand, you wouldn't
find me hanging around to answer to
creditors. That's where the fool is, not
in the fraud."

Zephaniah added, "He'll get twenty years — a year's transportation for every thousand. You can insult their daughters and rape their wives, but touch a penny of their money and they'll burn you alive."

I said, "Why did he do it?"

Zephaniah grunted. "Some might suggest he did it for you."

"A reasonable assumption, Frost?" asked Jones.

There was a silence between us, broken only by the sounds of distant hammering and the grumbling of saws; the carpenters were erecting the scaffold.

Zephaniah said with a chuckle, "There's something wrong with this conversation. At a time when we are about to be gibbeted, we're discussing a solicitor who has run off with the funds, a situation that is happening twice a week in Monmouth."

Together, we listened to the carpenters, and William Jones said, "The whole thing is unethical. Had we won the day, and removed this bloodstained Victoria from the throne, this is one of the first things I'd have altered. No scaffolds to be erected until after the guilty verdict — this lot

10

have been at it since the start of the trial."

"It is the way the Establishment does things."

"More," added Jones, "only yesterday I learned that the butchers come from Pontypool, my home town."

"Insult to injury in more ways than one."

I said, "The butchery is an outrage upon the dead. It is typical of the Whigs and Tories. Initially, of course, the Anatomy Bill was intended to frighten the life out of our colonial savages, who preferred to be arraigned before their gods in one piece; finding it worked abroad, they extended the privilege to us."

Jones said, "You talk with levity."

I answered, "Personally, I care little what happens to my carcass after the soul has fled," and Zephaniah said:

"Do you think we could have more sleep and less philosophy?"

"Well said. By the sound of what's going on outside, we've got to be up in the morning."

I lay there in the light of the coming dawn;

the single window of the cell reflected prison bars on the whitewashed wall with terrifying perceptibility. There was no sound now but the distant hammering and the steady breathing of the others.

The prospect of death did not terrify me; it frightened me into cold sweats of anticipation, but not the extremity of fear. So much had happened; catastrophe had followed calamity with such monotonous precision in the past weeks, that little more could happen to us. And the denouement to the tragedy, confronted as I was with it on the very day my guilt of High Treason was pronounced — my stepson's attempts to obtain false credit — had proved the final catalyst. God knows, I thought, what the effect on Mary would be. And God knows, also, what the effect of the Anatomy Bill would have upon her and the family . . . upon my sons, John and Henry and upon the girls, too — Elizabeth, Sarah, Catherine, Ellen and Anne, aged thirteen, a most impressionable age.

I tried to pray, but could not.

Lying there I began to analyse the talk between Zephaniah and William Jones, who, at the best of times, though coherent in oratory, was unusually flamboyant: now his speech, like Zephaniah's, through some diverse psychology, was couched in the same legal grammar and tonality that graced the defending counsel in court. I smiled as I lay there, and wondered why I was smiling.

Monmouth Gaol. Condemned cell.
Thursday 30 January, 1840.

Just before being apprehended, I read with disgust a pamphlet smuggled out of the women's prison in Cascades, Van Dieman's Land. "This," I told my companions, "was a statement by a prominent magistrate in England that, when ordering a child to be whipped, he took care that when a gaol sentence was also involved, the corporal punishment should occur at the end of the prison term; thus the child would be able to 'look forward to it in a torment of expectancy'."

"Great people, our magistrates," observed William Jones, and Zephaniah said:

"The theorem is being practised upon us, is it not? The erection of the scaffold

13

before the trial even began, is Melbourne's private message that he intends to murder the three of us. When, by the way, is Victoria's marriage?"

"Our gracious Queen and Albert? February the tenth."

"About ten days from now, eh? Is it the Whigs' ambition to lay three bloody heads on the pillow between Vicky and her lover?"

"It's a point," I said reflectively.

"Really?" Zephaniah sat up. "When have they ever been sickened by the sight of blood — on the gallows or on the hunting field — the political parties or the monarchy?"

Jones said, "But now the country is in a ferment about us, and heads are dangerous things to bowl around."

"Melbourne is the true enemy . . . "

I added, "And Lord John Russell. His squeaky voice has ever been my enemy. Anything that stands before him and his perverted interests are anathema — remember Dic Penderyn?"

Jones asked, "What the hell's an anathema?"

"Dic Penderyn?" echoed Zephaniah.

14

"Innocent? He was hanged because he was a Welshman. But don't range yourself alongside innocence, Frost. Or are you telling me that you marched down Stow Hill with pistols looking for ducks?"

It raised me. "Did you not also enter a plea of Not Guilty?"

"That's because I tried to save my neck, or would you prefer to lay your head on a platter for a Whig Salome? Let us plead what we like in public, mun, but let's have the truth of us in private. We're as guilty as bloody hell, all three of us, and you know it."

"Perhaps, but it will do us no good to become auntie confessionals at this late stage. The public fight for us because they believe us innocent. Lay a finger on a fencing post belonging to their precious Victoria, and they would bay for blood."

William Jones said placidly, "It is a state of education of the masses that will take another century," and Zephaniah grunted.

"Longer. In the year two thousand the fools will still be at it."

Nerves were becoming frayed, and a knock at the door put an end to the discussion; moments later Sir Frederick Pollock, one of my defending counsel, entered the cell preceded by the gaoler.

This, the son of a saddler and one of the most learned advocates of the day, had been retained by our Chartist friends; a year later, with the return of a Tory government, he became Attorney-General, and let this be recorded: none of us had complaint in respect of our defence, nor of the judges who condemned us. In retrospect, even when faced with the horror of such a death, I did not blame the judicial system in my country. Only in the selection of the jury did I take exception, and this was largely influenced by representation from London. Indeed, my lasting memory of the trial is the efforts of Lord Chief Justice Tindal to save us.

With Sir Frederick Pollock came William Foster Geach — one of my wife's two children by an earlier marriage; from where sprang his legal brilliance I shall never know — this, the Newport solicitor to whom the best brains of the legal profession had turned in defence of his stepfather, now deeply in trouble on his own account.

Sir Frederick said, "Again, my condolences upon the verdict. The jury ran in the face of the Lord Chief Justice's summing up — clearly he was working for an acquittal . . . "

Jones interjected, "And this is what you've come to tell us?"

William, my stepson, released me from his arms, and Sir Frederick answered, "The importance of the judge's remarks cannot be emphasized too much. The embarrassment he has caused to the Crown prosecution is far reaching," and William my stepson, added:

"The Attorney-General himself has criticized Lord Tindal, but the fact remains. Any jury but the one we were landed with would have acquitted all of you in the face of such advice," and Zephaniah said:

"Then we are to die because of a crooked jury? It would be better had you come to tell us not what might have been, but what is," and he rose in growing anger. "Does this not come of employing bankrupt solicitors? For, if I recall correctly, you yourself were in

17

charge of the jury selection!" And my stepson lowered his face.

Sir Frederick snapped, "Mr Geach was in charge of nothing — I employed him to help your cause, and this he has done!"

"Help?" cried Jones. "Christ, we're sentenced to death!" He thumped the table with his fist. "Lord Granville Somerset? Octavius Morgan, the son of Sir Charles of Tredegar — Frost's enemy? His grandson, the Honourable William Rodney — Sam Homfray, Bailey of Nantyglo and Ben Hall of Llanover — all three bloody ironmasters? God, had the Devil cast his net he'd have had a haul! What a hearing these would give to a favourable summing-up!"

Sir Frederick said softly, "Shouting and threats of violence will do nothing to assist you — this is why you are in your present position, all three of you," and he waved down Jones's further shouting. "Mr Geach here has worked long and arduously to save you. He has travelled the length and breadth of the country to raise Chartist support, it was he who arranged for Feargus O'Connor to visit you . . . "

Zephaniah Williams interjected, "That was a death sentence in itself — don't talk to me of O'Connor!"

Untouched, Sir Frederick said, "Palmerston and Macaulay are speaking for you. I myself am about to see the Prime Minister; Mr Geach here has petitioned the Queen."

"She'll make a bloody good ally, the bitch," said Jones, and Sir Frederick sighed, saying:

"This has been our greatest difficulty — allies and witnesses; even Daniel O'Connell has refused to speak for Chartism, saying that he had no available evidence."

"It isn't unusual," said I. "Who are the traitors? The victims in the dock or the witnesses in the ale houses?"

"We must go," said Pollock quietly.

"My mother sends her love to you, Father," said William Geach. "To you, Mr Jones and Mr Williams, she sends her respects, and will give her prayers."

"We can do with all the praying we can get," announced Jones. "From what I can see of it we're already on the scaffold."

"That's graveyard talk, and we can do without it!" I said.

"Aren't we already dead?"

"The time is up, gentlemen," said the gaoler; with his lanthorn and ring of jangling keys, he had the person of an Irish leprechaun.

Before he left the cell, William handed me a letter: opening it, I read:

My dear Stepfather,

Friends have deserted us, allies have been discovered. O'Connell is a great disappointment: he who often boasted he could raise half a million United Irishmen, has condemned you as traitors. Sam Etheridge, your printer friend, originally committed for High Treason, has been released on the reduced charge of conspiracy: there has been an attempt to implicate the preacher of Hope Chapel; it failed, and it will raise your spirits to know that ever he prays publicly for your liberation and the downfall of your enemies.

I have taken the liberty of transferring all your remaining property to my mother, lest this letter should find you unfairly condemned; which, you will recall, is a procedure which we earlier agreed, though it pains me much to do it.

Believe me when I say that I will labour ceaselessly in all your interests, and remain,

Ever your faithful stepson,
William Foster Geach

It saddened me to hear this of O'Connell, one who held my esteem and admiration: doubtless, this attitude was a direct result of the eternal animosity between the labouring Welsh and Irish; an unhappy divide between fellow Celts I had always striven to bridge. As early as 1798, at the time of the Irish Rebellion under Father John Murphy, Welsh regiments under English officers had suppressed Irish peasantry and joined with German Hessians in committing outrages against defenceless Irish populations: from those days, and earlier, to today when Irish escaping from the famines would work until they dropped for a sack of potatoes to undercut the wages of the artisan Welsh, this acrimony boiled and simmered.

It was a bitter situation that O'Connell should prove so ineffective in our hour of need . . . he who could have done so much to save us.

I was further saddened by the situation in which my young stepson found himself. His appearance was now sinewy and haggard; the worry of his recent bankruptcy, his trial for embezzlement and conviction on exactly the same day as my own, had reduced him from the confident young advocate of scintillating oratory, to a broken man: yet, despite his own tribulations, not once had he deserted my cause. Soon, like me, he would pay for his guilt; even while I climbed the steps to the scaffold, he would be removed to the hulks and the fate of Van Dieman's Land.

The fortunes of the family of Frost were at a low ebb, to say the least of it.

# 2

AFTER the visit of the lawyer and my solicitor stepson, we continued to languish in a torture of expectancy: sometimes, even in the long hours of the sleepless nights, we would awake to argue vociferously of where our tactics and policies went wrong — these hastened away the waiting; then, with the coming of each careless dawn, the first red fingers searching through the bars, we would awake from the shuddering, sweating drowse which some call sleep: awake to renewed hammering on the scaffold: in quieter moments, between the crowing of distant cocks, came the unmistakable sharpening of the knives.

"Well," announced Zephaniah, sitting up, "I wish them a fine edge to the steel. Having been a publican all my life, they are going to find my liver irresistible."

"Tell him to shut his mouth," said Jones from his blanket.

I rose, gripped the cell bars and looked

out on to the wet drizzle of a morning: the peak of distant Pen-y-fal, I thought with my mind's eye, would be shrouded in mist now; the roaming Usk, wandering in the valley with all the mystical symmetry of her years, would soon be garlanded with winter ice.

Strangely, Zephaniah's humour, in all its brave obscenity, did little to annoy me; in some obscure way it dulled the incessant turning of my stomach, which, as if no longer a portion of my being, was already being searched by the knife. The effect of this was to turn my bowels to water: I spent more time on the bucket in a corner of the cell than off it. The purge was enervating, and I was sweating badly.

Jones said suddenly, "Rumour has it that if you don't bribe the hangman, he doesn't hang you dead, but calls in the butchers before life is extinct."

"Carry on like that and you'll expire from a heart attack," said Zephaniah. "Next you'll be applying to be drawn, too, but fortunately for us, Judge Jeffreys is deceased."

I said, still staring up at the window, "Stay in date, Jones, and stay calm, too. The big thing here is to keep our dignity."

"It could happen," said Jones in a whisper.

"It could not happen. The surgeon is called in to pronounce one dead and nothing more is done until he signs the death certificate," but he persisted, and I remember thinking that if he carried on like this he would crack and infect the three of us. Chartism was disgraced enough without the gaolers having to carry us, shrieking, to the scaffold. Now, biting at his hands, Jones said, in gasps:

"One of the last of the Jacobean rebels to be drawn was of the Tredegar family . . . "

"For which they ought to be inordinately proud," interjected Zephaniah. "Had I known this, I'd have paid his relatives more respect."

"They behaved well at the Bloody Assizes," I added. "Would that we can follow their example," and Jones cried:

"Even while he was being drawn, he cried, 'God bless the Duke of Monmouth!'"

"That's where he made another mistake," said Zephaniah. "One pig in exchange for another. He must have been an appalling idiot."

At that moment — it was two days before our execution was due — the cell door grated open and the keeper of the gaol entered with the turnkey. This, a wizened shrew of a man in faded blue uniform, stood before us with a paper shaking in his fingers, and announced, reading:

"By order of the Home Secretary, the law having sentenced you to death by hanging and quartering, I am to ask you to instruct me as to the disposal of the portions of your bodies."

"Oh, God," whispered Jones, and sat down, weeping.

I asked, steadying my voice, "Better we thought you had come to reprieve us. Is this not the third time you have asked us for this disposal?"

It was always my belief, and still is today, that this harassment about the disposal of our bodies was an attempt by the Government to induce us to suicide. Further, we had the means: while knives and forks had been withdrawn from our eating trays, we had been allowed to retain our belts; at least, Jones and Zephaniah had been so allowed, but I didn't possess one. The turnkey said, jangling his keys:

"Show respect to the keeper, gentlemen. He wishes to know your answers."

"If he gives some replies himself," said I, and to the keeper said, "Come, sir, be kindly. Is it true that a petition is being raised to save us?"

"It is true," said he.

"Where?"

"In Merthyr and Blackwood, Abercarn and Risca; many are signing."

"Does Macaulay still speak for us?" asked Jones.

"Not now. Only yesterday in the *Vindicator* he said that your intention being to knock democracy on the head, the same should be done to you."

"Well done," said Zephaniah. "I always trusted that sod. And Disraeli?"

"The Jew says that you are being treated with the utmost severity." And Zephaniah replied:

"The man has imagination, doubtless. Well, keeper, dispose of our steaks mainly as you wish, this is the answer I send to the High Sheriff and the Lord Lieutenant of the Country. One leg I should like nailed over the door of Lord John Russell's office; the other on the entrance to the Prime

Minister's country seat. My head you can set on a spike in Parliament Square to delight the Whigs and Tories, and my two arms, suitably crossed, laid on the counterpane between Albert and his Queen." He went to the door. "Now go to hell, we've had enough of you."

I envied Zephaniah his brash courage in the face of the obscenity, and despised the whining of William Jones; one moment the romantic revolutionary who was fleshing swords to the hilt on the road to Malpas, but never arrived at Westgate Square; cocking his snoots at watching onlookers and now lying face down on the straw in tears.

As for myself: beneath the outward calmness which I fought to portray, I was very frightened.

The keeper of the gaol came again, with another paper in his hand.

"Gentlemen," said he, "the Home Secretary desires the prisoners to know that the Queen has been graciously pleased to respite sentence of death for a further week; but . . . " And at this he paused and smiled around the cell . . . "that after the expiration of that period, sentence of death will certainly follow."

Zephaniah stood like a rock. Jones burst into tears.

The knives turned again within me.

If this continued, I thought, it would be death by torture.

What we did not know was that the Queen had already reprieved us, and had remitted the death sentence to one of life imprisonment by transportation to Van Dieman's Land.

Presumably it was Lord John Russell, my old enemy, getting his pound of flesh, and afterwards Zephaniah said bitterly: "It is a pity, I think, that all three of us should suffer so much for the revenge of one bloody Shylock."

But others, thank God, abounded in the cause of justice, and one of these was the Lord Chief Justice Tindal, who had tried to save us at the trial.

Not less than two wagon loads of petitions had been sent to London; torchlight meetings were being held up and down the country; public disorder was again threatened, and the Government feared another armed Chartist outbreak — even an attempt to attack Monmouth Gaol and release us. All this we learned later; at the time we knew nothing of such agitation.

The cell door opened and my stepson entered again, followed by Mr Fitzroy Kelly, our senior counsel. My stepson ran into my arms, and I held him. Mr Kelly said:

"Gentlemen, it is my pleasure and relief to inform you that Her Majesty has been graciously pleased . . . "

I do not recall anything more; William was still in my arms, I remember.

"Mother sends her love . . . and the children . . . "

"Thank you."

*"Lags away!"*

It was a familiar cry, one we had heard countless times while in the gaol: it betokened the departure of the prison van taking men to other prisons, or worse, down to the Chepstow quayside for the little steamer that acted as a courier between Chepstow and the prison hulks lying off Portsmouth.

Earlier, at dead of night — somebody said it was two o'clock in the morning — there had been much hammering of footsteps and a jangling of keys: the gaolers had veritably broken in, roused us forcibly from our straw and hauled us out, bare-footed, into the prison yard.

There, while we dressed, we had been handcuffed and chained together: now there were eight of us, for Charles Walters, John Lovell, Richard Benfield, John Rees and Jenkin Morgan were hurried along, too; pushed and squeezed into a waiting prison van where five brawny constables sat, their batons drawn, ready to quell the smallest defiance. And the van, pulled by two stout horses, rumbled off along the Monmouth cobbles; a troop of Lancers with a pennant flying at their head, clattered their fine stallions alongside.

Soon we were on the open road leading to Chepstow, and I saw through the single barred window of the van the blue hills of Gwent shining in the rain. For it lashed us; it was a deluge of water, a tub-washing I shall always remember.

"All we want now is a ducking stool," said Zephaniah.

"It do come too late, mister," observed John Rees. "I reckon if we'd ducked a few, permanent like, afore we took on this daft old caper to conquer the country, we'd not be in this pickle now."

This was the father of Rees the Fifer, who had played his fife to us all the way from Blackwood, to help the march.

"Ach balls!" exclaimed John Lovell.

This was Lovell the Hercules; a man of great height and width, with bright fair hair hanging to his shoulders once, but now shaved bald against the lice of gaol: a brother to the Lovell who led the attack on the Westgate, and I heard his voice again amid the smoke and blood of that day, for he died in screams, writhing on the corner of Skinner Street.

"Listen, you," said Lovell, and leaned out to face old Rees, "Time was, if we'd listened to the likes of Mr Frost and marched earlier, we'd now be top dogs o'the country."

"Jesus, listen to it!"

"Aye, listen, Old Rees, or I'll take ye a couple when these rings are off me, old as ye are — I lost me brither in this lot, remember, and he were a man!"

The constable beside me grunted and slapped his baton against his palm, his eyes on Lovell. I said:

"Let it be, Lovell — you, too, Rees."

"Sorry, Mr Frost."

So we sat in the silence of men alive, but dead; bumping and swaying in the darkness of the van; listening to the clip-clopping of the horses and the ring of the iron-shod wheels. And when the dawn came raging over the hills, I saw through the barred window of the door a sun-flash upon water, and this was the River Wye.

Out of the van now, still chained together, we tramped in a chinking orchestra along the grass of the riverbank, with the towers of Chepstow castle lowering behind us.

How long would it be, I recall thinking, before I would see again this paradise of Gwent?

The rain lashed us; it bucketed, it fell in slanting stair-rods of pain that stung our faces, streamed down our bodies and overflowed out of our boots. And there grew within me a sickness. I had not eaten for two days, being unable to stomach the swill of the gaolers, and the unending diarrhoea, brought on by anticipation of the knives, had so weakened me that I had to lean upon Lovell. In this fashion, clinging to my companion, I reached the dock wharf where the steamer *Usk* was moored.

The Lancers arrived; one dismounted.

"The old Charter song's a bit out of date now, eh, Frost?" And the captain leaned above me as they set me down on the deck; he was young and extraordinarily handsome, his face bronzed with health and his white teeth shining.

I said, "But they will still sing it, sir."

"In a minor key, I'd say!"

"Perhaps, and if not for this burned-out generation, then for the next. Then you'll have a bigger haul to handle."

"My God, you accursed revolutionaries never learn, do you?"

"When you are older, you will understand why, captain."

The others joined me then — Zephaniah, Jones, Lovell and the other four; in soaked misery they squatted about me while the rain teemed down. The captain waved a hand. A trooper dismounted and clanked forward.

"Fetch a tarpaulin sheet and cover

Mr Frost before he dies on us," and the trooper replied with marvellous relish:

"If he dies, sir, he'll not be shouting that old Charter song over in Botany Bay — will ye, Citizen Frosty?" And he turned away, to come back with a tarpaulin sheet; this he draped over me.

"Do it properly," said the captain.

The trooper did so, arranging the sheet with care.

"Now get back to your horse, I'll deal with you later."

The captain stared down at me with expressionless eyes. Not a muscle in his features betrayed his thoughts.

"*Bon voyage*, Mr Frost."

He saluted.

A child was standing on the wharf above me; the tide was low. I judged her age at thirteen, about the same age as Anne, my youngest girl — she who was sent by God to replace James, who died six months after birth.

I am not a great one for organized religion, but I believe in the Man; yet I have always maintained the practice of never to call upon Him in travail. When

I lost James, the infant son we buried up at St Woollos (close to where my Chartist comrades now share their mass grave) I nearly lost my beliefs: only my wife's entreaties brought me back to Hope Chapel.

The child watching me now was of a fine Celtic darkness, having raven black hair and an olive sheen of skin; her features most delicately poised, were as fragile as lotus petals.

The rain beat down, splashing off the tarpaulin that covered all but my head, running in streams over the solitary child. Clearly, she was a fisherman's daughter, or one of the gangs of homeless children that infested industry — anywhere of activity found them; activity meant food.

Coming closer to the wharf edge, she foraged in her rags and brought out a piece of bread; sweeping rain from her face, she began to eat this, and her hands were blue with cold. The thought came to me then, terrifyingly potent, that this could be a vision of my own child — a phantasm of what was yet to be ... no longer the privileged child of the successful draper, once the mayor of Newport, but the bedraggled, half-starved incarnation of all my sins. The analogy caught me up, and raised me to a sitting position, and such was my loss of composure that the child stopped eating, and fear replaced her interest. Turning, she fled.

"Are you all right, Mr Frost?" It was Lovell again, cradling me against him.

I nodded. "Yes, perfectly."

Doubtless it was the weakening fever of the starve; this, combined with the knowledge of my imminent departure from Wales, brought home to me with sickening force the situation of my family. With so many mouths to feed and William, my stepson, in the court of bankruptcy, Mary would be dependent upon the sparse income from the Royal Oak; neither could she depend for a farthing upon my uncle, William Foster, who later took to himself a second wife. Lovell was still bending over me in the rain; other people, some apparently in authority, were standing around me.

"You . . . you have a family, Lovell?" I asked.

"Aye, sir. A wife and two good boys. Mind, she's got to take on me brither

Jack's three an' all now he's gone — he were a widower, you know."

I said, vacantly, "For God's sake, man, how will she manage?"

"Christ knows, sir. It . . . it's the way it is, ain't it?"

A voice said, "Get him on his feet, he'd better come below."

# 3

UNCHAINED from the others, I spent three hours in the steamer's sick bay, a narrow bunk in the engine-room where the giant pistons hissed and squelched, during which time I was brought hot cocoa by a man who said he was the cook. Nevertheless, the rest revived me, and I managed to keep down food; once clear of the Severn estuary, the little craft faced tempestuous seas.

At midnight two of the constables travelling with us, hauled me out of the bunk and on to the deck again; Chartist prisoners and constables crouched under a tattered awning in soaked misery: the rain lashed us, the wind from the Bristol Channel tore into us, heightening into a gale as we rounded Land's End.

Zephaniah, his hair comically spiked with water, had a word for it, as usual. "If these past hours is the punishment for Chartism, I'd call the bargain square. Where are we off to, for God's sake?"

39

"Brighton, for the bracing air," said someone.

"Dartmouth first stop, I reckon."

A point here: at fifty-six years, I was the eldest ringleader, though Old Rees, the father of the Fifer, was nearer seventy. Zephaniah was in the full bloom of health and strength; no physical imposition, however hard, seemed to ruffle him. Of the other Chartists, recently joined with us, probably Lovell was the youngest, while poor little Jenkin Morgan, retching and spewing in the scuppers, looked doubtful if he would survive.

"What you say, constable?" I asked the nearest. "We'll run for shelter?"

"Falmouth, probably, till the storm abates." His strangely open countenance (considering the job he did) with its clear, blue eyes stared into mine. Wiping water from his face, he settled deeper under his tarpaulin: things were easier now, for the wind had changed and we were running before it on a boiling swell; deep down into sea-troughs one moment, then hollering high on the crests when the paddle-blades thrashed air.

40

I looked around their rain-washed faces; men whose souls had died within the scaffold hammering.

These were the idealists of a cause now lost for a hundred years; who had gambled their all on reform of iniquitous laws that bound them to penury and the threat of the workhouse. Some had already suffered the violence of a state established by pious religions and corrupt politics: Richard Benfield, when wringing out his shirt a moment back, had the scars of the cat-o'-nine-tails — laid on heavy, by the look of him — from his neck to his breech.

"And more downstairs, mind," said he, laughing. "Twenty apiece on the backs of me legs. 'Serve ye bloody right, an' all,' said my missus. 'What happens now we're on the Blacklist?'"

"What did you do?" asked Zephaniah from the other side of the funnel, for here it was warmer.

"Laid one on the overman."

"But that didn't land you here, come off it!"

They thumped the deck, momentarily raising their flagging spirits.

"Christ, no!" cried Benfield, joyously, "I was under a pulpit wi' a bloody parson when the grain-raiders come through Llanhilleth, so I took the choice wi' a pike up me rear. 'Out you come, my lovely,' says old Dorky Evan — and do you know, he anna even here now — 'what you doin' under there wi' a parson, Dick Benfield. I'll tell your missus, I will,' and he had me out on the end o' his pike."

"'What about the parson then?' I asked him, 'for you're powerful enough with me, ain't you?'

"'You leave this old parson to me, son, and I'll change him for a slaughtered porker when we get to the village,' and he winkled that old preacher out on all fours, chased him down the aisle and through the churchyard while he howled for a pig-sticking."

"And then?" I asked him, and his voice quietened in a lull of the wind; the steamer rolled and dipped and we clung to each other.

The sea raced hissing down the scuppers and the masts swung over a leaden sky. The rain teemed down again. Dick Benfield said:

"I come on this outing to Newport, didn't I? My Lodge told me — I'm Blackwood, you know — that we were going to change things, for they once took my woman's clothes off the bedrail for Church tithes, and I've fed bread and skilly to my kids too long — they got rickets ... "

"You were telling us," prompted Jones, and I saw the constables raise their faces with interest.

I interjected, "You're not on trial now, Benfield. They got you for High Treason and that's the end of it — speak freely."

"Aye well, to change things, like. So I was outside the *Coach and Horses*, wasn't I? And I heard you tell of the new charter for the people, like perish the privileged orders and death to the aristocracy. So I took down me old man's fowling-piece and stole pit-powder from the foreman down my level — I'm a collier's gobber, ye know — I packs the gob and I made dropped lead for balls-shot, and followed the mob right down to Cwrt-y-Bella, near the weighing machine."

"And then?" mumbled a constable.

"Some said we was only taking a turn as far as Newport, but there ain't much sense in that, said the lads. So, near the weight machine I asked Mr Frost — remember, I asked you, didn't I? — what we was doing in the rain and where was we going — remember?"

I did not remember, but indicated that I did.

"And you shouted back to us — there was five of us, and old John Rees was one of 'em — remember John? You called for Hodge, the agent's man, Mr Frost. And he came, and you said to him, 'You here, Hodge? I'd have thought you'd be in the Feathers.' And Hodge said back, 'This is madness, Mr Frost. In God's name what are you intending to do?' And you said to him, 'All the soldiers in Newport are Chartists — in any case, over half of them are in Pontypool. So, we're going to take Newport town, blow down the bridge to stop the mail to Birmingham. And this will be the signal for revolution in the whole of Britain.' Remember?"

"He remembers all right," said Zephaniah.

"And that's why I come, see?" added Benfield. "It ain't no use shooting peanuts at this lot — this is what my missus says — she's a rare old terror when she

44

gets it up her apron — 'you put the bomb under Vicky Victoria, and I'll hop into bed wi' her Albert,' she says, 'there's more'n one way of killing a pig.'"

It had suddenly stopped raining; the wind was in a lull of conscience and a watery sun came out over a crested sea. One of the constables looked at the sky, and said:

"One thing's sure, they got the right lot, from what I heard now. But you'd be wise to keep your traps shut about it when you get to Australia."

I knew the pangs of conscience; Richard Benfield would be safe at home with his family, had it not been for me.

From Wales to Glasgow the Chartists were being rounded up; scores would go to transportation, hundreds to prison, to the treadmill and the whips.

I bowed my head.

The voyage from Chepstow to Portsmouth, normally a week's sailing, took more than a fortnight; such was the gale-ridden coast that we were often driven backwards before the wind; on one day we made more knots west than east, and we were forced into

Plymouth by the storm.

Here in port, lying exhausted upon the deck, we were visited by reformers bringing religious tracts; but who, when clear of the constables, gave news of efforts being made to obtain our release.

Merthyr Tydfil, apparently, where my son and Zephaniah's lad raised 27,000 signatures and formally petitioned the Queen, over 11,000 women signed for our release: even the Tolpuddle Martyrs, recently released from transportation, contacted the House of Lords without success. Poets wrote emotional prose in our defence, even one stupid play was performed which did more harm than good, for it turned our situation into false humour.

Soon, said a young missionary, someone was to move for a free pardon in the House of Commons, but this, through delaying tactics, led to postponement, and didn't take place until we were a fortnight south of the coast of England. In any case, the motion was defeated by ten to one.

Disappointing for me especially was that pseudo-Chartists, writing in our own newspaper, the *Charter*, were at pains to warn the movement that Physical Force Chartists deserved their fate; one such article having been written by the ever-moderate Francis Place. I could not help remembering Place's acquiescence in the face of Thelwall's revolutionary thunderings and the fire-eating verbiage of his friends like John Gale Jones, Horne Tooke and that emissary to the French Committee, Major Cartwright. But one thing was certain – the name of John Frost, he who sat at the back and said nothing during such fervent London debate, would now be whispered around the taverns with more than a little respect.

After a day or two the gales abated; again the ancient *Usk* raised steam and turned her prow to the east and the convict hulk lying at Portsmouth.

Truly, I doubted my ability to stay the course. All of us were ill with recurring diarrhoea and sickness, for the bread they tossed at us was mouldy, the fat they dipped it in rancid, and the water like bilge-rush. Is there anything more lowering than the growling pain of the guts and spewing sickness on a rolling, cascading sea? Or

RFAP5

anything more agonizing than to retch upon nothing, and strain on bowels that have long since turned to water?

The food we received on that voyage to Portsmouth was negligible. Later, from other prisoners, we learned that rations were often sold at Chepstow for the captain's profit; which guaranteed to bring servility to the most defiant prisoner.

Zephaniah thought it was unofficial government policy; I'm inclined to agree.

# 4

AFTER interminable rolling and pitching, when we expected every minute to be our last, the *Usk*, at quarter speed, battered and dishevelled, *chunk-chunked* into Portsmouth harbour; threaded a choppy path through countless men-o'-war lying at anchor, and came to moorings alongside a gloomy wooden wharf where lay the hulk of the ancient *York*, a battleship, once a glorious emblem of Britain's maritime empire, but now bereft of every shred of dignity.

In thanks for the riddling bow-shots, the thundering broadsides of her wooden walls, the old ship had been stripped of everything that had maintained her queenly vanity: carved balustrades and poop-deck ornament had been exchanged for the paraphernalia of the penitentiary — ring-bolts for chaining prisoners littered her decaying decks; balls and chains, neck-thrusts, spiked collars and branding irons replaced the swivelling brass. The great iron cannon that had blasted the French at Trafalgar and the Nile, had gone; the iron-studded porticos from which iron and fire once thundered had been closed to seal the escape of newer enemies — home-bred insurgents.

This, the *York*, filthy, rat-alive and vermin infested, was to be our home for the next week while awaiting the *Mandarin*, a sloop of 425 tons burthen which, as far as we heard, hadn't done the trip to Australia before.

"She do sound a bit flimsy to me," announced Jones, reading from a paper. "Six year old she is, built at Holton, and her captain's name is Muddle."

"That don't sound too good," said Lovell.

"So long as he knows the way," added Old John Rees. "But she do sound a little feathery — I heard talk that the old HMS *Tortoise* were a thousand tons, and the *Lady Raffles* comes nearer 60."

"How long do it take to Australia?"

"Four month — five — depends on the rust bucket."

"God alive and reigning, a four-month cruise, and at Her Majesty's expense!"

"You'll learn," interjected Zephaniah. "I heard talk that Jamey Muddle's a flogger."

"They'm all floggers. Or they weren't be there."

"Boozy old sea-dogs kicked out by the Navy on half-pension."

"What you think, Mr Frost?"

I didn't reply; I was hearing them in a wave of nausea and sickness; their repetitive argument based on expectation sharpened my growing animosity towards them. It was difficult enough to visualize the months of further seasickness without adding their futile assessments, and if the *Mandarin* and her master ran to form we could expect a voyage of terrifying discipline: these sea captains, products of the harsh discipline of our naval academies, didn't spare the rod when it came to punishment. Monarchs of their isolated kingdoms, hundreds of miles away from any restricting authority, they lashed and boxed and branded, often to death, their own Jolly Jacks who had offered their service to the Queen, or been kidnapped at the point of the gun.

Whigs and Tories cared little for a

sailor's life provided maritime profits to the Treasurer were maintained. Flogging around the Fleet was now a standard punishment for major crime; hanging a hundred feet up from a man-o'-war's yard-arm, death by ritual strangulation, was preferable to many for the sin of mutiny. Even Wellington, who once sentenced a man to a thousand lashes, was not to be compared with our Royal Naval sea captains in the name of sadism. In the roll of honour when it came to outrage upon the bodies of his sailors, including the ferocious keel-hauling, not even Nelson could be excluded.

So, what Captain James Muddle had in store for his coming guests, a couple of hundred convicts with no entitlement to pity, was yet to be experienced.

"What you say, Mr Frost?" They leaned above me, shaking me into reluctant awareness.

"Leave me. Go to sleep."

Shivering in the sleet-stinging February wind, I sat between Zephaniah and Lovell and we came alongside on the wallowing barge, pulled by naval ratings and guarded by six armed marines in scarlet and gold.

After futile attempts to climb the rope ladder dropped down to us from the deck twenty feet above, I fell in an untidy heap and took Lovell down with me. So a derrick sling was lowered with a net, and I was hauled unceremoniously upwards, as I later saw live pigs and cattle hauled to the deck for slaughter. Here was contrived a rotting log cabin into which filed the prisoners; I took my place with Lovell's arm about me.

"Right, manacles away!" cried a brutal-looking bosun, and he slapped his baton against his thigh with threatening intent.

The blacksmiths scurried about us, snapping off the handcuffs, waist-chains and leg-cuffs.

"Manacles away, B'sun!"

"Right you," bawled the Bosun. "Strip off!"

He strode among us as we took off our clothes. "Come on, come on, you lice-infested lags, this is a respectable establishment," and he emphasized his last words with blows across the shoulders of the nearest miscreants. "Hurry it, hurry it! I bet there's not a sow's son among you who's had a bath since the midwife. Come on, come on!"

Naked and dejected, shivering in the wind, we stood in an unglamorous line of angular, half-starved, pot-bellied scarecrows that some call manhood. Nearby a few half-clad '*jaunties*', trusted prisoners, were filling a large canvas bath with sea-water: steps led up to this, and standing astride it was a '*jaunty*' as big as Lovell; holding high a bass broom, he waved it jubilantly, shouting:

"In ye come, me lucky fellas! Up on the fo'c's'le wi' ye, me darlings and I'll scrub you cleaner than a bride before we marry you off to the Three Sisters . . ."

"What's he talking about?" Lovell whispered.

I knew, but I wasn't telling him; indeed, I heard, but scarcely contemplated it as a threat. Ice was lying between my brain and skull; I was shivering and my teeth uncontrollably chattering. I saw the bare buttocks of the man before me rise as I followed him up the steps to the bath. Surely, I reflected, the attempt was to kill as many of us as possible; certainly only the strongest could survive this attack upon the constitution. As for me, I was at my last gasp, and suffering the degradation of the older man naked among young ones. I recall grabbing the legs of the man before me on the top of the steps and fell into the bath with him, to wallow hopelessly in icy brine before being hauled out and laid on the now snow-flecked deck.

With Lovell openly supporting me, we were herded into the log cabin, given a coarse jacket and trousers, a felt hat and a pair of hobnailed boots. Then, kneeling outside in the snow we were shaved and cropped while blacksmiths double-ironed us with fetters at the wrists and ankles.

Boos and cheers from other lags greeted us as we were led below by armed marines.

"Welcome, me lucky lads!"

"Christ, look what's comin'!"

"Old Johnny Frost and his mob — come on, boys, give 'em a randy!" And cheers and groans died into cries as the bosun got among them with his baton.

I stood before my narrow bunk and stared down at the soiled palliasse shining with grease which was to be my bed; twenty-two inches wide and six feet long, while a man with a bloated face ran a tether wire though a link in my chains; this, running the length of the lower deck secured every prisoner; a slop bucket already brimming with urine and faeces was within inches of my pillow.

I knelt upon the straw mattress and lowered my face. Either side of me gaunt, emaciated men, long-termers or lifers, stared at me with cadaverous eyes.

Here was the essence of Man's inhumanity to Man: dimly lit lanthorns, hanging at intervals above the bunks, glinted on footpad and blackmailer, knifer and nark. Skeletal lags too old to die, were side by side with fresh-faced boys: official legislation decreed that men and lads should be kept apart, but not on the *York*.

Here were the pimps and procurers of the verminous courts and alleys from here to London; here the diseased and maimed shared court with innocence — the country's son who was going to transportation for the theft of a bag of turnips: here, in this very hold, not three years back, lay a young husband transported for the theft of a Bible. I looked about me at the scene, at humans who, after years in this hell-hole, had actually become putrescent.

It was a long journey, I thought, from this debasement to the comfort of Mary's kitchen; the ironed sheets of the bed she kept so white . . .

Later, while squatting with my mess-mates around an iron pot, fighting the sickness of a ravening hunger and spooning up a malodorous broth of barley and stale meat, I remembered again the starched white cloth of Mary's table; the gentle tinkling of cutlery as someone walked past, the serviettes . . . The only consolation was that John Lovell was put on one side of me and Zephaniah was within talking distance.

On my right was a stranger, a man of youthful vigour and a devil-may-care attitude. His almost beautiful Byronic features belied the male within, for he held disdain both for his surroundings and his gaolers, and was at no pains to conceal it. Talk had it that he was a titled man, one driven from court and had then taken to the road as a highwayman, but I didn't then have the proof of it. He spoke but once as I lay down upon my bunk in weariness,

"At your service, Mr Frost."

I turned to him. "I beg your pardon?"

"At your service, sir," he repeated.

Sleep took me then, coming out of a glaze of nausea and stink.

# 5

THE sun came up in elegiac beauty, rain-washed after the storm of the night; golden shafts shot down through the misted interior of the hulk upon the faces of sleeping men.

In the instant when I opened my eyes the lower deck exploded into the day's rhythm. A chorus of commands and shouts belaboured the foul air, with warders thumping down the footboards between the bunks and reviling and cursing everybody in sight. Men howled to descending batons, scrambling up in their jangling chains; competing with each other to stand rigidly to attention at the head of their bunks, still swaying from sleep. At entrance and exit stood two marines, their bayonets ready for the prod, eyes watching for the least hostility.

"They're just dying to shoot somebody," said Zephaniah.

"Ach, to hell, sir," whispered Lovell. "They're doin' their job, like us."

"Up decks, *up decks!*"

"Out and about, you bloody laggards!"

"Chains off!" bawled the bosun. "Mr Lawson, hurry along there, if you please! Up decks and about, for there's work on tap. Now come on, gentlemen, come on — liven the bastards up!" And the blue-coated warders scurried for his approval.

"I'll have him one day, that one," muttered Zephaniah.

"Shut up, you fool!"

A new strength, brought by sleep, had come into me, and I lurched forward to the exit, pulled by the communal wire, until it suddenly slackened and dropped. Those at the front cowered under the threatening batons of the warders; those at the back took the sticks across their shoulders in protesting cries, and the file bunched in sudden panic, protecting itself until the belabouring stopped. Never have I seen such unnecessary brutality.

Now the file moved on; slipping, sliding, we clambered up the narrow steps to the quarterdeck. Light and air struck me, the coldness taking my breath after the stinking heat of the bunks: here the sun slanted down in majestic fire, lighting up the tattered wreck that was once a ship, the wharf against which she was moored. Squat dockyard buildings, cluttered in the panorama below, lay against the bright green hills of Hampshire.

Once formed on deck we were numbered off, a roll of names being called: some two hundred prisoners were marched down the gangplank for work in the timber yards and stacking areas, each gang of thirty guarded by warders and armed marines: others remained on deck for the jobs of cooking, and cleaning the hulk, each small detail being in charge of a warder. We, the new intakes, were put on deck swabbing, and for a reason.

We were called into the log cabin in pairs; Lovell and Jenkin were followed by Zephaniah and Jones; I went in with the stranger in the next bunk to me, and we stood together before a table.

Here sat the hulk's commander, a tall, thin person with a sallow, aesthetic face and dressed in the faded, threadbare uniform of a naval mate. His grey, expressionless eyes raised to mine.

"Name?"

"John Frost."

"Sir," said he. The eyes momentarily shone.

"Sir," I repeated.

He shuffled papers with thin, pale fingers. "The leader of the misguided Chartists, they tell me. I congratulate you on landing in the predicament where you can do least damage, but I assure you that the mildness of your treatment here will not be repeated in Van Dieman's Land."

It called for no reply; my new friend shuffled his feet I recall, and raised his eyes to the ceiling. Even I was aware of his undisguised disdain, yet it passed apparently unnoticed. The commander continued: "You, and the rest of your infernal gang will sail from here on the *Mandarin* within the week, and I may say that I am particularly relieved to be rid of you in so short a time, which, clearly, is the wish of the penal authorities." Again he raised his vacant eyes, looking, no doubt, for some sign of hostility he could punish.

"For your information, if you do not already know, the convict code in the penal settlement to which you are being sent has no equal in severity in any part of the civilized world." He smiled up at me.

"Nevertheless, your life has been spared by our merciful Queen, Her Majesty having been graciously pleased . . ."

"Thank you," I interjected, and suddenly, as if planned to a moment in time, there came from the deck outside a man's hoarse scream, and the screams continued to a higher pitch as a whip swished and the thongs cut him.

The commander's eyes moved slowly over my face. The screams continued. Rigidly, I stood there, clenching my hands, and the flogging outside went on and on. Presently, there was a dull thud, then silence.

It was like the opening of a drama being performed especially for me.

The commander then said, "You may go, Frost," and sat back in his chair. "Next one up."

As I left the tiny office I saw my companion step in front of the table.

I was swabbing down with Zephaniah and the others when this man Richard Carling joined us.

"You did well," said he, swabbing laboriously.

"What do you mean?"

"The intention in there was to unnerve you into protest or argument. Had you done so, you would have finished up in the same position as that poor devil," and he nodded towards the mainmast where the flogged convict was being unshackled from the grating: he was in a state of collapse, his lacerated back running with blood.

"But why, why?"

"Why try to provoke you?" He grinned up at me and his eyes were good. "Because you remain as a threat to them; you were sentenced to death, and were reprieved. They think you got off lightly, and you did, make no big mistake. You are in custody, but your Movement remains, and you are the subject of much discussion. Better to be like one such as I — with good friends in high places, but nothing political: it is the politics they seek to kill."

I did not reply.

Zephaniah said, hearing the last words, "Let us hope they confine their dislike to dedicated Chartists, for I have left the Movement; henceforth I am the respected ex-landlord of an inn in Blaina." He looked my friend up and down. "And who may you be?"

"My name's Carling."

"What are you here for?"

"On a lady's whim — no crime."

"That's probably why you're here. It's the one thing they don't forgive you for. Highway robbery?"

"Marvellous guess!" exclaimed Carling, and his eyes shone.

"I don't believe it," said I. "Surely it was the lady, not her purse that convicted you. How long?"

"Seven years — and you?"

"The term of our natural lives."

"Aye, well the trouble was that you offended Victoria Regis; my little bitch was a long way down the social scale."

The warder, hovering nearby, suddenly straightened, saying, "There's too much gab — get about your bloody business, all of you."

Richard Carling said, "You get about yours, man, or it'll be the worse for you."

Zephaniah looked at me, one eyebrow slightly raised.

My newly found strength was short-lived,

65

for next day, with Zephaniah, Jones, Lovell and Carling, I was detailed for a labour gang ashore.

Now double-ironed and chained together at the waist, we were marched ashore and tethered to the end of a cart; on this two warders and a marine guard rode with batons and muskets at the ready: talk had it that every guard who let a prisoner escape while on 'Cosey' (the unofficial name given to work ashore) received fifty lashes from the bosun.

The work entailed loading pit props for the Welsh mines and larger timber, newly felled trees, from barges to the shore: here on the beach the loads were secured and dragged up to the road; with the pit props the work was comparatively easy; working with the larger timber was dangerous for the unskilled, and few of us were woodsmen or foresters.

The real danger came when a tree had to be lifted: earmarked, usually, for a ship's mast, it first had to be trimmed of branches; this was done by dockyard sawyers in attendance, men sullen of face and disposition, their feelings brutalized by the sight of constant beatings for the smallest misdemeanours. A man whose foot slipped in the mud, thus momentarily throwing his weight upon his fellows, might instantly be struck down by a baton; and then, fallen, belaboured by both warders until he regained his load. Thus one worked with dismal apprehension.

"Right, stand by her!" This was the first command. With the tree ashore and lopped of branches, we would line along it in our chains, taking care not to allow the slack of the chain to encircle your foot, for this, on the lift, would up-end and suspend you on the log.

"Bend and grip! Now come on, get hold of it!" And the warders would run up and down the line, cracking any rear which wasn't correctly positioned for the lift.

"Prepare to lift!" Grunts and groans from the slaves, and the rattle of their chains.

"Right you, *lift!*" and you would tense your back and stomach muscles to the strain and haul upwards: the great log lifts stickily from the reluctant mud; your hands slip and you grip anew, seeing behind you the sun-shadow of an upraised baton.

"Hold it on your knees — hold it, *hold it!*"

Hands are slipping and sliding along the trunk; the bark comes ripping off in torn fingers.

Clamped double now, with the log between your thighs and elbows, you pray for strength, for lose the weight and you thrust it on to your neighbour. Again the reviling voice, the lifted baton.

"Right, prepare to lift again so. Hold it, hold it — lift! And again so — *lift*, you lazy scum — *lift!*" And the baton comes slashing down. "Now come on, get your guts into it, or I'll take you all back for a sun-down flogging. This is a chain-gang, not a vicarage tea party. All right third lift up upon your shoulders. Lift! — jerk and turn — up, *up!*"

The log, fifty feet long and three feet diameter at its thickest girth, now lies upon our shoulders; this, for me, is where the trouble begins.

We were the draught animals of a new era of enlightenment; modern slaves of a new Pharoah called Victoria, who put her signature where uncaring ministers put their thumbs.

Now, too late John Lovell leaped to take the weight off me; as the man behind me and the one in front slipped simultaneously, their knees buckling under the weight, I took the full impact of their loads as well as my own: the log came down, wrenching my right shoulder and tearing the sinews, and the weight, loosened to the full, came bearing down upon me, forcing me to my knees. Instantly, the warders were into us, savagely striking with their batons, and the heavy circumference of the trunk descended, pinning me in the mud. I lay helplessly, impervious to the raining blows, which ceased, said Carling, when I fainted.

I passed the days in a haze of pain; still in the gang, still working, but with my right arm strapped to my body, and John Lovell, the herculean man, chained behind me to share my weight. Richard Carling worked in front of me, presumably to keep off the batons, said Zephaniah, for not a guard then approached me. But it could not last: a sedentary life of ease, with flabby muscles taxed beyond their endurance, began to tell their tale; and my old enemy, stomach disorders, assailed me. Streaming sweat,

I struggled on through day succeeding day, but at the end of the week, with the *Mandarin* making ship-shape out in the bay, I collapsed.

Light-headed, I lay in what they called a sick bay. In dreams of cooling water, my body racked and sore, I saw in the shimmering lanthorns the refracted light that played in Bettws woods; walked in riven sunsets along the banks of the Usk near beautiful Caerleon; kissed Mary after chapel; walked hand in hand with Anne, my youngest. And saw the sun descend into the sea below the spires of Newport.

"Tomorrow," whispered a voice. "The ship — the *Mandarin*!"

It was Richard Carling, bending over me, and the soaked rag he held was cool upon my face. Another voice, uneducated, hoarse; John Lovell's:

"Christ, Mr Frost, sir. You got to get on your pins or they'll bloody leave you behind!"

"Don't he fancy a sea trip, then?" And this was William Jones, grinning down at the end of the sick bunk.

"He do fancy it right enough, don't he?" cried Zephaniah, taking off Lovell. "He do

70

fancy it no end, but he prefers Weston-on-Sea to bloody old Van Dieman's Land, don't he?"

William Jones, I noticed, turned away his head and spat.

They gathered around me in the bay. Irishmen were there, long term patriots from England's Sorrow, who fought for their freedom once, were caught, transported, and returned to fight again: Dan Taply was there, not yet twenty whose girl-wife was cooking for Crawshay's mob up in Merthyr . . . transported for breaking into the Dowlais Truck Shop and stealing a loaf and a pound of accidents; the ironic local name for meat. Boyo Good-Turn was there, and Lucky, his butty, with seven years stretching before them for forming a Union in Benjamin Hall's constituency, the man who gave his name to Big Ben. Dick Benfield and John Rees, Charlie Walters (sometimes called 'Waters') and Jenkin Morgan, they were with me also, crowding under the dim light of the lamps.

"What you think, Mr Frost. Can you make it on your feet in the morning?"

"If he can't, he'll be left behind, that's the regulation," said Carling softly.

"God Almighty, what is this?" whispered Zephaniah, and his words quietened them. "If he's got the chance to vote himself to stay behind, why sail to Australia to be flayed alive?"

I replied, "I'll take a chance on it — anywhere out of this hell-hole."

"Then on your feet, is it, sir?" asked Dan Taply, his face becoming alive. "The sooner you're back on your feet, the sooner you'll get a taste for it."

I nodded, and put up my arms to them. "He's right. Raise me, and easy on my poor old shoulder, eh?"

They stood me on my feet, and waited in a circle about me.

"Now stand clear," I said to Lovell, and he did so, and swaying, I looked around their eager faces.

A man without comrades is dead; all the time he has them he is alive.

# 6

IN the year 1615 Britain ordered that 'anie robberie or fellonie (wilfull murther, rape, witchcraft or burglarie only excepted) . . . all those found guilty of same might be sent to the East Indies or the American plantations . . .' Further, it was stated that such practice could be beneficial to the Commonwealth and prove 'a greater terror than death itself.' Between then and the year 1700 some 5000 prisoners were so transported, and Blackstone's *Commentaries on the Laws of England*, which I read assiduously, so approved of the practice that he happily stated, 'So the wisdom of the English legislature had extracted rich medicine out of poisonous ingredients by applying the punishment to popish ecclesiastics'.

During which period, doubtless, many Catholic martyrs discovered a refuge of sorts far away from the flames of Smithfield, only to find themselves being 'married to the Three Sisters' — that is, bound naked to the blood-soaked triangles of Van Dieman's Land and flogged until the skin of their backs was removed.

Between the years 1660 and 1820, some 190 capital offences were added to the fifty-two already existing; death was the sole punishment for these; it was available to hanging judges for crimes varying from embezzlement to murder (attempted killing was only a misdemeanor up to 1802, unless maiming resulted) and piracy, to damaging a fence, or concealing the birth of a bastard child. While offences that warranted whipping, transportation, the treadmill or the house of correction included receiving stolen fish, the theft of more than a shilling or manslaughter.

On the other hand, stealing dead bodies, cabbages, turnips, or keeping a bawdy house called only for local imprisonment.

George III was particularly hard upon forgers, which was probably because he was invariably in debt; while his son, the Prince Regent, in applying the Royal prerogative of mercy when it came to reprieves, was hard on boys, whom he sent to the gallows with rigorous efficiency.

In the 18th century systematic transportation began to take the place of capital punishment, for the need was not only to rid the country of its felons, but populate the new colonies where better returns on investment were available.

Generally, some 2000 people were executed annually; the eight hanging days at Tyburn being a guarantee of Londoner excitement: mercifully, hanging diminished as transportation increased. Even more mercifully, progressive civilization had replaced the stake with the noose, and a disgusted William Cobbett could no longer complain of the foul stench of a woman burning.

Nevertheless, legal opinion was divided as to the efficacy of transportation as a punishment; many complained that it was no punishment at all, but these had not been subject to the vomiting of the roll and pitch; the scurvy, bilge fever, constipation, the nauseous smells arising from tattered prisoners lodged like packed sardines, double-ironed below decks . . . the hunger, and the beatings. The voyage to Australia was a major undertaking in itself, where, in the early years, the death rate was fifteen to twenty per cent, from epidemics ranging from typhoid to cholera.

Ireland, by virtue of her many uprisings, shipped some 8000 of her convicts to the Americas before Independence was won, and, since there was no Poor Law available, transported all those 'dependent for victuals', many such females falling prey to prostitution in houses of ill-fame awaiting them in the colonies. Harlotry, too, was endemic aboard most ships, one surgeon aboard recording that ' . . . the desire of women to be with the men was so uncontrollable that neither shame nor fear of punishment could deter them from entry into the seamen's bunks'.

The *Lady Juliana*, for example, carrying only female convicts, 'managed to provide every working seaman aboard with a wife — they nothing loathe', according to one of her stewards; another, Nicholas Bayly, stated in 1817, that 'it is customary, when female convicts embark, that every sailor be allowed a woman during Passage'. While a Mr Justice Field stated that ' . . . the women certainly were permitted to cohabit with the officers and seamen, and I am convinced that it would be impossible to prevent connection, even if their hatches had been nightly battened down'. He was clearly pragmatic.

No such romantic assignations attached to the clientele of the *Mandarin*, the convict ship we boarded on the 28 February, for there wasn't a woman aboard. Nor did we share the journey with Lovell, John Rees and their three companions; all five were in luck, their sentence having been reduced from transportation for life to three years' imprisonment.

I was in the *Mandarin* sick bay when they took their leave of me.

Lovell I would miss, but the rest were of small consequence to me in terms of friendship; all had pleaded guilty at the Monmouth trial, which had scarcely endeared them.

In replacement, three Birmingham Chartists were brought aboard in chains — Francis Roberts, John Jones and Jeremiah Howell — all distinctive Welshmen, who had been sentenced for rioting in the earlier July.

So Captain Muddle had 214 convicts in his charge; of these only six, to my knowledge, were dedicated Chartists.

"A nucleus for a successful mutiny, but it's God's wish, I believe, that we should have more," mentioned Zephaniah.

"Lower your voice! A mutiny?"

"It could be done," he added bassly. "Organize, and take the ship."

"Do not be ridiculous!"

"Your trouble, Frost, is that you never take a chance."

I did not reply, for Dr McKecknie, the *Mandarin*'s surgeon, entered the sick bay.

"I would have preferred to meet you under happier conditions, Mr Frost," said he, and offered his hand.

Such were the idiosyncrasies of the penal laws; one moment being beaten to one's knees by batons, next being greeted as a gentleman.

I suspected this Dr McKecknie of Chartist sympathies, certainly he was a radical; subsequent events gave proof of this.

He was a tall, distinguished man, his calm, smooth features unmarked by years of sea-going: About my age, he had seen service with the Royal Navy, retiring from active service with sufficient prize money to settle ashore to a life of squireen comfort with £1000 a year, 200 acres of rough shooting in Devon, a good trout steam and five servants. But the death of his wife had changed this, and when the sea called him, Dr McKecknie answered.

"Though what induced me to serve aboard a convict ship is beyond my comprehension," said he.

"Perhaps the need to inject humanity?"

His clear eyes snapped up at me. "I have never really examined the compulsion, Frost; suffice that I am here. And this one's safe — Captain Muddle is an excellent captain."

While speaking he had been examining me; the torn ligaments of my shoulder required rest, he said, and granted me a week in the sick bay. Daily spoonfuls of arrowroot he prescribed for my constant diarrhoea, and as quickly as he came, he left me.

Not a minute after he had gone, my stepson, William Geach, arrived.

Later, William told friends that I was "evidently dropping fast into eternity", and after seeing myself in the cracked mirror of the sick bay, I readily believed him.

Gone was the round lust of my middle years; I was as lean as Aaron's corpse, with the pallor of a starved ghost and looking older than Methuselah. And William Geach, for all his youth, looked little better. For he came with the worries of the world upon his shoulders: the possibility of being struck off the roll of solicitors.

It seemed enough at the time that he was with me; was up to date with national efforts to secure our reprieve and could tell me of the family.

"Mary and the children, they are well?" I seized his thin hands.

"They pine for you, and beg you not to seek further confrontation, Father."

"It's a luxury I intend to deny myself. What about the petitions?"

William said, "They arrive daily in Downing Street, are pulled in by the sack load, but God knows what happens to them then."

"And Macaulay's efforts? What of him?"

William sighed. "His intentions appear to gain him internment in Westminster Abbey — he is about to begin yet another history of England; I doubt if his interests extend to saving Chartists."

"You are bitter?"

All about us was the apprehensive scurrying of cleaning, swabbing orderlies under the watchful eye of the bosun at the sick bay door, who also had an eye on us. This meeting had been granted by Dr McKecknie, but it wasn't generally approved of.

William said, "The Whigs never change. Disturbances which threaten their property are anathema to them; Macaulay is a Whig before he is an historian; his glorious revolutions are centuries old."

"He continues to speak against us?"

"He compares you with the barbarians who marched under At'tila the Hun. You have but one strong voice in Parliament, and that belongs to the Jew. But comfort yourself that you have a hundred thousand voices like Disraeli's in the streets."

"The people!"

Zephaniah joined us, saying, "Then more's the pity that they did not follow us before, it is now too late for words; this old crate takes us off tomorrow."

William moved his great dark eyes over me, and I knew the inner suffering of one pledged to keep his personal secrets which, later, I learned in full: now he said:

"James Hodge, your enemy in Blackwood who testified against you, remember him?"

"What of him?"

"As the people of Merthyr ran Abbott out of town for false testimony against Dic Penderyn, so this will happen to Hodge; many accuse him of being a Government spy. If he stays in town he may not survive."

Later, I learned that when a bloodstained note was thrust under Hodge's door and his windows were broken, he left town.

"And Israel Firman, what of him?" demanded William Jones, swabbing within earshot, and my stepson said:

"His house is blockaded, the people will not allow him home. Yesterday, the magistrates paid to remove him and his family to Newport."

"He'll get short shrift there!"

"Nobody will drink the ale of Barnabas Brough, he is already bankrupt: indeed, every witness for the prosecution is being ostracized; collieries and ironworks are being forced to discharge their informants because men loyal to Chartism will not work with them: such a terror is among them that some coal-masters are supplying them with arms with which to defend themselves."

"This," said Jones, drifting away, "is excellent."

My stepson raised his smouldering eyes. "It is not! It is threatening the very ethics of non-violence for which we are fighting. It is people like you who were fleshing swords, but not arriving, who have brought us to this pass. If those who are shouting for violence now had supported moral force, my father would not be here . . . " He rose, his eyes on Jones. "Blood would not have been spilled at all, had Wales listened to him."

"Right," called the bosun at the door. "Visitors away!"

I took William's hands in mine; he appeared wasted and old; only his eyes were alive with the old desire for a fight. This, the humble Newport solicitor that the great lawyers, Pollock and Kelly had taken to their hearts. I knew a sudden and overwhelming sadness that he was not of my loins: from where his brilliance came, none would know; but it was enough that he was of Mary's blood. I said:

"You are in trouble, William?"

He bowed his head.

I asked softly, "You will not tell me?"

"You have grief enough . . . "

"Is it on account of your defence of me?"

"It is not. Nor is it of any consequence to you, for I have brought it upon my own head."

"Does your mother know?"

He shook his head, and did a strange thing then: bending over the bed, he kissed me.

"Goodbye, John Frost," he said. Then added, "Goodbye, Father."

It was astonishing to think, later in retrospect, that he and I were so soon to meet on the other side of the world, in Van Dieman's Land.

# 7

ZEPHANIAH said, on the morning we set sail from Portsmouth, "Van Dieman's Land appears a promising place in which to spend a holiday." I replied:

"You've been talking to Dr McKecknie? That's what he told me."

"Indeed. He speaks highly of the place. So good is the climate that you can't keep people away from it. Altogether, if you include the penal settlements, about 20,000 villains like us have arrived there."

I wasn't in the mood for his irony, having just left the sick bay. Now, on my back, unable to move my arms because of the pressure of men either side of me, I shut my eyes to the coackroach-infested timbers above my face, and answered, "Be informed his figures are wrong. If you included New South Wales, which most patriots conveniently forget, the figure for Australia is about 120,000 to date, which includes 12,000 females. And that doesn't account for the numbers lost at sea."

"Mr Frost," said William Jones, beside me, "is in a happy mood."

"Face facts," I answered. "Five years ago the *Amphitrite* was wrecked and lost over a hundred women; a year later the *George III* was sunk with 140 men. Add to this death from scurvy, floggings and fevers and there's a sizeable chance that we'll never see the skies over Van Dieman's Land, a situation I find acceptable."

"You prefer death to transportation?"

"Eminently. You heard me telling Captain Shaw at the Kilbain just that."

"You'd take your life, you mean?"

"I didn't say that. When you two were advocating suicide in Monmouth, I was against it. That is the coward's way. But if this old hulk offers me a watery grave, I'd relish the prospect."

Carling, rattling his chains at the end of my palliasse, said, "Not I, Mr Frost. Actually, I'm much indebted to Her Majesty for offering me a change of air. Had I continued on my old path of boudoirs and duels with jealous husbands, I'd have turned up my toes. Besides, there are some splendid beauties in Paramatta," and he cocked up his head and sang in a fine tenor voice:

My true love was beautiful
My true love she was happy and gay.
But she's taken a trip on a government ship
And she's now ten thousand miles away

And an old lag down the gangway, hearing this, chanted from his bearded mouth:

Oh, Maggie May, you've gone away
To slave on cold Van Dieman's shore!
For you robbed so many sailors
And dosed so many whalers
That you'll not cruise down Lime Street any more . . .

"Aye, and that's the size of it," cried Zephaniah. "Have you seen 'em, Old Lag?" And he slapped his thigh, bawling laughter.

"I saw 'em proper, mister," shouted the old man. "For I been this way afore. And tho' I done most things in me life, I ain't done no Paramatta Factory beauties, that's why I'm here, cock an' all!" and he cackled laughter.

The *Mandarin* began to pitch and rough up when once she gained the open sea; the convicts lay in chained lines shoulder to shoulder; and heaving and vomiting began between decks: ragged, tattered wrecks of men (we slept little, most of us) were coughing and spewing into the gratings, and soon the warders came down among us, hosing down the bilges which were flowing with sickness. Amazingly, I was not now sick: all my dread of seasickness, which I thought would be my lot, vanished in those few hours when the *Mandarin* dipped her prow into a crested sea and shivered her shanks over the grey channel, making west for Falmouth.

Here, after storming into port with topsails blown away, we laid to for three days under the riggers and sailmakers. Battened down below hatches and double guarded by shore marines against escape, we knelt at the few portholes and watched the live meat coming aboard in a clucking, squawking chorus punctuated by bellowing old cows and shrieking porkers. Here a convict ship was lying offshore, especially chartered, Dr McKecknie told us, for the transportation of females; soon we saw these arriving at the wharf, some as young as twelve or thirteen, some as old as seventy; chained together in groups of twenty, all were carrying their blanket, straw bedding and their pot of oil-and-tar for killing the bugs. Barges closed in and they were herded upon these, standing in their chains while the rowers hauled them out to the convict ship. As they went they raised a cheer to us, and men waved from the portholes or stuck their arms out of the hatches.

"Most are prostitutes, of course," said McKecknie, wandering down the bunks. "And if they aren't now, they will be when they reach Australia."

"Some look comparatively decent," I suggested.

"I heard that some have no previous convictions," said Zephaniah.

"That I seriously doubt," replied the doctor. "These are mainly females who have rejected the sweat factories for easy money; occasional prostitution, but once they start they soon turn into whores and thieves."

"There's one who clearly isn't," said Jones, peering over my shoulder.

The last barge to leave for the ship passed on our port side and I saw its occupants clearly: true, the majority were depraved harlots, one could assess this by their ravaged faces and truculent attitudes. But down upon her knees, with her chains looping up to the nearest prisoner, was a young girl, and she was weeping bitterly. As I watched, the wind took her bright fair hair and waved it about her shoulders. She was barefooted and in rags, and I judged her age at little older than my Anne.

"She be a child-killer, that one, no doubt," cried Old Lag from behind me. "Lest they come for lendin' it out as dollymops, they're mainly floozies who got caught out — hayrick bundlers."

His was a foreign language to me; I turned away.

"In the name of God," ejaculated Richard Carling, softly.

And I saw through the smudged porthole a small pinnace tacking to the wind; leeward she came, her fore and mainsail billowing as she carved the waves. As she went about on the tack, Carling ejaculated, and I knew why, for standing alone in the stern was somebody he clearly recognized.

It was a woman of mature age. Tall and straight was she, with a fine prow on her, said Old Lag, and with the carriage of a queen. Bright silk was her cloak, blowing a white shroud about her in the wind; her gown was green, her bodice yellow.

"By Jesus, she be some woman, that 'un!" said someone.

"One thing's sure, mister, she ain't a doxy!"

"Where?" asked Dr McKecknie, bending to the porthole, and we sat clear for him. Nodding briefly, he announced with fine disinterest:

"The mistress of the captain of the *Lady Juliana*."

I glanced at Richard Carling; never have I witnessed such profound disbelief laid upon a face.

"You know her?" I asked.

"No," said he.

I could not sleep that night, but lay in the grip of a savage *hiraeth*, one fraught with longing, and not only for Wales.

Mary, I thought, would be abed with the children now; was she, like me, awake to the torment of our parting? My dreams of her came in a contorted imagery of pain, sharpened by the outrage upon womanhood which I had seen earlier. Over 200 women I had seen chained together like cattle, awaiting the horrors of a rat and vermin-infested voyage; of hunger, official cruelty and disease; to arrive on a foreign shore, sent by the Royal Pimp, Victoria, for, as one fine writer put it, 'wholesale prostitution in her colonies'.

Yet, standing alone among the poor, ragged creatures of the barges, was the beautiful woman of the pinnace, the mistress of the captain of the convict ship; and going to transportation was she, as surely as was the most calloused and depraved. But was she the only pure of heart to board the *Lady Juliana* I wondered, when a girl could be transported to a living hell for stealing a sixpenny bonnet or a cotton dress? Or a flat iron? A pair of paste earrings because they 'were pretty'? Or 'one-and-sixpence'?

These things I mentioned to Richard

Carling when, with the *Mandarin* running before a stiff breeze down the coast of Portugal, we were lying together in the sun; still chained, yet strangely free.

"Don't talk to me of British justice," said he, "there are people back home there stealing souls."

"Lord John Russell, for one."

And he smiled, saying, "I am privileged to have known a lot of them individually, but not that particular bastard."

"Like the woman you saw on the pinnace last week. You knew her, didn't you?"

"I didn't say so."

"You didn't have to. I could see it in your face."

Zephaniah and Jones, chained together, wandered up and sat down with us; in a group we stared across the ocean; the sun was a ball of fire riding high on molten clouds of morning. White horses leaped and cavorted to the distant horizon; somebody cried that dolphins had been seen off the starboard prow. At peace with myself for the first time in months, I lay back upon the hot deck and closed my eyes to the blood-red burnishing of the sun.

"You're a queer bird if ever there was one, Carling," announced Zephaniah suddenly. "We know why we're here — High Treason against the State, but why are you?" Clearly he was suspicious. Spies were everywhere.

Carling smiled. "If we can begin from the premise that I'm innocent of all charges, I might be tempted to tell you, but it really is the most randy old tale!"

I sat up, cross-legged. "Go on, tell us, for we're excellent listeners, and have all the time in the world."

"For the rest of our lives, son, thanks to the aristocracy," interjected William Jones. "You buggers are the curse of England," and he glared at Richard Carling.

I glanced up at this, and Jones added, "Aye, you can look. Sir Richard Carling — Dr McKecknie just told me — a Lord Muck sitting in the bloody middle of us."

"True?" asked Zephaniah, raising a bushy eyebrow.

"Reasonably," replied Carling, "if it was my father who fathered me. Am I responsible for what my ancestors did on boozy weekends?"

People laughed, but it was a surprise.

94

"Sir Richard Carling?" I asked.

"At your service, I said so before."

"God Almighty," grumbled William Jones, and Zephaniah said:

"Mind you, you won't be alone when we get to Van Dieman's Land — remember that character, Frost? Some months ago — Lieutenant Flynn was his name, wasn't it? Convicted at the Old Bailey of forging widows' pension tickets . . ."

"Sir John Flynn, you mean?"

"Aye, that fella! Queen Caroline awarded him the third-class order of St Ferdinand, and letters addressed to Sir John Flynn have been reaching him at Port Arthur!" Zeph slapped his thigh and boomed laughter.

The *Mandarin*, carving out of a lagoon of calm sea, suddenly swung her booms to a blustering wind, heeled, and came round in a welter of confused water; the captain's voice rang out, a wail above the wind;

"Alter course two points starboard!" Then: "Steady as she goes. Hold her!" And the man up in the crow's-nest bawled down:

"Sail a'comin' up port side, sir!"

"Say again, crow!"

The ship stormed on in thundering canvas and spume, and the crow's-nest repeated, "Ship on port, sir! I reckon I see'd the loom o' some'ut riding low . . . !"

"That'll be the French," said Carling, soberly.

We stared at him. He replied:

"A missionary caught me in Falmouth. Questions were being asked in Parliament, he said — *The Times* was full of it that the good old frogs would never let Citizen Frost be taken."

"You don't mean it!"

"Ah, but I do — don't your visitors tell you about the newspapers? Haven't you heard of John Frost, your namesake?"

I nodded, and he continued, "Years back he presented addresses at the bar of the French Convention; as a member of the London Corresponding Society, he's in touch with Anglo-French debates. Talk has it that his visits to France recently haven't been for debate."

"An intervention on the high seas to save John Frost?" Zephaniah laughed. "Tell me another — that French lot? Our Navy would blow them out of the sea!"

"Perhaps," said William Jones. "Now we

know why they slid us away at the dead of night with half the Army guarding us," and as he said this another wail came from the crow's-nest.

"Ship identified, sir. It's the *Juliana* fore-reachin' us!"

Zephaniah grumbled, "We're back to reality. The *Lady Juliana* — so much for the French navy," and he slapped Old Lag on the back. "You're in, sir! You've got some fast women coming up. And that's the nearest we'll get to frogs' legs for breakfast."

The clamour and commands quietened: men peered seaward at the topsails of the pursuing *Juliana*. Old Lag said, "It's the same wherever I go — the women are after me, sometimes it frightens me," and he leaped to his feet and did a little kick-step, rattling his chains. "And it do put me in a rare old mood for romance, lads. Mr Carling, what about this randy old yarn ye promised, then?" And he sat on the deck with his skinny legs akimbo, grinning from his toothless mouth. "Come on, lads gather round, for this little lad's goin' to tell us a shockin' tale o' ladies' pussies."

And so began a story so riveting in its depravity that I decided it was too abrasive for my conservative ears, though I listened just the same, and we called it *The Knight's Tale.*

# 8

SAID Richard:
"I was born twenty-four years ago of a love match between Sir Henry and Lady Elizabeth Carling, and would have been perfectly content with village life at Carling Hall, the family seat in Buckinghamshire.

"Unfortunately, as son and heir to the Carling fortune (which came mainly from American cotton plantations where the punishment for lateness at work was finger amputation) they put a starched collar around my ears, brushed up my quiff and packed me off to Eton. Here I learned to fag for older boys, resisted their sexual advances, and beat younger boys with the same dexterity with which I had been beaten.

"I learned Latin and French, and knew by heart the poems of Macaulay; I studied *The Lays of Ancient Rome*, read Shakespeare fervently, especially where kings and queens were involved; took to the field and horsemanship at the age of seven, and was blooded by the bishop when I was eight. In the college I sang *Non Nobis Domine*, and later, at university, took the daughters of landowners punting, and between dusk and sunrise and their black-stockinged thighs, I learned the facts of life.

"All in all, when I think back, I was a cadet eminently suited for entry into the Church or the Army, where all the sons of the aristocracy go since they're no good for anything else, but I couldn't make up my mind which to do, so my father did it for me. He, being a retired Major of Dragoons, decided that the wisest course would be to die for my country, so entered me in that capacity in the Royal Military College at Sandhurst where, in the year 1834 — just six years ago, gentlemen, I won the sword which is given to the year's brightest prospect.

"With this award and a commission bought for five hundred guineas I began a military career which would take me to many parts of the world. Here, before the age of twenty-one, I had put to death Pathans and Dervishes, black men on the Gold Coast and brown men in Persia, which delighted my father because he had done the same.

"Back home in Carling the vicar prayed for my success in such exploits, and the hope was that, covered with medals, I would die on the battlefield in time for the celebrations of 1837, when Victoria came to the throne.

"But this did not happen because I was cashiered. I will not make much detail here; suffice to say that the events are venal, for entering what I thought was the bedchamber of a lady of quality, I found myself in the sheets beside her husband, who was a dragoon in the Spanish Imperial Guard. Being Spanish, he naturally demanded satisfaction, so we met at dawn and I wounded him with the very sword I had been given at Sandhurst. My father approved of this; after all, mutilating Spaniards has always been an honourable English activity, but neither my mother nor the vicar could forgive the sullying of a lady's honour, and nor could William IV. So, with a price on my head, I took to the road."

Suddenly the day changed to a startling

cold, and the wind blew in mad blusters, bringing with it the land-based shivers of distant mountains. But not a man moved, such was his riveted attention.

"You took to the road?" I asked.

"I became a highwayman, a soldier of fortune," answered Carling.

"Like Robin Hood, sort of?" asked Old Lag. "Givin' to the poor and takin' from the rich?"

"Nothing so gallant, I fear, Old Lag. I was in need of ale and beef and my mare was neighing for oats. Therefore I worked the old Roman road to London until I found myself in Shropshire county. You've heard of Humfrey Kynaston, the highwayman?"

We said we hadn't, and I looked around the staring convicts.

Here were the brute-strong, bawdy relics of a broken community; the dregs of Newgate and a score of other gaols where only the near-primates survived: Old Lag with his cankered limbs and skinny shoulders bearing the weals of a thousand lashes; Timbo Weller, a pickpocket thief from the alleys of Lime Street, his jaw contorted and his mouth hideously snarling from the beatings of a gaoler's baton; Sole Bungy, the forger, the stringy, undersized draughtsman of Paradise Street, who always worked alone: Petticoat Boy, not yet twenty, his cheeks still rosy with youth, who pimped for fifty women along the Liver Docks in Liverpool, and a dozen others, mostly emaciated, ragged hooligans, the scum of humanity from a society of thieves and footpads which some called England. And us, William Jones, Zephaniah and I; we who plotted with others to bring the skirted vixen off the throne.

"Go on then," urged Old Lag. "What about this old Humfrey bugger?"

And Richard Carling continued his tale:

"Humfrey also was a gentleman of the road. He had set up headquarters at a village called Nesscliff, on the road to Shrewsbury, and lived happily off the spoils of the mail coaches. He carved for himself a cave in red sandstone — a small compartment for himself, a larger one for his stallion; this was concealed from easy view by a track through a wood, and the villagers, befriending him, would warn him of King's men or prying strangers.

"But, having long since been shot down on the roadside, he had no further use for his cave, and so I took it over, rent free, and operated from Nesscliff for years. I made mistresses of three Nesscliff wenches, roistered most nights at the old *Three Pigeons* tavern and, like my predecessor, made myself rich on the wealth of merchants, but never — and I repeat this — never once lifting a bauble from a lady's throat, or a ring from her finger."

"But you got plenty o' the other old stuff, I bet," cried Petticoat Boy.

"Indeed, I had more than my share of that." Carling smiled around at their eager faces.

"But it couldn't last, could it? The net that had tightened around Humfrey Kynaston, tightened also around me, so I distributed my remaining gold among the villagers, pleasured my three wenches at the *Three Pigeons*, and took off to the south, for Bristol. For news had come to me that a lady of high repute, one as rich as Midas, was travelling by stagecoach to Charing Cross in London. And she was more beautiful than the wife of Casanova!"

"Bloody hell," whispered Timbo Weller.

The *Mandarin*, caught in a sudden blast, heeled to port, her sails in irons and her timbers shaking as the booms came over; but not an eye moved from Richard's face; he continued:

"I stayed overnight in Bristol at the *Three Cups* inn within sight of the slave wharf: next morning, with the slave-selling in full spate, I sauntered through the courtesans and frock-coated gents, crowds of bawling hucksters and street criers. The slave merchants were arriving in their gilded broughams and chaises. For this was enormously wealthy Bristol, gentlemen, whose promenades and great houses had been built on the blood."

"For Christ's sake get on wi' it," whispered Sole Bungy, and Richard said:

"As I prepared to catch the London stagecoach, I paused at a stall which sold the products of the Indies; here I was intrigued by a small bag made of Moroccan leather and worked with intricate design. This small bag I picked up, asking its price — 'Two shillin', sir,' replied the stall-holder, 'and believe me, I'm robbin' meself.'

"'One thing's sure, my man,' said I, dropping it, 'you are not robbing me,' and a charming voice behind me cried happily:

"'Oh, come, sir — it would cost you three times that price in London!' And I turned to find a woman of marvellous beauty standing behind me as she bought another of the Moroccan bags."

"Jesus!" whispered Zephaniah, with pent breath. "It was the lady?"

"No!"

"The one you tried to sleep with — the Spaniard's piece, ye mean?" cried Old Lag.

"Be patient, he ain't got her in bed yet," said another, and as he said this a seaman's cry wailed from the crow's-nest:

"Here she do come, cap'n, sir. She's a'fore-reachin' us, like you said!"

We were on a long tack to sou'east and we hadn't seen the *Lady Juliana* creeping up upon us, and now she went about and plunged through our wake and the decks were alive with hurrahs as the convicts crowded to the starboard rail, waving and cheering as the ship, loaded to the gunnels with females, come roaring out of our shrouds: with her sails racking and straining to the windload, she drew alongside not 200 yards away, a fleet ship, while the *Mandarin* lumbered on like a drunken navvy. Now, overtaking us, the *Juliana* set her top-sails, and the women, clutching each other on the sloping decks, waved and screamed, and Old Lag's voice rang out:

"Stand by to board her, me lads — two miles of 'How's ye father' in six inch strips — we'll never see the likes of it ag'in," and a roar went up from the massed convicts who were clanking their fetters, and the females clanked theirs back so that a soaring orchestra of chains made music on the wind, with the women pulling up their skirts and the men dropping their trews to air their bums, and in no time the bosuns got among them with rope's ends and commands.

"Clearly, your story will have to continue at a later date," I said to Richard Carling.

"Aye, and don't forget," added Old Lag. "For you was about to go chasin' 'er butterfly, weren't he, Mr Frost?"

I could tell by the look on Carling's face that the statement was accurate. However, he suddenly added: "In every respect my tale is true, gentlemen; only one thing I have altered, and that is the places where her seduction took place, this being necessary to preserve my lady's honour."

Zephaniah, I recall, gave him a very old-fashioned look.

# 9

"**M**R FROST!"
Week by week a small number of us were freed of the irons; and I was up on the poop-deck, with my back against the rail, writing to Mary.

It was upon such occasions, unfettered, that I wrote my letters home to Newport, for by some strange quirk of psychology I could not communicate with my loved one when chained.

"Mr Frost!" The call was more urgent, and Dan Taply, a young convict with whom I had earlier talked, joined me.

The sea was bright blue and hazed; almost becalmed, and with Cape Fria's Land shimmering in the heat five miles to port, the ship rolled and yawed above bright, coral depths; the sails hung like dish-rags.

"You got a minute, Mr Frost?"

"That's a stupid thing to say." I put down my paper and pencil.

Taply, skinny, undersized, claimed

brotherhood with the Brynmawr Chartists, but when questioned later, Zephaniah, whose lodge encompassed that area, could not remember him.

"I've got a letter," announced Taply, looking about him.

"From home?" I asked.

"Not that kind, sir . . . "

"Then what's it to me?" and Taply replied, his eyes twitching in his gaunt face:

"Best you read it first, we say, sir . . . "

"We?" I folded up and put away the letter I was writing to Mary.

"The lads," came the reply. "We — that's about fifty or so of us — we bunk away from you, at the prow, port-side . . . we've been talking . . . "

"About what?"

"About getting better conditions aboard. That Lawson warder's a right bastard and Bosun's no better. We see you speaking to the surgeon-commander — yesterday Cap'n Muddle himself gave you the time o' day, for Hoppy Greg saw it . . . this letter . . . " And he took from his rags an envelope and pressed it into my hand.

The afternoon was hot, the air sticky, the

ocean burnished with sun. The wallowing hulk of the *Mandarin* appeared to be asleep; even the helmsman was nodding.

I accepted the letter, which was in itself dangerous. Down on the quarter deck the patrolling sentries wandered aimlessly, now one paused in his stride to look in our direction.

"Who's Hoppy Greg?" I asked.

"The fella who wrote the letter — he were Blackwood Lodge — says you'll remember him."

"A Chartist?" It surprised me to learn there were more aboard.

"Born and bred, sir, like me. And there's more'n us, too, I tell you." He leaned confidentially and I cursed him, for I had the letter now and he was in the clear. "I reckon there's fifteen or twenty of us who were at the Westgate. And about ten extra who was with Jones the Watchmaker, but he didn't get 'em past Llantarnum."

"That's all over now."

"Oh no, it ain't, sir! You and Zeph were the boss-men then, and you're the gaffers now, though we be here chained like bloody animals. We fought for the Charter then and we'll fight for it again, with you leading us."

The marine sentries had come together and were clearly discussing us, nodding in our direction. Taply continued, "We trusts you, Mr Frost. Hoppy says you'll know what to do."

The sentries apparently lost interest in us and began patrolling again. Relieved, I said:

"If your Hoppy Greg wrote this letter and was a Blackwood Chartist, why didn't he deliver it?"

"Because he's aboard this tub as a sailor — able seaman in the Navy once and they flogged him cruel in there, so he paid off and becomes a Chartist, don't he? Then he signed with Crawshay Bailey on the Black Seam, till he took up with Zephaniah and marched on Newport. 'Things 'ave got to change,' says old Hoppy. 'I was flogged in the Navy and starved by bloody Bailey, and me and my missus are decent chapel folk — we don't owe fuss nor fart to nobody, we don't,' says he. He's a right decent fella."

"You said he was in the Blackwood Lodge, now you say he was with Zephaniah Williams."

"Beggin' ye pardon, Mr Frost. But I just said that, didn't I?"

I pondered it; there were spies everywhere. I asked:

"Let's get this clear — he's aboard now as a member of the crew?"

"And I said that, too, sir. Don't you trust your own mates now?"

"Best make off. I'll talk to you again when I've read the letter."

"You're a right toff, Mr Mayor."

"Go now."

In the security of my own straw, I waited for night and in the glimmering light of the ceiling lamp, read the letter:

Dear Mayor Frost,

Being an educated chap and I write best of them, the lads ask you to lead us and take the ship. Just now we be two points port of Fria's Land, and not six mile by rowing. All the deck crew and all the soldiers are with us, to make a new life in South America if all goes well. Those who don't want it can row a lifeboat to Fria's Cape. There will be no killing. As for this captain, we fear

113

him like the grasshoppers that fly in the night, but we'll take the Dr McKecknie with us, for he's a gent. Long live the Charter.

The letter was unsigned.

I said to Zephaniah during exercise next morning, "What do you think of it?"

"I think it excellent."

We were chained together, walking in unsteady circles to the heeling of the ship, for a brisk wind had got her and she was making a sturdy beauty of herself, full sail to the wind.

As if voicing the scene, the Captain's voice cried:

"Hands to the braces and hold her at that! Starboard your helm, quartermaster — handsomely! Aye, handsomely!"

I said to Zephaniah, "You approve? You must be mad!"

"Then we'll turn up our backsides for kicks! God Almighty, Frost, what kind of man are you? Listen. With over 200 convicts aboard, we've got them ten to one, and the soldiers are with us."

"As they were in Newport?"

"If they aren't, it's the chance we take,

but they can be picked off one by one, the sentries first. We'll pen the rest in the stern compartment, then turn loose for Cape Fria all who don't want to come."

"And steer west for South America?"

"Where else?" He turned to face me. "It all sounds reasonable, unless you want to spend the rest of your days in the land of the bloody kangaroos."

I said, "Remember the Governor of Portsmouth — his departing lecture to us? That his troops had been told to act with great severity against any commotion aboard?"

"All right? It goes wrong, and they shoot the lot of us. I seem to recall you telling Captain Shaw from the *Kilbain* that you'd prefer death to transportation."

I changed the argument. "Should we tell William Jones?"

"No! It'd be all over the ship."

Later, I gave him the letter; Zephaniah read it and tossed it over the side, saying, "I still say it sounds all right to me. What have you got against it?"

"Where did he get the paper?"

"The paper?"

"The notepaper. I'm writing on bits I brought aboard; others are writing between the lines of newspapers. No writing paper is issued, so how did this Hoppy Greg get hold of his?"

"Out of the Captain's cabin?"

"No, that's headed, for I've seen it."

"From Dr McKecknie's cabin, then? He's got a private pad of notepaper."

"Did it have a watermark? the letter did. You were too sharp throwing it away."

"It went over the side, where it should be. You'd have got yourself flogged, carrying that around."

The bosun's whistle called us below for grub, and we clanked down below hatches: here were set a line of iron pots bubbling from the cook galley — one pot to a dozen men. Side by side, we knelt, Zeph and I, spooning up a sticky, foul-smelling mess of bone soup and bread decorated with floating red globules of the salt beef diet, which, with no fresh vegetables, almost guaranteed the scurvy. Already men were going down with this, especially fo'rard, for some unknown reason. The sick bay was filled to overflowing.

Teeth were already dropping out, mouths

swelling up like toy balloons; the stools of the sufferers were laced with blood when floating down the bilges above my head. Men could be seen bleeding from the nose while lurching around the exercise deck in the mornings, and I have heard men scream, not at the touch of Dr McKecknie, but at his approach. William Jones was complaining of a bleeding patch on his forearm that would not heal; I had a raw and painful scurvy patch widening under my left arm.

For decades it had been observed that while farming and town children were subject to rickets, the children of the sea-ports who dipped their bread in the gutting buckets to make it savoury, were usually clear of the deforming disease: this began medical research into the reasons for scurvy, and the antidote — fresh vegetables and the juice of lime — was discovered; hence the later nickname of 'Limies' given to visiting English ships to American ports.

Such luxuries on convict ships were confined to the crews, and the convicts suffered in consequence; disability caused by scurvy while at sea was rife, and death was commonplace. Whig and Tory governments — having expelled the miscreants from the English shore — cared little how the expulsion was effected: death by scurvy aboard meant one less sinner to keep in the penal colony.

Now Dr McKecknie, who sometimes made visits to the communal eating-pots, was standing beside me, and he gestured to Lawson, our stern-bunk warder, saying, "Release Frost from Williams, bring him to my cabin, and stand guard outside the door."

Zephaniah, blowing on his spoon, said quietly, without an upward glance:
"Something is in the wind."

No luxuries attended a surgeon-commander aboard a convict ship: a bunk, table, chair, and a tiny port hole was all McKecknie was given. Still in chains, I stood before his desk, and noticed the notepaper on the pad before him. The gold braid of his collar rank, on an otherwise insignificant blue worsted uniform, gleamed in a sun-shaft. He said, abruptly:
"I will come straight to the point, Frost. You have received a letter suggesting you

should lead a mutiny aboard, and seize the ship?"

I hesitated, and he saw it. We stared at one another. McKecknie said:

"It would be better to tell the truth than have it flogged out of you. You are not a young man and the consequences would be disastrous. I ask you again. Have you received such a letter?"

"Yes."

"What did you do with it?"

"Ignored it, and threw it over the side."

"That was not wise of you. The action made you an accessory to the crime, you realize that?"

"I do now, sir."

"Was it signed?"

"No."

"How did you receive it?"

"I discovered it under my straw."

"You discovered it under your bed, and it was unsigned."

"Yes."

"I hope you are not lying to me. If you are, and Captain Muddle gets the truth out of you, the business will be out of my hands. It is only because you are still on my sick list that I have the power to interrogate you first, do you understand?"

"Yes."

His calm eyes moved over my face. "You remember the terms of the letter?"

"I can recall the general trend."

"State it."

"It gave the ship's position . . . ."

"Wait," McKecknie interjected. "How and to whom was the letter addressed? Did it not begin, 'Dear Mayor Frost . . . '?"

"It did."

"Then why didn't you say so? Continue."

Anger coloured his face, and I added quickly: "It said that I, being educated, should lead an action to take over the ship and sail it to the Americas; that there would be no killing, and that all who did not want to be involved would be landed on Cape Fria."

"A straightforward mutiny!"

"I assume so."

He rose. "You assume so! God alive, man, your assumptions amount to stupidity and your loyalty as treasonable as that for which you were sentenced! Do you realize the implications? For not divulging this letter to your captain you could be hanged! Clearly, this movement — which not only affects the crew, I hear, but some of the soldiers aboard — is one inspired by your damned Chartists. Yes, we have discovered the ringleader; one named Taply, who has confessed to brotherhood of the Brynmawr Lodge, and a seaman called Greg is his accomplice." The doctor glared up at me. "Was not your friend, Williams, leader of the Brynmawr-Nantyglo Chartist Lodge?"

I nodded.

"Did you confide the terms of the letter to him?"

"No, sir."

"Then he knows nothing of the venture?"

"Not that I am aware."

He rose again. "Let us hope for your sake that's the truth, for Williams is at this moment being interrogated by the captain. Knowing Captain Muddle, he may decide to flog the lot of you."

A silence came between us, one of a small unspoken friendship; an interlude fraught with male understanding and respect, each of the other's situation; McKecknie said, quietly:

"Doubtless, you suspected, from the start, that the letter was a trap set for you — come, you're an intelligent man."

"I suspected it, but didn't have the proof. Where, for instance, could a convict obtain notepaper of quality? Such a letter could have been written by my enemies long before we left Portsmouth, and sentence of death could have been passed upon me while at sea. That would have delighted the Whigs, placated the Tories and brought confusion to our petitioners." I bowed to him. "Let us pray that this is the end of the matter."

McKecknie opened the door and Lawson, the warder, entered; the doctor said:

"Not the end, Frost, but the beginning. It will be necessary, in order to put an official seal of disapproval upon the affair, to flog one or two at dawn." He smiled at me. "Shooting the innocent bearer of bad tidings has long been the fulcrum of international law. But understand that I have no hand in it."

I returned to the hatches in a fever of apprehension that Zephaniah, in his evidence to the captain, had told the truth. I was surprised to find that he was awaiting me.

"Tell the truth?" said Zephaniah. "To this lot? The only time I'll do that is before

122

the hand of St Peter. But somebody, I fear, is going to catch it."

"A fella called Taply," said William Jones, arriving at my straw. "And a seaman called Greg. The bosun's limberin' up — they're getting the cat at dawn."

This was the first occasion when I had been forced to witness a flogging. Even the thought had a sickening effect upon me: that a man could be tied into a helpless position by his fellows and his back, breech and shoulders flayed in order to exact revenge for misdemeanour . . . it appalled me. And the instrument constructed for this bestiality would have found no place in a jungle of animals.

# 10

THE *Mandarin* was still becalmed. At dawn the sun flung off his veil of night, exchanging a hunter's moon for an orb of astonishing brilliance and we sweated and fumed on a glassy sea.

Earlier we had lain shoulder to shoulder in exhaustion by heat while the ship, creaking and groaning in the hot bowl of night stank her bilges in the fetid air. Even the rats were ill with heatstroke.

An hour after dawn, herded up from below, we were crowded into a massed circle around the mainmast, all 200 of us, our bare feet crinkling to the scald of the deck.

Here had been vertically lashed a ten-foot-square ship's grating, and before the grating, flanked by armed soldiers and two brawny seamen stripped to the waist, was Captain Muddle: in full braided uniform was he, with Dr McKecknie, his eyes cast down, in attendance. Short, wide and hairy, the captain cried:

"The evidence, for and against, having been heard, we are here to witness the administration of punishment for the crime of suspicion of mutiny." He lowered the official paper from which he had been reading, and his voice rang out over the sea:

"Had it not been for the loyalty and alertness of crew members who, from time to time, have reported to me the foul design of taking the ship and sailing it to the Americas, we all might now be in the grip of piracy. For mutiny, let it be known, is a brother to piracy, and is not to be tolerated. Indeed, had I the power, I would hang the guilty ones from the yard arm, but I have prayed to the Almighty One for guidance and have been advised of a lesser sentence, and it is this: that Seaman Greg, who, I am ashamed to declare, is of my ship's company, and Convict Taply, one who assisted him in this malfeasance, be brought to the grating, each to receive fifty lashes; this is the punishment granted me under the laws of Transportation of Felons." Captain Muddle raised his face to the sea of men about him, and added, "After which both will be stapled to the deck on bread and water, without shelter, for a week."

The convicts shuffled uncertainly in their chains; the sun beat down. Without the surgeon's intervention, I thought, Greg and Taply would be lucky to survive it.

"Issue the cat," cried the bosun, and a sinewy, undersized creature, the keeper of provisions and accoutrements, came forward and presented the whip to Dr McKecknie, who took it, studied it momentarily, and handed it to the bosun who tested it in his hands and swished it through the air with obvious pleasure; giving it to the nearest flogger, he said:

"There it be, me lad, and lay it on proper."

Later, I examined this implement of torture.

It was constructed of a short wooden handle of about two feet long; this, interlaced with plaited rawhide thongs of equal length, extended nine tails, each about three feet long; thus it earned its name, the cat-o'-nine-tails; the thongs were knotted at intervals and had the strength and consistency of wire.

"Bring the man Greg!"

I lowered my head and stared down at the white deck, but in pity looked again as the man was led up from the chain locker; he came between two warders, with Lawson, the head warder leading the trio: he came naked, chained like the rest of us, hands manacled and with fetters on his ankles; but also, in his arms he carried a forty-pound cannonball, and this was linked to his waist. Yet he came with a small, indefinable arrogance, a man defiant to the world and its tortures; and his very nakedness enhanced this so that he appeared as one contained; clearly he despised the proceedings, and Zephaniah muttered beside me:

"Some man."

I nodded, now hypnotized by the preparations for the cruelty.

First they unlocked the cannonball and freed Greg's wrists from the manacles; then the bosun freed his ankles; this done, Greg was now spreadeagled vertically against the grating and his wrists and ankles tied to the vents. Meanwhile, the brine bath in which the flogged men would be immersed, was being filled with sea water, and there was no sound but the hissing of the swell, the dull thumping of deckspars where the sails hung dejectedly in the windless air, and the metallic clank-clank of the bilge pumps.

"Bring the man Taply!"

Next the Chartist who had given me the letter was brought from 'tween decks. They thrust him, squatting with bowed head, naked, in the small circle about the grating.

"Right, lay on lashes!" cried the Captain, and Dr McKecknie, taking a notepad and pencil from his pocket, began a dull chant, counting the strokes.

Flexing his muscled body, the first flogger laid back the whip, took a pace forward, and brought it down on Greg's back. The flesh was sliced, the skin laid open in a bright red weal, and Greg screamed. Blood droplets gathered along the wound, instantly to be swept away by the next fearful stroke. Again and again the naked man screamed, each cry being followed by the dull tone of Dr McKecknie:

"One, two, three, four . . ."

The bosun cried, his fist up at the

flogger, "Come on, man, put your back into it!"

I stood in an apathy of sickness, the bile rising to my throat; the convicts clanked their chains. The marines tightened their hold upon their muskets, eyes switching along the swaying ranks for a hostile movement.

Within ten strokes of the whip, Greg's back was a lacerated mess of blood and rippled skin. Something touched my hand, and I saw, gleaming scarlet upon one of my knuckles, a single stain of blood, and this was Hoppy Greg's; and I noticed men in the rank nearest to the grating wiping it away from their faces. Again and again the whip curled back; again and again its rawhide thongs descended, punctuated by the victim's shrieks.

"Thirty-three, thirty-four . . . " intoned the doctor.

The first flogger was sweating with his efforts; it streamed down his hairy back and soaked his waistband; it brought wide, black patches upon his trews where they stretched over his straining buttocks, and his black-maned head was gleaming sweat; clearly, he was tiring, and strangely (although I understand it better now) Greg had ceased his cries: he simply hung there by the wrists, his knees akimbo, his bloodstained body shuddering as the whip came down.

"Right you, out!" bawled the bosun. "Next man up!" And he took the whip from the first flogger and tossed it to the second one.

"Wait," commanded Dr McKecknie, and the men stood back.

Reaching the flogged man, the doctor raised his eyelids, and turned to Captain Muddle, who asked:

"He's unconscious?"

"No, sir."

"Then get on with it. To fifty he's sentenced and fifty he'll have. I'm not having mutiny aboard my ship, you hear me?" And he swung to us, his face livid with sudden anger. "The next talk I hear of Cape Fria and the Americas will be your last. Just another word of it one word — and I'll flog the lot of you between here and Cape Town! Lay on, bosun! And lay on strong!"

And the flogging began again. The bosun cried:

"I'll 'ave a do of it myself, beggin' your pardon, sir . . ."

"Just get on with it, get on with it!"

Through half closed eyes, appalled by the inhumanity, I saw creeping towards my feet across the white-burned deck, a thin trickle of scarlet; then another, and another, and the blood gathered speed as the swell slanted us.

"Forty-eight, forty-nine, fifty," said Dr McKecknie. "Punishment finished, captain!"

"Cut him down, if you please, bosun!"

I raised my face as they carried Greg past, to recoil at renewed shrieks when they threw him bodily into the brine bath. Here two warders, unnoticed by me until now, were waiting with deck brooms. Vigorously they began to scrub salt into his wounds to prevent infection.

"Stand by, bosun — the convict Taply, if you please!"

Taply, skinny, his ribs showing beneath his wrinkled sides, begged, with his shackled hands together in prayer, but they dragged him, his naked toes flexing, and tied him to the grating. I heard Dr McKecknie say:

"My respects, sir, this one may not be up to it. The flesh of his back . . . the man is wasted . . . "

"And my respects to you, good doctor," replied Captain Muddle. "Twenty-five on the back then, and the rest on his legs and buttocks," and hearing this, Taply wailed, his head turned at the grating:

"Don't flog below the breech, sir. For God's sake don't flog below the breech!"

"Continue, if you will, bosun," said Captain Muddle.

Not even by this stupid name shall I remember him.

We were but four days out from Cape Town and although Captain Muddle relented in one respect, he assigned for us a different punishment.

With his disciplinary powers curtailed now, said he, in view of our better behaviour, all convicts would henceforth have all their shackles removed to allow freedom of movement throughout the ship. This was nothing new; through the voyage so far we had been granted intervals when chains were completely removed sometimes for as long as a week at a time — it happened, it appeared, on the captain's whim.

"He reckons he's got the measure of us, that's why," said William Jones.

"After what he did to poor Hoppy, he's got the measure of me," added Zephaniah. "What think you, Frost?"

"Sadism is a sickness, it comes and goes on the wind."

"It ain't nothin' like that," announced Old Lag. "Greg's a tough 'un — he's all right, but they reckon l'il old Taply's nigh near to snuffin' it. Muddle's a'feard o' a corpse to handle."

Old Lag, with previous experience of transportation — seven years for lifting a gentleman's watch in Cheapside — was probably right, but in the event Taply did not die then, although something in me did. Until that flogging I still had some hope for Mankind.

It was tried even more severely when we endured the few days of 'down the hatch' punishment. This wasn't unusual, said Old Lag, following suspicion of mutiny.

"I'm complaining to my Member of Parliament the moment I get home," said Richard Carling.

For they crowded us into the bunks 'tween decks, and battened down the hatches.

The effect of this is best described by another convict in another time, John Boyle O'Reilly, who was transported in the *Hougoumont*, the last convict ship to Australia:

When the ship was becalmed in the tropics, [wrote O'Reilly], the suffering of the imprisoned wretches in the steaming and crowded hold was piteous. They were so packed that free movement was impossible; the best thing to do was to sit on his or her berth, and suffer in patience. The air was stifling and oppressive. There was no draught through the barred hatches; the deck above them was blazing hot. The pitch dropped from the seams, and burned their flesh as it fell. There was only one word spoken or thought — one yearning idea in every mind — water, cool water to slake the parching thirst. Two pints of water a day was served out to each convict — a quart of half putrid, blood-warm liquid. It was a woeful sight to see the thirsty souls devour this allowance as soon as their hot hands seized the vessel. Day in and day out, the terrible calm held the ship, and the consuming heat sapped the lives of the pent-up convicts. Hideous incidents soiled the days and nights as the convict ship sailed southward with its burden of disease and death. The mortality among the convicts was frightful. Weakened and depressed by the long drought, the continuous heat and the poisonous atmosphere, they succumbed to the fever.

Let John O'Reilly speak for me, such is the truth of that description. I have little to add except the words of Captain Hill, the commander of the military guard aboard the *Surprise*, who described the shackles used on that ship as akin to those used aboard the *Mandarin*.

The shackles are made with a short bolt that drop between the legs and fasten around the waist, so that they could not extend one leg from the other more than an inch or two; thus fettered, it was impossible for the prisoners to move, but at the risk of breaking a leg.

Such irons were known as 'slavers', being hand-downs from a Slave Trade which was still active; such leg irons, having been used on the blacks, were transferred to Britain's penal system. I have not been so shackled, but I have seen men who were.

While it was heaven-sent to be free of chains of any sort, it was hell to be put under the hatches. We lay together shoulder to shoulder, all 200 of us during the four days it took to reach the Cape: amid the stench of vomit and buckets brimming with urine: dreaming in that foul atmosphere of cool air and falling water . . . of the green fields of home: listening to the monotonous creaking of the spars, and the groans of the mutilated Greg and Taply, who were stapled to the deck above us.

Man, vain Man, I thought, when clothed in brief authority, do such things as make the angels weep.

Unknown to me, Zephaniah, of all people, was about to make an invaluable contribution in that direction.

# 11

TWO days before we reached the Cape of Good Hope, Captain Muddle relented; the hatches came off and a fine brisk air blew the length of the ship, which was now scurrying along merrily in the arms of a little sou'wester: freed of shackles, we all came up on deck.

My letter to Mary already written, I decided to inform Feargus O'Connor, compatriot in our Chartist venture, of my situation.

*Mandarin* at Sea
Near the Cape of Good Hope
4 May 1840

My dear O'Connor,

So, my dear fellow, your prognostications were wrong; you have not proved yourself the true prophet, either as to the punishment or the extent. You ought to have known the Whigs, they are ever the same: there is everything in them to despise and nothing to admire. What do they care for Law or public opinion, if opposed to their interests or the gratification of their passions?

On the 22 February Mr William Geach, my stepson, came to see us aboard the Hulk; his appearance and spirits were not at all promising, and when he left us he promised to return and inform us of the Queen's answer to the petitions of the people on our behalf. But the day before he was due to come, the Chief Mate of the *York*, our enemy on the Hulk, informed us that he was to convey us to the *Mandarin*, the convict ship then lying off Spithead. Almost immediately, with no opportunity to say farewell to our best loved ones, we were put aboard a barge, and near dead with cold and half starved, taken to this ship. So ill was I that many thought that a few days only would terminate my earthly career, but the surgeon-commander, a Dr A. Mckecknie, received us with much kindness and promised to make us comfortable during the voyage, and well has this gentleman redeemed the pledge. I hope the Chartists will not forget this, but they will shew themselves as sensible of kindness as of cruelty.

Farewell, my dear sir,
Truly yours, John Frost.★

"To whom are you writing?" asked Zephaniah.

"Feargus O'Connor."

"Isn't that a waste of good paper? Uncle Feargy proved himself a physical force Chartist in the bath. One bang from the redcoats and he'd have been off back to Ireland."

"Perhaps so, but we'd have done better to listen to people like him, Place and Lovett, I think."

"Oh aye?" He became expansive. "I was a moral force Chartist once but every damned one of us knows that only a kick up the backside will work. If we'd let daylight through a few Whigs and Tories and hanged a few bishops, we wouldn't be here now."

Richard Carling joined us. "Yes, you'd have your heads on spikes in Parliament

★Text reproduced in an abbreviated form — with kind permission of Newport Public Libraries.

139

Square and the rest of you in strips," he cried.

"That's always been my ambition, mind," said Old Lag, and our Chartist companions, Roberts, John Jones and Jerry Howell, followed him to us, rubbing their wrists after freedom from the irons, and Old Lag added, "Old Olly Cromwell had his 'ead stuck up there, didn't he? And what's good for him is good enough for me."

The sun shone, the *Mandarin* buried her nose into a heavy sea and threw it over her shanks as the wind filled her sails, and I looked around my companions one by one.

Somewhere on the port side a sailor was playing a mouth organ and dancing to the tune of a hornpipe, and the convicts, gathering about him, were clapping the time, and there was growing on the air a singular spirit of festivity born of this new freedom. So many of us had expected a watery grave after the sinking of the *George III* and the *Neva* that all were a little surprised to find themselves alive, and Hope, though a restless bedfellow, is also a happy riser.

And so, pounding down the southern

sea-lane, with all sails billowing to a friendly trade wind, it was a ship's company of a different hue; and when the dim blur of blue land grew in shape on the port horizon, a cry like a dying gull wafted down from the crow's-nest:

"Cape of Good Hope coming up portside!"

With the tumultuous water of the Atlantic falling behind us and the warmer winds of the Southern Ocean coming up, we greeted each other in a new fellowship.

"What about a bit more o' that old yarn you was tellin' us, Dick Carling?" cried Old Lag.

"What old yarn's this, then?" asked Roberts.

Timbo Weller was there, Petticoat Boy, Sole Bungy the forger, and poor old Greg, his back split deep from his flogging, "and God help that bloody captain if ever I get him in an alley," said he, "l'il old Taply's legs'll never be the same, he fair cut the muscles off."

"Come on, start off, lad!" This from Old Lag, slapping Richard's back, and he put up a gnarled fist. "He's goin' to lay the fair wench out for bed-time, ain't you, Sir Richard?"

I gave them a grin and a sigh; they didn't have much and I commended the tale despite my inherent bias to a prim Non-conformity. I watched them gather around with intent faces. Dr McKecknie wandered up then, saying:

"Is this a private tale, or can anyone listen?"

"Make way for the doctor," said Richard, and the tale began.

"You remember the little Moroccan leather bag I bought for two shillings at the slave stall?" asked Richard, and some nodded. "Well, the lady bought one as well," said he, "and this is something you must remember."

"What is all this?" asked Dr McKecknie, coming closer.

"It's a story of theft and sexual depravity, sir," said I, "and you'd do well to abandon it at once."

"Indeed, I shall not," said McKecknie, and leaned closer, and Richard continued.

"I took my seat in the London coach, sitting opposite the lady, and she was clearly a foreigner — from that clutch of French aristocracy who are possessed of sparkling eyes and snowy bosoms."

"Bloody hell and hounds!" whispered Old Lag.

"At her waist, which I could have spanned with two hands, she wore a corsage of wild flowers; her bodice was white and embroidered with silk, her skirts purple and voluminous; upon her head was a black mantilla, and her back hair fell to her bare shoulders in tight ringlets like ten pounds of curly black candles. But, it was her eyes . . . They were green, like the eyes of a lynx. And her jewels . . . !

"I asked her, as the coach started off, pursued by dogs and urchins:

"'You are French, Madame?'

"''ow you know?'

"'By your dress and your accent,' I answered. 'Forgive my presumption, but may I pledge you my protection? I am also bound for London.'

"'I am bound for London? 'Ow you know that?'

"'You appear to know the prices there. Further, one so beautiful, can only be bound for London. For the season, may I ask?'

"'To meet my 'usband, monsieur. He

'as booked a room for us in the Charing Cross 'otel.'

"Now, most suitors would have been dissuaded at this hint of rejection, but conquest is only worthy of the prey if the chase is hot; her jewels, which had brought me to her side in the first place, suddenly assumed minor importance."

"They always take orf their earrings, mind," interjected Old Lag. "That were the first thing my old girl ever took off."

"For God's sake!" said Zephaniah.

Richard continued:

"I had now decided on a foul design; cold, wet journeys along muddy English roads shouting 'Stand and deliver' was rough stuff compared with this. For here, sitting opposite me, was the double reward of loot and love. Planned judiciously, one could well serve the other.

"'Your name, monsieur?' the lady asked.

"'Sir Richard Carling, ma'am,' and she nodded prettily, saying:

"'Madame Le Roy, monsieur. I am delighted to meet the English aristocracy.'

"The coach clattered east for Marshfield, on through Calne to Marlborough and an overnight stop at the Crown Hotel.

"Here we dined together on duck and green peas while the other guests, mainly chinless aristocrats with their wives and lovers, chatted intimately, but no woman compared with the beauty before me. Beyond the bow window where we sat, a hurdy-gurdy was playing a little minuet that sweetened the night; upon the hurdy-gurdy man's shoulder sat a white turtledove, and this, at intervals, sang to us.

"'Do you know the song of the turtledove lover, monsieur?' Madame Le Roy inquired.

"I confessed that I did not.

"She pouted prettily 'so lonely was she for a mate that she sang to the trees for one. She was a long way from home, you see . . .' and I replied:

"'Were I her lover, Madame Le Roy, I would fly a thousand miles to her window,' and, reaching out, touched her hand.

"'How very gallant! But Charing Cross is not a great distance,' and she shivered with suppressed anticipation. 'Oh, monsieur, I am dyin' for my 'usband!'"

Zephaniah said, with an audible grunt, "From what I hear, Carling, she'd got her hand on it."

"Mind you," added Petticoat Boy, "I've

'ad 'em that way, like — once they've got it they reckon to sit on it."

Richard said no more because the warders cried:

"Up in line, lags, up in line! Approachin' shore, so stand by for fitting irons!"

So we stood on the slanting deck shoulder to shoulder while Lawson and his gang snapped on the manacles and leg irons, and with Table Mountain looming up on a sea of cobalt blue, it was the nearest we got to freedom that day.

I said to Richard, "You'll finish that long-winded tale of yours one day, God willing."

"God," he replied, "has nothing to do with this particular story."

# 12

AS I later told Mary, the Cape of Good Hope was a significant milestone on my journey to exile. Having embarked the *Mandarin* in a state of collapse and spent days in the sick bay under the attentions of Dr McKecknie, my health now was better than could be expected for a man of my years. Further, though I thought I'd be a prey to seasickness, this fear was unfounded; compared to many I was a veritable sea dog.

At Falmouth one of the missionaries allowed aboard to save our souls, had generously given me a tattered copy of *Pilgrim's Progress* which I again read avidly. But Bunyon's heavenly prose did nothing to prepare me for the hypocrisy of what followed on the *Mandarin*'s deck, when we dropped anchor in Symond's Bay, Cape Town.

"All hands to a religious service; prayers for Deliverance!" cried the bosun, and went around stirring people into speed with his rope's end. "On deck aft, below the poop!"

And there we gathered in a massed throng; a packed circle of zoo convicts in their chains around the squat figure of Captain Muddle in full uniform, with ceremonial sword. And with a Bible in one hand and the other uplifted to God, he shouted:

"Revelation 20, verse 11, I read from the book of God, which is the holy book, 'And I saw a great white throne and him that sat on it . . . ' Next verse, 'And I saw the dead, small and great, stand before God: and the books were opened, which is the book of life, and the dead were judged . . . ' Next verse, and mind this carefully!"

His small, black eyes glared at us from under their ape-like brows, and he shouted, shaking his fist at the sky, "'And the sea gave up the dead that were in it . . . and they were judged every man according to their works . . . '"

Silence, save for the lapping of water and the crying of gulls, and Muddle shouted:

"'And I saw a new heaven and a new earth . . . and there was no more sea. And

I heard a great voice coming out of heaven, saying. Behold, the tabernacle of God is with men, and he will dwell with them, and they shall be his people . . . and he shall be their God . . .'"

I watched this man and knew the reason for him; that his soul, within the limits of a confining intelligence, was on fire; it was the intellect of a Torquemada, the Dominican friar of the Inquisition, filled to the teeth with God and to the belly with cruelty; yet no better, or worse, than a thousand of his fellows like John O'Hara Booth, the Commandant of Port Arthur whom I was soon to face. And now he cried, his features working with an inner emotion:

"'And God shall wipe away all tears from their eyes; and there shall be no more death, neither sorrow, nor crying, and neither shall there be any more pain . . .'"

Not far from me I saw the face of Hoppy Greg; in profile I saw him, his arms shrugged to the rack of his torn shoulders, and his was the face of fury: near him, with a ragged blanket thrown over his thin body, supported by warders, was little Taply, the broken Chartist. And

I looked again at the sadist Muddle, and saw that tears were upon his cheeks . . .

Repeatedly I have been accused of being Godless, and falsely, for while I believe in the Man, I reject his black-clad disciples of dishonour; their cant has made ignoble the most noble of pursuits, and here was one such hypocrite before me and here I quote the historian Wade.

"These self-appointed priests, they bawl at the card table and howl in the playhouse; they tally-ho, shoot, hunt, they brandish the coachman's whip and roister with the drunks. And remember, too, that these jovial bishops, filled with the Holy Ghost, have the cure of souls, while their wretched curates starve on a threadbare stipend, their labours wasted in the profligate and dissipated lives of their parochial superiors."

Allow me to give a dissertation on the plague called Bishoprics, which can be interpreted as a newly discovered religious pestilence contemporary with parasitic fleas currently affecting rodents. Typhus owes its first historical mention to the Book of

Samuel, where it is described as an epidemic among the Philistines, the symptoms being a swelling of the lymph glands, mainly in the groin. But such disease is not confined to microbes; it is integral with the doctrine of Church and State — a combining together to enlighten the few and hoodwink the many, and the swelling induced by this policy is a swelling of the guts.

We complain, do we not, of the poor rates, of charges for the army, navy, government offices and courts of law. But what are these compared to the sinecure wealth of our bishops who proliferate about us like demented lemmings, to say nothing of their aristocratical rectors and vicars? Is it really conceivable that, when Christ owned nothing but a blood-stained rag, we employ His fat prelates and sit them on elevated thrones in sumptuous palaces attended by gorgeously attired menials to wait upon them with holy smoke and autocratic heraldry? Contrast this pomp with my impoverished minister of Hope Chapel back in Newport, who receives for his service to the poor less than the pay of an Irish hod-carrier.

I subscribe to this. For it was later

written by finer exponents of the literary quirk than I, that Britain should not be satisfied until the last English king is hanged by the guts of the last bishop, but let Wade of the *Black Book* have the last word: By their sanctimonious pretexts these monks have possessed themselves of the benefices of the kingdom and perverted them for their own enrichment. Their establishments have become abodes of luxury, indolence, sensual crime; even many unnatural practices have become endemic. And who can expect from societies so depraved either charity or hospitality? The rich and powerful never sympathize with indigence; as a motive to indifference they regard the poor, who will always be with us if they have their way, with cruel and unjust suspicion; zeal in their welfare they call mistaken benevolence. Yet the poor are the very prey upon which they batten for their privileges.

In the past I have been indicted for High Treason upon the monarch; if the above be High Treason upon her servants, the priests and monks, I plead guilty now.

The convict ship, the *Lady Juliana*, crammed

with her ballast of females, was anchored in the bay. Fleeter than us, she had earlier been moored at the supply quay, there to take on provisions; this done, she was warped out, to make room for the *Mandarin*; and we convicts, decked to the ears in the old slave irons, crowded at the wharf rails to see the animals, provisions, and fresh water come aboard.

I have just glanced at my diary.

It is the sixth of May.

Surely, we are about half way through our great journey. And this, the Cape of Good Hope, is a great meeting place, a showpiece of Britain's maritime power.

Many men-o'-war, mainly brigs, were anchored in Symond's Bay.

"What are this lot doing here, then?" asked Jerry Howell; he had joined me at the rail with his two companions, Francis Roberts and John Jones.

"They are on the way to China," I answered. "In support of the Opium War."

"To stop those Chinkos smoking opium, is it?" asked Old Lag.

"To induce them to smoke it," replied Zephaniah.

"Why, for Gawd's sake?"

"Because there's money in it," answered Richard, his eyes narrowed to the sun.

Below us the loading activity quickened; blacks, their near-naked bodies shining like watered coal, trailed their loads into our holds past white Afrikaner overseers in a cracking of whips.

I indicated the brigs. "Narrow draught, so they can navigate Chinese rivers. The Chinese, forced into signing British treaties, are now themselves harvesting the Indian poppy under the muzzles of British guns."

Later, Gladstone was to say:

"I am in fear of the wrath of God for our national iniquity towards China."

And the men who were soaking that country in the juice of the poppy, were actually coming aboard us, to pay their respects to Captain Muddle; one, young and fresh-complexioned, clearly straight out of the English climate, paused beside me.

"Mr Frost?" He glanced meaningfully at my companions, who dutifully shuffled away.

"Yes?" I answered.

"My name is Jennings. I am from Newport."

154

I wanted to grasp his hands, but his nervousness at the meeting was betraying itself in anxious glances at his fellow officers, and he said softly:

"Probably unknown to you, there have been many petitions for your release — from Merthyr alone one of 17,000 names has been delivered to Her Majesty. My squadron left Spithead weeks after you; being fleeter, my information is more in date."

I answered: "Mr Jennings, I apologize for my appearance. When you return home please make no mention of it."

He said, "The Tolpuddle Martyrs, they have also petitioned . . ."

"I am glad."

The sun was bright upon his young face. "Lord Teynham, with a petition of 1500 names, took it to the House of Lords . . ."

"That was before we left Portsmouth."

"And Mr Leader moved for a pardon in the House . . ."

I smiled to cheer him, for clearly he was endeavouring to lift my spirits. "Examine it, Mr Jennings; you are little more in date than I."

"But in this last instance, perhaps . . . ?"

"Tell me."

"Your two main accusers, Hodge and Israel Firman . . . "

"Are being ostracized and insulted," I interjected. "Hodge has been run out of Blackwood. Yes, I know these things, too. Could you but tell me that my wife has ceased her tears; that my children are cared for, that my stepson is now free of the accusations made against him — this would alleviate a lot of the pain."

"I can do none of these things."

I bowed to him, a ridiculous movement when one is in chains; amazingly, he saluted me. This the second one.

"God be with you, Mr Frost. You have a message, if I get home?"

"*If* you get home?" I questioned.

"The China expedition; we are in the process of convoying opium from India to China; the Emperor doesn't approve of it, to say the least. Bottled up in the Yellow River? Death by a thousand cuts!"

"Well done the Emperor! Admit it, it really is a shameful business."

"One worthy of the Whigs," said he.

The reply surprised me: they exist, these

156

small idealists, in unusual places: later, given time, they grow into revolutionaries.

"Don't forget the Tories," I said. "And God speed you home, young man; when you get there kindly visit my family."

In the event, he didn't. His ship foundered in the Yangtze-kiang, according to a later letter from Mary.

Later still, history recorded, that during the sack and burning by French and British troops of beautiful Peking, the soldiers were so sated with loot that they were treading rubies, amethysts and gold (because of its weight) into the mud; only stooping to pick up diamonds, while acceptable females were sent to official brothels.

"It is what is called colonialism for the benefits of the natives," said Zephaniah. "No doubt the God you worship can see some value in it."

With shrieking pigs and bellowing cattle aboard, and some of the excellent Cape salt beef; with tubs of fresh spring water to replace the stinking vermin-infested slime we had been forced to drink, we crowded on all sail, and on the twelfth of

May 1840, exactly a week after arriving at Cape Town, we pulled out in pursuit of the *Lady Juliana*, who had all Old Lag's hopes aboard.

"Get after 'er — come, beat us about — *after her!*" he cried.

But she was still the fleeter, and with hours she died from a white dot on the horizon of the Indian Ocean, into nothingness.

# 13

**I** WROTE in my diary:

For the past fortnight we have been clipping along at a fine pace, settling beautifully into the arms of the trade wind, and probably for the first time I am at peace with myself. The very helplessness of one's situation endows the spirit with a sense of retirement from conflict. While, from the time I can remember, mine has been an opposition to authority; discord and dissensions are all gone now, I can let the world by like squawking Kilkenny cats. I long for one thing only — the arms of my beloved. But if I disclose one thought, speak one word of adoration or desire, it is seized upon and gloated over by a score of censors. Oh, my darling, how can I tell you of my need of you? In the light of the creaking lanthorn I see the shine of your hair, the whiteness of your breasts; can it be so corrupt to lie here in felon's straw and dream of you beneath me? Can it be that never again will I know the velvet smoothness of your body? Or see you suckle a new child of my loins? Remember me, your husband, for I have loved no other; remember again the madcap escapades of our love-making when the moonlight of Bettws bound us, and the world was gusty in the honeying sweetness of our touch — remember? Now I forge all our vagrant, empty dreams and mould them in your thighs.

*"Frost!"*

It was Lawson's command, ringing down the line of outraged sleepers; I sat up on the palliasse.

"Yes?"

"Report to the doctor."

"Dr McKecknie?"

"Come on — there's only one doctor!"

I carefully folded away my diary note and put it into my jacket.

Despite my every attempt to stay presentable, my clothing was in rags now. The daily conservancy of deck scrubbing on hands and knees, the filthy bilge-scraping and emptying of disgusting pails and pans had slowly decimated the suit in which I had come aboard.

On the *York*, the prison hulk, we had been given Grey Garb prison clothes, but had to hand these in when taken to the *Mandarin*. Indeed (and I reflected with some humour) the scarecrow apparel on me now was the same suit I had worn in Monmouth courthouse: more, now I come to think of it, it was in this very frock coat, waistcoat and trews that they had pronounced me Mayor of Newport!

The top-hatted gentlemen, the wives, the sweethearts and the courtesans, the titled personages and the tradesmen so dear to my heart, would have died of apoplexy had they seen me now: with my gray hair down to my shoulders and my beard straggling to my chest. Gone was the fine-cut suit, the black curve of a quality stock — always the sign of a well-dressed gentleman, he of the high quality calfskin boots . . .

But the boots had long vanished, I fear; now replaced by calloused feet and broken toes, and let me state this while I think of it — no toe unused to harsh treatment, complains more than when broken in the bilges aboard a convict ship; no shin more agonizing when the skin is broken — a kick in passing from a warder's hobnailed boot.

"Come on, come on! Do I have to drag ye out of there?" Lawson again.

Sod him, I thought, let him wait.

Sod them all.

Old Lag, did they call him?

Old Lag; *me*, they mean.

I was becoming as ribald as the rest of them.

Old Lag, Old Lag, *Old lag* . . .

I was surprised to find Zephaniah in Dr McKecknie's cabin; more, he had his manacles removed.

"And his," commanded the doctor, and Lawson, with clear reluctance, removed mine.

"Ye realize this is dangerous, sir?"

McKecknie said, "It is not the least dangerous, these men are gentlemen."

Lawson dropped the manacles on to the floor and slammed the cabin door after him with disapproval. Zeph nodded me a wink of greeting, but I didn't return it, for I was watching McKecknie.

"Please sit down, both of you," said he, and we obeyed.

Rising from his desk he brought a decanter of wine and three glasses. These he filled with meticulous care, smiling up as he allowed for the ship's sudden slant to wind'ard.

"I expect you are wondering why I've brought you here?"

Zephaniah frowned up from under his heavy brows; a strange trick of the lamplight shadowed his features, turning him into a primate, but he did not answer; the doctor handed us each a glass.

"A toast, first, to the *Mandarin*? She has brought us this far with no complaint."

"I'll drink to that," said Zephaniah, and drained his glass.

I sipped at mine, for I needed a cool head.

This entertainment of convicts by a member of the crew was against the Laws of Transportation. It could end in severe punishment, not only for the doctor, but for us. With the smallest excuse, Captain Muddle would flog the pair of us. Then McKecknie said:

"This meeting, gentlemen, is with the official approval of the captain."

The wine was good; it played its Italian sunshine upon my throat.

The doctor said, "Back home, I understand from fleet Naval despatches, speculation is rife about the actual intention of the Chartists . . . "

Ah yes, I thought, here it comes.

From the very outset of our journeying; indeed, before we were removed by prison van from Monmouth gaol after the sadistic cruelty of the keeper and turnkey there . . . who had delighted in asking us as to the disposal of our bodies, when all the time they knew of our reprieve; the construction of the scaffold even before our trials officially began; the bitter treatment aboard the steamer *Usk* that took us from Chepstow; the brutality of the hulk while awaiting the *Mandarin* . . . All was perhaps contrived to serve one end — our subservience born of gratitude, for the kindness shown by McKecknie . . . ?

This kindness became suspicious when the doctor had forewarned me of the dangers which had ended in the flogging of the mutineers. Few humanitarians existed in the medical profession aboard convict ships; indeed, the opposite was the case, for these doctors were usually only those who volunteered to serve in the face of the brutality they were bound to witness. I liked Dr McKecknie and wanted to trust him, but there existed in my mind a nagging suspicion concerning him.

Chartism was not ended in Britain; indeed, our convictions had lit a flame of agitation for our release. Conversely, our opponents in churches and chapels back at home, would be saying that only Divine Providence had saved the Throne, and that we were in the place where we could do least damage.

Nothing achieves more than kindness in the face of adversity; so had Zephaniah and I been served up as psychological packages about to be suborned into repentance and confession? And had Dr McKecknie been planted by a watchful government which had spies and accomplices?

Now, in the cabin, McKecknie said, "It is being argued in Britain, I hear, that you are guiltless of the charge of High Treason levelled against you . . . " and I interjected:

"That isn't what the Whigs and Tories believe, that is why we're here."

He nodded. "But that is not what the people think; on every hand they petition on the grounds that you were falsely sentenced, and the Government is being faced with public disorder to gain your release."

"Excellent."

"But is it excellent?" He sipped his wine, watching me. "Has there not been enough political upheaval? Chartism is over, is it not? But, although the pig has had its throat cut, it refuses to die."

It angered me, but Zephaniah only smiled. I said:

"Chartism isn't dead, Dr McKecknie. The people will not let it be abandoned. Our fight for the Charter was a result of the failure of the Government to put right the wrongs . . . had it done so our movement would have died in the cradle."

"And meanwhile, though you claim to be a patriot, you can stand by and watch your country go up in flames?"

"You are over-dramatizing the situation, Doctor. Moral force Chartism will prevail over physical force in the end."

He got up and wandered about, glass in hand. "And it was this belief that made you plead not guilty to the charge of High Treason?"

I did not reply, and he added, "For it appears to me passing strange that men of such conviction should so perjure themselves if they believed otherwise. You were sentenced for trying to replace the monarchy with a republican state. If the people believed that it would quieten agitation at home."

I said, "What would you have had us do, Dr McKecknie? Hand our bodies over to the butchers?"

"So you lied?"

"Of course we lied, and so would you have done."

"I doubt it. It is a question of honour." He turned to Zephaniah. "What say you?" and Zephaniah answered:

"Let Frost speak for me, he was my leader."

A silence came between us broken by the creaking of the ship's timbers and the thumping slaps of water breaking along her shanks. I said, "Doctor, what do you want of me?"

167

He made a small, grotesque face. "Your signature to a document."

I didn't reply, and he added, "I make no apology — I know this is what the Government wants — just a simple statement of fact that you were rightly sentenced for the crime you committed. The people clearly hold this in some doubt so they agitate for your pardon, which proved successful in the case of the Dorchester labourers. You were clearly guilty of High Treason, Frost. You know it, I know it, and so does the Government, but the people do not accept it."

"An affidavit — in writing, you mean?"

"An affidavit countersigned by Captain Muddle — it would be a legal document."

"And in return?"

"In return?" He lowered his glass.

"Don't tell me there isn't a reward for such a document!"

It was out; sweat sprang to the doctor's head and he raised a weary hand and wiped it into his hair, saying:

"While nothing at all has been offered, no doubt an easier passage could be arranged when you are landed at the penal settlement. You have knowledge of administration.

The commandant there could do with another clerk . . . "

"And him?" I nodded at Zephaniah.

"He has been a collier. Would a position as a superintendent of mines suit you, Mr Williams?"

"Passably."

"Nor must we forget Mr Jones, the third of the trio. As a watchmaker he could be gainfully employed with boy apprentices."

"They sound like sinecures, doctor — are the salaries good?"

He sat down at his desk and glared up at me.

I liked him then and I like him now; I will always be grateful for his kindness to us, me especially, when I came aboard the *Mandarin* close to death; but even today I am not certain if he was doing what he considered right for us, or was in his country's political grasp. Anger was now in his voice:

"Don't become too fickle, Mr Frost. Port Arthur, when you get there, could quite easily change your attitude."

I knew a sickness in my stomach. Port Arthur was the hell that every convict feared; one presided over by a commandant whose reputation for cruelty was echoing around the world.

I glared at Zephaniah who had shown no surprise. "You knew this?"

"Yes."

"I told him earlier, but pledged him to secrecy," said McKecknie. "It could, like him, affect your decision. Will you prepare and sign the document I suggest?"

"I will not."

"That's a pity; Mr Williams here has already done so. Because you are his leader, your signature would have been more important, but I suppose, like everything else in this life, we can't have everything." He knocked upon his desk; the cabin door opened and the warder entered.

"Iron him and take him away," said McKecknie.

I was still awake, and fuming, when Zephaniah returned to his straw beside me.

"Well done," said he. "Now you can't look upon Port Arthur as a holiday resort."

I fought to control my anger. "What have you done, for God's sake?"

"Given him what he wanted."

"You've signed a document confessing to High Treason?"

He answered wearily, "I've written him a letter telling what we were up to. God Almighty, man, we knew what we were doing from the start, didn't we? All I've done is make a clean breast of it."

"You've sold us out!"

"Oh God, don't start that . . . " And I cried, sitting up:

"It'll ring round the world and make bloody fools of us. Dear Jesus, I've done some shameful things in my day, but I've never curried favour with the bastards!"

"Ach, go to sleep, old lady!"

A voice came up from the straw ten bunks down, "Bloody hell, lads, go to sleep. We've got to be up in the marnin'!"

They slept, but I did not sleep.

With dawn, just before the clang of the bell and the threats from the warders' batons, Zephaniah awoke, and said:

"Your scruples do you credit, Frost, but I've learned my lesson. The people at home, apart from family, don't give a sod for us. They can petition for the next ten years and we'll still be here, and you know it. They can change the Government from Tory to Whig and still we'll rot. And when he told me we were headin' for Port Arthur, that was the end of it for me. From now I'm having whatever's going, and to the devil with you and anything to do with Chartism."

Before we landed at Port Arthur, on the pretext that I might change my mind, I asked to see Zephaniah's letter and made a copy of it. For the sake of history I repeat it here:

The *Mandarin*
25 May 1840

Mr A. McKechnie Esq.
Dear Sir,
    Although being induced thro' your kind treatment and persuasion to make this manifestation of our designed and prepared plan to overthrow the present Government of England and establish a republic, I beg to be excused giving names of persons concerned in the affair for reasons which are obvious

and require no explanation to a mind like yours. The following are the chief particulars and had we been cautious and judicious in the proceedings it would have been a difficult matter to defeat us. From the neighbourhood of Merthyr 5000 men were to march up to Brecon Town, in the Dead of Night, & there attack the Soldiers, which was anticipated would soon surrender themselves as they were so few, not exceeding 30 in number, and many of them fresh recruits; then take all Arms and Ammunition and Provisions the Town contained: about the same were to march to Abergavenny from Rhymney, Tredegar, Sirhowy, Ebbwvale, Beaufort and Nantyglo, but as the soldiers there were billeted in Public Houses, about one hundred chosen men heavily armed was to enter the Town the day previous, not altogether, but few at a time, and there obtain lodgings at the billeting houses and when the Body entered, which was intended to be in the Dead of Night, a signal was to be given to the fresh lodgers, who was to open the doors and let them in and immediately leave the Soldiers and arms — 36 was the number of Privates there stationed, and all with the exception of two was agreeable and anxious to join provided it was a general outbreak — to take Newport as the Soldiers was stationed in the Union Workhouse; it was proposed to send down from Blackwood on Saturday, and Sunday a large number secretly armed, to join the Newport Chartists & take the Soldiers on their Way on Sunday Night when they returned to the Barracks from the Public Houses, which they generally resorted to on Sunday Evenings. This was the chief reason why Sunday was fixed upon for the attack. This plan was not adopted because Mr Frost said, let me have two thousand armed men, and Zephaniah Williams with them, we will accomplish our object with little trouble & as for Brecon and Abergavenny we will afterwards soon secure them — To take Cardiff about the same number was designed to enter there from Taff Vale. In all these said places there were a great number of Arms & Warehouses which contained powder. Likewise on the Hills at the Iron Works there were many Powder Magazines which were all to be taken too, consequently in a few days we would have from 80 to 100,000 Men well armed. A Steamer had to be despatched to the Powder House that is on the River Side near Bristol and convey therefrom all it contained & bring it to Newport. The Blast Furnaces & Foundries were to be appropriated to cast cannon and manufacture Arms of all descriptions. Glamorgan and Monmouthshire contained about 30 Associations & in each from 100 to 1300 Members, pretty near all organized & a great number of them Armed. The said allotted number would leave sufficient behind which were to take possession of the Magazines & Provision Warehouses in the Country, likewise to take and imprison all the Aristocracy and Magistrates & if any of them made the least resistance they were to be put to death. There was a certain number which was not to escape death under any consideration whatever, likewise all the Police. As soon as the day was agreed & fixed upon for the Attack, Messengers were despatched to the North of Wales with the information, also to the North of England, from thence despatches were to be sent to Scotland, London, Manchester, Birmingham; Sheffield and Bath received the information by our Messengers where every possible preparation were making. Why Wales was fixed upon to commence was because there were so few soldiers. England was not to move until they found the Welsh Mails did not arrive as usual in time, which was to be taken for granted that a successful attack was made in Wales. It was therefore thought and believed Troops could be spared to be sent to Wales, except it was from the West of England which could not arrive in Newport in less than a week, by which time we should be prepared with sufficient Cannon & Ball. The river was to be blocked up with trading vessels. If sent by land they were to be attacked on their way in every possible place; in Bath & its neighbourhood there were five thousand ready armed men, and there were spies in all places watching the movements of Government. If any preparations were made for a march of Military from any place, that was to be taken as a sign Government was informed of Our design, which was immediately to be communicated to all places, that so might be prepared to meet them. I know nothing of the preparations made in England, and who were the leading men, but what I was informed by Mr Frost & one of the messengers after he had returned from there giving them the intelligence of our preparations and the fixed time — from what they said there was every preparation possible making particularly London, Bath, Yorkshire and Lancashire, where they are strong and courageous.

This I hope and trust will not be made use of to my prejudice either to my interest or reputation,

I have to be etc.,
Zeph. Williams

P.S. Had we succeeded at Newport on Monday the 4th November 1839 We had proclamations ready printed which were to be immediately posted all over England, offering Fifty Pounds a year to every soldier that would volunteer with the Chartists.

Z.W.*

While there was not a word in that letter with which I disagreed, every line revolted me. For my part, at the time, I would not have lifted a finger to lighten the lot of these bloodstained Whigs and Tories, and Zephaniah's defection to the enemy I thought shocking.

Much has been written since by Establishment historians anxious not to offend their political masters and with most historians ringed by the literary nose (there being no profits in history), successive recorders have been content to dilute the truth of Chartism.

Add to this the need for governments to expound the sanctity of property and deny the possibility of public disorder in the midst of agitation, and the Chartist Rebellion first becomes a riot, then a minor disturbance of the peace, then nothing

*The above letter, copied from the manuscript, is by courtesy of Lord Tredegar's library, and used with the permission of *The National Library of Wales*.

more disagreeable than a march of protest.

Similar governmental treatment was accorded the Peterloo Massacre of 1819 when it was happy to confess to the killing of two or three people in Manchester. But, according to the newspapers of the day, the killed and wounded numbered 'upwards of four hundred' and evasive coroner's inquests were held on the bodies of the slain.

All governments being agreeably content to minimize threat to public disorder in the purpose of 'what is good for the people', their paid historians follow suit with commendable ambition. Similarly, lesser historians have 'followed the leader' in dilution of the facts of the Chartist Rebellion, and will continue, I suppose, to misinform the generations.

Let me now inform the generations.

Our intention as leaders of the Chartists on that day in November 1839 was to remove Victoria from her throne and form a republic based on the principles which had succeeded in France.

Speculation as to the planning, lack of militarism and pathetic organization may continue, but let there be no more doubt as to our intentions, for which we were found guilty at Monmouth. And so, while Zephaniah's facts were right, his timing, in my opinion, was palpably wrong, and I continued to resist it.

# 14

WITH the expectation of Port Arthur looming on the horizon despair settled upon my mind. Under the Tasman Peninsula's probationary system, four stages of punishment were specified by Sir John Franklin, the present governor: rigorous punishment, such as flogging; the chain gang; labour under a private employer; the ticket-of-leave stage, and finally pardon. After a pardon a convict could be free to return to his own country were his application sanctioned, if he could raise the fare. This last was most difficult. The island's economy had been ruined by the vast convict intake; a year after I arrived more than four thousand men and women were arriving annually; the economy was now based on virtual slave labour.

As if in realization of the misery to come, Captain Muddle released all convicts from their irons, doubled the armed guard, and allowed us to roam the ship. All we

Chartists gathered together on the poop deck in the sun while the ship, her trial by storm over, clipped along on a crested, azure ocean.

For the best part of a week the wind had blown great guns, rising from storm to a fierce hurricane, and while the ship tumbled about merrily in great troughs and wave mountains, we were all battened down below. With the hatchways even slightly open to save us from suffocation, the sea poured over us in torrents, especially down the mizzenmast hatch where I was situated. Heavily ironed, with shackles that would take us all directly to the bottom if the *Mandarin* foundered, we lay in soaked misery while the rats, in a panic as great as ours, swam desperately around our half submerged faces.

But, on the twenty-first — yesterday — the wind relented, and to lift from our minds the fear of Port Arthur, Old Lag shouted:

"Now come on, lads, gather round for the next instalment!"

"That Carling yarn?" cried Zephaniah, "God spare us!"

Roberts, Jones and Howell, the Birmingham Chartists were there, two of whom later shared my chain gang; poor Taply, who was to die later; Hoppy Greg who was now a convict, Petticoat Boy and Sole Bungy; Timbo Weller with his hideous grin and Richard Carling were there too. They squatted on their hunkers either side of Old Lag, who bawled:

"Lest I get the stiffers back, where was you last, Dick lad?"

"He was kissin' her!"

Interjected Roberts, "But I was inspecting a very different orifice."

"Come on, Carling, let's have it," shouted William Jones. And Richard continued the tale:

"If I recall, I left the tale while dining with Madame Le Roy at the *Crown Hotel* in Marlborough; being determined on making connection with her, I actually tried the door of her bedroom that night, but she had locked it against me."

"You dirty young bugger," said Old Lag.

"And next morning," said Richard, his hands going to the tale, "she was starched up and frigid with me, so I determined to set her by the heels overnight.

"Now, listen! When leaving Marlborough we took on another passenger, a portly gentleman with a large stomach.

"'The morning is fine, is it not?'" said he. 'God smiles upon three travellers, and that is excellent,' and he kissed Madame Le Roy's hand, entered the coach and eased his great shining backside into the seat. Thereon, he began to snore rhythmically to the clattering hooves and grinding wheels until suddenly, with the lights of Reading coming up, he became an architect of chaos, for he leaped up and shouted:

"'Murder! Calamity! Highwaymen!' as the stagecoach lurched to a halt.

"My lady was terrified, of course, so I consoled her, and with my arms about her stared through the window into the face of a man with a lantern, who said:

"'Nothin' to be a'feared of, lady — just a routine check. Special constable from Marlborough I am; me and the landlord 'ave ridden hard, ain't we, sir?' And the Crown landlord, whom I recognized, cried in tears, 'Thieving swines! Impecunious buggars, I am ruined!'

"'Beggin' ye pardon for the landlord's language, dear lady,' said the constable, 'but the fella ain't himself. The night 'fore last, his guests, one and all, 'ave been dished and diddled — there's scarce a penny left in the 'ouse, poor sod. So just a few discreet inquiries, ain't it?' And he raised his lantern into my face. 'Name, kind sir?'

"'Sir Richard Carling, at your service,' said I.

"'And you? You don't look savoury to me,' and he prodded our portly gentleman.

"'Me, sir?' wailed he, 'I am only a poor man trading between Marlborough and Reading. I am innocent of any allegation of theft!'

"And to my horror the constable took hold of our gentleman and shook him to rattle his bones, yelling, 'Landlord, I do believe we've found the vagabond. For 'ere we have a gent of the aristocracy and his lady travellin' in peace, and 'ere we've got this 'ooligan,' and he hauled the old boy out on to the road. 'Where was you, Ebenezer Cooper, at the hour o' four o'clock the day before yesterday mornin' before the streets was aired, eh? Can't you see the guilt on 'is fat face, landlord? You tell your innocence to the magistrates, me fine chap, for I reckon we'll find all we're lookin' for in these bags of yours,' and there came two thumps as the poor man's boxes hit the road, and the last I saw of Ebenezer Cooper was him standing in tears in the arms of his accusers.

"The coach clattered onward, and Madame Le Roy said, 'Summary justice, no doubt. It seems that they know him. The people one has to travel with! Tonight at Reading we could be murdered in our beds.'

"'Not while I am around,' I said, and patted her knee."

The *Mandarin* slanted to the wind; the sea danced in spume and flashing sunlight. We lay in indolent attitudes of peace, listening to the story: Richard said:

"There was more going on in the Labour in Vain inn in Reading than a Tipperary cockfight. The sign of this inn is a fat lady bathing a little black boy. Gentlemen, the cobbled yard when we rode in was crowded with ranting, strutting actors from *Romeo and Juliet* to the witches of *Macbeth* for travelling players were in Reading, their leading actors being the famous Sir Roger Martin and Lady Thora, whose jewels I had originally come for . . .

"As we descended from our coach we were surrounded by pantomimists, buffoons, harlequins and columbines: tumblers and posture-masters shrilled their commands to young ladies under tuition; lace-bosomed serving maids raced to do the bidding of contortionists and prancing ballerinas . . ."

"Hell!" ejaculated Zephaniah, "he don't half tell a tale!"

"It was a mêlée of sound and movement," said Richard, unabashed, "with more ale and gin going down Thespian necks than in a dozen beer-shops. Soon, after making ourselves known to the landlord, we dined early, Madame Le Roy and I, then retired to our respective rooms."

"And ye travelled from your room to hers . . . ?" asked Old Lag.

"Not immediately," continued Richard "Earlier, Sir Roger and Thora had visited our dining table; she descending into a most elegant curtsey when Sir Roger introduced her, and asked:

"'You are French, madame?'

187

"'From Brittany,' replied Madame Le Roy.

"'And this is your husband?'

"'No, my 'usband is awaitin' me in London. This is my escort,' and Sir Roger fixed me with a gimlet eye, and said: "'You are a fortunate man to be entertaining such beauty, sir. Have you and I met before?'

"'Not that I am aware,' said I, and made a mental note to lay my hands on all jewels, both Le Roy's and Thora's, before I was officially recognized. But it was clear to me that madame was now upon her guard, for she said to me before we parted at our doors:

"'Sir Richard, I am fearful with all these actors in the 'ouse. In France, all actors are thieves, and I 'ave many lovely jewels . . .'

"'Think nothing of it,' said I. 'Should you need me in the night, just knock upon the wall, and I will enter and protect you.'"

The *Mandarin* was rolling in tropical heat; the sun slanted down in rays of incinerating light; the red-coated marines sweated and fumed in their emblazoned uniforms of brass and braid; for once we convicts were thankful for our rags. Richard continued as Dr McKecknie came up and sat nearby, smiling:

"About two o'clock in the morning I awoke with the intention to begin my theft, when a woman's scream echoed through the inn; and she screamed again and again to a growing commotion, which sent me to the casement in my night-shirt.

"Flinging open the window, I saw the Thespian revellers of the night spring into activity down in the cobbled yard as a little fat man, clad only in a short vest, came galloping in at speed pursued by men with riding-crops. And these were endeavouring to lay their crops on his little bare bottom.

"Round and round the upset tables he went, howling as the swipes landed, leaping over sprawled drunks and dishevelled maids, for a great love making had been going on, I can tell you.

"On, on he went, breaking wind as he skidded within feet of me: propelled by a lucky one, he vaulted a barrel, flew through an open gate, and cantered for open country pursued by Thespians.

"Now whips were cracking, horns

blowing, and the drunken actors rose with their maidens and began a general pursuit of the little fat man, who, from what I heard later, had apparently curled himself up on the chest of the landlady in the early hours without asking the permission of the landlord. He, seeking wifely solace, had embraced the suitor instead of his wife. And as Sir Roger mentioned later in the courtyard, 'To be cuckolded is one thing, sir, but in one's own bed is abominable.' 'Mind you,' said the landlord, 'he do tend to come randy round about September,' and he put an arm around his spouse. 'She ain't the only one's been done, ye know, 'ave you, my beauty? Six fair ladies in one night he did right in the middle o' Reading,' and he bowed to Sir Roger and Thora who joined him, ' . . . Concentrating mainly on married couples, he do slip through a window wi' a happy knack, and he's up a wife's nightie afore ye can say Jack Robinson,' and he patted and consoled his plump lady, adding, 'Never you mind, my flower, we'll 'ave him sure enough,' and said confidentially to me, 'They got no chance, see, sir, for he's in an' out like a bloody jack rabbit — a week last Sunday, among the stalls o' Reading market, he did an alderman,' which sent his wife into a flood of tears. 'Oh, I'm undone, I'm undone!' cried she. 'You bloody will be,' said her husband, 'if you leave that window open again — that's the third time this week you done it,' and she wept on, her great breasts shaking with surly grief and outrage.

"Now, this incident made me apprehensive; if such an evil could befall a fat landlady in bed with her husband, what chance had my lovely madame got, in a bed all alone? And now she, all a-flutter, was standing at my elbow in the court-yard, and Sir Roger bowed low, sweeping up the cobbles with his nightcap, saying:

"'Dear lady, pray compose yourself. I will find this seducer and flog him within an inch of his life. Allow me to escort you back to your bed.'

"'Allow me,' said I, and took the slim arm of the beautiful Madame Le Roy."

"For God's sake, don't tell me you're finished?" cried Dr McKecknie, getting up.

"Sir," answered Richard, "I am not even started."

# 15

TO Old Lag's uncontained delight, the female convict ship, the *Juliana*, was anchored in Storm Bay, having arrived at Hobart Town two days earlier; the women lined the rails and waved greetings as we slid past them on the morning breeze. Many and varied were the descriptions levelled at these, the refuse, it was said, of British womanhood; as I pointed out to Old Lag, but with little success, these paramours were scarcely worth having as escorts; indeed, I later saw the 1837 Commission of Inquiry into Transportation, which said:

'They [such women] are as bad as it is possible for human beings to be; they are shockingly dissolute, drunken, everything that is bad,' and another writer stated, 'What shall I say of the female convict, acknowledged to be worse and far more difficult of reformation than the man? Her character is immodest, drunken, and she uses the most horrible language . . . you can have no conception of her depravity.'

"Ah no," whispered Old Lag confidentially, "you're too hard on 'em, Frosty. I can see from 'ere they're a right good set o' little bunnie tales, that lot," and he sighed in anticipation.

The early sun shone down with topaz brilliance on the white-coated waterfront of Hobart; the Derwent, surely one of the loveliest harbours in the world, shimmered and glittered in refracted light. Zephaniah said, joining us at the rail:

"You want to get yourself posted to Cascades, Old Lag, and pick yourself a dollymop out of one of the parades. The bosun was telling me that there was a bit in the *Colonial Times* about a club they've got running in the gaol called the Flash Mob — they come and go when they please to the taverns, climbing in and out of the windows of the military barracks."

"Knock twice and ask for Nelly?" Old Lag's eyes were like saucers.

A man behind me, I think it was Parson Job, the Cheapside forger, was saying, hands clasped, "Oh God; be Thou my help and refuge . . . "

Another cried, "I'm turning this into a holiday, I am. I'd not change this for Porthcawl any bloody day."

"It'd suit me, if only I'd brought my little missus . . . "

"They say the governor's coming aboard when we get in."

"And a right old sod he is!"

"So long as I don't land under that bugger Captain Booth." Which was where I was going to land.

Two days later, after visits by Government officials, the schooner *Eliza* came alongside and we three — Zephaniah, Jones and I, together with the other four Birmingham Chartists, were bundled down the gangplank into her.

Port Arthur, our destination, we were told, was reserved solely for convicts who were proven miscreants during the voyage; but something special was required, it appeared, of convicted Chartists, and with us, too, came young Taply and Greg.

It was Saturday July the fourth, the time of America's great celebration, when the *Eliza* landed us at Port Arthur.

What a Fool's Song is life, I reflected: one moment wearing a mayoral chain of office, feted and respected; next moment shuffling along in leg irons, filthy of person, bearded to the chest and in rags. Yet they had promised we would not be treated as badly as the rest.

Lined up on the quay the Superintendent of Convicts, a Mr Cart, called our names and partitioned us off. William Jones was to be sent to Port Puer, the boys' prison across the bay; Zephaniah was to go to the coal mines. I, it appeared, was to have the plum job as a police clerk in the office of the Commandant, Captain Booth.

A word about Port Arthur.

Situated on a peninsula, it was connected to the Forestier Peninsula of Tasmania by a narrow strip of land known as Eaglehawk Neck; one so narrow that it could be guarded by fierce dogs. The only other escape from Port Arthur was by sea through shark-infested waters.

The alternative to escape was the company of Lieutenant-Governor Sir John Franklin: his predecessor, Governor Arthur, with the assistance of the able commandant

I mentioned earlier, having turned the penal settlement into a hell-hole.

Other settlements on Tasmania were Port Puer, earlier mentioned, to which William Jones had now gone; there the young offenders numbered up to 600: the coal mines to which Zephaniah had been sent was opposite Sloping Island. Other convict outstations abounded, but I was yet to hear of these.

Of Port Arthur itself I saw little until later; my early view being first a wharf, boat and store houses facing the sea, and, as I was taken into the compound, the elegant commandant's residence in spacious grounds and a high steepled church.

The commandant's administration hut, where I was to be employed, was surrounded by a small military barracks; four convict hutted barracks, one with brick cells for solitary confinement (the solitary system was an innovation recently introduced by Captain Booth for hardened offenders) and a variety of small buildings ranging from the Commissariat Stores to the bakehouse, kitchens and doctor's quarters; in those early years Port Arthur was mainly composed of semi-permanent hutting.

Another probation station, situated on Flinders Bay, was quite new, apparently; housing consisted of primitive bark hutting where some two hundred lags worked under the eye of a certain Mr Smith, who had achieved a reputation for brutality. This included the application of bayonet pricks to that portion of a man's anatomy usually reserved for the punishment of schoolboys: the heavily ironed working gangs goaded into greater speed suffered such injuries that the soldiers finally refused Smith's orders.

I made a mental note to keep clear of Flinders Bay.

Female convicts were also imprisoned on Tasmania.

Twenty years before, in Governor MacQuarie's day, the original accommodation for women was a single long-room storey built above the men's gaol in Paramatta; later, female convicts were housed in the island prison on Tasmania where there were two factories, one at

Cascades in Hobart, the other at Launceston. A description of Cascades, which was converted from an old distillery reads:

> The capacity of the building is so unequal to the number of wretched inmates, that their working rooms resemble the hold of a slave ship; so fetid is the air after the night's inhalation that the turnkeys, after opening the doors in the morning, escape rapidly to avoid semi-suffocation . . .

Punishments inflicted upon the women were vicious; in early years an offender could be forced to wear an iron collar weighing about fifteen pounds; with its long iron spikes projecting either side, the apparatus gave the woman the appearance of horned cattle. Another punishment was the barrel-dress, in which a woman could neither sit nor lie down; she could receive cuts from a cane on the buttocks or be flogged through the streets 'tied to the back of a dray'. And the treadmill, dreaded even by male convicts, had a terrible effect upon women: built originally to suit the height and strength of men, a woman had to keep climbing the treads to avoid falling off. Operated for hours at a stretch it produced cramping pains in the loins and brought on haemorrhaging and miscarriages.

Here, at Cascades, as at the earlier Paramatta, young children were undernourished and their mothers suffered punishment for pregnancy.

Within minutes of my arrival in the commandant's office, I passed Captain Booth in a corridor; he delayed me.

"Frost?"

His eyes possessed the coldness of a man who conversed with stones.

"Yes, sir." I removed my cap.

"You are here as a police clerk — a copier, you understand? Do as you're told, ask no questions, and work with a will. Come up in front of me for the smallest breach of regulations, and you will regret it. Now get yourself cleaned up. Mr Cart will give you details of where you will sleep and eat; if you do well you can stay out of the yellow and black."

This was the yellow coat and black trousers most convicts wore, the standard issue.

"Thank you, sir."

My first impression was comparatively reasonable.

Later, I walked in evening sunlight around the esplanade; here substantial stone buildings, tasteful cottages and luxurious gardens turned the bestial into the enchanting — 'Port Arthur, the beautiful woman,' as somebody put it, 'who at heart is a whore.' The elegant steeple of the church reared skyward — this, built by apprentice boy labour but a few years before, appeared to stand at prayer over the glittering bay. But down the aisles of this holy place shuffled the manacled and leg-ironed convicts; not far away stood the Silent Cells, Booth's latest horror . . . and beyond it the white-walled lunatic asylum whose shrieking inmates sullied the gentle quiet.

In a small corner of the office, discreetly away from challenge, I watched Mr Porter JP, the penitentiary's resident magistrate. Of a girth to fit his name, florid of countenance and with his stomach sitting on his knees, Justice Porter dozed until stricken into alacrity by an unusual situation — the clang of a bell, the slam of a door; the shrill commands from the military parade ground outside. The screams of flogged men would wake him instantly. Then, the confusion over, he would again droop into a sleep of flustering snores.

On sight I did not like Justice Porter, who was there for sentencing miscreants; I'm sure he didn't like me, which was important.

"You'll learn, Frost, you'll learn," he used to say. "Been a magistrate yourself, 'ave you?"

"Yes, sir."

"Different kettle of fish — chalk and cheese. Damned useless lags, the scum of the earth. Next lag up for sentence — come on, Frost, come on, smarten yourself." While reading the charge sheets he snorted snuff; this dripped in yellow trickles of saliva down his pearl-buttoned waistcoat.

I said, "Number 18694, sir, Convict Wilde. Accused of absence without leave — two days, sir. Found in a tavern in Hobart — temporarily attached to a wharf gang there stationed at Cascades." I lowered my copy of the charge sheet.

"Posing as a ticket-of-leave man, Captain Booth tells me."

"It doesn't say so here, sir."

Perplexed, he stared up at me with rheumy eyes, and I saw beyond him the punishment yard and beyond that the parade ground shining like a newly minted sovereign in the light of the morning.

"All right, all right, bring him in!"

Wilde was one of seven brought in that morning, not a week after I had arrived; they stood in their chains outside the door, awaiting trial and punishment.

In regal authority Porter perched himself upon his magistrate's chair. The first prisoner, ushered in between two Javelin Men, drooped before him.

"Number 18694, Wilde is that you?" asked the judge, and Wilde bowed his head.

I judged his age at twenty. Undersized, rickety, he was clearly one of the thousands of disreputables picked by fate off the streets of a city; his shoulders were narrow, his features sallow: I glanced down at the charge sheet. Theft of a gentleman's watch in Cheapside, life transportation.

"After a woman, were you?" Justice Porter leaned forward with revived interest.

"Only lookin', sir," mumbled Wilde, and raised a swollen face.

He had been picked up in a tavern by soldiers; clearly he had been fist-beaten on the way to detention. Justice Porter said:

"Women, you call them? Lying, ignorant, unchaste whores of lust and drunkenness! You people put your cocks where I wouldn't put my walking stick."

"Only lookin' at the marriage mart, sir, then went down for a drink. I . . . I was on me way back, sir, when the corporal took us . . . "

"Silence! Before you compound the felony! By God, I'll teach you dirty young stripers to come up before me for immorality. Prayer is what you need, sir, prayer to your God," and I saw past him two floggers slicing the air with their whips.

Most Mondays we had minor 'deserters' working in labour gangs in the vicinity of Hobart who made their way to taverns. The temptation was great, for every Saturday morning the Cascades Marriage Mart would be performed; this would entail the female inmates being paraded for the choice of any ex-convict or settler who wanted a wife.

Many such 'wives' instantly became mistresses; or worse, ended in brothels. Often a pimp acting for a brothel agency would arrive to look the women over: if he fancied one to suit his purpose, a word to the female warder would suffice, and the woman changed hands for the price of a coin; if she refused, this then subjected her to the rigorous subjection of the prison matron, a bovine-looking creature with the morals of a sow.

Now Justice Porter went to the open window and called in his high, squeaky voice, "First this morning, flogger — a Paramatta Romeo, so lay on hard — the buttocks mainly, to cool him," and returned to his chair. "Next, Frost, and look lively."

They stripped Wilde naked, bent him double over the 'Bum Table', with his wrists and ankles tied and his backside 'turned to the sun', and his screams sullied the beauty of the morning.

Soon the morning 'quota' of punishment was reached — all five triangles being occupied by writhing, shrieking prisoners until the ground beneath the triangles was soaked with human blood. But I will always remember that morning for another incident.

Coincidental with the sentencing of a tenth prisoner, a messenger arrived demanding Justice Porter's presence at the church where, apparently, the commandant himself awaited him. With the prisoner — one too old for flogging, I thought — on his knees and beseeching mercy, the judge reached for his hat and, turning back at the door, said:

"I'll deal with this one when I get back. Meanwhile give him fifty to be going on with."

By some unaccountable change of mind, or perhaps as an answer to my prayers, Captain Booth, suddenly disturbed by the close proximity of the whipping triangles and the shadow of the hanging scaffold which, sun-shot, lay across his desk at afternoons, had them all dismantled and transferred to an area on the other side of the parade ground.

Now the screams were but whispers on the balmy summer air.

Immediately I was settled in, I wrote to my wife:

Port Arthur
Van Dieman's Land
July 21 1840

My Dearest Mary,

The words Norfolk Island and Port Arthur convey to the minds of the English people places of extreme suffering. They are penal settlements, to which, generally, persons are sent, who, being prisoners, have committed their offences in the colony. The punishment here is great, but the persons who are sent here are frequently old offenders . . . There are various reasons assigned for sending us to Port Arthur, but as it is impossible for me to be acquainted with the facts, I shall merely state that this is a place to which the worst of men are sent, and where human misery may seem to be at its greatest extent. We are told that we are here to perform certain offices. Zephaniah Williams is to be a superintendent at the coal mines; William Jones fills a situation at the juvenile establishment at Point Puer, and I am now in the office of the commandant, that is, the governor of Port Arthur. I am acting here as a clerk, and am in excellent health. The climate is milder than in our own country; the situation of the settlement must be healthy; we have a fine open bay before us.

So much, my love, for this part of the subject. You are aware that all letters sent from, and received by, every prisoner are read by the Commandant, and though I believe that that gentleman would not be very particular in a correspondence between a husband and a wife, yet it is a great check to that freedom of communication, which, to be affectionate, must be unrestrained. Politics are, I believe, forbidden; yet it is a subject very much connected with my affairs. There are various matters of a public nature which affect our situations; I shall, however, leave that subject until I hear from England. I am of the opinion that my letters will be perused by others besides the gentleman who rules here. I suppose the Colonial Secretary would be glad to have a peep at the letters of his old correspondent. Well, I trust that if Lord John Russell should break the seal of my letters, he will have so much of the gentleman about him, as to send them according to their address . . .

It was a mistake, and one which, the moment it was posted, caused me worry.

It was an infinitely greater mistake when one of my daughters, in the enthusiasm of learning of my well being, sent it to *The Times*, which published it.

# 16

A MONTH or two after entering the office of the commandant, there came upon me a fierce and corrosive loneliness; worse than the isolation of the spirit, it was an illness of the soul. It was something more than the loss of my family and friends that afflicted me, but akin to apoplexy of the mind.

Man's ingredients can elevate him above a wounding, public and personal; he can rise above shame and defamation, provided there is one beloved in whom he can confide; victory and triumph play a noiseless trumpet if there is no one there to share it; alone, defeat and grief become a scald to the senses. I would have put my hand in a candleflame and watch the sinews wither and snap, could it but lift from me this fearful pain.

My days were filled with the agony of others, my nights with this tossing emptiness.

Now my friends began to arrive for

sentence in the office, and I saw Justice Porter not as a dispenser of inhuman punishment, but as a snouted pig in a starched white collar; the bulging pearl-buttoned waistcoat was replaced by a teated belly; the treble squeaks he uttered became snorting grunts; lace-frilled hands were cloven hooves.

Pig and I reserved for the first prisoner of the morning a horrified stare.

The prisoner before us was of herculean size, a giant of bulging strength that dwarfed the two warders and redcoats who had escorted him. Scarcely a rag of clothing covered him, save that which drooped at his loins to cover his nakedness. Yet he stood proudly, his manacled wrists stiffly at his sides, his head up and his eyes blazing in his bearded face. There was scarcely a square inch of this man's skin that did not register the cut of the lash; his face, even, dripped blood from the slashes, and I knew, without being told, that he was a victim of Mr Smith, the overseer at Flinders Bay.

"His charge?" barked Pig.

I read from the sheet a warder handed me, "Found to have tobacco in his possession.

Given three hundred lashes of the cat-o'-nine-tails — now showing dumb insolence."

I looked up at the prisoner and he stared down at me; there was upon his face utter disdain. The door opened then and Captain Booth entered.

"Is this Hendriks, of Flinders?" he asked.

Booth was a big man; he had the accent of the Irish bogs on him, and the big, rangy shoulders of a hod-carrier, more than a military gentleman. His brass buttons gleamed upon the wide expanse of his chest and he carried himself with the elegance of a man in authority, but he was a pygmy compared to the prisoner before him.

"Can't break you, eh? Sure to God, if Smith canna whack 'em he always sends them down to me. Dumb insolence, is it? Well, me foine fella, would ye care to show me some?"

The man spat at his feet.

"Take him down to Silence," Booth commanded; turned, and left us.

History has it that Port Arthur church is cursed by the ghosts of two men; one who was murdered during its construction, some say in one of its aisles; another committed suicide by leaping from its steeple the day after it was completed; certainly, it was never consecrated. An even better reason for this would be its close environment with what was called Victoria's Hell on Earth, the Silence Block. Of brick construction, this was designed to replace the lash for the really obdurate men such as Convict Hendriks who, with his fine physique and golden hair, was clearly of Scandinavian origin.

Chained between two warders, his legs free of the irons for walking, but carrying a forty-pound ball in his arms, they marched him off to six weeks' solitary confinement.

The Silent System was the product of Captain Booth's evil genius; some prisoners, he had discovered (and I had noted the names in plenty in the book of records in the office), could not be broken; their spirits remained gloriously defiant, even to the point of death.

One such man — little more than a lad, really — I lay witness to myself. I see that I later wrote:

One of the regulations of Port Arthur is that punishment must be received respectfully! Fearful that I should not appreciate the effectiveness of the system, the authorities put me into the yard in which local flogging was administered.

One day a young man called Wilde was brought in for thirty-six lashes. I never saw any man receive punishment with such firmness. He moved not a muscle, and when the flogger loosed him from the triangle, he walked to his clothes with a contemptuous smile, and began to dress. This look interpreted itself to the superintendent as dumb insolence. He was taken back to the office, charged, and sentenced to a further thirty-six lashes.

Here's a beautiful system! Here are laws which English judges tell us are 'the envy of surrounding nations and the admiration of the world'. These are rules which Sir Eardley Wilmot said, ' . . . should tend to regulate the prisoner's mind, to soften his heart, and thus lead him to the path of virtue in this life and to the humble hope of a happy hereafter'.

The following day we took the bloodstained Hendriks down to Silence.

Here, from the moment I entered with the charge sheet, waiting warders indicated by gestures that we were to remove our boots; Hendriks's chains were removed to save their chinking.

Standing in our stockinged feet in a little passage, the door, its rebate lined with thick wool, was carefully closed behind us.

With two warders leading, and me following the prisoner, we were taken to a tiny office where sat the official gaoler. With a finger to his lips he put out his hand for the charge sheet; the paper crinkled sound, I recall; this brought his frown.

We waited while he read the charge; then he scribbled a brief message; I was taken back to the entrance; Hendriks, prodded by warders' batons, went in another direction.

Each prisoner in this silent place was confined in a tiny cell, of which, it was said, there were twenty: even the passages were carpeted and warders wore carpet slippers so that no human sound was heard, except on Sundays.

On Sundays, when for the good of his soul the prisoner attended church, he was put into a box in which he sat; one so constructed that only the chaplain could be seen; the faces of possible friends and other malefactors were lost to him. Even at times of exercise his face was covered with a mask which had apertures for the eyes; any attempt at whispered messages to another prisoner would be instantly rewarded by a beating.

Not far away was the asylum, and it was said in Port Arthur that anything over six weeks' detention was a one-way ticket to it.

Let Captain Charles O'Hara Booth be remembered by posterity, if not for his decade in Port Arthur when he lowered the town's name into degradation, but for his evil genius. Under him suffered men of intellect and high standing, the Irish patriots; none could look to this compatriot for the smallest pity.

The next prisoner up for sentence was Old Lag, and his pathetic attempt to greet me on entering the office was shut off by a blow from a warder.

Old Lag, in company with Greg, the sailor from the *Mandarin*, came with Timbo Weller, Petticoat Boy and Sole Bungy, the counterfeiter; all five, the occupants of my hut, had been arrested for stealing firewood. Led by Greg, whose back was still split deep and crusted from his earlier beatings, they had absented themselves for a few minutes from log hauling to gather twigs for the hut fire. Earlier, they had snared and gutted a rabbit — these existed on the Peninsula in excessive numbers, but still counted as game under the Colony's law. At a time when a poacher could be transported for life from England for treading on a partridge egg, the crime was considered horrendous.

"Fifty lashes apiece," said Justice Porter. "Twenty for absenting themselves from the nominated place of labour; thirty for the rabbit, which I hope has been confiscated."

So I had the shame of making out the charge sheets, filing them, and standing on the parade ground with all five triangles occupied by my friends, counting the strokes for the superintendent until the punishments had been inflicted.

It did little to advance my popularity in Hut Ten, even though I tended to each man's dressings.

Greg, his back now badly mutilated by cross-scarifying, was ten days in the sick bay of the hospital. Fortunately, having been numbered in rotation as we came off the *Eliza* at Port Arthur, we had been allocated bed places in the prison huts as they were vacated. Thus, I found myself with a palliasse bunk next to Zeph with Richard Carling on my other side: Sole Bungy, with Timbo, Petticoat, Greg, Roberts, Jerry Howell, Old Lag and the dying Taply, were in my vicinity; the other occupants were mainly soldiers.

Until then I had not realized that, out of the 212 convicts aboard the *Mandarin*, a sixth or more were from the army. The Chartists transported for the attack upon Newport were considered officially to be both 'treacherous and probably intelligent'; such convicts it was said, will be 'absorbed in small groups to various stations on the Island', and the policy was to be applied to Hut Ten.

"It's a little pleasing," said Zephaniah, "to know that we're still a threat to law and order."

Since, in the words of Sir William Molesworth, a late Secretary for the Colonies, '. . . no human being could be made unutterably wretched without becoming in an equal degree depraved, for the extremes of misery and immorality are generally found to be existing together . . . ' he could well have been speaking of Norfolk Island.

This tiny penal settlement, lying hundreds of miles east of Australia's mainland, had no parallel in terms of penal ferocity in the world, save for the exception of Port Arthur itself. Proof of this is the evidence of officers resident there who reported on the order of Lord Glenelg.

I make an early reference to Norfolk Island since, together with Port Arthur, it bears comparison with the biblical Cities of the Plain.

The Rev. R. Stiles, Norfolk's resident chaplain, stated in a report that:

blasphemy, rage, mutual hatred and the unrestrained indulgence of unnatural

218

lusts are the things which a short residence in the prison wards of Norfolk Island must necessarily familiarize the convicts here . . . and in order to preserve discipline, attempts were made to terrify them into good behaviour; minor and trivial offences were erected into high crimes, and severely punished as such; in short, the convict code has not its equal in severity in any part of the civilized world.

Therefore Norfolk Island, to which so many intellectuals were sent — the fervent Irish leaders of that country's constant rebellions — possessed the double tragedy: the destruction of the sensitive. I have no hesitation in saying that this soiling of decent manhood was an official policy of revenge.

We in Port Arthur, suffering under the sadists, even more dreaded confinement in Norfolk Island for its outrages against humanity; its perversions were with us in every waking moment.

It was with me particularly, I recall, during a visit of Sir John Franklin to our settlement, lest by some ill-advised remark as police clerk, or even a facial expression, he could find me so displeasing that I could finish up in Norfolk Island. There are times in life when it is best to keep a low profile; mine, in the office of the commandant, was high.

Sleepless nights assailed me in expectation of this visit, for I remembered vividly the words of a friendly superintendent who was present at a visit by Governor Arthur. One apparently never knew where one stood with governors.

"The convicts," said he, "were drawn up for inspection, smartly to attention, washed and stitched up as best they could to make a good impression. And Governor Arthur stopped occasionally to ask of them simple questions. The inspection finished, the governor said, 'These are your convicts, Captain Booth?' 'Yes, your excellency,' answered Booth, 'one and all convicts.' 'You surprise me,' replied the governor, 'I'd have thought they were gentlemen.'

"Nevertheless," said the superintendent, continuing the tale, "while inspecting the prison huts and the little gardens where the prisoners were growing vegetables, and seeing some fish drying on a line, the governor said, 'Gardening and fishing, eh? I will have no more of this. Dig up the gardens and stop them fishing. Keep them constantly at their convict's work, you understand? Constantly!'"

I looked upon the impending visit of Sir John Franklin, with apprehension.

Governor Arthur once controlled Van Dieman's Land; fortunately, it was before my time. Were it possible to lay before the world the conduct of this man who was the author, with his Devil's handmaiden, Captain Booth, of such misery and depravity, Hell would prove unequalled.

Men were driven to robberies, violence, and murder; solitary confinement followed, road-parties, flogging and hangings. The juries who tried a man for bushranging, say, were composed of military officers handpicked by the governor. Victims were strung up by the neck six, eight or even more at a time, for offences for which this Governor was the primary cause.

Arthur came to Van Dieman's Land poor, and became the most bare-faced jobber in the colony. Possessing himself of beautiful estates and the most valuable property on the island, he employed prisoners by the hundred for the improvement of his properties. His salary, a trifling sum, was nothing to the half a million dollars of American money he amassed in the twelve years of his tenure. Yet this notorious thief would flog a prisoner half to death for the theft of a fig of tobacco from one of his government stores.

When removed from Van Dieman's Land, Arthur was sent to Canada, and there he continued the same ferocious disposition towards his prisoners. Approved of at home, he then left Canada for India and high office. He was promoted to a general, created a baronet, and was made a member of the Privy Council when back in Britain.

These are the fiends who live in success and splendour at the expense of impoverished and tortured people; and such things will continue in my generation all the time the aristocracy rule.

What manner of man was this new

governor, Sir John Franklin, then? Of milder disposition than Arthur, men said. And yet I could not shake away the dread that somehow, in some strange way, he would prove to be my Nemesis.

# 17

AS a police clerk, mine was a sedentary occupation; one removed from the rank and file of our hut. As such I was scarcely popular, though all recognized that if detailed for a task one had to do it.

Some, however, volunteered for antisocial activities, and heading the list of these were hut trustees, flagellators (floggers) and Javelin Men.

Hut trustees occasioned only minor dislikes and were tolerated in the bawling and swearing when they roused us in the mornings, but floggers came into a different category, and were hated, while hangmen like Solomon Bleay went in fear of their lives.

Floggers must have had bad dreams, especially when George Grover of Richmond Gaol (north of Hobart) was found murdered, thrown over a bridge while drunk.

Floggers, paid seven pence a day by the Commissariat, made their own tools of the trade; it was perfectly usual to see them constructing their cat-o'-nine-tails while sitting in the sun. First they would cut the whipcord to the required lengths, tie the eighty-one knots, soak the whole in brine and lay it beside them to dry until each cord of the knout became the consistency of wire.

At least the hangman Solomon Bleay performed a social service by ridding the world of the worst example of human-kind, but these flagellators induced in me disgust when they entered the office.

The relationship between flogger and victim is a contest; the flogger gratifying his lust to give pain by using all his strength to break the will of his victim, the flogged often determined to die on the triangle (and many did so) rather than give a groan.

I have no wish to sicken, but the truth must be told. The sight of a man's back, even after the standard thirty-six lashes, was unbelievable, and I have seen men, day after day, receive as many, to a total of 600. The back by then is cut to the bone and the ground beneath the triangle soaked with blood.

Some men never completely recovered; madness would often follow continual beatings. Way back in '31, Francis MacNamara, transported for seven years for the theft of a scarf, received 650 lashes 'in fourteen doses', three and a half years in the chain gang; solitary confinement in the 'Silent Cells' and three months on the treadmill at Carter's barracks. Being a poet, he wrote what is now the famous Australian song, 'Moreton Bay' in which he expressed his feelings about the hated convict system.

> For three long years I was beastly treated
> And heavy irons on my legs I wore;
> My back with flogging is lacerated,
> And often painted with my crimson gore.

Even in our hut we had an example of a man whose physique simply could not take the outrage upon him.

Little Taply, who had been flogged upon his back, buttocks and legs, was slowly dying. In and out of the camp hospital, they seemed able to do nothing to combat his slow demise, except subject him to more horrifying pain when they stripped away his bandages. He was still breaking stones on the road, too, working next to Richard Carling, who did all he could to lighten his loads. The little man, towards the end, didn't have the strength to lift the seven-pound hammer. Blood and pus were soaking the waistband of his trousers, and running into his boots.

We all did the best we could for him, but my constant applications to Captain Booth achieved nothing . . . at a time when one could see the maggots actually working under the flesh of Taply's back. And his legs, swollen to twice their size, gave him the appearance of a man with elephantiasis. It should be added that there was no Dr McKecknie at Port Arthur. The one we had seemed to be perpetually drunk; certainly it was so when he was present at floggings.

It astonishes me to see the ease with which men in cruel authority persuade those of lower intellect to conspire against their fellows; more, to ill-treat and torture them for less than the wage of Judas. The worst of these were the Javelin Men ('prisoners of the Crown with indulgence') who enforced their authority as gaolers with pointed sticks, using them as goads. One of these in my time, but at Richmond Gaol, was Jabez Brown, infamous in the vicinity of Coal River.

Now it was dusk and the lads were coming back to the huts after their fourteen-hour stint on stone-breaking in the wharf area. They came linked with a wire cable, to cheat escape; this, fixed to a padlocked belt on each man would later be unlocked by the hut trustee, whom I wouldn't trust as far as I could throw him, said Richard, carrying in the big iron pot that contained the evening meal.

So we gathered around Taply's sick bed and began to eat, spooning up the filthy mess with gasps of disgust.

"Christ," said Richard, "this is worse than usual — who's on tonight?"

"In the cookhouse? Old Joeboy Jones from Swansea," replied Old Lag. "Who called the cook a bastard? Who called him a cook?"

"What is it — monkeys' brains?"

"I know one thing," cried Big Hendriks, now back from the Silent Cells. "I'd like to hear Dick Carling's tale when I'm finished this steak and kidney."

He was unbreakable: as handsome as a Greek god, with his golden hair and beard to his chest, he'd spat at the feet of the Javelin gaolers when they brought him into the light, blinking at the sun — and got away with it.

"That's right," spluttered Old Lag. "How goes it, Dick?" and Richard answered:

"Bugger you all, you're not listening to the yarn, you're only after the cocky bits."

"You can say that ag'in, me son," cried an Irish soldier. "When I get clear o' this bloody place I'm robbin' a bank and laying meself on a woman wi' a pink petticoat right up to her thighs; and I'll see the sun go and come and I'll never rise at all, at all."

"I got a woman like that at home," said somebody, "but her petticoat were black, and her legs were made o' silk and cream . . . "

"Ye'll drive yourself nutty, ye slags, talking o' women," said Big Hendriks. "You can't trust 'em, mostly, you know. I knew one, next door but seven to us in our village, and because her old man was courtin' some bangle earrings, she glued his cock to the bedpost."

They shouted laughter; even Taply smiled.

"My old girl's as frigid as two penn'orth o' starch," bawled someone. "It'd take a bloody fire engine to raise a tit on her, but she fell for the lodger, she did — took the cord out o' my nightshirt and put it in his."

"I got sons and daughters," said another, coming to us, and he squatted on the floor. "Tommy Ructions, they do call me; I got a woman an' a half back home in Nanty, and the kids all sleep together, top to toe, on me grandfer's feather bed. Goin' at the seams is that bed, and our pastor do say that they're the only brats in the valley that need plucking before he can start 'em on the biblicals."

"I got six boys," cried another, "all sitting around wi' their spoons whenever we have a sheep's-head-Sunday. 'Come on, Mam,' they shout, 'let's be bloody 'aving it,' — gasping and blowing at the steam and banging on the floor with their spoons, and that old sheep's head, down in the pot one minute and popping up the next. 'Hey, look, Mam, look!' shouts our Bobo, aged five, 'it's eatin' the bloody carrots!' 'Bad language, you'll go to bed, mind,' says my missus. She's no woman for goin' to Turkey for love, love, love."

"Ach, to hell, mun — there's always a fancy man around the corner!"

"Like mine," said another. "But not lately, for 'er legs are botherin' her: not that they ever bothered anybody else."

And Roberts, the Chartist, said, "I got a girl back in Brum, and the Devil himself stitches her garters . . . "

"And I got one waitin' — if she waits — back in West Brom. She's a vain well set-up piece, but I'm getting her milked, nourished and bedding for sons — six sons I'm goin' to have . . . "

"Oh aye, you can have 'em! There's only one set o' balls going up my stairs, and they're mine."

"Mostly I use me butterfly net . . . " I watched them; listened to their bawdy banter. It was all very well to play the game of piety, but these were men without women; yet for all that, filled with the purity of manhood: I knew their longings, the fierce erections of the loins that had to be fought in manhood's decency.

I longed for my wife with a desire that was more than physical; after making love to her, she would give a sweet, sad sigh that was like the ending of the day, and I would wait for this sigh while closeted in pillow darkness. Making love to one absent is but a graft upon a love remembered, and in the hot nights the knowledge of what once had been filled me with a furious indignation. It was a genesis of hatred and disdain of all my life now stood for; I'd have given ten years of what remained to me ... for the touch of Mary's breast.

"How about another instalment of that yarn, then? — come on, Dick ... " and Richard said:

"Aye, you're a randy old bunch, but I suppose you're entitled to something ... " And he continued:

"You'll remember that during that first night in the Labour in Vain tavern, I still hadn't got my hands on Madame Le Roy's jewels ... Well, realizing that I needed more time, I visited the stables and, by a small strategy, interfered with one of the stagecoach's wheels, which meant another night's stay to effect repairs. Little did I guess that this would allow the Reading rapist to strike again . . .

"Sure enough," continued Richard, "just when the clocks were striking midnight, screams and shrieks rent the air, and out on to the landings we all trooped in our night clothes — old girls in red flannel, young ones in silk and lace and old gents in tassled nightcaps, and right in the middle of them was the Labour in Vain landlord, and he was hopping mad."

"'He's back,' said he.

"'Who?'

"'The rapist. He's back, and he's just done Lady Thora.'

"'He hasn't!'

"'He bloody has,' cried Sir Roger, and out of the bedroom came he with a duck fowling piece, howling to raise the churchyard, and Thora behind him. '*Au secours! Au feu! Au voleur!*' shouted Sir Roger. 'I've just been cuckolded — and in me own bed! Oh, woe, oh woe!'

"'Don't take it hard, love,' said Thora, patting him.

"'But I am dishonoured!'

"'One thing's certain sure, Rog,' said

Thora, 'I know'd it wasn't you. Besides, it's me who's been 'aving it, my beauty,' and she whispered to the women about her:

"'I tell ye what, girls, I never know'd a fella like him — got a real happy leg on him, he has,' and she seized a broom from a maid and swung her foot over a windowsill, shouting, 'After him, girls, don't let him get away!' And she hitched up her nightgown and joined the mob of ostlers and footmen in pursuit.

"And just at that moment Madame Le Roy arrived on the landing, and I've never seen anything so beautiful: all in white was she, with her black hair tumbling over her shoulders.

"She said, softly, 'I was asleep. What 'as 'appened, monsieur?' So I explained in delicate whispers into her ear, and she said back:

"'Oh, Sir Richard, I am terrified in this dreadful 'ouse! Please do not leave me again until I am back in the arms of my 'usband . . . promise, monsieur?' And her dark eyes begged of me."

Richard turned to us, emptying his hands at us. "That was the situation, you see. After that, I couldn't do otherwise."

"Of course not — you have our deepest sympathy," said Zephaniah.

"Well," said Richard, "I thought I'd pay Madame Le Roy one last respect, so I returned her to her room with the assurance that I was on guard outside her door. Then I got into my own bed in the room next door, and lay there, listening to the night. You understand, gentlemen, that with certain fish you have to play it cool, and it was her jewels I was after, as you know, not Madame Le Roy. And just when I judged her to be asleep — I tell you, I had actually got my feet on the floor with the intention of robbing her — when the door of my room opened, and she stood there.

"'Sir Richard,' said she. 'There is a mouse in my room. First there are rapists, now mices — may I come in with you . . . ? And share your room? Oh, sir, promise you will 'ave me?'

"'Madame, you can bank on it,' said I.

"And believe this or not, in her hand she was holding the little Moroccan bag she had bought in the Bristol slave market, and she said:

"'Also, I am afraid that someone will

235

try to steal my jewels, so I bring them with me,' and she sat down upon a chair and put the bag in her lap. 'You sleep in the bed, monsieur, I will sleep 'ere.'

"'Madame,' I answered, with great respect and bowing, 'I would not hear of it.' And I took her hand and raised her up. 'I shall take the chair, you must have the bed. I am an English gentleman, madame, it cannot be otherwise.' Although in my nightshirt, I did it gallantly.

"'But I am a French woman, sir,' said she, 'so may I make a suggestion?' And she smiled at me in moonlight from the window. 'We can both 'ave the bed, if we put the bolster down the middle — 'ow does that appeal to you?'

"'Very greatly, Madame Le Roy,' I replied, and she got in one side (taking care to put the Moroccan bag under her pillow, I noticed) and I, after placing the bolster between us, got in on the other side, and I lay there, let me tell you, with a racing heart, and listened to her breathing.

"The clocks of Reading chimed again; two, then three o'clock, and my beautiful companion was clearly fast asleep. Indeed, to my astonishment, she was actually snoring. So, I carefully got out, took my own Moroccan bag — I had bought one also, remember? — slipped it under my own pillow, and got back into bed again. Then, when I was absolutely certain that madame was in deep slumber, I carefully pulled her Moroccan bag from under her head and replaced it with my own.

"Now I was in a very strong position. Madame Le Roy had her head upon the bag which held my shaving brush and razor; while my head was happily resting upon the bag containing her jewels. Indeed, so content was I with this situation — not actually having to enter her bedroom and rob her like a common thief — that I began to doze, and nearly dropped off. And then it happened . . .

"I was amazed to see two small fingers walking along the top of the bolster dividing us. I tell you, I simply could not believe it. And then, after the fingers came an elegant hand, and this began to slide down my side of the bolster.

"Gentlemen, I thought I must be dreaming, for this was no tavern wench, this was a virtuous, married lady. Quite naturally, my mind turned to pursuits removed from jewel robbery, and when the fingers started walking across my chest and a long, white arm slid over the bolster, you can imagine my condition. And then that same arm got under the bolster, flung it away, and the two arms of Madame Le Roy went about me hard and strong, and she whispered:

"'You realize, monsieur, I 'ope, that if I did not believe you truly to be my 'usband, I would not be doin' this? Oh, Roberto, oh, *Roberto!*' And she pressed her lips upon my mouth . . . " Richard paused. Old Lag said huskily, "Go on, Dick boy, come on, let's 'ave it . . . "

"That's right, lad, ye can't stop now," said I.

But he did stop then, because a voice from the door of the hut bawled:

"Is John Frost in here?"

"I'm John Frost," I replied, and got to my feet, and two Javelin Men came in with chains, hauled me to the middle of the room, and, while all watched in astonishment, manacled my wrists and took me into leg irons.

"What's all this about?" I demanded, and Hendriks, like some avenging primate, seized me from them and thrust them away, shouting:

"Ye'll explain, you pigs, or you'll never get him out of here. He's one of us. What do ye want with him?"

One of the Javelins replied, "You'll be out of our way, big ape, or we'll take the cat to ye. If he's John Frost he'll be leavin' on the night tide — on the *Eliza* down to Hobart Town — in chains, that's our instructions. For an interview with Sir John Franklin first thing in the mornin', and I tell you sure — if you're wise, keep off o' this, for I wouldn't be in his shoes for all the tea in China."

In beautiful moonlight, they dragged me down to the wharf where the little sloop was waiting, and we sailed for Hobart on the night tide with not a word of explanation.

# 18

THE schooner *Eliza*, then under Captain Hurburgh, was a sleek little craft of some 150 tons. Built to provide convict transport to Hobart and the dozen or so seaborne semaphore outstations on the Tasman Peninsula, she was used mainly as the governor's yacht, and many were the military and civilian parties held aboard. Indeed, there appeared to be a celebration of sorts going on now, for, hurried aboard at Port Arthur, they dragged and prodded me past the supercilious glances of ladies in off-the-shoulder gowns of bright hues; their escorts standing protectively about them from the moment I appeared.

I recall being strangely pleased at the reception; this, apparently, was Frost the feared revolutionary; not an ageing convict now dressed in the hated black and yellow garb with *Felon* written across his shoulders. Their attitude reduced the base shame of the manacles and shuffling leg irons.

Hauling me aft, my feet dragging, the two Javelins clipped the manacles under the starboard rail aft, a quiet place away from sight. The moonlight glistening on the rippling tide-swim of the estuary was indescribably beautiful, I remember.

Within moments Captain Booth came; gorgeously attired in epauleted naval uniform, he regarded me with revealing disgust.

"Stand up properly for the commandant!" bawled a Javelin Man.

I did so, and Booth said softly, "Well, ye asked for it, sure to God, and you're goin' to Hobart to get it. If I had my way I'd given ye fifty to be goin' on with, for all your age!"

I said evenly, "I don't know what I've done wrong."

"Ach, do ye not, now? You soon will. For not only have ye made a bloody fool of me, but ye've trod on the toes o' the governor himself, and now you'll pay for it in blood." Turning abruptly, he left me. Faintly, from the companionway where the guests were gathering, came the sound of music.

It was an all-night party, one conducted

with decorum; occasional couples, wandering close, were gently turned away from the criminal by the Javelin Men. Greeted by dawn, we slid gently into the Derwent on engine, and men of the 96th Regiment formed up on the Hobart quay as the gangplank went down.

Other chained prisoners were awaiting inspection by the governor, but the Javelins hustled me to the head of the queue. Commands were barked; blue-clad warders clattered to attention. Somebody shouted, "Bring Frost, the Chartist," and I was surprised by the unintentional flattery; next moment I was hauled into a spacious room decorated with flags and coats of arms . . . and found myself facing a vast mahogany desk and the loose-featured, impassive face of Sir John Franklin.

He was at least ten years my senior: balding, his straggling muttonchops accentuated the grip of his senility; his voice, when he spoke, was as weary as his eyes.

"You remember this?" He tossed me a newspaper and I stared down at it.

Momentarily the eyes blazed. "Pick it up and read it, man!"

I did so, recognizing it as a letter I had

written to Mary at least a year ago. The governor cried:

"Now aloud — go on, read it — where underlined by the Home Secretary . . . "

I read tonelessly, and people about me strained to hear.

" . . . You are aware that all letters sent from, and received by, every prisoner are read by the commandant, and though I believe that that gentleman would not be very particular in a correspondence between a husband and wife, yet it is a great check to that freedom of communication, which, to be affectionate, must be unrestrained . . . "

I hesitated. Then Franklin commanded, "*Continue!*" And I saw in his eyes suppressed fury. I obeyed, reading aloud:

"I suppose the Colonial Secretary would be glad to have a peep at the letters of his old correspondent. Well, I trust that if Lord John Russell should break the seal of my letters, he will have so much of the gentleman about him, as to send them according to their address."

The room's silence was broken only by the ticking of a clock. Franklin said, his voice low, "You agree that this is your letter?"

"Yes, sir."

"And you agree, do you not, that it performs a cunning and vicious libel upon the integrity of a gentleman of honour, our respected Colonial Secretary?"

I said, "Sir, this letter was censored and passed by the camp commandant at Port Arthur. It was not my intention . . ."

"Yes, indeed! And it is to Captain Booth to whom you will answer for the embarrassment you have caused him. But the fault and guilt lie with you. You would have been flogged had the commandant had his way, and thoroughly deserved it. But you have also grossly offended against my own office, for it is here, on this desk, that such specific complaints land, and it is I who will have to send a letter of apology to the Home Secretary whom, no doubt, you still look upon as a political adversary." He rose. "I will now teach you that this is not so. You are a felon under detention, and as such you will now undergo two years' hard labour in the working gang on Brown River — and the very first complaint I receive as to your conduct from the overseer there — the first, you understand, and you will be flogged and put into working chains. Next prisoner."

Let the point be made: the severity of the libel had now come home to me, and with its magnitude came realization of my stupidity. Kinder men may have ruled in Tasmania: but my punishment at the hands of one like Governor Arthur might have been such that I would never have survived it.

All in all, considered in retrospect, the sentence was fair, but I was now being sent back to the discipline of Captain Booth: the prospect was chilling.

But there was undying consolation — Chartism must still be alive back home. Clearly, they were fearful of public protest, or the sentence would have been infinitely worse.

For three days I lay in a cold, damp cell in the infamous Richmond Gaol north of Hobart, while awaiting the return of the *Eliza* from transporting convicts further east. But at least I was guilty; Aborigines who had preceded me in this room, were not.

Here, members of the Stoney Creek tribe were imprisoned 'without charges of any outrage committed', and the full story of their tragedy has yet fully to be revealed to the Australian people.

With the coming of the white man to Tasmania, the true-blooded Aborigines were hunted down and shot like wallabies: 'King Billy' and Truganini, the last male and female of the ancient race, died after the white man's coming. I could not help reflecting, as I dozed there in the dark cell, that I was lying in noble company.

On the fourth day in Richmond, two Javelin Men came for me, and after a short journey by trap to the wharf, they bundled me into the *Eliza*; she seemed full to the gunwales with convicts bound for Woody Isle and the Norfolk Bay station: one now growing in importance since the building of Captain Booth's convict railway striking north from the Port Arthur estuary. I was landed on this wharf, in chains.

This railway was the dream of Booth's heart.

It was five miles long, and obviated the sea route from Port Arthur to Hobart Town; since its opening, the Norfolk Bay station had become a collection point for the shipment of stores and dispersal of convicts to the outstations. But I was a little surprised to discover Zephaniah Williams in chains with a dozen other felons, awaiting shipment south. By a turn of good fortune, my guards said:

"Wait here with this lot," and went off.

"My God," said Zephaniah, looking me up and down. "The things you see when you haven't got a gun."

His humour had not deserted him, even if his looks had. Clearly, double ironed as he was, his clothing ragged and ripped about his body, he had been in trouble. One eye was nearly closed with heavy bruising and the stripes of a cane were upon his half-naked shoulders. Recognizing me, his friends pressed about us, whispering, gesticulating; scarecrows of hunger, these, who once were men. Zephaniah said, "Tell me what you've been up to?"

"Said too much in a letter home. And you?"

He eased his big shoulders uneasily to

the chains. "Tried to escape — bloody madcap, Frost — don't tell me."

"Where are you off to now then?"

"Port Arthur, for sentencing." He squinted at the sun. "You?"

"Brown river. Labour gang — two years. Is Jones still at Point Puer?"

He nodded. "Practically taking the cloth, they tell me — God bless the Queen every other minute, and grace before meals. Jesus, how did we get mixed up with such a world?"

"It's not the world, it's the people."

He said bitterly, "He was pissing around Ponty looking for reinforcements while we were at the Westgate with hatchets and muskets. But we should have known what he was long before that."

"This is why revolutions fail."

The men about us were too intent for our health, hanging on every word. Zephaniah said:

"Write to my missus if they top me, eh?"

"What? For escaping? They can't do that!"

"Can't they?" said a man nearby. "Christ, you don't know 'em."

Zephaniah said, "My two companions are still at large — don't ask me how, but we got through on Eaglehawk — somewhere up in Forestiers they knocked off a guard."

"They killed a guard?" I searched his face. "Were you with them?"

"No. They collared me in hours. William Jones put the word out."

"Jones?" I ejaculated. "He betrayed you?"

Zeph nodded. "That's how low we've sunk. Somehow he got hold of it from some people who were privy to what I was up to."

I bowed my head. Zephaniah said, "Don't take it bad, Frosty, he's not the man we knew," and here he hesitated, adding, "Things have happened to William Jones in Port Puer Boys' Prison . . . too delicate even to mention in letters home."

"God Almighty," I said.

There came a silence between us. Prisoners about us craned their necks to hear us, and Zeph said, "You . . . you know about my Llewellyn?"

I awakened to his change of mood. "Your son? Of course!"

"If you make it home, get up to Blaina and have a look at him. Joan says he's just won a Charlotte Guest eisteddfod purse at the last Abergavenny . . . the harp, you know. He's brilliant."

I nodded.

"They . . . they might have come out here if this hadn't happened."

"You'll see it through," I said.

The Javelins came with soldiers of the 96th: rough ones, some of these, assisting me along with their musket butts, and the last I saw of Zephaniah then was standing in his chains.

"Goodbye," I said.

To my amazement, he winked.

One thing was certain, I reflected, I should never have taken charge of this rebellion while people like Zephaniah were about.

The probation centre at Brown River, mainly a logging camp, did not long accommodate me. Within a month I was again in trouble with the law through a man to whom I did not respectfully touch my cap. Sick of him, defiant of a system that demeaned a man's self-respect, I exaggerated the action from a touch of the forelock to a grand genuflexion that was almost a prostration.

Too late I found he was Superintendent Smith.

This entitled me to an immediate transfer to Impression Bay, a logging and sawyer station where, apparently, things would be even harder for me. My belligerence was growing with the realization that they were clearly reluctant to flog me.

Meanwhile, under a Mr Armstrong, an engineer of some repute and no-nonsense, Impression Bay, with its working gang of a hundred convicts and guard of some twenty soldiers, was beginning to make its mark upon geography.

But I did not know, as I took my place in the working gang, that not seven miles away, at Saltwater River, my stepson, William Foster Geach, had also joined a labour gang.

What with one and the other of us, Mary would have her hands full, I thought.

So had I. Along with the heavier labour in the punishment gang, I was also to endure two weeks of the Silent System.

This is what drives men mad quicker than pain.

At Impression Bay, dale, wood and water combined to make an enchanting whole: it was a panorama of beauty, every feature basking in the ethereal loveliness of 'a spotless empyrean' as one writer put it — the vaulting eternity of the sky.

Here abound sweeping kingfishers to remind one of England; here the kookaburra laughs away the impudence of the mynah, and occasionally sings the beautiful lyre. Black swans mate and bring forth in this paradise; the blue crane stands in scornful majesty on the marshlands. I've heard it said that thirteen kinds of birds are found only in Tasmania — tits, green parrots, robin and currawong; here waddle the platypus; forester kangaroo and wallaby, about since primitive man, infest the hinterland: Tasmania's temperate climate seduces to the vast rain forests tropical butterflies of every shape and hue; unwittingly, one perched on my hand, a riot of green and gold, and covered it down to my fingers.

Trust Man to bring his sadism to this Elysium loveliness.

Our working gangs numbered five, each consisting of about twenty men; a few, under extra punishment, being in chains. Each gang was lorded by a convict overseer, and the whole controlled for discipline by Mr Armstrong, a colourless individual who always appeared to be within vaporous dreams of higher calculus. But he came to the point the moment I arrived.

"You will work with Gang Four; you will take commands, but will have no occasion to speak under any circumstances, understand? Neither will anyone speak to you, except in writing to command you. If you need anything, or the necessity to draw attention to any circumstance, you will do so by indication — a sign — nothing more. If I have the slightest trouble with you, I will send you down to the commandant at Port Arthur, you hear me?"

"Yes, sir."

And he raged with total fury, "I told you not to speak! There are no more chances, Frost! Because you are undergoing Silence, you will not share the company of the gang when off duty; to this end I have allocated you to a palliasse in the Commissariat store hut; there, off duty, you will be responsible for the safety of tools and implements. Make a sign that you have heard me!"

I raised a hand to him.

"Overseer! Take him away!"

Men glanced up, their heads lowered in obedience to the overseer's watchful eye, but spoke no words as I joined them at labour. Armstrong had been known to become engaged in intricate calculations of bending moment, torque and sheer — the new wharf on Impression sands was apparently his darling — during the antisocial business of flogging.

Exclusive of the carrying gangs, there were watermen, grubbers and gardeners, quarrymen, splitters, tramway hauliers and a dozen other men of trade. Half an hour before evening muster, a ball was suspended at the yardarm of the semaphore as a signal to those working away in the bush to return at the double ... or be listed as absconders.

Log rolling was the main activity at Impression, and upon this Gang Four was engaged. The logs would be floated in from 'luggage boats' and we would wade chest deep and get under them, dragging them out of the sea. This was all right when traversing flat sand, but again, the shoulder loads varied considerably with a man's height, and the inequality of pressure (or a stumble by the man before or behind one) could bring a load of more than 200 pounds crashing down on to a wet and bruised shoulder.

The chain gang working close by were engaged mainly in stone-breaking; certainly all chains were removed from men in the working gang, for fear of accidents. But the French felons of the Bague were not only put into irons, but, being habitual absconders, were linked together by a tether chain. Upon this the overseer would often haul, dragging manacled men to their knees in the process.

I could have wept for these French patriots, whose only crime was that they had fought for their country. Neither Britain nor France made attempts to draft an international convention for the protection of their prisoners.

Every dusk, with the red sun glittering and hissing as it sank into the sea horizon, the gangs would repair to their lice-infested bark and wattle huts: there to be locked in until dawn, when the Javelins would come bursting in with rope's ends and furious commands. At least I was spared this rude awakening, and opened my eyes to the blank ceiling of the little compartment I owned at the end of the stores.

Lying there I'd listen to the riotous confusion of scurry and clang as the breakfast mess tins were gathered by the day-turn orderlies — every convict took a turn at this — serving the 'skilly' (a glutinous mess of watery soup upon which floated the remains of last night's supper). And anxious were the eyes cast to the top of the tables, lest generous helpings at the top starved those at the bottom.

Then the bearded, cadaverous faces would spoon up the broth: shining eyes is what I most remember, for the eyes of the half-starved glint and reflect an animal lustre in the fight for survival. Next do I remember the gnawing pains of the half-empty stomach and the sickness that rises to the throat when the stomach's bile is active . . . without sufficient to eat upon. And yet, in retrospect, after a week or two of hard labour carrying ship's masts and yardarms, with all surplus fat slowly stripping away, my body began to react to its new disposition. The muscle pains and cramps faded, and I felt revitalized, reborn. From flaccidity and superfluity, new bands of muscles appeared: new strength replaced the careworn inertia of approaching senility. It was a fight for survival in which I flourished.

That was the physical aspect; the mental aspect was a different story. And from that there was but one escape down a golden avenue of fantasy; all other paths, within the Silent System, lead to madness.

# 19

OF all the punishments meted out to me in my life, the one that left upon me the deepest scars was the Silent System of those weeks' hard labour at Impression Bay. No man is an island, the poet said; by nature he is gregarious with his fellows, finding it imperative to exchange his views with another of his kind.

Isolation from womankind is torture enough, severing his natural spiritual and physical outlets; but divorce from sound is a circumcision of the mind. It was no coincidence that the asylum in Port Arthur was within shouting distance of the Silent Cells where prisoners, their faces masked to counter recognition, their lives a vacuum of silence, soon began to howl like chained dogs. Hendriks was the only man I knew to survive unmarked out of the Silent Cells.

Had I been denied escape into the past, which I had assiduously practised during earlier imprisonments, I doubt if I would have escaped mental derangement during those two weeks of silence. Then, as often happens in the affairs of men, the sublime became the ridiculous . . . there was an influx of new prisoners for the expansion of the station, and many of my old friends arrived to join my labour gang.

Hendriks arrived, and with him came Greg; Richard Carling and Old Lag, Roberts the Chartist, and young Wilde who was defiant of his floggings; Sole Bungy, Timbo Weller of the hideous grin, and, almost unbelievably, Petticoat Boy, plus John Jones and Howell, the Birmingham lads.

On the day the *Eliza* delivered them to my station, two Javelin Men arrived that morning at the Commissariat Store hut — a confining, verminous and ramshackle shelter which scarcely kept out the rain; they released me from the extension chain that allowed my toilet, and led me, unmanacled and free, into the sunlit air.

"Good for you, Frost, now ye can chatter," said one. "Report to Hut Five down on the beach." These were reasonable Javelin Men.

And already sitting in Hut Five,

contemplating their new surroundings, were all the comrades I had in the world.

The eyes of men can kiss a male greeting; they leaped upon me, they slapped my back in their uncouth banter, they flooded me with questions about conditions on Impression Bay, and what kind of a bastard is this man Superintendant Armstrong, and who's in charge of Gang Four?

"Taply died, ye know," said Hendriks.

"Soon after you went to see the governor at Hobart," said Richard. "They sent him over to Dead Man's island; fair's fair — Captain Booth let Petticoat and I go over there to bury him. 'A man's got a right to be buried by his friends,' he said."

"God, he's changed!"

"Talk has it that he's just finishing his term. This time next year he'll be retired, they say."

Roberts said, "Did you hear what happened to poor old Zephaniah?"

I told them how I had met him weeks ago.

"Two years in the chain gang. I don't think I'd come out of that," said Petticoat Boy.

"He will," I replied. "You don't know Zephaniah."

"And William Jones still teaching the lads over on Point Puer."

"Don't talk to me about William Jones," interjected little Sole Bungy, and cried in his shrill soprano:

"They do tell as how he be gone all queer, like saying grace at eating, and he's very fond of boys."

"You can say that twice," said Richard Carling. "Living in the lap of luxury, they tell me," and Timbo Weller put his hand over his twisted mouth and added:

"He'll do all right at Point Puer, mind — you don't get flogged for changing your sex."

"You've proof?" I asked.

"Ah, well not exactly, but I talked to a fella down on the docks and he said 'Jonah' Jones had changed his mode of living."

"He might have, but that doesn't mean he's changed his sex," I said. "There's enough filth round here without us adding to it by scandal; William Jones is supposed to be a comrade."

It brought upon them an unusual quiet.

My mounting joy that I would be allowed to work with my friends was short-lived: I was undergoing punishment labour; they were not. Nevertheless, my application that I might share their hut was granted by a doleful Armstrong. This was on a Monday; had I left it to the following day, I would have been rejected. For Tuesday was the day that Armstrong was transferred to Port Arthur docks and Superintendent Smith, my old enemy of Brown River, arrived to replace him. And the first thing Smith did was to put Big Hendriks and the others on the cart-hauling from Impression through to Cascades and on to the Norfolk station, which entailed them being away every other day. Log piling was going on at the head of the convict railway; every spare tree cut down at Impression was shaved, sawn into handable lengths, and transported on iron-shod wheels by gangs of six. And on the very first day that Smith arrived, young Wilde and Old Lag, working a double-handed saw after tree-felling, broke the blade.

"Christ Almighty help us," I heard Timbo Weller say, for I was working near them.

Saw blades were in short supply; there was scarcely a greater crime in the Colony than breaking one. Superintendent Smith arrived at the scene, took one look, and said:

"Thirty-six apiece," and his voice rose and he shouted around the group of sullen men. "And thirty-six it will be for anyone breaking a blade now I've arrived."

To this day I am convinced that he seized the opportunity to assert his authority at Impression.

Two gang overseers seized young Wilde and Old Lag and bundled them down the beach to the flogging triangles, which was unusual, but within the law, for a superintendent had the authority to order up to thirty-six lashes without an appearance in court.

Armstrong was meticulous in having every man appear before a magistrate for sentencing and punishment, although a night's confinement in the Belly Bot (a box contraption little bigger than a coffin) was his normal punishment for minor offences, such as dumb insolence, or being caught roasting a Hawkesbury duck, the convict's name for a cob of maize which could often be picked at the roadside.

Superintendents varied in their views on crime and punishment. For instance, it was the law that no convict should catch and eat reptile meat; the daily rations, Captain Booth held, were amply sufficient: to supplement them was to encourage hoarding to facilitate escape. So, while Armstrong merely admonished sawyers for snapping a saw blade, he kept to the book when it came to the 'fiddle', as we called it: such as sneaking away to gather wild peaches or nuts which often grew in profusion near the camps, while an overseer's dog might get short shrift if it took a midnight walk.

As to saws, Armstrong knew about metal fatigue, and Smith did not.

"String them up," said he, and the gangers pulled the shirt down Wilde's back and tied him to the triangle.

With the broken saw laid at the feet of the flogger, the punishment began. We stood in a half circle, about 200 of us, and not a man there raised his face as the floggers laid it on. Wilde, still a lad, bit upon the stick and made no sound: blood soaked his waistband and his buttocks were stained crimson when they untied him. Nor did he even stagger when he walked to his clothes, but did not raise his face this time lest Smith accused him of insolence.

Next, they brought Old Lag to the triangle.

It was midday. The sun burned down. The sea, flat calm and hazed, was the colour of cobalt; coloured birds were singing in a rush of wings across the vetch grasses, the hair of the dunes.

Old Lag was old, if not in years; nobody knew his age, but his body had long wilted to life's privations, bringing him to premature senility. His muscles sagged, his straggling beard drooped on to his wizened chest, and Hendriks always worked behind him in the log loading, to take the strain if Old Lag's foot raised him on a mound. Now the old man stood to attention while the floggers 'stripped him down': motionless he stood before the triangle while they hauled his arms upwards to tie his wrists, then kicked his legs wider while they knelt to tie his ankles.

"He do look like someone's grandfer,"

whispered Hendriks beside me. "You say we try a go, Mr Frost?" And Richard Carling, behind us, said:

"Don't be a fool, Hendriks — look."

Perhaps Smith, by some strange instinct, expected trouble that day; we shall never know; but a troop of six marines with muskets at the ready appeared suddenly on the brow of a nearby slope, and stood at ease there, looking down while Old Lag was flogged.

There was no sound but the sighing of the wind, the cracking of the cat as it descended on Old Lag's blood-stained back, and the doctor's shrill voice as he counted the strokes:

"Twenty, twenty-one, twenty-two . . . "

The flogger was tiring; he paused and tossed the whip to his 'second', the man who had flogged Wilde; the grasses whispered about us; high above us a lark was filling the sky with a shrill, cadent song. 200 convicts in their yellow and black raised their faces to one man . . . the flogger who was taking off his coat; and Old Lag hung by his wrists on the triangle, and turned his body once in agony, and I saw that his chest was black: a danger sign, the blood escaping from the lacerations of the back muscles.

"What kind of men do we call ourselves?" said Hendriks.

And as if that whisper was an unheard sign of suppressed fury, a low murmur came from the massed convicts.

"God, no!" said Richard.

The flogger hesitated. Old Lag straightened, tensing his body for the laying on. Superintendent Smith, having momentarily turned away, came back and stood in the circle: bending his cane over his stomach, he glared around the faces of the men. But still the murmur grew from scores of throats at first, then more; a defiant grumble that spread along the packed ranks, until Smith's squeaky voice rang out:

"*Lay on hard!*"

The man hesitated, looking fearfully over his shoulder.

"I say lay on, or you'll have it yourself!" Smith waved his arms in growing nervousness, shrieking, "Overseers forward! Come on, overseers!" And these shouldered their way through the convicts and ranged themselves about him.

"Drummer up!" cried Smith, and a drummer, always present but rarely used at unimportant beatings, came forward.

Gradually the clamour grew from 200 half-closed mouths as an accompaniment to the steady beating of the drum, but no whip was coming down; it was waving uncertainly in the air while Old Lag cowered under it. And the grumbling rose higher, like a moan: down came the marines in a single-file trot. Reaching the triangle, they halted under Smith's orders, turned about and presented their muskets at us. Smith, now almost dancing with uncontrolled rage, yelled:

"First flogger up — and flog that man!"

Up came he, and began to flog his mate, who momentarily covered his face against the lash, then turned in desperation and began to flog Old Lag.

"Lay it on, you scum!" yelled Smith, running around the triangle. "Harder, harder!" and the marines, I noticed, began to check their priming as the grumbling grew into a chorus of derisive shouts: so we had the spectacle of the first flogger lashing at his 'second' while he was lashing at Old Lag; and to complete the sadism,

Smith himself began to bring down his cane upon the first flogger's back, making a trio of indiscriminate beatings, while the drummer tried vainly to match the time. The men began to stamp on the ground with their boots and, some being chained, it made an obscene and awful symphony of pain, interspersed with Old Lag's screaming.

Suddenly, his head drooped sideways; a sign of unconsciousness.

As if cut by the flash of a knife, everything stopped: the shrieks, the flying whips, the cane, the drum.

In that silence the doctor went up to the triangle.

Silence.

Smith, red-faced and infuriated, cried, "How many?"

"Thirty, sir," said the drummer.

The doctor said, and we heard him clearly, "I would advise a cut down, superintendent, the man's unconscious."

"Thirty-six he's due for, and thirty-six he'll have, by God!" shouted Smith, and stared around defiantly at us. "Lay on, floggers!"

The two men approached the triangle

again, their whips laid back.

"Wait, sir," said the doctor, and turned Old Lag's face to the sun, "wait, I say . . ." and he put his hand to Old Lag's temple, then the other around him to feel his heart, and the hand that came away was bloodstained.

"This man is dead, Mr Smith."

Later, we washed him clean and laid Old Lag out in his coffin, and took him over to Dead Man's Isle, which was something Captain Booth always allowed; indeed, said Richard Carling, he's quite meticulous about it, as was the coroner — 'Death from natural causes'.

We buried him between young Taply, and the man who threw a stone at William IV.

"He's in good company there," said Hendriks.

While working in Gang Four at Impression Bay there came to me sickening proof of what I had daily seen on paper, when in the office of the commandant; iniquity when reported second-hand is never so substantial as when seen.

I was now surrounded with a new and

horrifying debasement — homosexuality.

"Didn't you know?" asked Hendriks. "It's happening all over the Colony."

"He's had it easy in the old man's office, mind," added Roberts. "You want to get up in the morning, Mr Frost."

Later, in my *First Letter* to the people of the United States, I wrote (it being impossible to get it published in England):

I was on the Tasman Peninsula for three and a half years and, as a clerk to the commandant, was able to become an observer of both the conduct of the authorities and the morals of the prisoners — men of all grades of society and transported for different offences. Among these were men of talent and good breeding, and I saw with deep regret how depraved so many of them had become. Even highly gifted men indulged in moral crime so debasing that it is beyond their repentance. I tell you, not ten men could be found in the Cities of the Plains — Norfolk Island and Port Arthur — uncontaminated by the filth of Sodom and Gomorrah.

During the administration of Sir

Eardley Wilmot it was commonly reported in Hobart Town that a great number of convicts recently arrived from the peninsula were in a wretchedly diseased state as a result of their perversions; each new outstation having become its own arsenal of moral crime, misery and a disease for which there is yet no name. And yet, when the Duke of Richmond gave notice to the Government that he would move for a committee of inquiry, there was not a single member of Parliament who, though completely aware of the depravity existing in this Colony, would support its debate: such is the irresponsibility of power in the hands of vicious men.

Richard Carling said in the hut one night, "The lads are right, John Frost, you've been behind the curtains too long. Things are happening over in Point Puer which puts Norfolk Island and Port Arthur in the shade."

"Tell him, boy," said Sole Bungy, nudging young Wilde, and the lad, his back still crusted from his wicked flogging, said:

"It do not sound decent," and sat on his

straw with an averted face.

"If it's that indecent and you tell about it, perhaps Mr Frost can write about it, and smuggle it back to England."

"He'll tell my name and my mam'll find out."

"No names, lad," I said, "I swear it to you, so tell me," and the boy said:

"First when I come here on the *Asperous,* they sent me over to the Point Puer workshops — I were sixteen then — and worked in the pattern shop on the trades — you know, cuttin' the taps and turns for the moulders in the fire-smithies . . . " He hesitated.

"Go on," said Petticoat Boy.

"It be awful dirty, mun."

"You tell it clean, my chap, and it'll be less dirty for other decent lads — tell Mr Frost."

Wilde said, "One night, soon after I arrived, I were asleep in me bunk and in comes four or five o' the heavy 'uns — you know — blacksmith's strikers and hauliers. 'Joey Wilde,' they says to me, 'there anna no proper feed here, nor skirts to cuddle and coon, save one, and she's fair dinkum — come in to Sarah's and lookin'

273

out for the likes o' you, for she's got her pecker up for one day sailing off to England home and glory. You coming?'

"'Aw, shove off,' says I. 'There ain't no skirts this side o' Paramatta Females, and that's bloody miles off for I saw them prancing and got flogged for it,' — didn't I, Mr Frost? You was there, wasn't you?"

I nodded.

He frowned around the faces of the squatting men, saying, "I tells you about Paramatta Females, for I went there for a girl, see, for whatever I tells, you ain't ever goin' to call me a fancy Dan. I anna that."

"Don't worry, boyo," said Roberts, coming in late and squatting on the floor beside him.

It was raining outside, I remember, the only way Tasman can rain: cats and dogs and tub-wash bucketings, and Joey Wilde said:

"I tell you lot somethin' more. Before I left Portsmouth I took a girl to bed and put her in the family way; that's me, I'm decent."

"Without a doubt," interjected Richard Carling.

"What happened — did you go with them?" I asked, and Wilde replied:

"I just told you — you ain't knockin' me up on that one, I told them, so you piss off and let me sleep. And this got their tuckles up and they grabbed me, and tied a gag in my mouth, for I was hollerin' to raise Puer Point; and they heaved me outta the hut and into the scrub, all four of 'em, and two more came, and I laid one out. And there, in the dark, they stripped me jack naked, and four of 'em held me, and then you know what . . . " He lowered his face.

We did not speak at once. Then I asked softly, "This happened to you, but to no others, as far as you know?"

It angered him. "Jesus, Mr Frost, didn't ye hear of it in Captain Booth's office?"

"I heard of it among men, but not at Puer Point, with the boys being taught the trades . . . "

"Then I'll tell ye, sir. It happened to every one. Every time a new boy came, the bigger ones got hold of him."

I knew this, of course; day by day I had read the records of Port Puer as I had done with every other outstation, but I wanted the proof of it from a trainee's lips, and now I had got it. Wilde said:

"I . . . I couldn't get clean, see? For weeks I'd go down to the sea and wash all over till I was near a pink lobster, scrubbing meself with sand. And then I thought I'd never get right again till I'd done a clean woman, so I took French leave and 'sconded and took to watching the wives in the streets, and old girls like my mother. I know'd they'd flog me for laggin' off, but I reckoned that was fair, like . . . I tell ye, Mr Frost, you take a beating and you get clean again, my mam used to tell me. She was a right old girl, with a fist on her like a man, and she wore a lavender bonnet. And if she knew what happened to me here in Port Puer, she'd come right over and kick the bloody place to pieces." He stared at us, his eyes moving over our faces. "Boys are no good, so I come to work with men like you. You're a good clean lot, mind."

"Maybe, but I reckon you're the cleanest man here," said Richard.

"You think so, Mr Carling?" His eyes were bright.

"I'm sure so, Mr Wilde," said Hendriks.

"This filth can be laid at the door of Captain John O'Hara Booth, who condones it," said Richard.

I did not take issue with him at the time, but Richard was quite wrong, for after a year in his office I knew Booth intimately. While Booth was a moral pervert in the mould of Sade, one who could inflict horrific punishments on helpless men in the cause of discipline, he was no supporter of homosexuality. In terms of where and how the boys of Puer Point slept, a state conducive to unnatural practices, he sent a plan to the Government in London by which, for a small financial outlay, this might be avoided: the answer came back that the Government disapproved of any such alterations. And this from grave legislative assemblies composed of nobles, gentlemen and bishops, who commenced their daily duties with a prayer. And Lord Derby compounded the indifference to human suffering by stating:

For the past four years the system of religious instruction in the penal settlement has been productive of the most beneficial results. The condition of the convicts under the improved probation system is most satisfactory.

In a case similar to that which Joey Wilde described, and under the governorship of Colonel Arthur, another young man of about Wilde's age resisted all attempts upon his person when working in the coal mines, a hellish place in which many diseased men existed.

Underground, six men laid hold of the lad and violated him. And despite all attempts to hide the matter by threats and blandishments, the lad would hear nothing of it and persisted in his allegation. The men were apprehended, committed to Hobart Town, tried by the Supreme Court there, found guilty, and two were sentenced to death; two of the other four were sent to Norfolk Island, there to carry on the same practices.

# 20

FOR two years I worked under Superintendent Smith at Impression Bay, one of the worst masters in the colony: had it not been for the comradeship of the men of Hut Five, I am sure I would not have survived it. Day after day, from dawn to dusk, the work was the same; Gang Four, with Big Hendriks now its ganger, felled the trees and shaved them while we, the punishment men, carried them down to Impression beach for the cart-hauling down to the railway at Norfolk Bay.

I was nigh sixty, an old man by any standards, yet my body had been revived into a new, youthful vigour; every muscle I owned was hard and strong. I had never felt better in my life.

Those were the days of sweat and slog under reviling voices and threat of the whip, but when the shadows lengthened and my friends swarmed into Hut Five, there always came to me the same vigorous warmth of their companionship.

"Hey, you!" cried Petticoat Boy, coming in out of the sun, and he slapped Richard's back in passing, "You don't ever guess what we saw today coming in on the railway."

We were all sitting or lying in attitudes of exhaustion on our palliasses; nobody even washed until after an hour of rest.

"Lady Godiva," muttered Hendriks, his eyes half closed.

"And bloody nearly, too, me son," said Petticoat, squatting nearby, and he elbowed Timbo and Sole, both of whom, like him, were away for days at a time, working on the Convict Railway. "Tell his lordship, lads," said he.

"I reckon it was that piece we saw on the *Lady Juliana*," said Timbo.

"You know, Sir Richard, the lovely skirt standing on the pinnace in the harbour o' Falmouth?"

Richard gave them a grin; they knew him by a variety of titles, it was a banter he had to take.

"I tell you it was her, though," added Sole, sober serious, "for I was pushin' right close to her. Sitting on the wagon like a fine duchess she were, in a white lace frock and a big straw hat, with her nose up."

"Cost ye sixpence to talk to her."

I noticed the smile fade on Richard's mouth. "Alone?"

"Christ, no, mun. Her old man was with 'er, weren't he? All decked up in navy blue and scrambled eggs — Captain somethin' or other, they said he was. Come ashore to take up a post in Cascades, accordin' to the overseer."

"And a fine house all ready to go into," added Timbo. "And I tell ye this, Your Grace, I was wind'ard of her, and she smelled as sweet as a nut . . ." He roared bawdy laughter. "You try pushin' a bloody old wagon wi' that lot within two feet of ye!"

"Tell 'em to pull the other one," grumbled Hendriks, getting up, and suddenly Joey Wilde cried:

"That's the same lady I saw in Cascades last Sunday. Dear me, she's a jewel of a woman," and an Irishman bawled from the other end of the hut:

"Be God, he's seein' skirts all over the place, so he is! Sure, when it comes to females he's a foine administrator."

"It's true, I say," persisted Joey. "A lovely high-steppin' piece, and gabblin' away like a foreigner."

"French?" asked Richard, suddenly interested.

"How should he know?" said Hendriks. "He cannot even speak English."

And Sole made wine-glass signs in the air with his hands. "With lovely golden hair hanging down her back and tied with ribbons . . . "

Richard glanced at me and shook his head.

"Not the same one," said he. "Madame Le Roy was blackbird dark."

"Madame Le Roy?" asked Petticoat instantly. "Hey, your lordship, that reminds me — what happened to the end o' that courtship yarn you was tellin' us?"

"Yes," added Hendriks, now trimming his fine beard in a glass. "We never did hear the tail of it."

"What yarn's that, then?" asked Joey.

"Dear Jesus," said Timbo, "now Joey's on to it, you've got to tell us. The last we heard you were in bed with her, remember?"

"That last night in The Labour in Vain

in Reading, wasn't it?" Hendriks asked.

"Aw, come on, Mr Carling," cried Joey, "be a sport — I anna heard any o' that!"

"Nor me, me lovely fellas," said the Irishman, joining us.

He was nearly as big as Hendriks, and his looks had gone, for his cheeks were scarred with fire and his hair was tufted and burned off; in the 1798 Irish Rebellion, he said, the German mercenaries sent in by England had put upon his head a cap of pitch and set it alight, the burning cap of the Hessians. "And then England had the bloody audacity to send me here, be God," said he, laughing. "And all because I tried to free the beloved country!"

"What's your name?" asked Hendriks.

"Mike Flynn, and I've just come in."

"Come and sit by me, friend," said Hendriks. "And you tell your tale, Sir Richard, or you'll never hear the end of it," and Richard began the last episode of *The Knight's Tale*, saying:

"Especially for Joey Wilde, then," and we all gathered around while the rain of dusk, for this was August, beat upon the hut windows, and the story continued:

"Now, you'll recall that, against my will, I was taken to bed by the French beauty, Madame Le Roy, who brought her jewels for safe keeping into my room . . . " Richard's voice was a whisper and I took the opportunity to look around their tense, eager faces.

"And you'll remember madame throwing her arms about me . . . "

A chorus of shouts and jeers received this.

"But, be fair," said Richard. "Apart from my three serving-maids in the Three Pigeons back in Nesscliff, I'd had very little experience of such a situation. But, I was prepared to sacrifice myself on the altar of womanhood if I could get my hands upon her jewels."

"Gawd, hark at it!" cried Petticoat Boy.

"And this I did. I pleasured the lady not once, but thrice, let me tell you, all in the space of an hour, and Madame Le Roy, with a sigh of contentment, slept."

He paused, looking around him. "Indeed, it was scarcely sleep, it was like a fraud of death, and from time to time her red lips would whisper, 'Oh, Roberto, my love. Oh, Roberto . . . '!"

"Ye seduced the creature?"

"I did," answered Richard, "and then, most carefully I eased her Moroccan bag from under my pillow — remember, I had changed it for mine? — and got a leg out on to the floor. But my other leg got its toe caught in the sheets, and I lay there half in and half out, till milady shifted over, and I was free. Off with my nightshirt then and into my trews; wave arms into my shirt and tunic, on with me boots and I was away through the casement without ruffling a feather . . . and dropped eight feet down into the hotel courtyard."

"Ye left her? That was a dreadful thing to do!" whispered Joey.

"But I had her jewels, you see," said Richard. "And within five minutes I had one of the stagecoach nags out of his stable and I was on him and away over the countryside like a witch on a broomstick."

"Ye got away with it?" asked Petticoat, his eyes like saucers.

"Well, I'd got about five miles along the London Road when I heard pursuing hooves, and when half a dozen stallions came abreast of me, I reined in the

285

stagecoach nag, and a voice bellowed from the dark:

"'Halt in the name of the Queen!' And the moment I did so, a pair of special constables pulled me off my horse; a moment later I was surrounded by dragoons, and their captain had a levelled pistol.

"'Sir Richard Carling?' he asked.

"Being active so far away in Shropshire, I had made the mistake of stating my real name in Bristol and Reading; now I was paying for it. Clearly, Madame Le Roy had betrayed me in more ways than one.

"The Captain seized my Moroccan bag, 'Give me this. I have reason to believe it carries money and jewels stolen from the Crown Hotel in Marlborough and the Labour in Vain stagehouse in Reading, the property of Thora, the actress.'

"'On the contrary, sir,' I answered. 'The bag contains my own money and the jewels of my wife, whom I am meeting at Charing Cross this very day.'

"'You, Sir Dick,' replied one of the constables meaningfully, 'ain't goin' nowhere, beggin' ye pardon, for accordin' to the French madame at the Labour in Vain, not only 'ave you lifted Lady Thora's, but you've stripped our French cousin as well,' and he opened the bag and peered into it by the light of the moon. 'Stone the bloody crows, Capt'in, it's empty!' and he turned it upside down, and to my astonishment, out fell my razor, shaving brush and soap and something else — two small, cheap earrings; the constable picked them up. 'Ay ay!' said he. 'And what 'ave we here, my lovely?'

"A voice said, 'That's Thora's stage earrings — worthless paste,' and I recognized the landlord of the Labour in Vain.

"The constable twisted his waxed moustache, watching me. 'I'll say one thing for ye, sir, you've been pretty quick on the fence . . . '

"'That's what he's done — he's got rid of the lot, damn me!' asserted the landlord.

"I cried bravely, 'I have done no such thing!' and I appealed to the dragoon captain. 'I am an honest member of the aristocracy going about his lawful business, and this is quite outrageous. You'll be hearing from my lawyers.'

"'And you'll be hearin' a bit from the lawyers of Her Majesty the Queen,' said the constable, taking my arm. 'So I'll trouble you to come this way and we'll sort the matter out in court. Meanwhile, ye can cool ye heels in the Reading lock-up, for the dirtiest thing that's happened to me tonight was to see that beautiful little Frenchy cryin' her eyes out, you agree, Capt'in?'

" 'I do indeed, you cad,' said the Captain of the Guard, sent me a look to kill, and galloped off.

" 'This way, my charmer,' said the constable, 'for we knows all about your little capers now, from Marlborough via Reading to Nesscliff up in Shropshire and back return journey, including serving-maids in bed at the Three Pigeons.' "

"It was a fair cop, mind," said Petticoat happily.

"The sharpest, thanks to Madame Le Roy," replied Richard. "Got to hand it to her. Later I heard she'd made a business of it under a variety of names. The French highwaylady of the London Road, they called her — after putting the finger upon me, she disappeared with the loot."

"And you haven't seen neither hide nor hair of her since?"

"Not a whisker."

"Is that exactly true?" I asked him, later.

Replied he. "Except when I saw her at Falmouth."

"And now on the Convict Railway? The lads aren't fools, you know."

"As the mistress of the captain of the *Lady Juliana*, come ashore to live at Cascades? I doubt it, but you can never tell — that lady got around."

"And if she proves to be Madame Le Roy?"

Richard smiled. "Then, my friend, I'd take a trip to Cascades to visit her, and I promise . . . the lads in this hut would live on the fat of the land."

I replied, "If it is the woman you think, and she is living in Cascades, it'll be with an important man, and you could find yourself on the triangle."

"That's the chance I take, for I reckon she owes me something. Seven years' penal servitude for a night in the feathers?"

"What do you propose to do?"

"I'll tell you after I've done it," said Richard.

He didn't waste much time.

That night I saw a figure moving in the hut, and it was Mike Flynn, the new Irishman. I sat up in my bunk.

"Will you lay quiet and snore," whispered a voice. "For the least ye know about this mad caper the better, sir."

"I know it all now," I whispered back. "Is he taking you with him?"

"He is, for me back's broad for carryin' the tins out o' her larder, he says, and it just could be — if it's the lady he thinks it is — he could suffer a wee delay."

"No doubt," I replied, and in a single shaft of a stricken moon, watched Richard and Flynn slip quietly through the door.

I looked at my watch; it was just gone midnight; there would be a hue and cry all over the Peninsula, I reflected, if they were not back by dawn.

Before the first flush of morning stained the sky, Mike Flynn returned; he had a sack upon his back as big as Burglar Bill's — all the delicacies imaginable, food we hadn't seen in years; rations from the old French campaigns, tinned beef and mutton, dried fish and roo meat fresh from the shooters; wheaten bread, and a precious cask of goat's milk which we drank at once, and fired the cask in the stove to prevent discovery. We stored the rest away from the eyes of the Javelins, and then gathered around Mike Flynn like anarchists crouching over a bomb, and he told us: "Sure to God, we were nearly nabbed by a patrol outside Cascades, but we took the beach road and waded in the swim to clear the Javelins' dogs. And I tell ye this, that fella has the nose to sniff out a woman, for we cut inland until we came to the administrator's house. 'Michael,' says Sir Richard, 'I'll lay me back teeth that this is the place, for once ye lay eyes on the bitch you'll realize that for her only the best is good enough . . . '"

Joey's eyes were like stars in that dawn light, I remember, Mike continued:

"He bade me stand in the shadows, and up he went on the ivy creeper, hand over hand, till he came to a balcony. And damn me, he had a casement door open as if he owned the place, and next moment, he was in."

"Inside?"

"Like a wraith in the night. God help the Pope, I've never seen the like of it. I tell ye, it was as if he knowed every nook and cranny o' the place, and the woman, too, for after me shiverin' and sweatin' for an hour or so, out he comes again wi' the loveliest creature it's been me privilege to see, with golden hair down the back of her, nothin' down the front and showin' enough bum on the pair of 'em to murder a bishop."

"No clothes on?" whispered Joey, swallowing hard.

"Not a stitch between 'em, I'm tellin' ye," whispered Mike. "And I sat there in the bushes with me eyes on stalks."

"Is this all true?" I asked.

"It is so, as true as Irish ducks, Mr Frost. I swear it by the nails o' the holy Cross, I do. Just like Adam and Eve they were, if I wear a pauper's shroud."

"Dear me!"

"Like as if he'd known her all his life," said Mike. "And doin' it so I would see, ye understand?"

"Cod 'em along, Michael," said Petticoat Boy. "You tell a fine yarn, ye do. Next ye'll 'ave me dreamin' of laced up girls and parasols."

"Ach," cried Mike, "you're the peak o' low taste, the bloody lot of ye! Don't you believe me, Mr Frost?"

"If you tell us where you got the food from."

It raised him to his feet. "Sure, he lowered it down from the balcony! He did, I'm telling ye! First he swung the creature up in his arms, then comes back on to the balcony with the loot and lowers it down on a bedsheet. 'Michael Flynn,' he whispers down to me, 'take this back to the lads and tell 'em there's more where it came from, and with luck I'll see ye in time for roll-call, lest I change me mind.' And he went inside and closed the door."

"He never did!" exclaimed Joe, his mouth open.

"Providence and mercy spare me," said Mike, sighing. "Didn't he have a foine, prancing woman impatient inside — what do ye expect?"

There was a silence. I said, quietly, while they all looked at me for judgement, "The food's here; it is what Dick promised us. I believe every word of it," and Mike answered:

"God increase your plenty, Mr Frost, and bad cess to any who don't. For tho' they're helter-skelter bloody liars in the place I come from, I'd ne'er twist the truth on a comrade."

I said, "I believe Dick Carling knew a sight more about that woman and the administrator's house than we give him credit for."

"You can say that again," said Michael Flynn.

The dogs were brought out when the Javelins reported him missing an hour later: the military in barracks down in Port Arthur were alerted; the garrisons at Norfolk Bay, Impression and Cascades began to scour the country. But they didn't find Sir Richard Carling. Rumours abounded, and we in the labour gangs caught their whispers . . . that the wife of the administrator in Cascades was absent, too: talk had it that an escape had been engineered; that a small boat had been discovered on the sands north of Eaglehawk Neck.

Meanwhile, Richard had disappeared as completely as if the hand of God had come down and lifted him off the Peninsula.

# Book Two

Book Two

# 21

## *In dreams of home*

MY bunk space in Hut Five was the first behind the door; often, when off duty, I would arrive to find the hut empty of occupants: divided into three labour gangs, one gang, with Zephaniah as lead convict, worked locally at general conservancy in the administrative area; the two others, with Richard Carling in charge of one and Francis Roberts the other, were employed on wharf-loading at Port Arthur docks. Therefore, with the unequal hours, I found myself spending much time alone. This, of course, was before Richard disappeared.

Books were hard to come by; *Pilgrim's Progress* was a soiled, disreputable object now, for I'd read it a dozen and more times. A few tattered fragments of Gibbons' *Decline and Fall of the Roman Empire*, once possessed by a United Irishman who had obtained his ticket-of-leave, was now my sole companion.

And so, at sunset, I would lie in the straw and focus my eyes and rivet every nerve and sinew on to a single, focal point — the hypnotic miracle of the glaze. So, although my being might be lying on a foreign shore, my mind then walked the hills and dales of my beloved country.

Plinlimmon, I saw, and Cader Idris, the Mountain Chair of the Clouds: I heard strange sounds above the rolling slopes of the great Van Rocks of Brecon, and this was the cry of the slaves. Lowering castles built their battlements in the cloud formations of my mind. The Teify, Towey, the Severn and the Usk meandered through the green lands of home like capricious Welsh maids.

All this I saw in the eye of my mind; the inner eye that assesses and disposes all things, great and small, beyond the chained body. Glimmer and glance . . . bright beams the hypnotic light; now to wither and dance before the half-closed eyes of the prisoner; and then come soporific visions.

And all that had been enacted in my past life, now came winging back to me with irresistible force and clarity . . .

None of this is easily achieved; the abandonment of one's sensitivity to the distress of others I found necessary to this therapy; and only a self-induced slumber was inviolate against external threat. The cry of a gull, for instance, could be interpreted by the brain as a human shriek; the sighing of the wind translated into moaning: and while the coarse banter of the returning occupants did not awaken me, the chinking of their chains could rake me back to consciousness.

From the beginning of my early experiments I had concentrated all my faculties upon a given object. And, by some strange quirk of the situation, there existed near the latch of the hut door, a tiny wane in the woodwork; nothing more similar to the Cross could I surely have found — but more, since the last rays of the sunset always fell in this direction, the door, when shut, presented to my eyes this minute shape of glory.

It was like looking into the eye of God. I had heard it claimed that sunlight glinting on gold makes easier the hypnotic process; but how much better was my small aid of sanctity! Its glittering gold offered more than internal peace: hand in hand with escape from reality went a seraphic, holy balm.

In this sunset dream walked Mary, my wife, in the woods of Bettws. Strange and interpretive visions of the past assailed me and brought personal joys, and griefs.

In recording these images they became in no way progressive; all were flash visions suddenly glowing out of my early manhood, from the time I can remember to the fateful years that brought me here, to the other side of the world. And, as they appeared before me, untutored and unrehearsed, so I have set them down in the room where I am writing this. My mind traverses the years of Gwent . . . back into the mists of Time.

*Home. Newport. 1802 Monmouthshire*
Stow Fair in Gwent, when one is young, can be rhapsodic, the most colourful event of your life. *Calan Mai*, the first day of summer . . . !

"Yes," cried my grandfather in his small cracked soprano, "well may you remember its religious connotation. For, while He is ascending from St Woollos on a cloud of divinity, you and the town are behaving like limbs of Satan. *Away with ye!*"

And I went up the stairs in the Royal Oak, our public house in Thomas Street, like Baal with St Peter behind him, collided with Gran on the landing, and ran back down again.

"Hey!" cried she. "Wait, you!"

A word about my grandmother.

Five feet eleven in her socks was she, with a big bustled bum on her and a bosom that cuddled and cavorted to drive the men demented when she went along High Street in summer, and she had an eye for them all, though she was knocking sixty.

"Come you in," said she now, being Welsh, and she sat down at her dressing table and turned her face this way and that, grimacing at the mirror.

I entered her bedroom and stood decently for her, since her word in our house was law. Now she puffed and powdered and slapped the spare chin under her chops, and said:

"John Frost, you are eighteen years old on the twenty-fifth of the month, are you not?" (Her use of my full name meant trouble.)

"Yes, Gran."

She pouted at herself. "No doubt you think it impossible, but I vividly remember when I was sixteen, and I was married a year later. I knew where I was going, but you apparently have no idea. To date you've been indentured to your grandfather as a cordwainer and apprenticed to a Cardiff draper. Now, having broken both contracts, you are lazing around the public and kicking your heels in the inns and taverns. Your mother thinks the world of you, but your grandfather and your Uncle William don't think much, and neither do I."

"Not my uncle," I said.

"Perhaps not, but he thinks he is, and so, it seems, does your mother, so it's best to go along with it. Who, in the meantime, is Becky Crosscut?"

"Daughter of the Chinese sawyer."

She grunted. "Chinese I can well believe, with a name like that. But she's also the barmaid of the Sloop and Betty, I understand," and she turned on her chair and took my hands and her fingers were strong and cool upon mine. "Listen, boy. I know you want to discover the facts of life and that to do so it's no good nibbling at green apples, but Becky Crosscut! Really!" Shocked and appalled was she. I said bravely:

"She is not my girl!"

"I'm delighted to hear it, for the moment she is I'm up High Street to see her father. *Ach-y-fi!*" And she shoved me away to rouge up her cheeks. "You young boyos are all the same. You think that floppy rabbit's ear you've got is every woman's pride and joy, but get the wrong side of it and it becomes your greatest enemy. What time is it?"

"Close on midday."

"Then I've got to run, for the Abergavenny coach leaves at one," and she rose to her full height and pulled on a summer straw hat all black lace and veiled, and she looked like Juliet must have looked before she pulled the blinds on Romeo. Now she bent to me, kissing the air with her lips an inch from mine, whispering, "Bloody old grandma, innit? But someone's got to pull your ear and Grandpa won't. Love me some?"

"Ay ay."

"Then mind what I say or I'll belt you

myself up Stow Hill and down return journey, so let's hear no more o' this Betty Crosscut."

"Where you off to, Gran?" I asked, to get her goat, for I wasn't born yesterday, I knew what was happening.

"I tell you that, *cariad*, and you'll be as wise as me."

Rumour had it that a tall straight chap, an ex-colonel in the army, used to meet her every fourth weekend at the Abergavenny Angel, and he don't come all the way from Brecon Barracks to polish 'is boots, so she can talk, said Becky Crosscut. Don't do as I do, but do as I say, ain't it?

Mind, she looked like sino-relations, did Becky, with eyes so slanted at the outer corners that I thought they were never coming down, otherwise things were normal; but if she was Chinese, I was a Portuguese mariner. And she can keep her opinions to herself when it comes to my relatives.

Some gran I had.

Never seen the like of her in a month of Sundays.

So I stood outside the King's Head hotel and waved at her as the stagecoach went off to show her I knew, and I bet that put one up her apron.

My mother was the antithesis of my gran, a real old Biblical reformer; a most pious woman for a publican was she, and knew the Scriptures. "Strong drink," she used to say, "is the wine of wickedness," and she paid an annual subscription to the Newport Temperance Society to advance their aims for the soft stuff since she, ever since my father passed on, only served a very mild brew. Mild or not, it had some effect on the drinkers, because come 'Chucking Time' as Grandpa called it, most had to be assisted on to Thomas Street with broom handles. We weren't physical people, as I remember it — we had no chucker-out, but with Grandpa only five-foot-two and my mother inclined to the Quakers, we had to call for Gran when there was trouble in the tap-room.

"Emmy, Emmy!" my mother would wail, and under the bar flap would go Gran; a fearful sight was she; with her bosom like a ship's prow and her hair piled up to ten feet tall, bare-knuckle pugilists in full fight used to quail before her — largely because they knew she had a knuckle-duster under her skirt. And so, what with Gran, Grandpa and my mam, Pa and 'Uncle' William Foster calling at odd times (I suspect for romance) the only one normal in the Royal Oak, was me.

Now, on that Fair Day the navvies were flooding into our tavern, opening their gullets, pouring down the quarts without a swallow and barging each other about in horse-play. Never have I seen the likes of 'em before or since; little wiry slips of the north country, mainly, with muscles as hard as the stone they quarried. Among them worked Irish giants, men of handsome, Latin faces, laughing eyes and chests like doormats, and you couldn't understand a word in ten from them. With yellow mud caked to their shoulders and yorks under the knees of their moleskin trews, they'd swarm in from the cut and hammer the bar for ale.

"Sixpence down and two quarts, me dad!" And they'd start a commotion of ale and argument you could hear down in Cardiff.

Mind, I was always fascinated when Grandpa got a sixpence, for he had ambitions to retire to the country, and I never knew if he intended Gran to accompany him, or not. Up to the light would go the sixpences, then between his teeth, the test for silver: and while I've seen scores of them enter I've yet to see one emerge, especially when followed by a quart of stout. And every Monday morning I used to have to 'repair to an apothecary' for a draught of opening medicine 'in case the women needed it'. A walking money-box was Grandad, but I never managed to catch him fishing for his sixpences.

My father having died soon after I was born, my mother consoled herself with another, who passed on to Bethlehem as well, and thereafter we were pestered with the visits of Uncle William whose desire, it would appear, was to become a publican. And it was about then that he decided to take a hand in my affairs, with the suggestion that I should go to boarding school in Bristol, for I kept asking Mam for another father, so off they sent me at the age of twelve and I returned speaking reasonable English three years later; and was taken into Grandpa's room to learn from him the trade of bootmaking. But I soon tired of soles and stitching, so Uncle William, now a respected businessman and a constant visitor to the house despite the presence of Mam's third husband, sent me to Cardiff to learn the trade of tailoring. But I didn't succeed in that, either, at least, not until later years, and then it reached family ears that I was becoming interested in radical politics. And Uncle William, who was now an alderman, decided that I was too dangerous to have around. So he got rid of me permanently.

Let this be understood — I did not like my Uncle William, and this dislike was generated in the fantasies of my childhood.

Normally of a gentle nature, when the roaring of a baited animal in High Street would send me under the bed in tears, I could sleep in perfect peace in the knowledge that Uncle William was at that moment hanging by his testicles from a hook in the cellar, a punishment I had pronounced upon him two weeks earlier: more, I would dispose of his remains in the band-saw mills of Tredegar Slip without the rites of a Christian burial. This done, I would sit at the table wide-eyed with perplexity, and, like Gran, wonder where the devil he'd got to.

My radicalism actually sprang from Gran, who would always remain seated when 'God Save the King' was played in public, an act which got her ostracized by the best people and beloved of the worst, for the navvies working on the new canal coming into Newport adored the delinquency and we garnered most of the trade; the Royal Oak was just the place to sing revolutionary songs, and after a skinful there, you could stagger, if you still had legs, over to other iniquitous watering-holes where met criminals who, like the Dorchester Labourers of later years, were actually taking secret oaths and trying to form a Union of Workers.

And so, with the 1798 Irish Rebellion recently suppressed by our General Lake with appalling savagery, and the French Revolution a resounding success just over the Channel, the military in Newport were sharpening their bayonets and the aristocracy were trying to insure against damage to property. There were pools of potential bomb throwers all over the county, said Uncle William, getting out his

Riot Act, and the way your Gran is going she'll end in the Tower of London.

"Kill the King!" cried Gran one Saturday night in our tap-room. "This has always been me ambition," and she waved a bottle of stout within inches of the navvies' noses. "For what is kingship — have ye stopped to think, you heathen lot? — I'll tell you. It's crowns and coronets, white wands, black rods, lace, maces, wigs, silk stockings and buckled shoes — more like a state of cannibals. Can ye hear me at the back there?"

"They can hear ye down in bloody Swansea, woman!"

"And what do we get out of it — we, the working classes?" and she climbed up on the bar and waved a fist. "Nothin'! Ye leap up like a bunch of turnips when they play 'God Save the King', but do ye know what you're saving him for?" Her voice rose. "So his son, the Prince Regent, can whore and spend your taxes, make merry with the London gamesters, consort with the Whigs, buy jewels for his harlots and tailoring for his gents. Do you know that he cleared the poor from their hovels so he could ride at ease to Regent's Park? And he's a Hanoverian German, remember, like his father and grandfather — the beggars aren't even English. Do you understand me?"

"Aye, mostly, missus," said somebody.

"And how can ye, you dumb scuts, for you're not even educated — and this is how they want you, drugged by work and ale. You drink yourselves silly in here, then go home and beat the women who bore you . . ."

"Watch it, mind!"

"Threats and fists — the same old thing, isn't it?" And Gran leaped down into the sawdust and shouldered them aside, and they made a path for her, thrusting their brutalized faces into hers; ravaged by labour, bulbous-nosed and thickened, these faces; yet there flickered in their eyes a grudging admiration for the woman who faced them without cowering; and now she shouted from the door:

"'God Save the King', eh? The biggest idiot was John Bull who composed the thing. I'd save him. I'd have him out from under his gilded domes — for he's the real King, the Regent — and kick his backside from here to Aberystwyth!"

"What's wrong wi' that old girl, ye say?"

"She dunna like the King, she do say."

"He ain't done naught to her, 'as he?"

As Gran mentioned once, there's not a lot of hope for us, but I was to hear her words echoed in important places up in London, and I tell you this — young as I was, I learned a lot from Gran. But her mind, as politically colourful as a tropical butterfly, made her an unworthy bedfellow.

This, I believe, was why Uncle William wanted me removed from her unsettling influence.

# 22

MY Grandad passed on to the Upper Palace and we laid him to rest in St Woollos, the mourners carrying him up Stow Hill on a black mahogany bier.

There was a lot of sniffing and wiping and what a lovely old chap he was, but half the mourners owed him money and were pleased to be rid of him. He suffered a minor discomfort of the stomach, and the death certificate said 'intestinal debility', which I put down to a surfeit of sixpences. My mother appeared paralysed with grief, and it was all Uncle William could do to prevent her falling into the open grave. He, Uncle William, was clothed in his usual stoic demeanour and the gaggle of businessmen present were there on his command.

Like the fingers of a giant hand with its heel in the sea, Newport beckoned along her tramways and new canal all the wealth of the South Wales valleys;

opened her warehouse maws to the tumble of black gold flowing down from the mountains. And speculators, dazzled by the glint of gigantic profits, came storming in. At a time when life was rich and turbulent, the immigrants of foreign lands flocked into Newport across her bold, unsculptured hills: sloops and coasters, giant four-riggers crowded into our docks between Castle Green and Moderator Slip; financiers killed each other in the face of Mammon.

Houses of ill-repute sprang up, mushrooming their tawdry doors along the river and cramming Corn Street and Bakehouse Lane with pimps and their painted whores, and if you dropped a penny down Skinner you'd kick it to Cardiff before picking it up. Scandinavian sailors and Japanese ladies were dancing the hornpipe on the cobbles of High Street: Welsh colliers clog-danced to tin whistles, Spanish dancers whirled their fandangos in their black hats and flowing mantillas. The Norman lord who conquered the ancient kingdom of Morgannwg would have had a rag baby if he'd come back now to find a wild, lawless frontier town teeming with hucksters and shysters, ballad singers and harpists, circus acrobats, pick-pockets and nymphs of the pave. Even the sky changed colour, now shot with a roseate hue as the molten bungs of the Top Towns' ironworks splashed the heavens with rainbow colours of red and blue and gold.

People like Uncle William and the Protheros and Phillipses who came after, schemed and wheedled and plotted to lie in the womb of the God of Profit. And the aristocracy like the Morgans and Beauforts, their vaults already lined with gold from careers ranging from land enclosure theft to piracy on the high seas, opened their banks to another flood of wealth.

Give me private enterprise, said Gran, and I'll show you public criminals.

Meanwhile, my politics, influenced by Gran, were becoming a trifle left-of-centre, as she called it, for when I wasn't trying to manoeuvre Becky Crosscut into compromising positions, I was selling pamphlets in Westgate Square announcing 'Down with the King and off with his head'.

"What?" demanded Uncle William, "is this?"

This happened before Grandpa was cold in his grave; our tap-room, decorated with black drapes and lilies of the valley, was even colder.

"Cobbett's *Political Register*, sir," I answered.

He became choleric. "You have the effrontery to bring such radical clap-trap into the house at a time like this?"

"Oh please, Uncle William, don't upset yourself," whispered my mother, while my third father, Bill Roberts, a fishy fisherman, stared at me like a dead cod.

Gran, aloof and removed on the other side of the room, gave me a wink. It was a pose she adopted in the presence of Uncle William; a planned disregard for his ambitions to ascend to the upper class.

"You realize that such trash is against the law of the land?" Uncle screwed the pamphlet in his fist.

"He realizes that you're making a damned fool of yourself," interjected Gran. "When the likes of you don't know the difference between Twopenny Trash and Parliamentary statements, it's time the lad formed his own conclusions."

"Oh Gran," wailed my mother, "leave it to the men!"

"How dare you!" muttered Uncle.

"I dare because this is more my house than yours, William Foster. And if his stepfather won't speak up for him, I shall. If you want the lad out of it, pack him off to nowhere, but don't compound the eviction through Cobbett's political rhetoric, for you're not fit to clean his shoes."

One moment the lady of elocution, next the street harridan with the manners of a shrew, for now she added:

"Get rid of him if you don't want him — so far he's had three blutty fathers, and now he's got you." She wagged a finger in my face. "If ye had any sense you'd give this lot the whistle, which I intend to do now your grandpa's gone," and she strode among them. "For I'll tell you another thing, this town's going to the devil. Its corruption stinks — find me an alderman who hasn't got a hand in the till — you included, ye buggar!" And she braved up to Uncle William and put her chest on his, then turned on my mother, crying, "And for God's sake, Sarah, do stop snivelling!"

A tidy old bitch I had for a gran, bless her.

"Therefore," said Uncle William portentously, as Gran stamped about, "in anticipation of general family agreement, I have taken the liberty of purchasing a single ticket for you on the steamer *Speedwell*, at present lying at Moses's Jetty; she departs for Bristol in the morning. Here, also, is a letter of introduction to my friend in a Cloth Hall in Bristol, for in clothes, I understand, you are vaguely interested. This will enable you to learn the drapery trade, earn a small income, and keep you away from doubtful company, both in this house and out of it."

"Oh, thank you, thank you, William," said my mother, very damp.

Now, I didn't particularly want to work in Bristol; firstly, because I had recently exchanged my waning interest in Becky Crosscut for another who rejoiced in the name of Ophelia Ball, which was not her name, although her father was a pawnbroker in High street. Indeed, I had an appointment to meet her a week next Friday for the last *Calan Mai* I'd enjoy before I left home.

"That's right, lad," said Gran, kissing me. "Take so much, but no more — you go when it suits you," and she patted and smoothed me and went bright in the eyes like grans do when they're cuddling up to grandsons. "A good boy you are for giving up that Becky Crosscut."

She didn't know, of course, that I was about to give Ophelia Ball the sailor's farewell.

I was alone for once, up at St Woollos, for this is where the fair was held. From here you could see the old Usk shining her quicksilver at the sun, and the traders jockeying for wind, their sails ruffling on the clear morning air. And up came Ophelia, all peaches and cream; God, women smell beautiful. She breathed upon me coming up from her curtsey; all flouncies and lace under a white, summer hat, and the air was perfumed.

"Hallo, John Frost," said she, and her dark lashes spread wide upon her cheeks.

"Ay ay."

"What you doing now just?"

"Lokin' for books."

"Books?"

"Study books. The *Tredegar*'s due into Moderator slip at ten this morning. I've been waiting weeks for this one."

"What one?"

"Blackstone's *Commentaries on the Laws of England*."

"Dear me, I thought you was penny dreadfuls, like me."

She looked the part, did Ophelia, but it stopped there.

"Come," I said, and took her hand, and the sun burned down in smells of bombazine, worsted and cotton ruffs, for the townspeople were flocking up Stow Hill now and the drunks were stopping at every other door where the ale casks waited, and there were protests and tempers and "Come on, Alf, for Gawd's sake," and "Hold it, Gert, I'm entitled to a quart," and come nightfall, with the fields full of deads and randies all around St Woollos, the ghosts of other drunks would walk. It is astonishing to me, said Gran, how many births and deaths we get nine months after *Calan Mai*, but it's all part of livin' and dyin'.

"Where we off to now, then?" asked Ophelia.

"I'll tell you where you're off to after dark," said I.

"Oh dear me!" said she, giggling plump, which was encouraging, for it's when they're giggling that you get them, remember.

Mind you, it's a hell of a thing to be nineteen years old and randy. You've got this damned thing and you don't know what to do with it, for it gets in the way of everything you intend. And yet there is an innocence in you when you are walking side by side with a girl, in the sun. Later, I had a basketful of children, by my lover, Mary Morgan, and the manhood wilts, I think, in lover's repetitions. For, just cast your mind back — to those early delights when you wanted to, but didn't dare; when you were afraid to ask her in case she said 'yes'; when your arm touched her arm in a sunlit lane, and the shivers went up and down your spine. When you were dry in the throat, hypnotized.

The curve of a sweetheart's breast is the sugar-sweet essence of lovemaking; a balm to the raging senses of the man; the fragrance is so often sweeter than the flower . . .

So it was with Ophelia Ball that *Calan Mai* — and I tell you this if you're a bosom man, like me, she was the one to be seen with.

Down by the West Gate old Duck-Eye Higgs and his lot from Derbyshire were decorating the well on Bane's; apparently they do these daft old things up in Derby. But pretty it was, mingling their local lore with our Welshness; gorgeous to see the little English children carrying their little buckets of clay and wild flowers . . . building a circle of bright colour around the circle of bricks, in thanks to God for water, on Ascension Day.

Down Bakehouse Lane which some call Market Street, Ianto Lloyd and his relatives from Flint were dancing along in line, stamping their boots on the cobbles and throwing up brightly coloured handkerchiefs, with old Jones Cloth-Hall, the draper, as *Cadi*, to lead the procession. In his element was he, dressed in white and scarlet robes, with one half of his face painted red, the other half black, one half of him a witch, the other a sweep.

"Oh look, oh look!" cried Ophelia, and clapped her little plump hands together.

They thrust their begging bowls for the poor at us; they came with garlanded dancers covered with spring flowers, and a great rattling, rustic frame hung with silver spoons and merry little trinkets gleaming in the sun. Urchins scampered; sunlit faces merry with joy and laughter. Couples, old and young, were arming each other to the screeching of the fiddles, for now the Irish had got among us.

Now arrived Scrumper in the procession, the mock-mayor in his chain of office — gold thread and onions — followed by his attendants carrying buckets of earth and water; a young man one side, a girl on the other, the symbols of Father Rain and Mother Earth, and the garlanding of young lovers in the act of love. Now, back up at St Woollos, Scrumper *Cadi* knelt before the closed door of the church; and to perform the act of divination, thrust a knife through its keyhole, crying:

"*Dyma twca, ble mae'r wain?*" which, being translated, says: "Here is the knife, where is the sheath?"

*Watch nob, come closer!*

From the people a little girl came forth, and she was dressed in white; in white denoting purity, the little virgin knelt before the church door, she being the divine sheath, who from her loins would bring forth her kind; as May Day, the first of the summer, raises up her signal to the planter in the earth.

"Come to the dancing, come to the dancing!" And I took Ophelia's hand, stopping only to kiss her, and we ran down to Corn Street like mad things with her black hair flying out behind her; bumming up her skirts went she, and I've never seen such twinkling pantaloons in my life; she stopped the colliers in their tracks and brought up the fists of sweating wives.

Ay ay, make the most of it, I thought; I'll have those off come sunset.

Jews' harps and squeeze boxes were shrieking, a few old girls out of the Griffen Inn (and this was some place, let me tell you) were dancing knees up, bottles in each hand, and a few old drunks turning up their toes in the gutters. And all up High Street, right up past old Napper's and the

King's Head were suddy bowls of soap and water, with widows and sweethearts from nine to ninety, all prospective brides, down on their knees, doing the washing. Socks and long johns, vests long and short, briefs and belly-binders — with a chemise and petticoat and breast-puddings here and there to get their blood up.

Singing and laughing at the sun, even round the whipping-post they were hanging out their smalls; dainty little silk things, drawers as big as balloons. And the men, give them credit, were filing up to the washerwomen of their choice, tendering their garments. For one sock offered to a washerwoman on Ascension Day was a contract of marriage tendered, and more than one breaker of the code has gone into the town Pill the day after *Calan Mai*. Indeed, such is its dignity that more than one maid-servant, washing in her bowl, the custom of *ffatio*, has seen a carriage and pair stop nearby and a liveried footman descend . . . to put out a hand and raise her . . . and advance her in dignity to the head of the table . . .

Cinderella? Ugly sisters? A prince? They've got nothing on the Welsh when it comes to romance.

You don't believe it? Then listen to this.

"That girl over there, she's giving you the eye," said Ophelia.

I was swinging her around in the dancing, and the band, with its head well down into its collars in case of Irish confetti, was playing *bomb, bomb, bomb!*

"Don't be daft!"

"Look now, stupid — she's at it again!"

The people were crowded about us, shouting, laughing girls and men, with big Irish hustlers doing tarantellas on the cobbles and the drunks from the *Griffin* staggering around without a leg under them. And I saw, in a sudden break of the people, a girl in a white dress. I saw the upward tilt of her chin when she smiled, the sideways glance of her sweet come-hither beneath her shading parasol; and lifting the hem of her dress out of the mud, she sent it again. You'd have to be a monk at Pentecost to miss what she was up to. On the blind side of Ophelia I landed her a wink.

"Look, look!" cried she, outraged. "She winked!"

"I know," I said, "it's damned disgusting."

I did not know that that wink would change the course of my life ...

Now the sun of midday was a molten ball, and near the Westgate Hotel we could hear the bull being made ready for baiting, which never failed to sicken me.

Now we were among the tinkers and pedlars. Gingerbread stalls vied with the Punch and Judy, and *What the Butler is up to* competed for favour with roaring lions. At the bottom of Skinner Street, where later I saw Jack Lovell dying, Baker's Royal Theatre was putting on a drama performance. Here low comedians bawled their tasteless jokes on the cobbles where the horses were slaughtered, and over in Wombwell's Menagerie pigs and boars were about to fight to the death, but all we saw was one doing a pig. And the drinking booths outside the Bull and Six Bells were flooded with clients washing their beards.

Obnoxious stinks arose from the rickety-rackety slums where wizened faces peered down at us from papered windows. Fruit baskets, filled with decaying rubbish, had been churned into a gangrenous mess of mud and filth, and night-soil poured out of the windows. Contentedly chewing the cud, sheep and cattle sought the shade of decaying courts and alleys.

Here lived the poorer than the poor; ragged, emaciated, mainly from the Irish famines, they lay in a thieves' kitchen of gamesters, prostitutes and cutthroats. It was a morass of ruin and misery that should have made our burgesses blush, but only elicited, said Gran, the endless political promises that never came about. The puny child beggars who scampered around the alleys and picked over the garbage for morsels of food, continued to invade Newport right up to the time I myself became its mayor. In daylight, with astonishing courage — for they risked a hanging — they pickpocketed and burgled unwary householders, to retire by night to their verminous straw, six to a bed — there to watch the perambulations of the harlots and their clients until the uncertain dawns. All my efforts to eradicate Friars' Field during my year of office came to nothing;

it needed a decade of dominant effort displayed by a man of genius.

"The bull's a'comin'! The bull's a'comin'!"

Up at Bull's Field they had cut off his ears, filled his nostrils with pepper and put mustard into his eyes. Now, pawing at the ground, head raised and blindly bellowing, he opened his bloodstained mouth and roared defiance at the sun, and you couldn't see Church Road folk for dust. Down the hill he came at a gallop followed by a contingent of youngsters, each one after the longest hair on the bull, for this won a prize, according to custom. And every time he stopped to barge down a stall or toss a huckster he was surrounded by shrieking, clawing lads who beat him with sticks or prodded him with goads.

"The bull's coming!"

"Oh Gawd!" said Ophelia, "I'm off."

He arrived in Westgate Square, this bull, a full ton of beef, with his nostrils breathing fire at anything he called human. And in front of him flew the colliers and ironworkers he had collected on his way down from St Woollos: portly burgesses

329

still in their chains of office dragged at the hands of hysterical wives; skirts up to speed escape came the matron stall-holders; old girls in scraggy black, young ones in their Fair savageries, and youths lagging behind to jeer at the tossing fury of the bull who, maddened by rage and pain, slowed to a halt, confused and perplexed; then, roaring anew, he was off again, and catching a goatherd and two billies coming down High, tossed the first and drove the second full pelt along Skinner.

"Save me!" shrieked Ophelia, and went like the wind with the billy goat after her and me after the billy. We upended two drunken navvies coming off a sloop, pulled down an awning stall where fat women were duffing up butter pats, and the last I saw of Ophelia was bum up over a table as the billy goat hit her: up in the air went she, skirts flying over frilly pantaloons, and I closed my eyes as he got her again.

Very delicate was Ophelia, I recall, rubbing the affected part and saying ruefully, "Oh, me ha'penny, me ha'penny, I reckon he's split me difference," and that's the last time I'm coming to *Calan Mai* with you, John Frost.

Which was an end to the affair, as far as I was concerned, since you can't make love to cripples. For I was a gay young dog in those days. A girl had to be ready for all eventualities.

The last thing I remembered was not the grief of Ophelia Ball, but the eyes of the girl I had seen before, now standing near with other spectators.

With an eyebrow slightly raised she surveyed me with sustained interest, then whirled her parasol, and was off.

But the wink she left behind her was real.

*Diawch!*

After laying fresh sawdust on the tap-room floor, polishing the snug mahogany and hosing out the spittoons, I stripped to the belt, went under the yard pump, then changed into my Sunday best, for the Lord, Grandpa used to say, do put great store on personal appearance, like no tide marks around the neck or garden under the fingernails.

Now, knickerbockered, well braced up under the crotch, my hair smarmed down with Belston's bay rum, a starched white collar under my chops and a tall glazed hat holding down my years, I pushed myself along Thomas Street and over the road to the King's Head for the afternoon mail coach off to Bristol. And the route, please note, is important.

The mail goes only as far as Chepstow Ferry; there, with the coach passengers, it is handed over to the Aust ferrymen which runs a service to Avonmouth; passengers disembark there and catch another stagecoach which transports them, and the mail, to Bristol. Later, at my trial for High Treason, much was made of 'ludicrous' attempts to make contact with Bristol and the North when the mail, in fact, stopped at Chepstow: nothing, in fact, is simpler.

The ferryman takes the mail in his safe keeping.

All last night it had rained and now High Street was a quagmire of mud and blood, especially around the baiting ring-bolt in the middle of the road. Here had been baited the bull, to make him tender.

Never would I use Uncle William's ticket to Bristol on the *Speedwell*, all the time I could travel by coach, for the countryside in Gwent is glorious at this time of year. Newport town was still celebrating *Calan Mai*, of course, and I wanted one last look.

Bum-Baccy-York, the tinker from Bradford, was still in the stocks for Drunk and Incapable, with Cheap-Jack Joey, his mate, the mountain fighter beside him; old Jack Shite, the road-sweeper, was plying his trade of brooms and dungcarts, and plump housewives with deep divides were down on their knees on doorsteps, scrubbing their little circles of purity into a world of stink, and I was proud of my town.

The celebrations were still in full swing, with giant colliers and fat women coming down from the iron towns; rumbustious, with their molars awash at this time of the morning, they came six abreast, taking the place by storm.

Gaitered and waistcoated, with their muttonchops sprouting black and gold, came the top-hatted gentry with the fair sex on their arms: broughams and chaises and traps were clip-clopping up to the King's Head entrance where liveried footmen, ponced and powdered, were bowing and scraping, for there was a dinner or something happening which all the Quality attended.

But this was High Street! Down in Friars' Field, Madog's and Castle Green the crippled children of the Top Towns would wave their amputated stumps in hope of a penny: Moll Walley and Dulcie Promise would be breasting along for clients; Poison Ivy and Iron Man Cass, the pimp, would be on the waterfront pulling in the sailors.

I could hardly reach the coach for the hotel crowds, and here Polliana Poll, our local soprano who used to play hell with Handel, was singing with a glee chorus behind her:

Come *Cadi*, sing to *Calan Mai*!
Men and maids, girls and boys,
Sing summer carols, dance with joy!
Harps and fiddles greet us all
On this the first day of summer!

I was just getting into the coach when along comes Becky Crosscut arm in arm with Ophelia Ball, doing her best to limp along, so I got into a seat by the window, pulled down the blind and sank into my collar. For it's a hell of a thing for a

Romeo when the enemy ranks get together and start checking cross-references, such as What did he tell me last *Calan Mai*, and What did he do to you a week last Sunday?

My life, as I mentioned earlier, has changed a lot: I didn't do the Grand Tour because we hadn't got the money, but I got around Gwent quicker than most bachelors of the day; but that was then, and this is now, and the sweetness of my youth has died in the hands of the world's corruptions.

# 23

## *Memories of Bristol and London*

IT is better, say the Chinese, to light a few candles than to forever curse the darkness, and with this proverb Gran agreed. But the candles being lit by a decadent English Parliament in the face of the hideous pantomime called the Slave Trade were few and far between. And, while my days were spent either in the cutting rooms of Ifan Hughes, Uncle William's prosperous draper friend . . . or entertaining the roisterers and layabouts of his clientele, my nights were spent (as if drawn there by some sadistic magnet) on the slave wharf near Bristol's Broadmead and Wine Street. Here I fruitlessly endeavoured to lighten the misery of our black brothers, known unofficially as the Black Gold . . . a mouthful of food here, the intervention in some specific cruelty there.

Justly, to Denmark, belongs the honour of first abolishing this disgusting trade in humans, upon whose blood Britain built her major cities. So wealthy became Liverpool, for instance, that she actually voted £10,000 to oppose the Abolitionists. Only in 1807, fifteen years after Denmark's action, did England abolish the trade on paper, and it was twenty-six years after that before the Emancipation Bill was fought and won by a dying Wilberforce; which included a sum of twenty million pounds (£37 per slave) to compensate the criminal slave owners, many sitting in the Commons and the Lords. Nevertheless, slavery continues in the British Empire during Victoria's reign, and interest in suppressing it appears negligible. Even as I write this, the filthy trade is active: for instance, in Hong Kong and Malaya, child slavery under the *Mui Tsai* system still flourishes under our Union Jack, and this excludes the three hundred thousand British children of near slavery, who languish in sweat shops and factories at home. Victoriana has much to answer for.

I did not become a revolutionary because of my time in Bristol, for which I garnered a sharp and lasting hatred, but my experiences in the slave market there sharpened my focus on Man's inhumanity to his fellows.

By a strange coincidence, Richard Carling met the engaging and beautiful Madame Le Roy in this same city some time later, he bound, without then knowing it, to another form of slavery in Port Arthur. But, unlike Richard, having in no way drunk Bristol's pleasures of wild women, I put the place behind me and took the stagecoach to London, arriving at the Bear and Lion hotel in Charing Cross with a soul as white as a St Peter washday.

With the domes and spires of London town sliding down the temples of the sun, I left the inn and entered the crowds of Charing Cross; immediately to be surrounded by throngs of milling, frantic beggars. With their Devil-dust clothes in rags about their half-naked bodies, they thrust their clawing hands at me with a ferocity born of long starvation — worse than anything in Newport.

Among these, unseeing and uncaring, strolled the London dandies with a nonchalance born of privilege. Drunks, tipplers, bawdies and prostitutes vied with each other for a claim on the stranger, and in the end I was taken to thrusting them off with the same ribald threats I heard from the dandies.

Harlots with powdered wigs and bulging bosoms touted their wares at tavern doors where verminous hags suckled skeletal babies; while from within blasted and thumped the merrymaking of the town; a Hogarthian mural of lechery and larkery. And through all this passed the city tradesmen, frock-coated and top-hatted among the hurrying artisans in their standard gray and black fustian jackets and trousers; these, naturally, took my eye.

The sun burned down in golden light, flashing on the high-stepping charioteers — the traps and broughams, wherein sat gentlemen elegantly dressed for the evening in broadcloth of rich design, and ladies in silk gowns and lace bowed or delicately fluttered hands, the epitome of everything Gainsborough. All was perfume, elegance, poverty and utter confusion . . . on the streets; and above the streets where wan faces peered down, just as in Newport, an imprisoned population of the old and infirm, the starving and the diseased, gave themselves up to defeat and putrescence.

"John Frost!" cried a voice, "All is not lost! John Frost, John Frost!"

On the edge of the Strand the crowd was thinner, but bystanders were gathering at a central point, and I saw, through gaps in their ranks, a man standing in a pillory: with his hands and head trapped in the board, he was wagging his fingers and acknowledging a dozen shouted greetings.

"Ho, John Frost! We're here, too, all isn't lost!" And I saw, as I pushed closer, that women were laying flowers at the prisoner's feet and putting posies into his hands. And then the crowd took up a new chant, repeating my name.

It was scarcely believable, and I asked who he was of a passing man.

"Ach, he's John Frost, so he is! Are ye a political chap?" And he peered. I said I wasn't. Bog Irish, this one.

"Ah well, me son," replied he, and did a little hopscotch on the road and his face was a bunch of laughs, "Tho' I'm Irish me'self, I've a soft spot for this one, for all he's English."

"Why is he pilloried?"

"For speakin' his mind to the bloody

English King, for that's a useless gunk if ever there was one. And it needs a comedian like Frost to spill his guts to the people. Are ye Irish yourself?"

"Welsh."

"Ah, midear, we can't have everything — so I'm up to pay me respects to the lovely fella. Are ye comin'?"

I said I was, and followed my companion to the foot of the pillory when the crowd rushed from behind and young men ran up with saws and axes.

The sun was down, I remember; the night was curling its shadows into premature darkness. The hatchets and axes rose and fell, and they chopped John Frost free. With the people waving and cheering, they lifted him shoulder high and carried him down to Newgate.

"Where to?" I cried above the hubbub.

"To prison," said my friend. "He's in and out o' the place like a bloody jack rabbit, and he's got six months for sedition. What are ye doin' tonight?"

I hesitated, and the Irishman cried:

"For if you're a stranger, mun, I'll show you around. Mind, I'm a member o' the vulgar-tongued classes, not a gent like you, but I'll show ye where you can scratch your arse wi' a few midnight goings on — do you get me? Bad ale and lovely women — are ye with me?"

He peered at me in the dusky light, the crowd had gone, and then said, "Lest you're one o' the Holy Ghost people, I'll show you a street that'll raise your pips, son — t'is a street o' tits, and every one a nutcracker."

I didn't reply, so he peered again. "What's your name?"

I got going.

"In the name o' the Pope, what's wrong, me darlin'?"

But I was gone.

Faintly on the wind I heard the sound of people in chorus, and they sang:

Thelwall and Gaol Jones leave the Strand
To organize revolt on sea and land.
John Frost, John Frost, *John Frost!*

It was a strange foreboding that struck me. As if Fate itself had decreed a path to a pillory, that one day I would take.

Unknown to me at the time, the first step along that path was to Number 16

Charing Cross Road, the home of the London tailor, Francis Place, to whom my Bristol draper, Ifan Hughes, had given me a letter of introduction.

It was a night for funeral clothes when I stopped in the shadows of the city's bay windows and knocked at Number 16. Almost immediately it was opened by a little gnome of a man in a top hat who peered at me with smoky eyes.

"Yes?" One word told me that he was educated.

I said, "Sir, I have a letter of introduction to Mr Place. Is this the right address?"

"It's a Parliamentary fact, sir," came the answer, and he raised himself to his full height of five feet, adding, "You have come through the market?"

"Beg pardon?"

He groaned. "A perfectly simple question, young man — did you come through the market?"

"Why, yes."

"That being so, you'll have seen the price of things — the butter is rancid, as you probably know."

"I . . ."

"Unless, of course, you arrive early to

343

bribe the cow. Artificial beans are added to the originals to add weight, chicory is mixed with ground coffee, tea diluted with sloe, cocoa adulterated with fine earth, and tea leaves dyed and roasted and palmed off as new. Port wine, which the poor consume, is manufactured with sugar and dye, flannel stretched, chalk mixed with flour. It is all, I assure you, an unmitigated fraud — I'd go further, sir — a venal rascality."

He was unhinged, of course, but I thought him delightful, so I entered his world, saying, "And the rich?"

"The rich are less deceived, of course, since they purchase from approved dealers who would be ruined by a charge of fraudulent practice — certainly, I assure you, in my constituency . . . "

"Constituency?" I was still on the doorstep.

The little man removed his hat and bowed low. "Mr Horne Tooke, sir, Member of Parliament — a free-thinker, graduate from Cambridge, lately a vicar who contended, and still does, that Jesus was the first socialist. You've heard of me?"

"Most certainly." I took off my hat.

"What name shall I say, sir?"

I hesitated.

"Come, come, boy — surely you have a name!"

"John Frost."

He peered up at me in the light of the street lanterns. "God forbid, here comes another one. Don't trifle with me, John Frost is in prison . . . " and then his eyes opened wide, and he clutched me, crying, "Why, of course, *of course!* The Bristol indenture lad," and he patted his head. "Intellectually failing, you know. Welcome, welcome, but come tomorrow when Mr Place will appraise you upon the ignoble influences of Church and State, given in his library to newspaper men, revolutionaries, prospective drapers and other misplaced dissidents. Half-past seven, sir?"

I bowed to him, but he raised me with a cry:

"No, I forget again, sir — not Church and State — he is to denounce the criminal aristocracy."

At dusk next day, having been ushered into the basement library of Number 16 Charing Cross Road, I sat among jowled and collared gentlemen of large stomachs and larger intellects; Mr Horne Tooke, M.P. (who gave not the slightest intimation that he had seen me before) appeared to be Master of Ceremonies, because before Mr Francis Place arrived to begin his quite astonishing oratory, Mr Tooke announced a final list of important guests.

"Mr John Gale Jones!"

A round of applause as Jones entered; tall, slim, vital; his dark eyes swept the room; he who was a member of the London Corresponding Society and a constant visitor to the French Assembly.

"Mr John Thelwall!"

Men stood up when Thelwall came; the fierce revolutionary whom men called 'Citizen Thelwall'; he who likened a crowned despot to 'a bantam cock on a dunghill' — nobody was safe from his oratorical barbs; a man in touch with secret Jacobin societies and on the top of the list of all Government spies. He took his seat beside me with calm assurance; small, compactly muscled, his dominance slowly crept out and contained me. Now entered the most important guest.

"Mr William Cobbett!"

The son of a peasant, this one; ardent reformer and vicious critic of the Government, he wrote from impulse, striking about him with savage wit and irony; lately the hero of his *Political Register* of which my Uncle William so vigorously disapproved.

I had come to this address with a letter of introduction to serve an apprenticeship in tailoring; by some irony of fate I had landed within a nest of political vipers.

"Gentlemen, our guest speaker tonight, Mr Francis Place!"

This, my prospective employer, was young — a little more than thirty years; with his bulging forehead and calm demeanour, he looked the intellectual he was — about to abandon progressive politics, men said, to make a fortune in the drapery trade; presumably this was why I had been sent to him. But, from the moment he opened his mouth I knew him for an astonishing orator:

"Gentlemen," he began, "may I first greet the distinguished assembly, worthy rather of a baronial hall than a humble basement in Charing Cross. Such guests!

347

Thelwall and the indefatigable Cobbett, whom the Parliamentary gods preserve," and he raised his hand. "I see our ancient benefactor of the French Assembly, Major Cartwright, at the back — agitation and reform is really to the front this year. To John Gale Jones, our perennial gaolbird, we give our respects, likewise to the initimable John Frost who went to Newgate yesterday for sedition and took his pillory with him." His voice lowered. "But at least we have his namesake present by a strange coincidence — John Frost, sent for indenture to me by Ifan Hughes, my business partner in Bristol," and he bowed to me. "Later, sir, we will talk more officially." And his dark eyes, crowned in their broad forehead with a flaring mass of bright hair, moved over me.

This man was a king-maker; once a maker of leather breeches, the hardships of that trade had calloused his hands and forced him into radical politics. Now compared to the leading political thinkers of the day, he later secured Sir Francis Burdett to a Parliamentary seat, and ranged his theories with men like Jeremy Bentham and James Mill. Later still he was the fulcrum of the Duke of Wellington's failure to form a government, and almost single-handed opposed and vanquished the Workers' anti-Combination Acts. Now he cried:

"No introduction is necessary when the subject, gentlemen, is the aristocracy, for, like all delusions of witchcraft and demonology, their fictions become most preposterous when they claim divine right. But claim this they do — often — and it is far too commonplace a drollery even for mirth.

"There was a time, as you know, when Lords were petty kings with their own dungeon-castles, there to torture, imprison, even execute their fellow-creatures with impunity. And the lords then deputed their power down to the squires, who sought fit to employ such monstrous usages as *borough-English* and *child-wit*, which, if you don't know, claimed the trifling perquisite of spending the first night with the brides of the tenants of his estate, and the latter claiming a tax on women in his employ who gave birth without his permission. Thankfully, we've killed off such offences against our kind, but their existence is sufficient to make the name of aristocracy, in any age, an insult to human dignity."

Place took a breath. "Under the tyranny of the Stuarts, the Commons happily brought one monarch to the block and abolished, thank God, the House of Peers, the home of sleepy foot-proppers and lay-me-downs. But the return of the second Charles and his Parliamentary corruption annihilated the powers of the Commons and gave back to the Aristocracy its irresponsible ascendancy!

"What right, I ask you, has a single generation of men to gain such aggran-disement, when their estates have been in the first place stolen from the people and then handed down by robbers who died when William Rufus was a boy?

"It is an indefensible grievance that certain families of the Realm enjoy masses of property obtained by theft; soil which is the common inheritance of the entire community. And why do I make these chinless blue-bloods the target of my animosity? I shall tell you, gentlemen! It is because this same aristocracy is about to obtain a Commons Bill which will allow them greater theft of our inheritance by yet a further Bill sanctioning land enclosures. If the cottager builds a shelter and that shelter contains a roof constructed from the land – slate or tile – then under this new, obnoxious law such shelter will become the property of he who encloses the common land.

"Listen, these aristocratical stupidities cannot continue. A farmer can be transported for a minor debt, but the peer can thieve on the highway with impunity. The peer, unlike the commoner, is not required to give evidence upon oath, but only upon his honour! If a man scandalizes a peer, it is not judged to be common scandal, but *scandalum magnatum*, an horrific and vile offence. If a peer gets up a bubble company and dupes investors, you cannot imprison him or make him bankrupt, and if, in fury and frustration, you knock him on the nose, this carries a frightening punishment.

"And I could go on and on, but will not, except to warn you of the dangers of poaching. For the Lords have passed laws granting licence to spring-guns and man-traps, which will take your legs, and a hare down your breeches will send you to Van Dieman's Land: they may carry arms, but God help the pastry-cook who possesses a pea-shooter, for he will go to the House of Correction . . ."

After the meeting had dispersed I stood with my letter of introduction clasped in my hand, and Mr Place disengaged himself from questioners and approached me.

"I commend your patience, Mr Frost," and he bowed. "You come for indenture and land yourself in coffee-house politics!"

"I was enthralled; I tend to forget what I'm here for, Mr Place."

"To be advanced in the profession of draper. Since I need the money for a rising family, I'm about to begin the trade in earnest."

I gave him a smile. "And abandon politics?"

He nodded. "Drapery in the window, sir, reform in the basement."

"All moderacy?" And his dark eyes shone. He replied:

"Preferably, where it works."

"When it works, Mr Place, for that is rare."

"*Aha!*" He slapped his thigh. "We have

a radical, eh? Beware, or Thelwall will hear of it and chastize you!" He peered at me with renewed interest. "All you young pups are the same, but I applaud you." He made a face. "Your grounds for physical force?"

"It is the only language they understand."

"And the Parliamentary process? What of democracy?"

"It cannot exist all the time they hold the guns."

"And when we hold the guns?"

"Then will come change."

It was the only occasion when I was given the opportunity to talk with the great; all too soon broken up by Cobbett's waggish banter and Place's cold irony. But Thelwall, I noticed, was watching me carefully from the other side of the room.

For over two years I worked in the Place drapery establishment; by day, receiving distinguished clients and cutting them to measure: these were mainly the fops of the turf and Regent Street, who confined their days' activities to the racecourses and their nights to revelry and women of the taverners' beds. Place, it appeared, had no qualms about being in service to such clientele: and so, I was sewing pearl-buttoned waistcoats, and taking notes of Thelwall's fiery speeches, most of which came from Cartwright and the French Assembly.

This man, not Francis Place, fascinated me. His revolutionary fire scorched the coffee-house debates; for while Place delivered homilies about progressive achievements within the law, Thelwall was outright in his condemnation of the iniquitous liaison between Church and State.

And while Place held court in Charing Cross Road, John Thelwall tub-thumped his furious eloquence in the seamy alleys of Billingsgate. Unknown to my friend and mentor, I would slip out into the dark alleys and head like a fugitive for Sarah's Court, there to knock three times upon a stable door and be granted entry by one who rejoiced in the name of Sarah Bumkin, a ragged shrew of a woman with hands like claws. With a ha'penny in Sarah's grubby palm, one could sit at the back and listen to the maestro at his best; be instructed in every aspect of Tory theft and Whig corruption, the appalling profligacy of George III and his useless son, the Prince Regent.

These were the winter nights when I divested myself of the parochial tricks of the draper and opened my callow mind to the furious doctrines of men and fire — not mere radicals, but self-educated scholars who had studied the tenets of the French Revolution: John Gale Jones, for instance, now out of prison for sedition (his friends fed his family); a man chosen by the London Corresponding Society to tour the provinces and explain the repressive acts of 1795; such men, and all were wonderful orators, opened up new vistas of my mind, pushed at doors I had never opened, and Thelwall was at it now, crying:

"Corrupt offices and corrupt gifts — of titles, contracts and money — this king has even built up a party known as 'The King's Friends'. And while insanity may abound within the royal head, there exists, also, the cunning of the lunatic . . . a cunning, my friends, that would evince the admiration of a Temple lawyer, for it is not lacking when it comes to his Civil List — here it is, a litany of silent theft and shameless extravagance!" He

355

paused for breath. "It is a tale of noble vultures, all of whom we will expose to the public gaze for what they are — tricksters, footpads and thieves in the royal kitchens and bedchambers. What say you, Newport lad?"

What say I?

This I know. It was upon the rock of such persuasion that I built the foundation of my radical beliefs; beliefs which, most strangely, I had heard in earlier days at my grandmother's knee.

It was owing to the constant entreaties of my mother for me to return home that took me back to Newport, and, in retrospect, to my fate.

There were, however, certain consolations; one of these was Mary Morgan, the beauty who winked at me during Stow Fair, but she couldn't wait for me and had married, and her name now was Mary Foster Geach.

Meanwhile, the dream of fair women and London's politics were over.

# 24

"WE meet again," I said to her. How to tell of her with only words available?

"Have we met before?" she asked, askance.

"Mary Foster Geach," I answered, "you know very well we have!"

Her two children were with her, a girl and a boy. Momentarily I joined them in the walk through the woods, our feet crunching on the refuse of a thousand autumns. Vaguely, I recalled being told by somebody that, while I was away in London, she had married, and I mentioned this.

"Soon after William was born, my husband died," said she.

"I heard that, too, and I'm sorry."

The boy, seeking my hand and finding it, stared up at me with sober serious eyes; bright blue those eyes . . . eyes I

357

was to remember on the other side of the world . . . William Foster Geach, later my solicitor . . .

"Uncle William took us in for a while," Mary explained. "In his last term of office as mayor, we lived with him after my husband's death, in the Mayor's House. But now we three have lodgings in Bettws parish . . . this is why we're walking here today."

I said, bravely, "Uncle William gets about. I didn't realize he was your relative, he's also supposed to be mine."

She smiled, and the sun shone; her teeth were even and white against the curved redness of her lips. "Uncle William seems to have a finger in everybody's pie. But, he's been good to me since my man passed on."

She looked at me through half-closed eyes; the children quietly pestered her skirt for attention, but she gently thrust them away, saying, "And you, John Frost? Still single? I'd have thought you'd be well cut and carried by now — what was her name — Ophelia?" She put the tip of her tongue between her teeth, and her eyes were mischievous. "Or was it Becky

Somebody or Other?"

"Errant wanderings! I've been to London and met real people since then."

"Are there not real people in Newport?"

"I am beginning to think there are."

The children, tired of isolation, had wandered away hand in hand. A small embarrassment came between us; the language mainly of eyes that say everything.

She was beautiful, I thought: her dress, full to the ankles, and bustled, was of quality, green in colour; hand-worked lace — and I knew this when I saw it — was at her wrists and throat; she looked part of the summer, steeped in sun; her broad-rimmed shade-hat was white, and lying upon her shoulders. She was a girl when I'd left Newport over eight years ago; now she was a woman, and the power of her stole out into the sunlight, and held me. She said, huskily:

"They . . . they tell me you've taken a tailor's shop in High Street . . . "

"Taken? I've been there five years — old Edwin Thomas's premises."

"And . . . and that you are doing very well."

359

"Where does that come from — Uncle William?"

We walked on side by side. "You don't like him, do you?"

"No, and the dislike is mutual."

Young William returned alone, immediately seeking my hand. Mary said, "He has no inhibitions with you; I've never seen him show interest in any other man. Even my own husband, for the short time . . ."

The boy's eyes were constantly upon my face.

"How old is he?"

"He's three, Mary's a year older."

Those riveting, bright blue eyes . . . Lifting the boy, I held him against me and his warmth merged with mine.

I did not know, at that first meeting, that the destiny of William Foster Geach, aged three, was irrevocably linked with mine.

The astonishing coincidence was that Mary Geach, like me, looked upon the recent thrice-times mayor of Newport, William Foster, as 'uncle'.

On the face of it, it appeared that this one was an uncle to everybody.

And so we had met again, Mary Geach and I.

In those days, with the influence of Grandpa still upon me, I used to worship at the Mill Street Congregational Church, and apart from occasional soirees, and earlier, into the company of people like Becky Crosscut, it could have been said that I'd seen the light. Indeed, I can lay claim to being one of the founder members of Hope Chapel, which although not yet officially registered, was used by Mary and the children for all things religious.

It was at Bettws Parish Church that she and I were married late October in the year 1812: I was twenty-eight, Mary a few years younger — a marriage, I must add, which was severely frowned upon by our 'uncle' William Foster, and was in no way applauded by my mother who wanted me back in the Royal Oak to take charge. It was not an unreasonable request, for William Roberts, her third husband, appeared to be upon his last legs. William Foster, meanwhile, once a fervent visitor to the tavern, had now cooled off in the company of a lady called Margaret (who was known in the Royal Oak as a vixen) to whom, apparently, he was going to give his hand.

But, more importantly, my beloved Gran had died, and I felt her loss with sickening emptiness. Every portal, every corner of the Royal Oak abounded with her effervescent personality. Sitting in front of the dressing-table mirror in her bedroom, I could hear her voice. And every Sunday morning I would make a pilgrimage up to St Woollos where she lay with Grandpa, and put a flower upon the mound that covered her.

She, at least, would have approved my radicalism and romantic sensibilities, which translated themselves into amazing nuptial benefits. For eight children were born to me in the course of fourteen years — John, Elizabeth, Sarah, Catherine, Ellen, Henry Hunt, James (whom we lost within six months) and Anne, who was born in July 1826. And so, no less than eleven of us shared the small premises above my tailor's shop in High Street, Newport, which was known as one belonging to a master draper comparable with the best to be found in London.

When William Foster died, he continued

to influence the Frosts as much from the grave as he had from the mayor's parlour. Possessed of much property when a merchant and builder, he owned a group of houses in Newport known as Foster's Court and considerably more near Cardiff. He showed his dislike of Mary's second husband — always referring to me as 'that bumptious young radical' — by leaving all his possessions to his second wife, Margaret.

Thus Mary's marriage to me was the source of the greatest financial injury to both her and my two young stepchildren. Because this injustice rankled within me, it needs this account, for out of the ensuing family quarrels with Margaret, to whom all had been given for no good reason, there was sown within me seeds of discord that coloured my actions; a rancour which forged a train of events that landed me in Van Dieman's Land.

At that time I wouldn't have conceived anything to be more ridiculous.

Newport, meanwhile, was becoming the Mecca of enterprise. Many prophesied that this was going to be the second

Birmingham; a new Black Country whose arms were open to the flood of output rushing down the valleys from Blaenafon to Sirhowy and Pontypool to Risca.

As the immigrants of farmland evictions and the starving of Ireland poured into the Top Towns, so they were cornered by prospectors who offered them slave wages. Irish, in terror of the new Poor Laws, were prepared to work until they dropped, undercutting the wages of the itinerant Welsh.

New lines of communication sprang up. With the canal crowded with exports from Newport to Blaenafon, a branch tramroad was constructed to connect us to the vast Sirhowy and Tredegar Works; this passed through the grounds of Sir Charles Morgan's Tredegar Park, a Golden Mile which added to the piracy of his ancestors in excessive tolls.

Added to Parliamentary approval to exempt Newport of duties levied on coal and culm was the extension of the Monmouthshire Canal over a mile beyond the town: this achievement, serving the second highest tidal waters in Europe and excellent port facilities, forged the foundation of Newport's prosperity. Speculators poured in, hammering the place for profit.

New names arose in the financial markets; men like Thomas Prothero, the grandson of Edward Prothero, a humble currier of Usk.

Thomas Prothero, of illegitimate birth, arrived in Newport a few years before my return there from London, and immediately set himself up as an attorney. Admitted as a burgess in 1807, he was appointed to the post of Town Clerk. This, the man who became my adversary, arrived with scarcely a shirt to his back: in less than two decades he boasted a fortune of over £20,000.

Others were not slow to realize Newport's potential. Land grabbers like the Duke of Beaufort, already fabulously rich through the eviction of their tenants, bought up prime land in the paths of canal and tramroad: Sir Charles Morgan, who owned large slices of Newport by ancestry (and bank bullion through ancestral piracy) leased to relatives over 200 acres, upon which they proceeded to build Tredegar Warehouse and Quay; an act unsuccessfully opposed by the freemen of the town. Thus, great and small were the practised corruptions, when fortunes could be made upon the embryonic body of the town. The Welsh Industrial Revolution was now in full spate.

Despite attacks upon his professional conduct by brother attorneys, Thomas Prothero, with the reins of Newport in his hands, continued his path of sharp practice and corruption. He intimidated witnesses, split fees with auctioneers, charged extortionately for loans, and a multiplicity of briefs where one sufficed; overcharged for legal work in procuring Parliamentary Acts for town improvement; had financial interests in every available commercial undertaking from the docks to canal construction, coal speculation and turnpikes.

It is upon record that Prothero and another speculator, Tom Powell, induced colliery owners' to sell them coal by contract at eight shillings a ton, then raised the price to eleven shillings . . . and obstructed port facilities for other owners who refused to comply.

These were but a few of the corrupters

366

to whom I addressed myself, at personal cost . . .

Meanwhile, up in the Top Towns, in places like Merthyr, Dowlais, Aberdare and Blaenafon, another form of commercial piracy was abroad.

Here the Crawshays, Guests, Homfrays and Harfords, hard on the heels of Anthony Bacon ('Bacon the Pig') were vying with the Baileys of Nantyglo as leaders in a new genre of exploitation. The earth was tunnelled and pinnacled in a vast explosive upheaval of Wales's green and pleasant land. Incoming immigrants were channelled into back-to-back housing, ten to a room and four to a bed on mattresses that never grew cold. Top Towns' riots against working conditions and hunger grew with increasing ferocity in the midst of military oppression: outrage followed outrage on the body of mankind. Up in the mountain towns and down in the valleys of the Rhondda the mailed fist of profit, backed by force, began to cripple the new generations where the expectation of life went down as new millionaires were born. For the iron and coal towns were becoming inhabited by a new breed: the ragged, hungry refuse of pit and furnace when the fly of a winch or the drop of a cage entered new names on death statistics.

Squeezed by the vicious Poor Laws, which promised servitude in Houses of Industry, whole families, blacklisted by their employers for minor offences, were surviving in caves, quarries and culverts. Parents were hammering at the doors of the bridewells, offering themselves to the treadmill, to save their destitute children. And all the time the Irish, scarecrows of the starve, came funnelling down the roads from the sea-ports. While ironmasters like the Crawshays dined off gold plate in a putrescent sea of their making, the poor plundered the poor and the starving stole from the hungry.

And as the graph of human misery reached new heights in mutilation and death from a dozen endemic diseases, so the graph of Newport's profits rocketed, and the unpopularity of men like Prothero soared.

Meanwhile, having myself become a burgess of the town, I considered it in the public interest to curb the excesses of the 'Get-Rich-Quick'.

"You'll regret it," said Mary.

I lowered my newspaper at the dawn breakfast table; God knows why I read the damned things for they never had anything good to say about me: their radicalism being confined to landowners' complaints about the disagreeable nature of their tenants.

"You mean I shouldn't undertake it?"

"I mean that to publicly attack men like Prothero is to court a libel action, and that's something we can't afford."

The difficulty was that you couldn't ignore her opinion. Like most women of the period, she babied, breast-fed and napkinned from morning until night; the house was full of protesting infants competing for all her favours and none of mine.

Now as an active leader of the burgesses I was much in service to the community. Enjoying honorary appointments on committees ranging from public health to street cleaning, turnpikes and the docks, I found little time for domestic afflictions; all these Mary bore without protest, even though she had not yet fully recovered from her confinement with Ellen, our fourth daughter, born in the autumn of 1820. She was a sickly baby, indicative of James, who died. Now there was no sound save the crying of the street vendors down High Street and the occasional rumble of iron-shod wheels. It was firelight; little flames flickered upon Mary's face, nunlike in its quiet repose. She said:

"Sometimes I think you're getting too involved, John." She wiped stray hairs from her forehead and shifted the baby on to the other breast; nothing in the realm of true nobility, I believe, can compare with that of a dutiful mother; the palatial trappings of pageantry make no comparison with the beauty of a woman suckling her child. Mary lifted her face and I saw her in profile; Welsh dark and beautiful still; she said:

"True, William and Mary have now begun their own lives, but we have five young children and this one, my darling Ellen, is ill. You are a good father, John, and I know your importance to the community. But, sometimes I dream . . . " She lowered her face.

"Of what?"

"That you are but one against hundreds, and you cannot cry for the world."

I said, "People are poor, Mary. All over the valleys. You don't even have to go beyond Newport to see the distress."

"People will always be poor. Long after you and I are gone, this place will be crowded with beggars."

"Of what else do you dream?"

"That men like Prothero and the Morgans are too strong for you. This letter you propose to write to Prothero, for instance, could land you in serious litigation."

I got up and wandered the room. "If so, it's the first time that one citizen complaining privately of the behaviour of another, has landed in the witness box," but she ignored this, saying:

"You tell me that you intend to accuse him of using his position as agent to Sir Charles Morgan to browbeat his tenants; of over-charging for legal services, and corruption over the Corporation Wharf. But Morgan's in this up to the hilt, too, attack Prothero and you attack Sir Charles."

She was simple-minded, this one, but in no wise a simpleton; if a man finds the issue complicated, he does well to put it to an intelligent woman. I said:

"The letter will be a private one, I tell you."

"Then keep it so," said Mary. "You contested Prothero over the issue of Uncle William's will and it cost us money. Your business is flourishing, the voters think well of you; beware of the words you commit to paper."

I momentarily knelt and took her into my arms; Ellen snuffled in sleep; the firelight flickered upon her tiny, snubbed features. Bending, I kissed Mary's breast, and as if affronted, she took a breath and tucked it out of sight.

"You are still mine, you know," I said.

She kissed my face. "You warn Old Sam to watch out too. Printers are the first in trouble, and I don't trust him."

I ignored this. "Truly, of what do you dream?"

Her shining eyes reflected the red light. "That one day they will take you away from me."

"Prothero and that lot?" I rose. "They'll

have to get up in the morning!"

But she was not placated; reaching out, she drew me down to her.

Until that moment I had not realized the measure of her love for me.

# 25

A WORD about Sam Etheridge, the one Mary mentioned, before I commend his foreman, John Partridge, who took over his printing premises in High Street.

Old Sam, seven years my senior, was to me a source of condolence when it came to radical politics; nobody in Newport shared my views with such fiery assertion. Sam's god was, like mine, the great William Cobbett; soon the author of *Rural Rides*, also the producer of the enormously successful *Political Register*. Sheaves of the great one's *Twopenny Trash* were eventually sold over Sam's counter.

On the proverbial shoestring, and with enormous gusto, Sam looked corrupt officialdom straight in the eye; be-whiskered and prematurely bent by endless quarrels with relatives and frequent excursions into the Poor House, this giant of intellect spent his life twisting the tails of local lions.

Like me, his radicalism had sprung from Cobbett's *Political Grammar*, which heightened his admiration of the French Assembly, and we soon began to work as a team. While Sam beat the Beaufort family about the head by exposing the enormous incomes it received from public funds, I concentrated upon the family of Tredegar.

Was it in the public interest, I asked in my pamphlets, that Lord Rodney, the son-in-law of Sir Charles Morgan, should receive three thousand pounds a year for merely signing his name to a receipt: while for signing his latest sinecure, Colonel Lascelles, as receiver-general of the taxes of Monmouthshire, also pocketed God knows what?

"That sally went down well," commented Sam, "but I suggest you might be over the top on this one," and he rolled a proof copy off his press, and read:

"May I suggest that these gentlemen of sinecures and cunning intrigue should give some thought to the inevitable consequences, because there is a new dawn beaming over the world, a new light of understanding by the great mass of the people. Revolution is in the air, heads are beginning to roll. So I take this opportunity to remind our much respected family of Tredegar, and Sir Charles as head of that dynasty in particular, that gentlemen similarly placed in France — some with even larger estates than that of Tredegar — have been delighted, after the Revolution, to accept sinecures as dancing masters, tavern fiddlers and even cordwainers, thus gaining the privilege of working for the first time in their lives."

"Excellent. Publish it," I said.

"It will cause a stir."

"Isn't it supposed to?" I added, "To drive home the message that it might be the first time a Morgan could 'walk the plank' — men better than he having done so in the cause of commercial piracy."

Old Sam said, "You will labour beneath a ton of lawyers and their papers."

"Not if it is the truth."

"Beware truth, John Frost. There is a new dictum abroad which affects printers and their pamphleteers — 'The greater the truth the bigger the libel'."

I said, "I don't believe it!"

"You might, one day. Our masters and their lawyers have invented the sin of truth. Indeed, I believe it is now case law, but I forget the circumstances."

"How does Cobbett get away with it?"

Sam examined his pipe. "I suggest that he has access to hornier secrets than us. That his inside information is greater than that which he actually publishes: anyway, this possibility, even, keeps the scandalized awake at night."

"And we have little or nothing, other than the facts we publish?"

"On the contrary, we have much. For instance, in this letter I have just printed for sending to Prothero. The one fact you should have omitted, you have put in — his fornication in St Woollos church."

The door clanged and a customer entered; a funeral card for a death in Caerleon, so the discussion halted; Sam dealt with it, returned, and said:

"Understand me, I am behind you in everything. I hate corrupt people as you do, and enjoy their destruction. But there are times when one pulls in the horns."

I nodded, smiling. "That's what Mary said recently."

"A woman's intuition?"

"Ah no, Sam. Mary is too intelligent for that. But she's frightened of Prothero; his strength she says, lies in Tredegar. But surely one can safely lampoon him in the churchyard — the biggest laugh of all would come from Sir Charles."

"Mary said all that?"

"Not precisely."

Sam lit his pipe. "Be warned . . . no better, let me read that part of your *Letter to Thomas Prothero* which I think his lawyers might find offensive," and he tore off a part of the proof, and read:

" . . . In the business of the so-called attempt of my client to effect a fraudulent bankruptcy, I accuse you, Thomas Prothero, in your capacity as undersheriff, of packing the jury at Usk, thus causing injustice to an innocent man.

"Trial by jury, sir, is the boast of Britain; a wretch who tampers with it is unfit to live. Indeed, a highwayman or pickpocket compared with him is an innocent character. More, I have proof that you, Thomas Prothero, have suborned a witness at that trial to perjury, and nor have I finished with you over the claims of the burgesses in the outstanding matter of the Corporation Wharf.

"Let those who practise religion by going twice to Church on Sunday give consideration to the sin of hypocrisy, lest they be seen on less auspicious occasions in compromising positions in that same churchyard — a subject, sir, which is as notorious as the sun at noon — and on no less an appropriate date as All Fools Day itself!

"I suggest you have a care, review the sins and omissions of your past life and devote the evening of your days to the business of making amends."

Sam screwed up the proof and dropped it at my feet. I asked:

"Well, what's wrong with it?"

"Everything, because it is true."

I said, turning away, "It's time it was told. Publish it and to hell with Prothero and all like him; by God, we'll cleanse this town of scum. Here is the money for it — four thousand copies — and keep it set up, for we're going to need more."

"Your wife is right, it's a mistake; stuff like this will land you in court."

"Then I'll lean on the justice of my country."

"My God, man, how naive can you be? We've got no justice!" He sighed. "Oh dear, what happens next?"

"The Town Hall meeting tonight."

"The Peterloo Massacre thing, you mean? I thought you weren't going?"

"Changed my mind, for it's important. It's being white-washed and I want the facts out in the open."

He said, facetiously, "There'll be an awful lot of die-hard Tories, there — prepare yourself for heavy heckling."

"I'll thrive on it. Are you coming?"

"It's a lot safer here, but I'll consider it," said Sam.

The hall, when I entered, was already full, and understandably. For long now I had been protesting, not only against the actions of the yeomanry cavalry against a peaceful demonstration in support of Parliamentary reform, but for the cause of Sir Francis Burdett who had written so eloquently upon the subject.

The front seats of the hall were arranged with Press representatives, all of whom could be guaranteed to give an inaccurate version of the happenings for the next day's readership. But this did not deter me because I now possessed the fellowship of the vast army of working-class people who inhabited not only Newport and its environs, but ranged up and down the Top Towns. A single broadsheet pasted on the doors of their inns and taverns would bring this army tumbling into Newport in support of the new demagogue who was bearding corruptors in their dens. Reform was in the air; the temper of the workers was rising. They were heady days, if fearful, and I felt myself upon the crest of a political wave.

The reception was deafening when I mounted the rostrum, and held up my arms for silence.

"Ladies and gentlemen, I greet you, not in my name, but in those who died in what is now universally known as the 'Manchester Massacre'. For, make no mistake about it, citizens, the killing and maiming of the working class affects us here in Newport as on the other side of the world.

"So now, not in my words, but in those of Wade, that great historian who has given me access to his proofs, I read from a document which is not dependent upon our follow-the-leader historians, but which establishes the factual truths and is in no way dependent upon obsequious grovellings, and I read:

This reform meeting was held on St Peter's Field. During the morning large bodies of reformers came marching into Manchester from neighbouring towns and villages. Two clubs of female reformers advanced, and a band of special constables took up a position in the field without resistance. When the chair was taken, the chairman expressed his confidence — to all fifty thousand men, women and children — of their peaceful demeanour and holiday spirits; nor was a single offensive weapon to be seen among them. Now, even while he was speaking, surprise was excited by the sudden appearance of yeomanry cavalry who, after pausing a moment to breathe their horses, brandished their sabres and charged right through the crowd and up to the platform: here the commanding officer took the chairman into custody, and a cry now arose among the dragoons of 'Have at their flags' and they struck down not only those around the platform, but with drawn swords dashed down all who obstructed their passage.

A dreadful scene of confusion and terror ensued; numbers being either cut down or trampled beneath the feet of the horses — men, women and children indiscriminately — while a body of magistrates — and mark this, I beg you — at the head of whom was a Christian minister, viewed the bloody scene from the windows of an adjoining house, where, believe this, they were supposed to have read the Riot Act, allowing no time for the people to hear it. The killed and wounded were upwards of *four hundred*.

Coroner's inquests were held on the

bodies of the slain, but the verdicts of the juries were so evasive that they led to no judicial proceedings. Bills preferred against individuals of the yeomanry were thrown out by the grand jury at Lancaster. And, to crown it all, citizens, Lord Sidmouth communicated to the magistrates, the commanding officer and the dragoons serving under him, the thanks of the Government for their prompt measures for the preservation of the public tranquility.

"And there, citizens, you have it, an instance of modified martial law sanctioned by a Riot Act nobody hears. This assembly to promote reform by peaceable citizens, unarmed, and without breaking the law, was held where such a meeting could do no possible harm. But such is the hostility of the ruling class that the smallest incident of our cohesion is assumed to be a threat to the Throne itself. However, such was the outrage to decent people that one, Sir Francis Burdett, wrote an eloquent letter to the electors of Westminster in protest at the bloodshed. He wrote:

On reading the papers I was filled with shame, grief and indignation on account of the blood spilt in Manchester. What! Kill men unarmed and unresisting! Gracious God! Women and children, too, maimed, disfigured, cut down and trampled upon by dragoons? Is this England? Is this a Christian country? Will the gentlemen of England support such proceedings? No! They must join the general voice that demands justice, and hold meetings throughout the United Kingdom to put a stop to this reign of terror and blood!

I raised my voice. "And the outcome, citizens? Sir Francis Burdett was indicted in the courts for a libel upon innocent yeomanry; he was fined £2000, and sentenced to imprisonment This, ladies and gentlemen, is the state of the country. At any moment now, I suggest that the doors of this hall could burst open and special constables arrive with batons and proceed to break our heads for daring to illustrate the growing terror under which we are now forced to live."

Loud and long was the applause. A chorus of shouts began, growing into a steady rhythm:

"Reform in Parliament. *Reform! Reform! Reform!*"

Men stood on their chairs, their fists clenched; one shouted:

"You lead us, John Frost. We'll follow!"

A woman shrieked in near hysteria, "Down with the Whigs and Tories!"

"Reform! Reform! Reform in Parliament!"

And then, as if the end of Act One of a drama was awaiting the fall of the curtain, the doors at the end of the hall burst open and special constables streamed in, forcing their way up the nearest aisle and facing me on the platform. With their batons at the ready they stared up at me.

I cried, "Well, you come with enough truculence. Are you also here to break the heads of a peaceful assembly? Show me, show me but one offensive weapon, and I'll dissolve this meeting now."

A voice came from the rear of the hall, and a group of aldermen approached; at their head was the mayor, and beside him was Thomas Prothero.

"Dear God, people, what have we here?" I shouted. "The mayor and corporation and the churchyard acrobat."

Prothero, squat and swarthy, glared up at me, and the mayor cried:

"This meeting is not only in disregard of public tranquility, but is being misinformed," and he turned to the audience: a good mayor this one; had I been an alderman instead of a mere burgess, I would have voted for him. He shouted to the hall, his voice clear and resonant:

"Not content with slandering one of the finest businessmen in the town, this speaker is leading you into conflict. For even supposing that the facts of the Manchester affair are true — and they are not — the justice meted out to Sir Francis Burdett is within the law, and the law, ladies and gentlemen, is inviolate.

"Indeed, the truer his allegations against the soldiers of the King, the greater the seditious libel, for the case against those soldiers had not yet been tried," and he turned to me now, saying:

"This is not the only tap-room barrister abroad tonight claiming knowledge of the law. The Burdett libel imputed that the dragoons killed unresisting people. Were this true, they could have been tried for murder, and had men like Frost here had their way, would have been indicted in the public mind before their trial by jury. Burdett was rightly convicted!"

Fists were raised, half the hall was now standing on chairs, and the reaction to the mayor's speech was deafening.

For the first time I realized the danger of this getting out of hand, but I was determined to stand my corner, shouting back:

"So now you tell us that it is not only lawful for magistrates to disperse an unlawful assembly, even when no riot has occurred, but if they do not so act, they are liable, by their negligence, to be prosecuted for a breach of their duty?"

"He did not say that!" cried Prothero, coming to the fore.

"Ah!" I said, "at last we have it! The true viper has been disturbed, has he not?" And the hall exploded into ribald jeers and laughter. "First we have the respected citizen, then we get the corrupt alderman. Loving mayors as I do in the name of democracy, let it not be said that I lie abed with monsters of appetite that infest our politics. 'He did not say that,' says the respected solicitor who capers in churchyards after dusk. I say he did, and under case law Regina versus Neale, any assembly attended with circumstances calculated to excite alarm, is an unlawful assembly. If that is so, good people, this very assembly is now in danger of having heads broken by the act of having assembled. Citizens! What freedom is this? Do you tell me now that Parliamentary reform is not overdue? Far better have your heads broken now and remember the assault, than delay until your children stand in chains. I cry again, Reform in Parliament, reform in Parliament!"

And the people took up the words, linking arms, and crowded in upon the specials, who stood indecisively. The mayor moved first.

"You will hear more of this, John Frost," he said, and led the constables out of the hall.

"I will see you in court," said Thomas Prothero.

"It was a victory, was it not?" I said to Old Sam.

"A most redoubtable one," replied he. "But whether you put Prothero in his place so easily when he begins his libel action — that is open to discussion."

# 26

SO often Mary had warned me of false optimism: this, I admit, was a character error; it has often clouded my judgement.

In no other instance was my judgement more clouded by optimism as in the Prothero affair.

"He will not sue, I tell you," I said to Mary.

"Don't be too sure," said she.

"How can he possibly sue in the face of the churchyard affair?" I asked Old Sam. "Possibly he could win on all other accounts, for I freely admit I have libelled him, but to the fact of his basic immorality I have a witness — he was actually caught in the act, remember — and this is proof of the libel stated."

"The greater the truth the bigger the libel, or do you conveniently forget?"

"Legal babblemouth, Sam. This sort of thing is shouted outside the courts by guilty men who are fearful of their guilt inside them."

"Really?" answered Sam, and there was about him an infuriating, cold indifference to my *Commentaries on the Laws of England*, the bible of my convictions.

"Remember it, chapter and verse," said Sam, "when Prothero sticks £5000 on your navel."

He was also a paid-up member of the vulgar-tongued classes, as he often proclaimed.

"£5000," said my lawyer, Frederick Pollock . . . later Sir Frederick Pollock who defended me on a much more serious charge . . . And Mr Thomas Denman, his senior, added:

"Yes, it is true. A considerable sum, Mr Frost. And the case is due to come before Lord Chief Justice Abbott at the Court of the King's Bench on March the first. The damages claimed are not excessive in view of the gravity of the libel."

I said, "My God, Mr Denman, I'd be forgiven for thinking you were acting for him!"

He responded drily, "Were it so, Mr Frost,

my task would be considerably easier."

"Furthermore," said Pollock, "your accusation that Prothero could select his own jury in Monmouthshire has rebounded upon your own head. Mr Puller, who represents him, made the immediate request that the case be tried in Middlesex, and the judge agreed. Your impetuosity overruns you, sir. Now the plaintiff will be able to claim that so loved and respected is he in Monmouthshire, it would be unfair to you to have the trial in the county."

"But we know the truth of that, don't we!"

"Of course we do, but the judge does not," said Pollock. "Therefore, considering the many points we have outlined, we both feel that it would be in your interests to plead guilty."

I stared at them.

"On the basis," added Pollock, "that the remarks in your letter to the plaintiff were libellous, even if the accusations are true."

Furious now, I replied, "Look, even if all else fails, no judge in Britain can ignore the fact that Prothero was seen in St Woollos churchyard on All Fools' Day with his trousers down."

"Had you stated that his trousers were off," answered Pollock, gravely, "the accusation would have been even more serious — the greater the truth the bigger the libel. Your intention to damage being further proven."

I shouted, "It is unjust and iniquitous!"

"It is also the law of England."

"Therefore you will plead guilty to the libel, but with mitigating circumstances?"

"I shall not!"

Denman closed his brief and took his leave of me.

"Nevertheless, we shall do the very best we can for you, Mr Frost. Good day," and they left me.

In the event my obstinacy was reduced by Old Sam's logical arguments and Mary's passionate pleas on behalf of the family, so I reluctantly pleaded guilty for mitigation of damages. It proved a mistake as all my dealings with these damned lawyers have been mistakes. The jury found me guilty on one count in respect of the *Letter to Thomas Prothero*, and the judge, whom I was to meet again, assessed damages against me of £1000 and costs at £316. The loyal crowd which greeted my arrival in Newport off the Bristol packet was some consolation for my loss of capital, but Prothero's victory rankled.

"Thank God you're back," said Mary, her arms around me.

She was four months pregnant with Henry Hunt (if her child proved a son, he was to be named after the great Orator Hunt, who had presided at the Peterloo Massacre) and the sight of her carefree joy and expectation gnawed at my resolve to get level with the hated Prothero, who was acclaiming his victory; telling how he intended spending his damages, and assuring a populace which detested him that he had ' . . . stopped the truthless allegations of Frost in time for summer'.

"But I've not finished with him yet," I told Old Sam amid the clatter of his printing press. Said he:

"In the name of God, man, won't you give a thought for your family, if not for yourself?"

"After I've published this," and I gave him a draft.

Sighing, Sam sat down and read it. It

was a full account of my trial, in two pamphlets; the first was an attack upon my counsel for their inefficient handling of my case — they had even refused to call my witnesses — the second included extracts from my Letter to Sir Charles Morgan which again challenged not only his right to the land he was acquiring in Newport (he and the Duke of Beaufort now owned most of Newport between them) but the manner in which his great estates were acquired in the first place. Further, I questioned Prothero's right to be employed by Sir Charles, on the grounds that he was a scamp and a fornicator on holy ground, and that I had a sworn affidavit giving proof of this. Sam said, sweating badly:

"Will you never learn? This is a repetition of the libel statements which has brought you close to bankruptcy!"

I cried, "The pressure is on to root out these corrupters and pickpockets, and once you've got them running you kick their backsides. Here's another, *A Sermon for Lawyers*, which may give the wasters like Pollock and Denman something to think about."

"And Mary and the children? If you get another action like the last one, she'll be out on the street. What about your property?"

"Don't worry. I've transferred all my interests in the Royal Oak into my mother's name, so nobody can touch that. Meanwhile, I'm working for the people. If things go badly they'll support me."

"Yes, I know. I've seen it happen with monotonous repetition."

"Give to the working class and they will give back to you ten times ten — remember Cobbett?"

"I think you've got your ranters wrong," said Sam, "but I'll take your word for it. You want these published, you say?" He held out the manuscripts.

I nodded.

"Any chance of payment?"

"Any moment. I'm off to borrow a couple of hundred from my esteemed stepfather. Bill Roberts is an astonishing character. When he gave up herring fishing and took on my mother, I didn't think he had tuppence with which to bless himself, but since my gran passed on he's been having the run of the place. Grandad Frost, too, used to swallow the sixpences . . . "

"Hand in the till? Your stepfather?" and I quoted Gran:

"Give me private enterprise and I'll show you public criminals."

# 27

RUMOURS in Prothero's circle were saying that he was preparing an action against me for libelling him again.

"It's the talk of the town," said Mary. "Only this morning in the Royal Oak I called in to see Mother and heard gentlemen in the snug discussing it."

"So you would overhear, I suggest."

"It could be, but the fact remains, John, the way you're going we'll be penniless!"

Mary looked strained; vendettas always embrace the family.

My stepson, William Foster Geach, was with her. Brilliant at school in Bristol, he was home on half-term: a sensitive hard-working lad who was Mary's pride and joy, and I would have given the world to call him my own blood. Mary said:

"John, if you won't consider me, think of William. His headmaster says he has a brilliant future — he's top in everything he touches. If he has a break in schooling now, it could be the end of his studies."

I answered, "Libel, like lightning, can't strike twice. Prothero can grumble at my pamphlets, he can set abroad rumours that he's going to prosecute, but he won't do it."

She said, sighing, "You've heard, of course, that he assaulted Sam Etheridge at the cattle show?"

"Of course. There's a lump between Old Sam's ears as big as a duck's egg. Doesn't it serve to show the measure of Prothero's desperation?"

"Yes, and he's pleaded guilty. The case is coming up at the Usk Quarter Sessions, Bill Roberts told me. Your stepfather thinks he'll get off." She gave me a meaningful glance. "Incidentally, isn't he the last man in the world from whom you should borrow?"

I replied, "He's made it out of the pub, hasn't he?"

"Perhaps so, but a debt like that affects your mother. If we can't pay it back, all sorts of domestic complications could ensue — it puts Mother in an impossible position."

"Tell me where else I could go for

400

credit? We've got less than a hundred in the bank."

"Then tell me, for God's sake, what we do if Prothero prosecutes again?"

"I'll claim the benefit of the Insolvent Debtors' Act. Then he'd get no damages."

"But you'd go to gaol?"

"Of course."

Mary said wearily, "You continue to astonish me. Me, the children — our property, even the roof we're under — you'd jeopardize everything to bring this man down. Why, *why?*" Her eyes were filled with tears.

"For the people."

"And where do we stand in this?" She stared at me passionately.

I replied, "You and the family are dearer to me than anything in the world. And whatever is endangered, I swear it will not be you. But I can't stand by and see these men thrive in the mess of their corruption. Justice and honour supersedes everything. The burgesses are crying for a lead, Mary. We will triumph in the end — trust me."

"Oh, my God," said she; and took William by the hand, and left me.

On the basis that Prothero would never dare to go to court within the environs of Newport and wash his dirty linen before a despising public, I would have staked my life on him remaining silent under my onslaughts.

In one pamphlet I had certainly libelled him; in a satirical poem entitled *The Wanderer of Usk*, already circulating with devastating effect, I had further infuriated him; and now rumour had it that he had taken especial exception to my public letter to *The Mayor and Aldermen*, which dwelt not only upon the private weaknesses of the incumbent mayor, but further taunted the arch-enemy. Happy in the knowledge that I was slowly exposing the godhead of the iniquity so rampant in Newport, I became lulled into a sense of security, until the night Sam Etheridge knocked upon the door of the shop.

He stood there in his ragged clothes and printer's ink, screwing at his cap, and said:

"I've just had a pint in the Parrot. One of Prothero's gamekeepers was in there. He says he overheard a conversation at Lapstone Hall yesterday — Prothero's sueing."

Mary put her hands over her face.

"Spit and sawdust talk, Sam — I'm surprised at you!" I said cajolingly.

"What the Parrot whispers today the courts do tomorrow. You'd do well to take it seriously."

"Get rid of my stock, you mean?"

"Even at half price get rid of it. What about the Royal Oak?"

"I've already transferred my interest to my mother. I told you."

"And clear all your debts, the judge will like that."

I interjected, "Aren't you involved?"

"Technically, yes, as your printer, but I don't think Prothero's after me. It's you he wants to break financially. You'll invoke the Insolvent Debtors' Act? — it's always a handy one."

Mary said bitterly, "So you're going to prison?"

"Only for a day or so," explained Sam. "It's a technicality. Don't worry, it will be all right, ma'am."

Mary stood between us, looking from one to the other in perplexity.

I said, "Well, if I'm going down, I might just as well be a sheep as a lamb," and went to my bureau and gave Sam two pamphlets, saying, "Publish these as soon as you can, preferably on my first day of imprisonment for debt — Bill Roberts is seeing to this, he's having me arrested before Prothero does, for I'm now flat broke."

"I'll read them back at home," said Sam.

The first paper was a further attack upon Prothero for causing the death of a woman in pregnancy — he had arrested her husband for debt: the second was a bitter attack upon the recent candidacy of a Whig of doubtful character. The bones of this I outlined to Sam before he went.

"Excellent," said he. "This will sit them up again," and Mary, looking sorrowfully at us, said:

"You two are the most obstinate and frightening men I have ever met. Do your families mean nothing to you?"

"Don't be like that, missus," said Sam.

The tap-room scandal of the Parrot proved correct. Prothero issued his writ, bringing me before a jury.

Found guilty, I was given bail to appear for judgement before the Court of the

King's Bench in November: meanwhile, arrested as agreed with my stepfather, William Roberts, for my debt to him, I entered Monmouth gaol intending to claim benefit of the Insolvency Act. But, when due for release after six weeks confinement, Prothero opposed it on grounds that I had given undue preference to some of my creditors; this substantiated, Justice Bosanquet (who later hanged Dic Penderyn and gained his niche in posterity), sentenced me to six months more in Monmouth gaol, which, in retrospect, were the happiest of my life.

With all financial commitments lifted — radical friends and supporters ran my draper's shop and contributed to the family upkeep — given time at last for the study of Welsh and French, I now concentrated upon making myself an even more formidable opponent to men of corruption.

Indeed, with Sam's assistance a veritable rush of pamphlets emerged from that gaol, one of which foretold that the day of revolution was at hand; enjoining them to spike the plans of corruption's aggrandisement; seize those of immoral practices

405

and put them into refining cages, and meanwhile put in bids at nominal prices for any stolen property they may wish to confiscate.

Lapstone Hall, I said, the mansion of the illegitimate son of the Currier of Usk, for instance this was a desirable estate that required an honest broker: as for my own part, I assured them, I had for some time coveted Werndee Farm belonging to Sir Charles Morgan, since, after the day of reckoning he would have but little use for it.

"For is it not a fact," I wrote in a pamphlet, "that men of great estate had obtained them mainly through the plunder of William the Bastard? Or stolen them from the Church during the turmoil of the Reformation? Or tricked their legitimate owners out of them by evicting them during the iniquitous Land Enclosure Acts . . . all corrupt bills forced through and against the will of the people? The great font of evil," I told them, "are the rotten boroughs; this is the Pandora's box from which flowed all national calamities, desolating wars and monstrous debt. By means of these the nobility have doubled their private revenues, thieved pensions out of the public purse, and filled, with their friends and dependents, every lucrative office in the army, navy, courts of law and public administration. Unfit, since they lack the necessary talent, to fill offices requiring ability or industry, these parasites condescend to fill profitable situations as clerks, ushers, messengers and registrars, but always at inflated salaries. Such leeches, gentlemen, most willingly carry the bags at the tails of those of more common birth, yet have the ability to call themselves superiors: only to these do the frustrated nobility pay homage . . . as a penalty for their own indolence and incapacity. But be aware, my friends, that all this is about to change. The working class is scratching and finding fleas, so watch your rears, you men of vast estate, for men of real substance are about to kick. And nor will it be, in the vast estate of Europe, the first time that this has happened."

And so, quite happily in my enforced confinement (for so well was I treated it was not imprisonment) the pamphlets poured out from the press of the indefatigable Sam

Etheridge. And while Old Sam concentrated his attacks upon the enormous emoluments received out of public funds by the Beauforts, I reserved my greatest venom for the family of Tredegar and the corruptions of men like Prothero.

Meanwhile, Mary had given me an addition to the family, and the Newport radicals drank my health at a dinner at the King's Head hotel.

Astonishingly, the authorities held little resentment to my outpourings; an assumption in which I was mistaken . . .

Mary said, in tears within my Monmouth cell, "You are to appear before Lord Chief Justice Abbott on the eleventh of February . . . "

"Abbott? The man who tried me last? *No!*"

"The same." She said, her voice breaking, "Look, I will try to raise some money for the defence. Can I not write to Mr Pollock and beg for his assistance? Perhaps we can pay him later . . . ?"

Mary spoke more, but I did not hear her. *Abbott*, I was thinking . . . *Abbott!* If ever there was a judge on the circuit who thought ill of me, it was he.

I wasn't wrong.

At the end of my confinement in Monmouth, I was committed to the custody of the Marshal of the Marshalsea, and in the February was brought up again in front of Abbott. Here I defended myself with little success, being sentenced to a further six months' imprisonment in Cold Bath Fields, London.

"You," said Abbott, "are nothing but a pest with your unfounded allegations, not only against members of the public but concerning the very standards and rules of the community by which we live. After imprisonment you will find security for good behaviour – for yourself for £500, and two sureties in £100 each. Take the prisoner away."

Manacled, without even a chance to say goodbye to my family, I was put into a communal cell in a cold, damp prison comparable only with the iniquitous Newgate, and shared with verminous, ragged companions, the very dregs of London.

In retrospect, Prothero could be forgiven for saying that he had stopped Jack Frost's mouth for good.

Shivering in an icy cold, eating with

criminals from a communal bucket and surrounded by pickpockets, footpads, extortioners and forgers, I had good reason to believe him.

# 28

ONCE out of prison, my business thrived again.

Hand in hand with the commercial growth of Newport, by dint of industry and honesty, qualities lost upon the majority of the enterprising businessmen of Gwent, I went from strength to strength. In the decade since 1820, the town had almost doubled its population, and I had quadrupled my takings.

Thousands of tons of coal was now flooding down to our wharves, and to carry this enormous load, Prothero, to his credit, formed a company to construct a locomotive railway.

Much happened in the year of 1830, and in terms of importance I will state them: firstly, the King died and was succeeded by his brother, William IV, in midsummer, which evoked national rejoicing: secondly, there was an agrarian outbreak which turned into a revolt among the half-starved peasants of southern England, whose wages were eight shillings a week: thirdly, my old enemy Prothero took to his bosom a partner, one Thomas Phillips, who, with Prothero, supported the view of the Duke of Wellington in his advice to the southern magistrates; here, for posterity, I repeat it, as I did at the time in a handbill:

I induced the magistrates to put themselves on horseback, each at the head of his own servants and retainers, grooms, huntsmen, gamekeepers, armed with horsewhips, pistols, fowling-pieces and what else they could get, and to attack in consort, if necessary, or singly, these mobs, disperse them, destroy them, and take and put in confinement those who could not escape. This was done in a spirited manner, in many instances, and it is astonishing how soon the country was tranquilized, and that in the best way, by the activity and spirit of the gentlemen.

Wellington.

Cobbett, in a letter to me, was outraged by the event, and I was distressed both by the brutality of the Great Flogger and the hunger of the people of Hampshire.

"I say it again, you cannot cry for the world," said Mary. "Surely, we have enough misery here."

"Perhaps so, but men like William Cobbett don't restrict their proposed reforms to their own cabbage patch," I replied. "Wellington's statement is a crime on the body of humanity; yet when Cobbett dares to state that it is useless to use coercion while public distress continues, he's indicted for it. But they will not silence him either by corrupt trials or public ridicule. Nor will they silence me."

"I had hoped you'd learned your lesson. A year's imprisonment and bankruptcy is enough for one man in his lifetime."

I said, "One is either in this world, or out of it, Mary. Anything less than protest is unchristian, as He whipped them out of the temple, the men of greed."

"Aye," she wearily replied, "And look what they did to Him."

Old Sam's logic was more practical.

"Like the Irishman," he observed, "a man's either with us or ag'in us; I know where I stand in the business of humanity."

"Cobbett's conducting his own defence," I mentioned. "God help them when he gets into the witness box. The Tories rule us with rods, says he, and the Whigs scourge us with scorpions."

"We can't all be Cobbetts, my friend," said Sam, "but you are doing passably well."

"And Mary?" I asked him.

"Never hang your hat on a woman's intuition," said he, "their hearts are on the wrong side of their bodies. The kitchen and the bed, this is their role. To them is the privilege of making life. To us, who cannot make a baby's fingernail, is the privilege of conflict."

I had never known Old Sam in such a philosophical mood.

"Meanwhile," he said, "keep an eye on this new one, Thomas Phillips. He has learned all the bad things from his master; is about to usurp him, and he is much more intelligent." He added, "Be content with small victories, meanwhile: your success in getting disallowed the cost of bell-ringing on Coronation Day was a stroke of bloody genius."

Satirical in his pamphlets, his sarcasm sometimes bordered on the contemptuous. He went on, "Reform in Parliament should be your aim, John Frost. Items like bell-ringing should be beneath your notice. The Reform Bill has been rejected; this is the nub of the case, and should excite protest. The only way to get reform is to raise the King and fifty dragoons, turn the old applewomen out of Parliament, lock the door and throw away the key. And you were right to denounce Wellington as the pauper on the public. Secret vote, equal voting districts and universal suffrage should be the right of every male citizen yes, you are correct in pursuing such political argument . . . but spare me, I beg you, dissertations upon whether your wife approves of you or not; and deliver me from a three-pound court action for bloody bell-ringing."

A humble printer in a shambles of an office in High Street; half-starved, bankrupt and tattered, yet I knew him for my intellectual superior.

"Who knows," said Old Sam, when I got to the door of his office. "The way you're going you'll soon be running for

415

mayor . . . if you widen the scope of your activities and disallow anybody, including wives, to tamper with your precepts."

In the following spring Old Sam, with the help of his new foreman, John Partridge, who lived in a cottage near me up in Gold Tops, launched our new project in the name of public dissent, the *Welchman*. Mary, as usual, had a word for it, and John, my eldest son, sitting in the kitchen with Anne, aged four, upon his knee, gave me a queer old look and a sigh when she said:

"John, this really is quite scandalous!" And she tossed the first edition on to the table. "That you should attack the ability of the magistrates is bad enough, but to brand parsons as drunken, unclean, hunting and shooting morons is disgusting!"

I replied, taking off my coat and hat, "The magistrates are selected for their influence or wealth, the parsons are corrupt and it is time somebody said so, and if we want religious dedication the Church should be disestablished."

"The bishops won't thank you for saying so!"

"Ours has just intimated as much: and

the curate of St Woollos, another dedicated young reformer, has just been dismissed, so I suspect he agrees with me."

"But not everybody, and that includes me." Mary's face was flushed with growing anger. "Can't you see that this perpetual antagonism towards authority is leading us down the same path we've trod before? It will end in debt and imprisonment!"

"Not this time, I'm a much wiser bird these days when it comes to libel."

In many ways I pitied her: money wasn't our problem now, but the eternal confrontations, the letters of protest were wearing her down. This was a womb-woman; one dedicated to the business of washing, mending, bottling and babying, and she kept her house as brightly as a pin. Politics were a gabble to her; her protests limited to those of her children; discord was anathema. Mary said now, close to tears:

"You have an excellent business; as a draper you are respected. Oh, God help me!" And she brought down her fist upon the table, rattling the crockery and sending Anne scampering down off John's knee. "For as long as I can remember I've been in the child-bed, scrubbing at the bosh or dosing kids for the colic." She hammered herself with a fist. "Where do I come in this life of yours? Reform in Parliament, political representation, secret ballot — and if they got it they wouldn't know where to put their cross — equal electoral districts! And now we've got this new agitation — the *Welchman.*"

She began to cry, her fingers forming a cage over her trembling mouth to stifle the indignity. "Sick to death I am of the fighting and argument, and tired enough to sleep for a week! Every damned knock on the door brings me to panic, in case they've come to fetch you!"

I held her: young John rolled his eyes at me, but I just held her.

It was the wrong time to tell her that I was considering abandoning my business — John was nearly old enough to run it now and devote myself to politics. Indeed, I had already sent a draft offering myself for adoption as a candidate for the Monmouth boroughs. And if Parliament disliked the idea of taking seat beside a mere tradesmen, I was about to warn them, in my next edition of the *Welchman*, that failure to do so could end as it had done across the Channel — in loss of property . . .

After a few days at home, when Mary was in a calmer mood, I put the proposition to her. Would she not find it agreeable being the wife of a Member of Parliament? It was an uplifting thought, I said and deserving of her consideration.

"In the name of God!" cried she, and picked up her skirts. "You just do not understand, do you?" And, white-faced, ran out of the room.

"There's more in this than meets the eye," said Sam.

There was. Her first-born son, William Foster Geach, my stepson, was in deep trouble.

I had long impeached the Almighty for not making Mary's first-born son my own son, such was my affection for him.

Brilliant in scholarship, he had qualified as a solicitor about a year ago, and was now practising in Pontypool, so we saw much of him.

Prospering, he had married into the Herberts, a county family, and confided to his mother all his success and happiness . . . with one exception: he had been indiscreet enough, in an effort to save time in some legal business, to send to a client a document prematurely witnessed by himself, for that client's signature. The client, unfortunately a friend of Prothero, took the irregular affidavit to the latter's office, and he, Prothero, with his partner Phillips, immediately took proceedings in the Court of King's Bench to get my stepson struck off the rolls.

This, of course, was another attempt by Prothero to get at me, but since William's defence was that no fraud had occurred, Prothero's attempts at a character assassination came to nothing.

Mary, however, was weeping bitterly when I found her face down on the bed.

"All right, there is something more!" Now her voice rose to a shout. "William is my son, not yours, and he is beginning to pay for the hatred you inspire," and I cried:

"He is paying, Mary, for his carelessness over a legal issue! Brilliant he may be, but it was the action of a fool!" And she turned upon me like a tigress defending her young.

"How dare you! You are the fool! You wallow in your titles of the poor man's friend and a guardian of the poor, but isn't it time you stopped these vendettas and remembered that charity begins at home?"

It was the only time we had seriously quarrelled.

# 29

ANEW era of self-help was sweeping over industrial Wales, led by the ironworkers and colliers of the Top Towns valleys. Aware now that the owners' economy worked on profit and not people, Benefit Clubs were springing up among the isolated mountain communities.

As a counter to the strangle of the Company Shops, which sold everything from a pin to a shroud, new advantages were now offered by private unions. For a penny a week a worker could be paid out sick pay of a pound a month, and his relatives given a coffin in which to bury him.

More, since few works provided medical assistance, small stipends could now be provided for workers' doctors; even free medical centre beds were envisaged for injured workers and their convalescence since no hospitals were yet provided by the owners. At a time when Crawshay of Cyfarthfa and Guest of Dowlais were living like Eastern potentates, applications to them for the provision of a wheeled stretcher were ignored.

Seeing the advantage of the Benefit Clubs, workers' leaders now used them as springboards for unionism, and the courage of the Tolpuddle Martyrs, under the leadership of George Loveless, was spurring the disorganized artisans of iron and coal into secret oaths of allegiance. Feargus O'Connor had declared that the Dorchester Six were not punished for taking secret oaths, as the Government pronounced, but for having been members of a trade union. Further, he stated that miscreants sent to the hulks should be replaced by the Prime Minister, the Lord Chancellor and the Secretary of the Colonies. One Member of Parliament begged the assembly not to vote one law for the rich and another for the poor, and quoted the rhyme of the poet, John Ball:

When Adam delved and Eve span,
Who, then, was the Gentleman?

Meanwhile, distress continued and resentment grew throughout the country.

In Wales, from Blaenafon to Swansea, the workers protested against low wages, bad housing and filthy working conditions, and this grew to a fever point among the crammed courts and alleys where endemic diseases raged: two out of five children were dying before the age of six and the expectation of life in Merthyr during epidemics, was under sixteen years — worse, even, than degraded Liverpool.

Aye, new leaders were rising among the people: and into this haunted field came one whose name will live in history, William Lovett.

Born in 1800, his career was over before he was forty, when he was 'dogged by disillusioned faith'. Yet in his short life he was the moving fulcrum who forged the People's Charter from British libertarian traditions; and, as importantly, formed in my year of office as mayor of Newport, the London Working Men's Association that sent its emissaries into every part of the country.

Lovett, as handsome as a Lothario and gifted in oratory, could, like Henry Vincent, 'hold a thousand men on the tip of his tongue'. He held the maxim that truth would always prevail like the sun in the heavens, and that public opinion is the great tribunal of justice to which the poor and oppressed can always appeal.

"I don't know if I agree with that," said Old Sam. "Men prefer an easier path to profit. Mammon, their eternal god, rejects all appeals to humanity."

"That," I said, "is typical of you, Sam. All ideals die in cynicism! But Lovett gets things done despite the sceptics."

"Don't tell me. I've just agreed to launch a Newport branch of the London Working Men's Association — more, I even told Lovett I'd do it with Baker Edwards."

"Mad Edwards? You're the one who's mad!"

This was Mad Edwards, as the papers called him; a man of tremendous strength and stature, yet one who laid claim to moral force for political ends, which is doubtless why Lovett had selected him. Sam added: "He's doing the talking, I'm printing his broadsheets, so I'll be slowing down on your work for a bit. Mind you, it's time we had a union of something or other here, though it'll be some time before it's active."

In the event, he was right; it was fully three years before Chartism took a hold in Wales, and then in the flannel industry of Montgomeryshire. Indeed I was mayor of Newport before a union was formed in the town.

With the passing of the Municipal Corporations Act of 1835, an election was held in the town. I won a ward, and became a councillor. Appointed as a Justice of the Peace, I also filled the roles of an Improvement Commissioner and a Guardian of the Poor. In November of the following year, I was elected mayor of Newport, and was now in a position officially to attack Prothero, Phillips and local corruption.

Meanwhile, Chartism was gathering force slowly, emanating chiefly from the countryside. I shared with Cobbett my hatred of all things industrial; mine, like his, was a romantic attachment to the green and pleasant land rather than the rapacious spread of dark, satanic mills. Sam, as usual, had a word for it.

"If revolution comes, my friend, it will be from the industrial areas."

"I don't agree with you," said I.

"It is patently true that our agrarian uprisings have got nowhere. In every case, ending with the domination of the gentry. Rebellion from land distress has failed because the peasants are not emancipated. This is not true of the industrial areas; here the workers are better organized."

"You talk of revolution," I countered. "I thought you were beloved of Lovett who stands for moral force; if you want physical force to change the order of things, you should follow O'Connor."

Sam said, "Pray don't mistake Lovett's honeying speeches for weakness. While advocating negotiation, he clearly states that, if all else fails, force must follow."

"It is something I have always realized."

We were walking together in the woods of Bettws. Later, through the mist of the years, I saw Mary again in the eye of my mind; young, her beauty untrammelled by the child-bed and living within a turmoil of argument and vendettas. She was proud, I think, of my political progress — which was now full time, for a manager was running my business interests — but secretly I think she yearned for the simple life. Sam was speaking, but I didn't immediately hear him; he said:

"I repeat, frankly, I have never thought of you as one prepared to employ physical force."

"Then you don't know me, Sam." He stared so hard that I added, "Beneath the skin of any lamb may lurk a tiger. Somebody once said that the only language the privileged understands comes out of the bad end of a gun. If a commodity is in short supply, those who possess it will not share it. It is the law of the jungle. A financier is to a financier what a tiger is to a tiger."

Sam said, "You quite astonish me. Your mayoral term has done nothing to educate you in political reason!"

"It is a world of rip and claw, Sam, and I've begun to understand it."

"And Unionism?"

I shrugged. "A means to an end. One has to have a cohesive whole before you can mount resistance. The Romans realized the dangers of cohesion, that is why their slaves were never numbered, lest they learned their strength. Until I was mayor I always thought that in an official capacity I could change things; influence the plans of those who channel their energies to private profit: garner support from decent men, bring to the courts the corruptives. But I find it isn't so, Sam. One can actually sit in high office and watch the corrupt become richer. High office is actually a quicker avenue to wealth for the unscrupulous and greedy, and power is always slipping away from the many to the few because the few are more vigilant."

"Christ," said Sam, "you are in a bad way!"

"Yes, aren't I? I opposed the recent election indeed, as the town mayor I proclaimed it after the death of the King, and as the Returning Officer I took not the slightest part in it. And the outcome? I had to swear in two hundred special constables to keep the peace, such was the bribery that flourished among the Whigs and Tories.

"My letter of protest to the Home Secretary that ten thousand pounds was paid in bribes and that the Whigs won because they bribed the most was ignored. For my pains I was falsely accused of myself receiving a bribe from a candidate," and Sam replied:

"I suggest, perhaps, that you protest too

much. Some say that if you can't beat them, you should join them."

"Die first, Sam."

"I've given serious thought to that as well. That will probably be the end of us."

He appeared to have said nothing out of the ordinary.

# 30

**I** ACTUALLY heard the great Henry Vincent at work before I met him.

Also, the occasion was probably the first time I'd had an insight into the activities of the Monmouthshire iron-workers, and this from sitting reading in one of the headquarters of the Chartists; the beer-house of John Lewellyn of Pontypool.

I sat incognito, and read in the newspaper:

It is an exciting time in Wales, one of fear and trembling of the well-to-do classes, and those who have goods and chattels to lose.

'The Chartists are coming!' is a cry that sends terror into the hearts of young and old: respectable people in the town keep their horses saddled and ready in their stables, hanging up their shawls, bonnets and overcoats ready at their bed-heads . . . for immediate flight, if necessary. For the name of 'Chartist' conjures up visions of plunder, rapine and murder.

'The Men of the Hills', as the ironworkers and miners are called, we look upon as lawless barbarians: and of a truth, they are wild and lawless in their ways, being given to kicking one another to death in their quarrellings.

In the town of Pontypool the Bloody Field is the scene of many a fight — the turning of a mug upside down in a tavern or the flinging of a cap into the air often being the signal that inflames the mob and sets it struggling like infuriated tigers. Woe indeed to the poor wretch who happened to be on the ground when the cry went up — "Give him a Morgan Prothero" — this being a Ponty cordwainer who made boots formidably armed with studded nails, for such boots are in great demand for kicking purposes, in addition to wearing.

At Blackwood, a man daring to work on after the Scotchers said 'stop' has had his furniture burned and his chattels broken, including both legs . . . when they were laid across a ladder and struck with a poker. One poor woman, whose husband escaped their vengeance, was shot dead among her children, and one of the murderers, accidentally wounded by a bursting gun barrel, narrowly escaped being buried alive alongside the dead woman in an attempt to prevent detection.

I folded the newspaper, looked around the faces of the clients, and saw little difference between these Pontypool froth-blowers and the customers who used to bait Gran in the Royal Oak in Thomas Street. The thick-necked, wide-shouldered colliers of the pits and levels; their features brutalized by excess of drink and labour, the skin of their hands and faces painted up with coal's mascara, the dust; the dust that stained their chests inside and out, and coughed up their lungs in streams of red saliva; these, I thought, might one day be my children.

As Hugh Williams, the leader of Rebeccarites, later met the lime-carriers on the roads about Carmarthen, and called them his progeny, so these were surely mine. For was it not such who called out in their pain for succour?

Not all these fought with the Morgan

Protheros, but cleanly; not all these lived as the papers reported it, in filth and degradation, but stood straight for their chapel and their God: not all these mouthed their dirty epithets and bawled their bawdy songs in the farting ale; these, who soundlessly called to me, sang in glorious harmony to their Creator; nurtured their wives and nourished their children.

Now, out in the starlit night I walked slowly down to the King's Head in Crane Street, and was in time to hear a man cry, his arms outstretched to a solid-ranked crowd below his balcony:

"So remember, citizens, to support the great rally and its march from Ponty to Blackwood on Whit Monday, with refreshments offered at the Coach and Horses hostelry where we will wet Finality Jack's obnoxious Reform Bill, and tell him where to put it. And now I introduce to you Mr Henry Vincent of London, the great orator who will pour it out to you like rum and milk!" And he stood back and handsome Henry Vincent took his place on the balcony, his hands up for silence and cried:

"My friend Mr Townsend refers to Lord John Russell, who states that his iniquitous Reform Bill is final. Well, I have news for the noble knight. His bill of reform is no more final than a grasshopper that flies in the night . . . " And he waved his arms for silence. "Does this Government really believe that men like us will stand by while the workhouses, their new penal institutions for an outrage on the poor, tear children from their mothers and part husbands and wives? I quote you Job, citizens — 'The congregation of hypocrites shall be desolate, and fire shall consume the tabernacle of bribery . . . ' What then? — do we assume that God is on our side because of a quotation? If God is not, gentlemen, then He must be sleeping, so I tell you this the decisions we take today, in the name of God or not — will be ours.

"We pray for equal electoral districts to head our forthcoming charter that will one day be the law. Do you know that in the borough of Old Sarum there remains today nothing but a thorn bush — a thorn bush, men, which has a nominal bailiff and burgesses, and returns *two Members* to Parliament, who, of course, are Tories! Can you hear me at the back? Take the hamlet of Gatton. Six houses exist in Gatton and has but one voter. This one voter unites in his person the function of magistrate, surveyor, tax collector and constable . . . and returns *two members* to the House of Commons, yet the great cities of Manchester, Leeds, Sheffield and Birmingham are excluded from representation in the House . . . while Little Appleby's right of the Parliamentary vote is *vested in three pigsties*."

He paused amid deafening protest, then cried, "Understand this, the situation is mad. Only an uncaring Government which thinks it has the country by the throat would dare to impose such an absurdity upon a people crying out for reform. Yes, indeed, says Job, protesting again, 'They conceive mischief, and bring forth vanity and their belly prepareth deceit . . . But it is a deceit, my friends, which will bring about their downfall, for we are going to take it to the streets!"

The town exploded into applause and a confusion of jeers and threats. Aye, I thought, the new Demosthenes; it was oratory of an order I had never heard before; not even Orator Hunt could compete with this.

So much, I thought, too, for the ethos of moral force . . .

Later, sitting in a private room of the tavern from which he had spoken, Henry Vincent surveyed me with dark, belligerent eyes.

I hold no brief for literary clichés, but these actually smouldered with distrust and suppressed resentment: this man didn't approve of mayors of any political persuasion.

Vincent said, "The Parliamentary basis is wrong. Is it right that an assemblage which ought to be a congregation of wisdom and probity should contain but a hundredth part of men of real ability and honest intention? You agree?"

I drank my ale, watching him; he drank water. An opponent of the evils of drink, he was forthright in his condemnation of taverns and beer-houses, believing them to be the cancerous root of poverty, and misery among women. I answered:

"The legislative power should lie in a filtration of the masses, not a landed few — a concentration of wisdom, integrity and patriotism."

"Of course. Power exists neither in eloquence nor strength, but the size of the vote. And while we are driven to the polls to put our crosses where our masters put their thumbs, we have no power." Vincent nodded to the window, where the crowd was still jabbering his praises. "Eloquence can spell danger, too, for it moves the mass to physical force. And it is not by force that we subversives will win the day, but by political influence. The real calamities of the country result from non-representation; equal electoral districts will prove as great an advance as a secret ballot. You know the Six Points?"

"I do."

"Will you forgive me if I ask you to name them?"

It was rather like being in school. "Certainly. Annual Parliaments, No Property Qualifications for Members of Parliament, Paid Members, Universal Suffrage the right of every male to vote Secret Ballot and Equal Electoral Districts, the point you were making outside."

He nodded. "Why put Annual Parliaments first?"

"Because it can be dispensed with, Vincent, you'll never get it."

"And Equal Electoral Districts last?"

"Because it is as important as the secret ballot, which in itself is a fallacy."

He smiled over the rim of his glasses. "You intrigue me, Frost. Why?"

I replied, "Of what use is a secret ballot when once the Whips come out? The candidates roar at us like lions and promise us the earth during their canvassing, swearing that they will represent our views. And then, the moment they take their seats in the House, call out the Whips. Our loyal Members change their minds to serve their parties. Thus we, the people, have lost our representation."

It stilled him. He said softly, "Anything else, Mr Mayor?"

"Yes. Equal Electoral Districts will become a farce in the hands of disreputable politicians. Even if you get it on the statute book, liaisons will be made between parties to break the laws the moment they get into office . . . and rig the boundaries to suit their purposes. If you read Blackstone's

*Commentaries on the Laws of England*, my friend, you will discover ample opportunity to break the law and stay out of prison. Knights, peers and paupers are not treated alike in England."

Vincent raised his voice. "And what of public opinion? Is this not the great tribunal of justice, to which the poor and oppressed can always appeal?"

"With respect, Mr Vincent, the fact that Lovett has written it does not make it imperative. Public opinion has not yet lifted a freeman off the treadmill or a saint from his pillory. Only a resort to violence can achieve that."

"You are a physical force Chartist, Mr Frost?"

"I am not a Chartist at all, sir; I know their aims but cannot see how it can work without the fists of men like Feargus O'Connor."

"Come, come, be fair. Feargus O'Connor also supports the moral stance." He smiled. "Perhaps he is less of a gentleman than most, prancing as he does for the big 'I am' but, while handy in a bar-room brawl, he only uses physical threats to achieve his moral aims."

I said, rising, "I must go, sir, before I get out of my depth. I have a printer friend at home like you; he is the intellectual, I am a humble mayor."

"Then I pray God I meet more like you. You refer to Etheridge?"

I nodded.

He saw me to the door. "My regards to Sam Etheridge; I seem to know him because Lovett talks of him. And speaking of William Lovett, who I'm due to meet in London tomorrow, may I mention your name?" He smiled and put out his hand. "Lovett found the printer, but missed the mayor, I'm thinking. He'll be surprised to learn that there is such a man as you in Newport . . . "

He appeared sincere, but knowing my shortcomings I could not sustain such a complimentary view.

# 31

IT is accepted that once a Government is established with a strong Parliamentary majority, its excesses become pronounced. The workers, therefore, knew that they could expect no help from a Government so determined in its policy of constructing two nations, the rich and the poor; two societies of people about which Disraeli was to protest so vehemently.

With the coming of the Poor Law Act of 1834 the workers were forced into renewed protest.

Three leaders arose. William Lovett operated from London; Tom Attwood had his headquarters in Birmingham, and the red-headed, volatile Feargus O'Connor, editor of the fiery *Northern Star*, pursued the violent course of 'fleshing swords to the hilt' in the north.

After my meeting with Vincent in Pontypool, it became the natural order of things that I should lead any Chartist organization rising in South Wales. To this end, after my year as mayor of Newport, I began to attend national meetings of the Chartists, while as far west as Carmarthen, Hugh Williams represented, with Hetherington, his branch of the London Working Men's Association now flourishing under Old Sam in Newport.

A new flag — 'Freedom's Tricoloured Banner' — began to wave at the London meetings, where great marches were organized to parade the workers' demands: a Freedom song was composed, rebellion was in the air: a new militancy was growing apace in Wales from Merthyr to Llanelli and Pontypool to Swansea. At a London meeting of the W.M.A. which Sam Etheridge and I attended, delegates addressed a meeting of 30,000, a massed rally that then marched from Blackfriars to Westminster and the Palace Yard, causing consternation among the Whigs and Tories.

The prairie fire, lit by Lovett's oratory and O'Connor's violent speeches, began to fan its flames among the flannel towns of Newtown and Llanidloes: slowly, inexorably, the aims of Chartism grew across the land

and new branches of the W.M.A. were established among the workers in the ironworks and collieries.

Socialism, the term coined first by the saintly Robert Owen, tore down the mantle of secrecy surrounding those new Bastilles, the workhouses, where the aged and sick were sent to die. Here the sexes were separated to reduce the birth rate of paupers; the young herded together with lunatics to meet the complaints of aristocrats who were being pestered for alms by beggars on the roads. Owen's *A New View of Society*, published two decades ago, again became the focus of social ambitions amid the flooding discontent, and during Thomas Phillips's term of office as mayor of Newport our town was riven with nightly torchlight meetings and banners calling for Parliamentary reform.

Talk had it, too, that the men of the mountains, those brawny, fiery workers of furnaces and pits, were drilling with mock arms in secret . . .

"There's a letter for you," said Mary.

There existed between us that coolness that comes with marital separation.

Recently, while sewing in her rocking chair by the fire, she had met my eyes across the twilight room, and I had seen the ungracious light of one whose love was fading. I could scarcely blame her. The constant worry as to what each day might bring had stained the family: confrontation is never the ownership of the confronted; it extends its tentacles of discord to every part of the family; that darling octopus that reaches to the farthest corner of the room and is never found wanting.

And while I tried desperately to confine the vituperation of politics to my own private actions, the personal threats crept their evil under the doors.

"Where?" I asked, coming in.

"Where what?" She could also be belligerent.

"You said there was a letter."

"In your study — where else?"

The years had embittered Mary: the child-bed where she had endured ten labours and two miscarriages had fashioned deep lines upon her face; yet much of this I knew to be my responsibility.

In retrospect I realize, but did not do

so in my younger days, that a maverick such as I should never collect about his person the trappings of family. In vain I remembered the days of our youth; the kisses of Bettws woods, the fevered nights of lovemaking when the moon above sleeping Newport was an orb of joy sliding down the window: now nothing appeared left of that affection save repentance.

I opened the letter in the study and read it walking into the kitchen: a stew was simmering on the hob, I remember, its smell delicious: the table was laid with a starched white cloth, the cutlery tinkling as one walked by. Mary's tablecloth was like Mary's soul, a raiment of purity: these days Hope Chapel was her only consolation.

"It's from Henry Vincent," I said, sitting down.

"Another trouble-maker."

"It's of small importance. He wants me to attend a meeting at Nantyglo."

"That sounds to me like Zephaniah Williams!"

"It is."

She lowered the sewing into her lap. "So now we've come to the atheists, have we? Zephaniah Williams who keeps a picture

446

of Our Lord above the bar of his public up in Blaina, and with an inscription underneath, 'This is the man who stole the ass'."

I said, getting up, "You've been reading the Tory press again." I sighed. "If you want a true perspective on the happenings of the day, you should read the *Vindicator*."

It angered her. "One is as bad as another. My God, I thought we'd be finished with the last round of politics when you ended as mayor, but now you're more involved than ever," and she pointed with her needle, her face pale with suppressed emotion. "I tell you this, John, the days are gone when I support you in this squabble and that one. In the old days when you were away, either with politics or in prison, I was behind you, for I had the comfort of William. But now he's gone, I've got nothing!" Suddenly she began to cry in gasps and wheezes, wiping her face with her hands. Standing above her chair, I held her. "Nothing, nothing at all, I tell you!" She stared up at me with a tear-stained face. "Man, you're over fifty-four years old — are you going on for ever? Where do I come in?"

I did not reply. It seemed enough to

stand there while her tirade of protest flooded over me. Flinging away the sewing, she stood facing me, crying, "An evil is coming, John — aye, you can laugh away the intuition of a woman, but this time I know it — and it is greater than a libel imprisonment, six months of parting here and there — it is something that will be the end of us!"

I took hold of her again. Initially resisting, Mary softened in the embrace.

I said, quietly, "My love, the evil is already here; for years it has fulfilled its purpose of greed and corruption. Listen, listen to me. Only last week a worker in Dowlais had to sell food to get the money to bury his child . . . "

Furiously, she interjected, "But not *my* child! Oh, can't you understand? Every damn time we have a scene like this you rake up some heart-breaking example!"

Her hair, I noticed, was thinning on the scalp, and I recalled with warmth the waves of perfumed blackness that once she owned. And, although the years of youthful passion were now lost in old age, I knew a small sweetness of desire that grew out of the tenderness into a faint wanting; and this wanting touched my loins: sensing this, Mary turned up her face to mine and I stroked her face and kissed her lips, and what began as youth's remembrance, ended in a gasping embrace.

I said, "I love you."

"And I love you, *cariad* . . . Oh, why can't things be different?"

There was a girl in a white frock standing on the edge of the crowds of *Calan Mai* long, long ago, before the world began . . . and she landed me a wink.

"Are we too old?" whispered the girl in the white frock.

"I am not," I replied, and kissed her again.

Somewhere out in the night, with the wind playing his doh-ray-me in the eaves there came a song; a fine, tuneless song of a watchman down by the river, and his voice was bass and pure, as hand in hand, we went up the stairs.

"O, my love, my precious . . . promise me? Promise?"

The moon, round and full after his heavy meal of June, was watching us through the bedroom window.

"I promise," I answered, and the girl

449

returned to me in the blinding darkness, as I divided her body and made her one with me.

The night was black with him and the errant winds of summer were blustering in dark places as the little cob clip-clopped along the road to Abergavenny; the iron-shod wheels of the trap sang a rusty song.

John Partridge, once Old Sam's foreman printer and now his successor, leaned back and looked at the moon which, appearing like a footpad from a witch's cloak, beamed down upon the milk and honey land. Lacking Sam's supreme intellect, John replaced it with native common sense; and his hatred of injustice was akin to mine. He said, bassly:

"Pity he couldn't come. I suspect it isn't just the branch W.M.A., though Lovett does keep him at it — it's the atheist, Zephaniah."

"With Old Sam? You surprise me!" said I.

"Oh yes, Mr Frost," said Partridge. "For anyone with Old Sam's intelligence, it's appalling, but if you want a lengthy dissertation on the benefits of Chapel over Church, start the argument!"

"You really mean Sam won't come to Nantyglo tonight because Zephaniah Williams is an atheist?"

"Either that, or he owes him money. Give him a month and he'll be back in the Poorhouse."

"Not this time. This time we've got the W.M.A. funds."

At Abergavenny we called into the Angel for a jar of porter to keep out the cold, then took the road up Black Rock to Brynmawr and on to Nantyglo.

Here the night had changed to red, for the furnaces of Crawshay Bailey were painting up the sky in rainbow colours, and away over the moorland Blaenafon was at it, too: this, the industrial world of blood and iron where the spit of a cauldron or the surge of a ladle emptied sleeves, tied trouser-leg with string, and glazed with fire the brightest eyes.

Once through Brynmawr the child labour of Bailey thronged about us; ragged, emaciated, they clambered upon the trap despite our efforts to push them off; not a few, but scores of tattered urchins;

many orphans, Zephaniah told us later; the product of dead parents now spewing from the ramshackle cottages that clustered around the ironmaster's roundtowers, his defence against his workers' fury.

It appalled me. Newport was bad enough in its filthy dereliction, but never had I seen such pitiful social conditions. Until now, the iron and coal Top Towns had, to me, been the frontier villages of a distant industrial revolution that was sending its iron and black gold via Newport to the ports of the world. But now I was seeing the tragedy of this success: the legless beggars with scraggy babies in their arms, rattling their begging tins along the road to Blaina in the River of Fire. And we drove on amid the treble shrieks of the tattered, hungry children, their eyes, large and wonderful in their shrunken faces, begging, begging . . .

"My God, I never realized. This is terrible!"

"Terrible, mun?" cried Partridge. "This is reasonable — you want to see Merthyr and Dowlais under the Guests."

"I didn't know! I just didn't know. I've only been up here in daylight."

"They come off-shift at night. You've been in Newport's politics too long, if I might say, Mr Frost."

I had no reply to him; also, I was thinking about Mary.

It was a pity, I reflected, that I hadn't brought her with me.

"But something, something's got to be done about this!"

"That's what Zephaniah Williams says."

Outside the Royal Oak in Blaina, Zephaniah's public house, a gaggle of old or crippled furnace workers sat, and they blinked away tears from their red eyes as we neared them, their movements slow as one or two raised hands in greeting to the strangers; which, Partridge told me, was caused by a drying of the joints through heat.

This, said he, was the refuse of Crawshay Bailey's iron empire; they who had been evicted from their company houses through age or infirmity, and rather than enter the Goitre Poorhouse, set up their straw beds in the disused ironworks called *Cwm Crachen*, the Hollow of the Scab.

My formal education into the problems of the industrial towns began that night in the River of Fire: it was furthered when I entered the packed tap-room of the tavern and followed Partridge up some stairs to the meeting in its Long Room.

Here, seated either side of a long trestle table were men of every class: bawdy workers straight from shift with their ale pots and smudged oaths; the more respectable, men of quiet demeanour; some with thick ears were clearly chapel pugilists, dangerous in a quarrel. At the head of the table sat a blind man, though his handsome features were unscarred by fire: he raised his face as we entered the room, and Partridge said:

"Mr Chairman, I am John Partridge, the Newport handbill printer: I bring, on request, Mr John Frost."

The blind man rose with lazy grace. "Ah yes, on Vincent's recommendation."

Clapping began and I stood in embarrassment. The blind chairman said, his hand up:

"Welcome indeed, and you, too, Partridge." His arm swept the room. "Lovett and Henry Vincent you know, of course, but may I present our guest of honour — Mr Feargus O'Connor, who has travelled from Lancashire to be with us."

This was the fiery Irishman (many said he was mad) whose father fought against English rule in the '98, and whose uncle, a general in Napoleon's army, bought an Irish estate . . . to house the French General Staff after their successful invasion of England . . . Big, florid of face, he was M.P. for County Cork some six years ago, but had resigned his seat to become a Chartist and attack the new Poor Law Act: now, editor of the brilliant *Northern Star*, he was waxing fat on its sales. Perhaps I was never a good judge of character; certainly Mary thought so, but I was right on this one, whom I disliked on sight . . . he who was to serve Chartism badly with his boastful confidence, and die a lunatic: thus are the plans of men brought to nothing.

Now, towering above me, he seized my hand in a grip of iron, saying, "For sure, the sight of a mayor always brings me to the knee o' true democracy. Pleased I am to meet ye," and he swung to the chairman. "Is this the lot, Gideon, for the sooner we finish the business the quicker we're into the ale. Where's Zeph, for God's sake?"

Zephaniah Williams entered, slamming the door behind him.

The moment this man, the landlord, met my eyes I knew in some unfathomable way that my destiny was linked with his.

"John Frost?" he asked, and his eyes were good.

I took his hand. He said:

"You've been a long time coming. Sit you down." His English was almost broken, the accent thick with Welsh. O'Connor shouted:

"Have ye no heart, Zephaniah? Where's the welcome?"

"The welcome's here," came the reply instantly. "Cool heads to start us, Feargus — I'll oil your gullet after — is that fair, Gid Davies?"

"Meeting open," said the blind man coldly. "The ale comes after."

The men stared up and down the table with surly apprehension.

After yet another official introduction, Feargus O'Connor rose at the table, and cried:

"I'm come down from the Midlands and North to see the state o' events in Wales, and let me tell ye, fellas, compared wi' the North you're not doing so bad." He glared down at us. "If you were a weaver in Leeds you'd be on ten shillings a week, and a bob a week less for a farm labourer in the South. But you, ye crass buggers, are takin' home twenty-two shilling if you're a miner, two bob more as a mason, three shillings more'n that for a smith and thirty bob for a fitter. Is this hardship? Jesus, Mary and Joseph, ye bring me nigh a hundred miles to gas about starvation, when you're livin' on the fat o' the land!"

The men muttered discontent, like bulls at an empty manger, and he bawled, "Christ, you'd be mutterin' if ye laboured for some o' the right bastards I've got back home up in the Black Country, I tell ye . . . " and a black-maned giant of a man with a blistered face, leaped up and cried:

"You've got some balls, mun, talking about the starve in Wales, and ye haven't been here five minutes!"

They thumped the table and banged it with their pots, and a little elf of a chap shouted, "Where did you get this bloody coon from, Gid Davies?"

"Send him back to bleedin' Connemara!"
"Is that a fact?" shouted O'Connor. "And is there a man here big enough to send me? I'm tellin' you straight, the Welsh leeks that ye are, there's more goin' on in starvin' Ireland than happens here in a month o' Sundays. For I've seen the bottomless coffins of County Connaught while the lot of you were on tits, and the foine people grazing in the fields in Mayo like animals before you'd got an arse between ye. Listen to me, me lovely boys, listen!" and he drew up his hands and held them before his face and I was astonished by the oratory that first infuriated them and then moulded them to his desires.

"All right, you've high wages because you're tradesmen, so I supposed you're entitled to more'n than a skinny wee weaver who was born to scratch a beggar's bum — so I'll set you free on that score, and I'll tell ye why. Why? Because I've ne'er in me good life seen such filthy livin' and working conditions since the midwife bathed me!" He pointed to the window. "Twenty to a room in Brynmawr, six to a bed in Nantyglo, and Crawshay Bailey livin' it lush in his foine mansion, wi' cholera and what-not breeding in the alleys within feet of where ye wives bear their children."

A man shouted, his voice breaking, "Come down and try it, Spud Murphy Man — it may be good enough for the bloody Irish like you, but it anna for us, for we're Welsh!"

"Sure to God!" cried O'Connor. "What do ye want off me? Isn't that just what I'm tellin' ye, be God? For your roots go back to the great Llewellyn and before that when ye kicked the Romans out o' these valleys. It's a proud and fightin' nation that you are, and it breaks my heart to see you under the heel o' these dogs of masters!"

"You watch your mouth, boyo! We're under the heel of nobody!"

"Order, order!" yelled the blind chairman.

And one got up and yelled back, "Order, did you say, you blind nincompoop? A chairman, are ye?" and Gideon Davies (he who was so soon to die) called:

"The speaker's on his legs, so give him a hearing!"

"He'll 'ave no bloody legs lest he sits down!"

And there rose to his feet another, and this was Henry Vincent: fine and handsome he looked in his unruffled calm, and he said, his hands up, "Gentlemen, you invited Feargus O'Connor here to address you he's had the first word, so give him the last. And this I vow. Before he leaves here tonight you will have confirmed him as your true leader, take my word on it. Quiet now, *quiet!*"

And O'Connor said, "I'm tellin' you, lads, and I mean every word, though it chokes me to tears to have to say it. For while you're paying your pennies every week into your benefit clubs and a bob a month for your union, the masters are sitting in their mansions eating game and drinkin' brandy while you're begging a loaf off their Company Shop. You ask off the clergy for fair dealing, and where does it get you? Deeper into the mire, double in the debt. Do you know that you're supporting thirty bishops, twenty-three useless bloody dukes, over a hundred marquesses and nigh two hundred earls and barons, to say nothin' of an army of peers of the Realm, these pansy buggers who parade around in summer hats and women's hose stockings! And you're begging off these sods for another farthing an hour! Jesus Christ Almighty. For this I vow, if ye downed their trews and checked 'em for inches you'd find 'em wearing petticoats and drawers, and not a set of balls among them . . . "

Someone at the back bellowed, "Right, you, tell us what ye want of us, you Irish bloody spalpeen!"

"I will," cried O'Connor, and set himself up with a prow of a chest, like a cock on a dunghill. "I want ye out in the streets, me lovely men out, out, *out*, and take to the clubs and staves. I want your women fashioning pike-heads in the kitchen, and your children wearing Prothero clogs. I'm a man o' peace, and threaten no one, but when I blow that bugle I want you out. Up in Leicester where I was last week — the cobbles are trod by armies of famished men and women, so if we can't clean up Britain with Parliamentary reform, we'll do it with the bullet, the bayonet and the pike. But first we'll raise a petition and present it to the House o' Commons, and if it's thrown out, I say God help them! Be prepared, if all else fails, to show your naked bodies to the muskets of the Redcoats, and spread the Charter throughout the land, lads — spread the Charter, O'Connor's Charter: let Britons, brave and bold, join hand in hand! Who's with me?"

He had mesmerized them. After a moment of silence, the place erupted with a roar, and they overturned their chairs to reach him first, slapping his back and pressing his hands.

Henry Vincent spoke next, begging them to be calm; William Lovett spoke last, warning them of the dangers of physical force, but by this time the men were supping ale: I did not speak at all, save to Zephaniah Williams, and said:

"God help us if the petition is rejected. This man has taken them by the hands and is leading them to the Devil."

"Meanwhile, there's a fine body of people gathering outside, and the tap-room's crammed, they tell me," answered Zephaniah.

"Isn't that the marvellous people of Nantyglo outside?" cried O'Connor, his nose against the window glass, and he stood back to take another swig of ale.

"Sure, I'd like to be goin' down there to talk to them."

I looked through the glass. As far as one could see the road was packed with people: men, women and children; and so quiet were they that we didn't know they had come. But the moment we showed ourselves at the door of the inn, a forest of arms went up and a deafening cheer split the night. Zephaniah cried, waving for silence:

"Aye, so you've heard about it, eh? The great O'Connor's here. And William Lovett and Henry Vincent — all come down to raise the Chartist petition. Reform in Parliament! Reform in Parliament!" And he thrust Feargus O'Connor to the front and raised his arm in a signal of introduction.

The people stood quietly; O'Connor shouted, "Good people of Nantyglo and Blaina, did ye think you were forgotten in the fight for reform? But, the crusade goes on wherever I may be — up in Lancashire, the Midlands or the southern counties — so get ye back to Crawshay's mansion and tell him Feargy O'Connor's loose on the mountains, and that we'll sweep the oppressors from the land, for 'woe to him that buildeth a town with blood, and stablisheth a city by iniquity' — says the Book of Habakkuk, chapter two . . . do ye know your Bible, you of the Welsh . . . ?" And he stared down at their silent faces.

A voice said, "We want John Frost . . . "

"Dear God," said O'Connor, "have ye no fever for the word o' the living God . . . ?" He emptied his big hands at them.

A woman shrieked, as Irish as he, "Would ye have me knock the head of ye with a naked broom, Feargus O'Connor? You're a divil of a one for the big talkin', for we've heard of you and your feyther kicked in the head by a horse."

"Aye!" bawled another. "Take your blatherin' elsewhere, O'Connor, and William Lovett and Henry Vincent wi'd ye, for we're down here and waitin' for John Frost. Where's John Frost?"

I was at the back and sank well down into my collar, but the single cries of my name became a sustained roar as the crowd stamped upon the cobbles, "John Frost! John Frost! John Frost!" And a little man, hoisted on to the shoulders of his comrades, bellowed from a toothless mouth:

"We've ducked the shift and walked the furnaces cold, Zeph. That's the bloody Irish yellin', but I'm a Welsh chap and there's a thousand like me. We want John Frost!"

My mind went back to my famous namesake, a man in a pillory who was worth shouting for, and I stood with a bowed head until rough hands seized me and propelled me to the front, and seeing me, the crowd cheered and shouted in a growing chorus:

"John Frost! John Frost! John Frost!"

"It's you they're after," whispered Zephaniah into my ear. "Say something, man!"

I raised my hands for silence.

# 32

COME the fateful year of 1839; Newport was agog with Chartism and its torchlight meetings, and the W.M.A. increased its brotherhood apace; Old Sam complained that he couldn't keep up with the demands for union membership. And while I continued my activities up and down the Welsh valleys by popular demand, I kept John Partridge busy with weekly broadsides explaining the theme of the new movement demanding Parliamentary reform:

People of Newport! As naught can be ruder, than is an intruder; no Marquess nor lordling our Borough shall storm: all shall now hear our call for Reform!

"That's a bit wishy-washy," said Partridge.

"Aye, but here's the next bit," I told him. "I'm calling for a meeting in the county to explain to the middle class the aims of the Union and Chartism . . . to put incorruptible men in Parliament; men aloof from the bribery and drunkenness of those who fill the Commons."

"You intend to name them?"

"I do not. I've been too long in prison for libel. The commoners know how common are those who govern them — they need no help from me. Poverty and distress follows in the wake of corrupt government, and this will be erased by the new Six Point Charter, the aims of which are upon the lips of all right-thinking men."

"It is voodoo — it's all been said before."

"No doubt, but we'll say it again — men will talk of it a century hence."

"Property is theft, you'll say?"

"Only to the extent that its possession is an insult to those who do not possess it; moderation is the aim. The great estates must be divided up, the sinecures and pensions abolished . . . "

"And the vote?"

"The producers of wealth, the workers, have as much right to the vote as the card-shufflers who doze in the debates."

"All this in a broadside?"

"Why not?"

"Because they won't understand it. Half

the population can't read, and the other half can only read in Welsh," said Partridge. "Why not incorporate the Charter aims in the W.M.A. speech you're giving? After all, there's a membership of 40,000 in this area alone."

I said, "Be honest. How can I deliver in competition with men like Vincent and William Jones? I'm just not up to it."

"Nobody can compete with Vincent. When his speeches don't prevail, he sings to them. But don't talk to me of William Jones; he has all the trappings of the agitator, and that doesn't work on burgesses — they're too middle-class. No, don't do it by handbill — go and talk to them."

"You think I can put it over?"

"It is their fault if you don't."

A new demagogue had appeared on the horizon — William Jones, a friend of Zephaniah; a taverner, like him, and a watchmaker by trade. Apparently, he was away up North on the night I met Henry Vincent in Pontypool, Jones's home town. A minor firebrand, this one, in the same mould as O'Connor, and with sufficient self-confidence in his romantic breast to replace him nationally.

"Romantic, did you say?" asked Partridge innocently. "Love is his first love, politics his second; he has 'em down Crane Street as fast as they can pull 'em from under him."

John added then, "And you want to watch him, for he spends more time up in Nanty fanning bloody revolution, than he does down in Pontypool."

I made a mental note of this. The Chartist movement, I was to discover, could have done without Jones the Watchmaker. As Hugh Williams, the leader of West Wales Rebeccarism was soon to find out, the scum always comes to the top of a brew . . .

But, in the wake of Jones's untimely intrusion, I knew a consolation . . . after the big meeting in the county, when my speeches on the advantages of Chartism were rapturously received, I was elected as delegate to the first Convention: later, at a huge meeting near Pontypool, speaking with Henry Vincent in the absence of O'Connor, I got my first taste of possible sedition, which can occur, I discovered, when within the heady elixir of oratory . . . and brought me into direct conflict with the Home Secretary.

"You're going great guns," said Old Sam, whom I met in the Westgate Hotel. He lifted his ale. "What did you say that caused the stir?"

A clique of hunting gentlemen in red coats came into the parlour, glanced at me, sniffed disdainfully, and went out again; always a sign, said Sam, of bourgeois success.

"Very little, in my opinion," I replied. "Vincent was in great form, of course, berating the Government as a gang of hooligans, hellhags and blood-suckers, all of which went down marvellously. Not content with that, he actually sang to all eight thousand, which had the women swooning."

"Yes, yes — but you?" He regarded me quizzically through his pebble pince-nez.

"I attacked the pensions, as usual . . . "

"The income of the Queen also, they tell me. Detail that for me." He was watching me over the rim of his pewter.

I shrugged. "If it is true, Sam, it stands examination."

"Was there not something said about the royal bedchamber?"

"Yes. I referred to the twelve grooms of her bedchamber each on a thousand pounds a year while the weavers starve. Grooms are there to clean one's horse, I told them, so what twelve of them are doing around her bed I was at a loss to think."

"That's sedition."

"Nevertheless, the truth."

"So was your allegation of Prothero's adultery, but you went to gaol for it."

"Not this time — all I've had is a letter from Lord John Russell. I've been noted for inflammatory speeches."

"Did you reply?"

"Yes. I told him where to get off. Vincent gets away with it. He said that the army supported the Charter, and that soon the Crown would come tumbling down into the hands of the people."

Sam said, "You're not nice to know. You're both sailing too close to the wind."

"Perhaps it's time we did. Handbills and verbal declarations change nothing. Sometimes I think Zephaniah is right; force is the only thing they understand."

Newport was bright with sun and activity when we got to the door of the Westgate, and a small sadness assailed me: in some forlorn way Old Sam and I were drifting apart. He said:

"Well, that bloody old Prothero once hit me on the head with his stick; since then I'm against physical force. I'm not your father-confessor, Citizen Frost, but in your present mood you'd go down well with the French Assembly."

"What do you mean by that?"

"That you're dancing to a different tune these days, and it's not fair to Mary — she's got the kids to think about and you don't think of anyone but yourself." He looked over the top of his glasses at me. "The present trend is physical force, and O'Connor's at the back of it, waving his arms like a bloody barbarian, and if you're going in his direction, count me out."

"I see. So we carry on begging, do we?"

"Yes, and it's a slow process, but Parliament can't resist for ever. Can't you blockheads see that they're just dying for you to take to arms?"

I didn't heed him, of course: already, I

think, I was too far gone. At the National Convention, with O'Connor himself in the chair, I declared to an ecstatic assembly:

"In the past six months the Working Men's Association has raised its membership to 40,000 in my county alone. So if Lord John Russell thinks fit to erase my name from the magistracy on the grounds of truthful speeches, the people themselves will put it on, for if necessary we'll take it to the streets. Further, if the House of Commons doesn't like it, and thinks to send me to gaol, let me say that there's scarcely a gaol in London where I haven't been already. Indeed, citizens, should any delegate present wish to avail himself of my experiences during incarceration, I am perfectly willing to enlighten him."

The applause was enormous: O'Connor and the delegates were beside themselves with approbation, and toasts 'three times three' were drunk in my honour.

The floodgates to my future as a leader of Chartism had been opened.

The debunking of Lord John Russell I found to be the touchstone of my new national popularity: now *The Times* and the *Manchester Guardian* hung upon my every public word; Vincent shrilled my political protests in his newspaper, the *Vindicator*, while O'Connor heralded my name on every banner of the *Northern Star*. Cartoons now appeared lampooning the Home Secretary as 'Frost-bitten Jack' and wondered what his precious Reform Bill would be like after the Welsh Citizen had done with it: surely, they said, the Poor Law Act was about to turn into a squalling baby.

Who, the papers asked, was this new footpad of the Welsh mountains who was turning Jack's stomach?

Vincent and I, now looked upon as *enfants terribles*, travelled the length and breadth of Britain, speaking at rallies and delegations and heading torchlight processions through towns and cities with banners demanding reform. A simmering revolution was beginning to boil: arms were being manufactured in the industrial districts, for we saw them being distributed . . . Yet at this stage, enjoying my own oratory and the passionate deliveries of men like Hetherington, Tom Cooper (once a chimney boy) and the fisty eloquence of O'Connor

. . . the fact of approaching violence made upon me no branding impression.

It appeared inevitable that Parliament would succumb to the demands of the people rather than face the ultimate — streets running with blood and gibbets in Palace Yard. And Vincent made no bones about informing them of the prospect. On a visit to Lord Russell's own constituency he declared to a cheering mob that not only was this a rotten borough, but suggested that John Frost might be induced to clean it up by standing against 'Finality Jack' at the next election. Why, he demanded, was the widow of William IV receiving a pension of £90,000 a year while young and old were being driven to the new workhouses like maimed goats? Why could not these dunderheads see that unless reform was granted to the people, England would endure the blood-bath of *La Place de la Concorde*, and that the Government could take it from him, the Welsh valleys, under the generalship of a man like John Frost, had all the geographical advantages of sustained resistance against the forces of so-called law and order.

Events were moving with breakneck

speed: but it came as some surprise to me that they were moving faster upon my own doorstep.

I learned this in the summer of 1839 when the illness of my mother brought me back to Newport.

In the spring of that year I was at the height of my popularity among the working class; even the middle class paid more than a courteous regard to one who was fencing successfully with national politicians.

But there occurred, after a week at the bedside of my mother, a happening which was to return again and again to me with strickening force.

It was dusk. The little cob had pulled the trap merrily up Black Rock, and I had entered the domestic defilement of Crawshay Bailey's iron empire. I had seen much of the tragedy of the Top Towns; their squalor and hunger. But, since compassion also has its limitation, I had grown to accept the open sewers, the heaps of rotting garbage that sent fetid stinks into the pin-bright little kitchens of the workers. But it was not this sight that appalled me as the cob clopped along. It was the sudden realization that, from a noble ancestry, my nation was becoming putrescent.

Out of this knowledge, wraiths of the future, like Macbeth's ghosts, suddenly made shape . . . three painted whores came out of the furnace smoke and, arm in arm, barred my way. I reined in the cob, and they thronged around me, their bosoms pushed high above their laced bodices, their skirts held up to show their thighs. The street lamp outside Zephaniah's ale-house glowed brighter, and I saw them more clearly.

"Come on, mister — sixpence for anythin' ye like," said one.

"Twopence apiece, my duck, if you can handle all three."

"Ach, bloody starvin' us, come on, gent, come on . . . "

Catherine, Ellen and Anne, I thought: but for a twist of fate, these three girls could have been mine. And somewhere, I thought, were three fathers, to whom the bodies of these were as precious as my daughters' were to me.

It represented for me the tragedy of my generation.

The tap-room of the ale-house was full when I entered; a ragged cheer of greeting went up as I climbed the stairs to the Long Room; two messengers went scampering away, I noticed, to spread the news of my arrival.

As before, the trestle table was occupied, but by only three men: Zephaniah Williams, William Jones the Watchmaker of Pontypool, and the tall, flowing figure of Dr Price of Merthyr. This, the half-mad visionary and eccentric of long, unruly locks and beard who spent his days driving around Merthyr decked in 'angel' robes in his goat-cart, waving a bardic sword . . . he who later made history by cremating his dead baby son. I had met this one before, and had placed him as a little above contempt: we could do without more lunacy in a movement like Chartism: this was Feargus O'Connor's prerogative.

Zephaniah said, "My God, Frost, you've been away weeks. Don't you realize that things are coming to a head?"

I sat down facing them. "Chartism is now nationwide," I said. "Think of it as local unrest and the cause is lost before it is begun." And Dr Price rose to his feet and cried with fine prophetic fervour:

"In the Name of the Creator speaks Henry Vincent!" And he raised his blue-veined hands to the ceiling, and cried, "'To your tents, O Israel,' and then with one voice, one heart, and one blow perish the privileged orders! Death to the aristocracy!"

"Excellent," I replied, "but cooler heads will win this particular affray, and this is why I have been employed on wider issues. In Glasgow I recently addressed a massed meeting of a hundred thousand. Even God couldn't be everywhere at once, this is why He invented mothers," which, strangely, brought clapping from Zephaniah, the atheist.

William Jones, whom I had met but once before, was watching me with narrowed eyes. I judged his age at thirty, this firebrand who kept the Bristol Alehouse in Pontypool. He said with droll charm:

"You've heard, of course, that Vincent's been arrested?"

I nodded.

The ale came up on a slopping tray; I drank deep, eyeing him.

"On the grounds of seditious language, they say."

"Wrong. Inflammatory language."

He smiled, but not with his mouth. "Strange, isn't it, how you seem to get away with it, and he doesn't? Dear me, Frost, the things you say!"

"Perhaps my luck will not continue."

"So, with Vincent, Townsend and Dickenson arrested, you just sit by and watch it?"

I got up and wandered around the room. "Tell me what I could have done to prevent their arrests. Newport's full of soldiers, so is Monmouth. More are arriving every day on the Bristol packet."

Zephaniah interjected like a man refereeing, "When the collieries and iron-works hear about Vincent there'll be hell to pay, and it's not only the men, either. The Female Patriots and Women Radicals will raise such a flood of drawers and petticoats that'll flurry the Whigs of Westminster. I mean it." He smiled. "Our hope is the Petition — how's it going?"

I answered, "One and a quarter million signatures so far, but I doubt if they'll present it within two months."

Price said, "Which means the end of the year before it's accepted?"

"If it is accepted," interrupted William Jones. "Meanwhile, take it from me, Mayor Frost, the people round here won't wait that long. They're sick to death of iron-masters and Crawshay Bailey in particular. Waving his bloody fists and telling Vincent to get off his property, but Henry handled him — 'Am I talking to a physical force conservative?' he asked him." I replied:

"Look, this is local stuff, and mostly nonsense. O'Connor says we should widen the protest, and he's right, so simultaneous meetings are being held all over the country — great processions from John O'Groats to Land's End. Every effort must be made to sustain the coming petition — everything possible must be done to portray this movement as one of moral force and social responsibility. If we let things get out of hand at this stage, we're lost."

Jones said, "Things got out of hand when they arrested Vincent."

Added Zephaniah. "Rumours are spreading that he's being beaten every day."

I sighed. "Then they must be countered, for it isn't true. These are tales being spread by Government agents to get us to move

481

too soon. Listen to me! Two thousand Specials have been enrolled in Ponty alone — you should know this, surely," and I elbowed Jones. "The Mayor of Monmouth has called for the prison's protection, Abergavenny is crammed with troops, and dragoons are marching into Blackwood for our Whit-Monday meeting," and Dr Price rose to his full height and said with a fine performance:

"Then let us meet them head on and have it out!" He raised his voice to a shout. "When such an evil as great as this shall be confronted, then let it be smashed with the very weapons it employs against us. For when the people are enduring so great an injury, nothing but the knife and the purifying flow of blood can remove the cancer!"

"Oh, Jesus, sit down!" said Zephaniah.

"But he's right!" protested Jones. "Everything's ready in the valleys. From here to Merthyr and over The Top down to Swansea, the towns are going on fire. One big attack would gain the day, I tell you! Arms are being made in secret, pike-heads forged, shot powder stolen from the magazines and stored under floorboards.

Wait too long, and we are lost. Strike now, before they are prepared to receive us, and freedom will be won!" His eyes were blazing.

I glanced at Zephaniah and he raised his to the ceiling.

It would be interesting, I thought, to discover what part Jones and Price would play when the revolution came . . . one probably under the bed of his Ponty beer-house, the other far removed from the drama of his operating table.

"There's another big crowd outside again," said Zephaniah.

The Nanty workers had come again to greet me, but not with the same peaceful intentions. Throwing down their firing-irons at the furnaces, blowing out their fires, they came in ragged squads of marching men. With their mandrels, axes, pod-scrapers, shovels and picks, they came with military precision, pushing aside overmen and foremen, howling down the protests of Crawshay Bailey, who shook his fist at them from Nantyglo House. They came singing, and with the banners of their lodges and benefit clubs flying: in a solid phalanx, like a Roman legion, they marched from Brynmawr and Nanty and Blaina works, and, surrounding Zephaniah's ale-house, they bawled in chorus, "John Frost, John Frost, John Frost!"

Zephaniah flung open the window of the Long Room, and I addressed them from there, shouting:

"Yes, yes, I know, men, you come shouting for Henry Vincent!"

"We shout for you, John Frost!"

"Ay ay, but Vincent's at the bottom of it, isn't he? And I, too, am here tonight because of him. I am told that all down the River of Fire there are men like you on the march to free Vincent from Monmouth gaol: and what is not known concerning him is being made up by spies and enemies among you. Beating him to death, are they? Starving him and others — is it so? I tell you and on my honour, that I know of this in detail. It is *not* so. If it were, would I be supping ale up here with nothing on my conscience while my friend lies beaten and starving . . . ?"

"We just heard, mister — they broke his legs!" shouted someone, and a man with a bandaged face called up to me:

"They done strangle his throat so he don't sing no more!"

"And he don't eat proper in days. He's English, mind, but he done all right for us, the Welsh. We say hie down Monmouth way and get the bugger out!" Cheers greeted this.

"Listen, listen to me!" I cried. "You call upon me to command you at every corner and on every page. If this is your wish, then I will do so. But give to me, then, the role of commander. For it is I, not you, who will give the signal for you to rise — aye, to free Vincent, if you like, but also to free the country from the yoke of this bloody oppressor that takes all and gives back nothing.

"And when you hear that word, I expect you to be at your posts and fearless of danger. But it is all too early now. The Chartists of the North, South and West are not yet prepared to rise, and the co-operation of all the lodges must be assembled under the clear banner before we do. Be patient, I beg you. Soon the great Petition will be laid in Parliament, and if that fails and Parliament is not dissolved, then I make a sacred promise to you — no longer will I argue, either to you or any assembly, that we keep the rules of Peace, Law and Order!"

This last was greeted by a mighty roar, and I was pushed aside and William Jones took my place at the window, shouting:

"Men of the hills! I have just returned from a mission to the Forest of Dean and I tell you this — the Foresters are armed and ready to back us. For myself, when you want a leader, I am prepared to sacrifice the last drop of my blood in your cause! I can't answer for my brother Frost who stands beside me, but I swear to you that if your enemies break the peace he mentions, I will be at them with sword in hand and trample their heads under my feet. I shall stand with Frost and Zephaniah Williams until this is a land of milk and honey, until every worker in this valley walks head high, for we will sweep away the evils that encompass us and run the aristocracy off the land of our fathers!"

No sooner had I closed the Long Room window, but Zephaniah said:

"Well done, Frost! You have made your decision."

I replied, "It is upon the Petition that

rest all our ambitions, this I made clear to them," and William Jones added:

"And doubly clear your intention to lead them if the Petition fails. My God, John Frost, I would not be in your shoes should the Petition fail these men, and you do, too."

"I shall not fail them. Isn't my word enough?"

"Yes," said Dr Price, "because they worship you. For my part, I shall only go to battle on the rules laid down in the meetings; I would never join a riffraff of drunken bawlers without an aim in view — the release of Vincent, if you like, but linked to an all-out engagement."

"That might mean killing a thousand innocent soldiers!"

"Aye — a hundred thousand if the Cause demands it," and he levelled a bony finger at me. "Understand this, mister. If you take me to the sword you will not hang a halter around my neck at the same time. For nobody shall take that sword from me, though it be at the cost of my life. What kind of revolution is this to be?"

I said, turning away, "A hundred thousand dead. My God, I cannot do it, I cannot.

Heaven and hell comes into this. Perhaps I am not the man to lead such an enterprise."

"You'll soon find out if you are, or not," said Jones. "You have promised to lead them. Fail them, and they'll run you out of Newport."

# 33

"*MAE'R Siartwyr yn dod!*" — "The Chartists are coming!" — was the cry that went rolling over the mountains.

It was whispered around street corners, bubbled through ale, shouted by the ranters, roared by the mobs.

"*Mae'r Siartwyr yn dod!*"

The Irish heard it and took up the cry; the foreigners from Spain chanted it; children joyously cried it; women fearfully whispered it behind their hands, wondering how they would feed their families.

And then, as suddenly, the chorus ceased; it was like the ending of a vast oratorio.

The rain began on the morning of Saturday November the second; a steady drizzle from overcast clouds as if the sky was weeping for what was about to come.

"It is a Tory God in a working-class hell," said Zephaniah. "Trust him to take a hand."

"We could have done without this," I replied, and looked at clouds leaden with rain and the promise of storms.

"It is the hand of a vengeful God at work," said the curates, under pulpits for safety, or peeping out from under beds.

Earlier, I had been away up North in England again, seeking support for my Welsh, whom I knew would rise. Despite my repeated speeches of warning, my threats of dire consequences should they move too soon, the colliers, miners and iron-workers of the great valleys had formed a solid phalanx of decision. Sick of poverty, disease, the squalor of living conditions, the exploitation of the Company Shops and the domination of masters, they threw down their tools and crowded the streets of towns and villages. From Dowlais to Sirhowy, Blackwood and Ebbw Vale; from Crumlin to Argoed and Rhymney and a dozen other bloomery hamlets, they crammed into their publics and taverns to escape the rain and listen to their leaders. They poured into the chapels and knelt in prayer; they raked out laggards from their beds and pulled them into line. The time of talking was over, they said; now it was time to act.

"First we will release Vincent and the others from Monmouth gaol!" This was a frightening cry, one spouted by the haranguers on pneumonia corners.

"And put Lord John Russell in his place!"

"By God, we will show them, these pigs who live in idleness while our children starve."

"Whigs and bloody Tories? We'll wig and crown the lot of them."

"Down with the waster Queen and off with her head! And roast the bishops of the Church alive like we once did in old Carmarthen."

And pasted on to every chapel wall was another hand bill, one smuggled from hand to hand under tavern counters:

We, the executive Government of England, do hereby state that before the week is out, we will be granted the Charter either by peaceful means or force if they drive us to it.

(Signed) John Frost,
President.

This was the work of William Jones, who, said Zephaniah, had been racing around the valleys; crying for the Charter as he galloped in fine style through the villages, bringing families cheering out of doors: stopping at times to deliver his fiery speeches of victory or death. This the actor in him, playing for the first time a truly dramatic role. Zephaniah, thank God, was cooler.

"What's it doing *abroad*?" he asked. By this he meant England; none I have ever met were more Welsh than Zephaniah, save perhaps his son, Llewellyn, the harpist, of whom he was inordinately proud.

We were in the long room of the Coach and Horses at Blackwood, a tavern used for meetings; downstairs the place was packed to the doors with men sheltering from the rain now lashing the thatched roof in a sustained roar. I answered: "The country is alive. God knows what the membership is in England. I say there will be a million men under arms: Parliament Square, they tell me, is packed nightly. From Heckmondwike to Bournemouth the country is teetering on the edge of a rising akin to the French Revolution."

But Zeph's mood was one of surly discontent. He asked:

"You saw O'Connor?"

"Yes, at a place outside Leeds. I addressed a meeting of about fifty delegates, and informed them that I had tried and failed to delay a rising, that our Welsh were becoming impatient . . . "

"But did you speak to O'Connor?"

"I did not. All fifty delegates were clamouring for his attention, though he indicated his willingness to lead."

"Do you recall his words, for I don't trust that beggar."

"Yes. A delegate said, 'Mr O'Connor, we are rising for the Charter in Yorkshire — will you lead us?'

"'When?' asked O'Connor.

"'Saturday next, November the second.'

"'Have you arms?'

"'Yes, all of us.'

"'That's fine then!'

"The delegate then asked, 'Can I tell that to my lads?'

"'Of course,' replied O'Connor. 'When have you ever heard of me deserting the cause of the people?'"

Zephaniah stared at me. "And then?"

"Then the meeting broke up in disorder — shouting and cheering and slappings on the back."

"It doesn't sound healthy to me," said Zephaniah.

I replied, "Nor to me. They had the same kind of vague assents in Paris, but at least they had the mass of the people behind them."

"And we have not."

"And we have not. But I tell you this. We have gone too far for retraction. Volatility and emotion are the traits of the Welsh; musicians and poets are better served by our national characteristics; today we prefer peace to rebellion. Perhaps our love of liberty died with the last Llewellyn."

"One thing is certain," came the reply, "we're about to find out." He added, "But you believe that England will follow, if we give a lead?"

"Yes. If we can take Newport with numbers enough — and that means the men of the valleys — and signal Britain to rise by delaying the mail coaches, O'Connor and the rest will follow our example."

"I hope to God you are right."

"One thing is sure," I said finally, "we've stirred up a hornet's nest and there is no going back." I went to the window and drew back the curtain.

Below me, packed like herrings in a barrel on the road outside, their faces turned up to the light despite the teeming rain, stood the men of the valleys.

"Right," I said, "We'll have them in," and opened the door and called down the stairs. "Delegates, please, all delegates!" And a score streamed into the Long Room: soaked men with rain upon their faces, the water streaming out of their sodden boots: bringing their smells of wet clothing, their breath misting the air, they took their seats at the table, and Zephaniah said:

"Listen, you. It is decided. We go tomorrow." I looked around their eager faces.

Zephaniah said, "I speak without notes lest such notes be found upon me. These, for your ears alone, are the chief particulars; more will be fed to you while on the march — can you hear me at the back?" And a man put up his hand. Zephaniah continued:

"From Merthyr district our captains

will lead their thousands upon Brecon town, capture it, and avail themselves of muskets, ammunition and provisions: another column will march from Rhymney, Sirhowy, Ebbw Vale, Beaufort and Nantyglo and seize Abergavenny — about a hundred of our boys have already billeted themselves in the town . . .

"Mr Frost and myself will lead two columns, one from Blackwood and one from Nantyglo; we will join on the march and take Newport; another column of men from Taff Vale will march on Cardiff, and capture it. Sunday is a good time. What soldiers there are, and there are few compared with us, will be drinking in the publics, and there are good Chartists about who will ensure that they drink plenty.

"But in any case, our spies tell us that most of the army are Chartist sympathizers anyway, so they will add meat to our bread." He raised his voice. "Are you asleep at the back, boys? For if you sleep on this you may not sleep again. Listen . . .

"All magazines in the pits and ironworks will be taken — our men are already billeted near the shot-firers. But, since we will need shot and powder for an army of a hundred thousand, we have a steamer lying by with armed men to take the Powder House outside Bristol; these will capture and bring to Newport every ounce of gunpowder, to keep it out of the hands of the army. Your furnaces, once Newport, the key centre, has been captured, will be appropriated to cast cannon and arms, for we will carry our attack beyond Newport — beyond Monmouthshire, even, and link with our English comrades in Yorkshire, the Midlands and the southern counties! No, do not look at me like that, for this has been long in the planning. Are you aware that in Newport district alone there are 40,000 Chartist paid up members? We will be many, they will be few . . ."

A man shouted, "How about the bloody magistrates, then?"

"If they show resistance they will be put to death."

"And the police?"

"Likewise, for special constables are traitors to our Cause; our aims are such that we cannot allow them to live."

"And the aristocracy?"

"They must be the first to die; alive they will plot against us. But no killing for the sake of killing, remember — only if they show resistance."

Sitting until now, Zephaniah stood, silent at first, his eyes moving over their faces, then said:

"This night messengers are going to North Wales, also to the north of England where the brave Yorkies are stretching at the seams, and Scotland! Aye, and London, Manchester, Birmingham, Sheffield and Bath — to inform them of our intentions to capture all of Gwent. Mind you, I know nothing of the greater designs, that are being made in England — only our leader John Frost knows of these. But this I can tell you. Britain's signal to rise will be our capture of Newport, so remember this. When we stop the mails to London and Birmingham, the cities of England will go on fire!

"For this is the day of reckoning!" His voice rose to a shout. "As our brothers in France gained victory over tyranny, so we will gain ours. Frost will drive his army in Blackwood, I will lead the column from Nantyglo; William Jones is even now rousing the men of the Eastern Valley. So, do ye know the password?"

"Beanswell!" They stood up now, bawling it, and Zephaniah cried back, beating the time with his hands:

"Then sing the last verse of Ernest Jones to guide the way for others — sing, lads, *sing!* 'Then rouse, my boys, and fight the foe . . .'"

And they sang with him, waving their glasses and pewters:

Then rouse, my boys, and fight the foe,
Our weapons are truth and reason.
We'll let the Whigs and Tories know
That thinking is not treason.
Ye lords, oppose us if you can,
Your own doom ye seek after:
With or without you, will we stand
Until we gain the Charter!

Up upon a chair now, Zephaniah shouted, "Aye, men, *Beanswell!* For if the iniquitous laws of England bind the hands of our Virgin Queen and she cannot be freed by our deputations and petitions, then the cannon of the people must, and blow into perfidy all her enemies, from her crooked politicians to the wanglers of the Pension List!"

They gathered about him, back-slapping him, raising him up in their arms.

Aye, I thought; a hornet's nest.

The die was cast.

# 34

IT was the morning of Sunday November
the third.

The mountain towns and villages
were jammed with milling people. Captains,
each controlling a ten-man squad, were
drilling them with military precision: arms
were being distributed under barked, regi-
mental commands, pikes exercised for
the cut and thrust, pistols secured in
stomach belts, muskets primed with shot
and powder and flourished by those who
had them. And the rain, relentless to
appeals by prayer, poured down in sheets
of water; the streets and cobbles of the Top
Towns were laden with slush and mud;
water butts were filled to overflowing,
brooks and streams burst their banks
and the flood water ran in waves to the
mothering rivers.

Yet such was the workers' cohesion and
the elemental barrier of the Welsh language
that those in authority heard little of the
warlike preparations. On the very day that

the *Merlin* reported that Chartism and its threat were ended, the manager of Abersychan's British Iron Company was hiding with his family in a mountain shed.

This, I prided myself, was a secrecy maintained by the tribal Welsh for the Welsh: no Welshman under English management was allowed to hold a position of trust and responsibility; now this national isolation counted against the common enemy and English domination.

Earlier, I had taken my leave of a tearful Mary: after exhausting journeys from town to town in Wales and England, and passionate exhortations to make the insurgency complete in comradeship, which, I assured my listeners, was a fight to the death, I reluctantly prepared to lead the Blackwood column.

With Lovett, Vincent, Dickenson, Edwards, Townsend and a dozen others in prison (from these I could expect no support) I was enduring a sense of isolation despite the presence of thousands of followers.

They came from all points of the compass:

waving their home-made pikes in a forest; they came with a military bearing despite the gale that battered about us. Wrapped in an old military greatcoat and with a red cravat to keep out the rain, I found a tump by the roadside, climbed up it, and shouted:

"Men, keep your military order! Ten-man squads follow their captains; muskets and pistols to the front, pike-men following. Keep together, for I'll take the boot to laggards: advance when you hear the shot," and I took one of my two pistols and fired it into the air.

The signal had a strangely calming effect: where before there were drunken shouts and threats, the men quietened into a low, threatening murmuring; now there was no other sound but tramping boots.

"Forward! On to Newport!"

They marched in a squelching of wet clothes and leather, and the rain sheeted down. William Jones, having arrived at a gallop on a fine gray mare, now led his horse, and marched beside me; a self-appointed liaison officer moving between the columns. I asked:

"What is happening at Zephaniah's?"

Jones wiped water from his face. "His men collected at the ale-house this morning; hundreds arrived yesterday afternoon."

"Yes, but are they marching?"

"Zephaniah assured me that he would meet you with his army at the Welch Oak Inn at Risca — he will be there."

"And your column, Jones?"

"It will reach Malpas by nine o'clock tonight, then we, too, will be in Risca three hours later."

"At midnight, remember!"

"In the name of God how many more times? Don't you trust anyone?" he asked.

No, in the name of God, I did not trust him. For this, as I mentioned before, could be the actor playing his role: this the failed Thespian, more proficient in the boudoir than any dramatic performance save Harlequin: verbosity was his essence, and, I suspected, cowardice his star, if the pantomime of this enterprise changed to tragedy. For tragedy would come at the end of it — I knew this suddenly and with stunning force . . .

With the firing of that pistol shot, the logicality of my situation had come home to me. Whereas, earlier, the wan faces of the three prostitutes of Nantyglo had risen before me out of the rain . . . they were now replaced by the faces of my lost children: Mary's tears as she said goodbye were suddenly a scald to my face. Now I wondered if I would ever see my loved ones again, and could have wept at the threat of such a loss. Too late my predicament had formed its true perspective. But, all such boats had been burned now. I had to go through with it. Jones was peering at me. "You all right?" he asked.

"Perfectly," I said. "Don't hang around here! Get away to Pontypool and see to your column. I want at least six thousand men in Newport by two o'clock in the morning, or I'll want to know why."

He mounted and rode off with a glance of surly contempt, and I stood on a *twmpath* and watched as the ragged, ill-kempt army of rain-swept and already dispirited men marched past me.

They came from the employ of iron-masters like the skinflint Guests of Dowlais; of William Crawshay, lord of Cyfarthfa, the 'place of barking dogs'. From the ironworks of old Sam Homfray and Crawshay Bailey they came; employers, all, of countless hungry children who laboured on coal tips in all weathers or delved for them a hundred feet down in the black dungeons of the earth.

Many, I saw marching past me, had the mark of the dandy-fires upon their cheeks — sores grown cancerous from exposure to heat: others who blinked away the tears of rain, had red-rimmed eyes that spoke of coming blindness, the puddlers' disease. Old men were there; a few I knew were veterans of the French wars — one at least had fought at Waterloo. Now he marched with military precision, his musket shouldered as he had been taught . . . and a little removed in pride from the others. Some were mere children; boys with fresh faces yet uncontaminated by iron or coal. Many there were with bandaged faces or hands wrapped in grimy rags; one I hadn't seen before had a wooden leg. And he raised a fist at me as he went by.

"Ho-ho, there, gaffer! Good day, Mayor Frost!"

I removed my broad-rimmed hat, beat the rain from my shoulders with it, and stood bare-headed. And they straightened

506

their bearing, seeing this as they marched.

Outside Abercarn a lad approached me, saying, "May I walk with you, Mayor Frost?"

"Of course."

"So I can tell my father that I walked with our Chartist leader . . . " He added, "You met him once — Samuel Shell — he formed the Ponty branch of the W.M.A. last winter."

"Ah, yes — did he not remove to Bristol?"

"Yes, sir, for trade was bad here. He took with the Dowlais Guests as a labourer, but debt got us at the Company Shop. 'So we're away to Bristol,' said my da, 'to make another start. And at Bristol I will march for Chartism, as you, my son, will march in Gwent' — he would never call it Monmouthshire!" He laughed.

The rain swept into us in gusty billows. His thin, eager face looked into mine. "We will win the Charter, sir?"

I gave him a smile. "God willing, by this time tomorrow."

"Or die doing it, eh!"

He could not have known that he was forecasting his own death. George Shell, whom they later found in the hall of the

Westgate, within a yard of the soldiers.

I led them along the mountain road down into the valley; and then, restricted, we took to the mountain tracks, which meant single file marching.

Here was no cover; where once the valley was clothed in luxuriant forestry, the mounds and lowering hills were like squatting men with pudding-basin haircuts. Once, in this paradise, primitive man had hunted, built rock caves, made fires, raised his families. Needing charcoal for his little iron bloomeries, he had forged his arrow-heads for the death of the sabre-toothed tiger, the bear and the antelope, and stripped the hills and valleys. Now, over this barren land there swept a lunar coldness; a wind of icy fingers that attacked us, and it rained.

It rained, but did not rain; it tub-washed, it sprayed splashing buckets from the clouds, and flooded the brooks; it sent the streams cascading across the sodden tracks where we picked our way: it burst from the wounds and crevices of the hills in volumes of white blood that poured in torrents down into the valley, and soon we were wading calf deep, losing boots and shoes in the sucking apparatus of peat and vetch grass.

I looked over my shoulder, seeing an army of groaning, cursing men floundering about in waving arms; prodding with their pikes to break the vacuum of mud and water that sucked them down.

Napoleon, I thought, miscalculated the weather in his advance on Moscow. Would history now record the stupidity of Chartist leaders who had made the same mistake?

Near midnight, with an opal moon spying down upon us from a rent in black clouds, we arrived, soaked and nearly exhausted, at the rendezvous we had planned with Zephaniah, which was at a place called the Welch Oak, a beer-house on the road from Risca.

Instantly the columns thinned; here was ale, warmth and a friendly landlord, and the captains could not hold the men. Bulging to the doors, the rooms were crammed with shivering miners who hammered the counters for ale, and washed away their misery with pewters and hot pokers.

I could not deny them this; indeed, I doubt if they would have obeyed me.

Seeking to show an example, I found a lonely rock outcrop and, resting out of the wind, opened my pack of bread and cheese prepared by Mary.

On the other side of the rock, speaking quietly, were two men; one was young, the other old.

The old one said, "Why are you fighting, lad?"

"Why are you?"

"For my children, to get them out of iron."

"Where you from, then?"

"From Nanty, same place as you, boyo, for everybody there knows the Mortymers. You did that Afron Madoc pretty well, remember?"

The young man did not answer, and the older one continued, "Two of his teeth my mate picked up on the tram-road and wore them on his watch-chain. *Diawch!*" And he slapped his thigh, whispering ironic laughter.

"Is Madoc here today?" asked the lad.

"Not likely, for he's six foot under, and I put him there. I had him before I left, ye understand? An eye for an eye, the Good Book says, and I had him for killing my girl. Ten years old, she was, and pretty, till he took her underground at the Garn — working at the face, mind, filling trams, and the roof came down and took her legs to the thigh. But I had all of Afron Madoc. I had him under ten tons at Llangattock quarry, but he died too quick for decency."

"Do not talk so loud," said the boy, and looked around, and I lowered my head below the rock. "And now?" he asked.

"Now I am fighting for the others, for my wife bore me nine. Three of them are working under the Coity, four in Crawshay Bailey's iron. It is a stink, Isaac, and it must stop, said my wife, and us with a four-pound debt at the Company Shop, and we are decent Chapel people, mind. It is dying this, mun, said she, not living."

There was a silence, then the man added, "I asked you before — why are you fighting, lad?"

"For my son and against *Cwm Crachen*, the old ironworks in the Hollow of the Scab where he was born. Do not ask more, leave it at that."

They got up then and went down to the *Oak* public, and in a sudden flash of the moon I saw the young man's face.

By some strange chemistry of remembrance, I could have sworn I'd seen that face before.

I had plenty of time to consider this because we waited hours in the storm; first for our Sirhowy men, who, in turn, had been waiting for the men of Dowlais and Merthyr, they told me . . . and then hours more for the column of Zephaniah Williams. And by the time he arrived the storm was at its height. Following our fierce commands, the men came off the ale and out on to the road again.

"Christ Almighty," said Zephaniah. "There are scores back there without a leg under them. What a bloody army!"

Now we marched side by side, Zeph and me, and the men behind broke into drunken, brawling songs: but some were there who sang sober, and two were the Lovells, Jack and John, of these one lived and one died: as I write this I can see and hear him, beating his fists in his blood on the cobbles of Skinner Street, and his voice was clear and strong as he shouted for the Charter.

Later, with Rees the Fifer at our head,

and Walters, Benfield and Jenkin Morgan behind him, we marched with a new spirit, for the dawn was raking the eastern sky. I asked Zeph:

"Where the hell has that William Jones got to?"

"He will be awaiting us at Pye Corner."

"The rendezvous was the Welch Oak!"

"One tavern's as good as another to Jones, and there's a few between here and Tredegar Park."

I looked at his face so firm and strong; the rain was flying off his broad-rimmed hat and running down his body in icy streams, he said, but he showed no sign of discomfort.

"And Dr Price? His was a big mouth for fleshing daggers into the aristocracy!" I complained.

"Perhaps he will arrive with the rest of the Merthyr men," and Zeph shouted above the wind, "Are all the Merthyr boys here, Lovell?"

"Every man jack — about two of the buggers," came the reply. "If I get out o' this alive, Zeph Williams, I'm giving a few of those a bloody outing. What the hell happened to the Crawshay mob?"

"What the hell has happened to these apologies for Welshmen?" yelled another. "They promised us ten thousand here, and I doubt if there's five."

The fife was playing merrily; the wind lashed us with needles of sleet; thunder rolled and reverberated, forked lightning flashed in astonishing brightness, splitting the world.

I cried to Zephaniah in a lull, "Five thousand here, you think?" And he looked over his shoulder.

"More like seven, I'd say, but half are carrying gin and home brew." I replied, wiping water from my eyes:

"We should have banned the taverns and locked the publics!"

"There's a lot of things we should have done," said Zephaniah. "We should have stripped Sam Etheridge's printing place, for a start."

"Why, what has happened?"

"Don't tell me you haven't heard! Last night Partridge sent a message. Mayor Phillips has confiscated papers from Etheridge's office . . . "

"And our plans for the attack?"

"Still in his office drawers. Perhaps I

514

trusted Dr Price, Frost, but you trusted Etheridge. Christ, I thought you knew — I sent word on, man!"

I bowed my head against the rain, saying, "If this is true, the Redcoats will be awaiting us in Newport."

Someone shouted, "Hold hard there! Hold it, I say!"

A horse and rider came galloping out of the rain. Zephaniah said, "At last, this will be Jones!" And he cupped his hands to his mouth, crying, "Where the devil did you get to — we waited hours for you at Risca!"

But it was not William Jones. The man, clearly a military courier, dismounted.

"Mr Frost?" he looked from one to the other.

"I am Frost," I said, and he stood to attention.

"A message from the Newport Chartists, sir," and he held up the lanthorn he was carrying, so I could better see his face. "I am a deserter from the 29th Regiment; the main body of our men have been sent to Pontypool and Abergavenny; some, but only a few, are in the workhouse up on Stow Hill . . ."

515

"Who are you and why do you tell me this?" I interjected.

"I am a fighter for the Charter, like you, sir. Under our officers we are treated more like pigs than men. Strike now at Newport and you will win the day. Delay the attack, and new soldiers will be in the town." He looked about him. "You don't trust me?"

"No," said Zephaniah.

The man said, "Examine my horse, stolen from an officer — look, his initials are branded upon the saddle: see, my papers," and he took them out of his pocket.

"True, the 29th Foot," said Zephaniah, examining them.

I asked the man, "How do you know that I intend to attack Newport?"

"Because Chartist prisoners are already being held in the Westgate Hotel; because Mayor Phillips has the Etheridge papers, I heard him say."

"You, a foot soldier, heard the mayor say that?" asked Jack Lovell now, joining us.

"I heard him, I tell you. I was in the Westgate Hotel parlour."

"The name of your officer?"

"Lieutenant Gray, but this is not his horse." He glared at our intent faces. "Believe me, or shoot me, as you wish. I am prepared to die for the Charter."

"You'll die, right enough," said Lovell, "if there are soldiers in the Westgate." He added, "I say take it from the back, and send some of us up Commercial Street."

Nobody answered.

"Go now," I commanded the man. "Go to Malpas and ride hard. Try to find William Jones's contingent — tell him, if you do, that we are marching on to Cwrt-y-Bella and that we'll meet him at the weighing machine."

"The weighing machine? At Cwrt-y-Bella?"

"You do not know it?" asked Lovell.

"I do not. I am a soldier and new to these parts."

"Go, now and find it, for it is important," I said, and he remounted and galloped away.

"You trust him?" asked Benfield, loitering near. "He had no military bearing. Never in this world is he a soldier!"

"He could be an *agent provocateur*," said Zephaniah.

"What's that?" asked Jack Lovell.

I did not reply. "You took a chance, didn't you?" said someone.

"Everything we do from now on is taking chances," said Zephaniah.

# 35

A FEW miles on, sheltering under trees, we again waited in wet misery; soaked, disgruntled men and boys with liquefied black pudding in their shot-firing tins instead of gunpowder, for the rain had got everywhere.

Sitting on the berms of the roadside, their faces averted to the sweeping rain, they pulled off their boots and showed me their chafes and blisters; some of their footwear, after years of the muddy oil of furnace compounds and pits, had now so disintegrated in the rain that it was better to hang them around your neck and walk barefooted; some, I noticed, were even throwing them away . . . and I thought of the ragged, bare-footed army that attacked the Bastille.

"How much longer, Mayor Frost?" one asked.

"A mile or two, mun."

"Then why don't we bloody do it, sir, instead of sitting round by 'ere?"

"Because we are awaiting Jones and his men of Pontypool."

"O, aye? Wait for that bugger?" The man spat obscenely. "We'll still be here on our arses a week next Monday."

The discipline, the respect in which they held me, was becoming diluted in this conflict with the weather.

I added, "And Dr Price of Merthyr — we also wait for him."

"That mad sod?" There was a chorus of groans and shouts, and they gathered aggressively about me on the road.

Zephaniah interjected, "Aye, but that mad sod, as ye call him, is bringing seven pieces of cannon."

"I'll believe that when I bloody see it, Zeph!" cried one, a man with a scalded face and one eye missing. "I see'd the drawings for 'em in Furnace Two on Crawshay's land, mind, but when I left Merthyr they hadn't made the moulds. He be a long-haired old loony o' a fella, nothin' more."

"Now say that wi' your mouth, mister!" cried a boy, coming out of the group. "When my Boppa Blodwen fell in the mould and got an arm took off in the

520

fire, he did her proud, did old Dafto Price: trimmed the stump tidy while she was bloody lying there," and he turned up his face to mine. "But he won't be here to fight the soldiers, Mayor Frost."

"Why not?"

"Because I come from Pentrebach, and afore that Pontypridd. And I seen that old chap standing on the Rocking Stone — bollocko, mind ye — beggin' ye pardon for the language, sir — ay ay, bollock-naked, and praying to his ancestors on the moon . . . "

"Yes, yes," I interjected, "but why won't he come?"

"Because my Aunty Boppa Blod, she do work for him, see — in his kitchen on the odds and sods — and two days back, before I left Pentre, she saw the old lad dressed up as a tarty piece, with his long hair in a bun at the back of his neck, making off. 'Where you off to, me sweet doctor?' she asked. 'Is it your wedding day?' and he gives her a flick o' his whip and galloped like the hounds of hell." The boy searched my eyes. "Maybe Jones the Watchmaker'll come with the Ponty lads, but Mad Dr Price, you won't see him ag'in, nor his cannon, and nor his twenty thousand terrors from Merthyr."

Zephaniah said, "God help us, we learn this from a boy."

The child said, "I heard him tell 'em in Political Square, see — you want your nuts shot off, my lads, said he, you march on Newport with that mad John Frost."

There was a silence. The men stared at me with narrowed, questioning eyes; the rain and sleet swept into us with renewed fury.

I cried, "We'll see who's mad, then!" And threw up my arms for attention. "We've seven thousand here — enough to eat Newport. Forward, lads, forward!"

"Aye, forward!" shouted Zephaniah. "And for God's sake rank yourselves tidy. Now come on. Stop the bloody gas, and *come on*!"

We had planned to attack Newport at two o'clock in the morning, but it was nearer six when I was marching at their head along the tram-road in Tredegar Park called the 'Golden Mile'. The tolls paid to Sir Charles Morgan for this invasion of his property was £3000 a year — one income he'd lose when we took Newport.

Reaching the weighing machine at Cwrt-y-Bella, two boys came hurrahing along to greet us, for the rest of the population, we learned later, were either in beds or under them: but there was no fear of the Chartists in these two, they who were later to testify at my trial . . .

I asked, "You live here?"

One boy stood to attention; the other bowed. "In Corn Street, Mayor Frost."

We shivered together in the icy wind. I asked, "Have you seen any soldiers?"

"Ay ay, sir. Now just, we saw 'em — a dozen or so marching down Stow Hill: they went into the Westgate."

A man behind me said with a groan, "They can keep the bloody Westgate, son, what I want is a dry waistcoat." I asked again:

"No more than those?"

The other boy replied, "Yes, Mayor Frost. Some drinking in the publics, and some more billeted in the workhouse at the top of Stow Hill."

I nodded, calling out, "Soldiers in the Westgate and Stow Hill workhouse. But they will not trouble us — all of them are Chartists."

"I hope so," said Zephaniah, suddenly beside me, but then ran back down the line, berating his mud-spattered, soaked and exhausted mob: their banners calling for the Charter, I noticed, were trailing behind them in the mud.

"You heard what happened at Cefn?" asked one of the boys, running beside me, and the other cried:

"The Chartists took a meat pie out of a woman's oven. 'Hold on to this, missus,' they said, 'and before it cools ye can have it back, girl,' and they put in their tins of gunpowder to dry."

The men behind me heard and shouted dull laughter, passing it down the line.

"Cefn, did you say?" I asked. "Not on this march."

"Malpas, ye bloody nut," said the other boy.

"Malpas, or Cefn — it's important — make up your mind."

"Malpas, it were — your pa's uncle, he's with Jones the Watchmaker, ain't he?"

"Aye, he done told me," and I came out to the road berm, took them by the scruffs and shook them to rattle. "Are you saying that you've seen a column marching though Malpas?"

"Aye, sir!" They looked aggrieved. "We just come from there. 'Tis William Jones, arguing on the road with Mr Prothero, the Prizefighter . . . "

"The home of Prothero?" I asked.

"The same, sir. And we heard William Jones tell him straight, sir. Wavin' his sword, he were, and shouting, 'I'll have a flag a-waving on top o' Woollos Church or be hanged doin' it!'

" 'You'll be hanged if you do, mind,' the old chap told him."

I leaped up on to a tump and shouted, "Men, listen. We will win the day. Jones the Watchmaker and his men are at Malpas turnpike!" And I asked of the boys, "How many men, lads, how many you think?"

"Hell, stuff me, Mayor Frost! Bloody thousands. At the Cock Inn, in Cross-ye-legs, they got an old girl out o' the bath to cook them *cawl*, and they've been drinkin' the taverns dry between here and Pontypool!"

I shouted down the marching line. "Jones is coming with thousands! The day is won, lads, so gather from Croesyceiliog your spirits for the march on Newport!"

Ragged cheers went up and down the line; the banners lifted wearily. One of the boys, ragged and wan, asked:

"Will it be better for scrumpin' lads like us when you become the Queen, Mayor Frost?"

A few around me laughed, but some did not.

I took the boys' hands. One added, "Like eating proper, an' all that, and warm?"

I nodded. "If I have anything to do with it," and pointed at the sky, for a sudden glow of bright sunshine began to flood the land, flashing on the roofs of the approaching houses, warming the chill of the wind.

The storm was over. The rain ceased; our soaked clothes began to steam with body-heat, as if in contrition for the icy terror of the night.

For the first time in two days I began to think of my beloved Mary, for every step I took now was bringing her nearer. And the grubby small hands in mine as I marched, took me back to the years of my own young children.

"Dress yourselves tidy!" yelled Zephaniah far down the line. "You're coming into Newport, lads, and the people will be watching. Hold yourselves proud and go like soldiers!"

I heard the thud-thud-thud of marching boots.

We Chartists at last were moving head high, and with dignity.

William Jones and his army, I thought, might even be awaiting us in Westgate Square to take over the town.

It was euphoria: it was the light-headedness of anticipated power that other men had known, and which I was briefly glimpsing.

A form of madness.

Still at their head I cried in a lull, "Now lads, we'll show ourselves to the town!"

The roar that went up was deafening: with a pistol in my hand, I led them in brilliant sunshine past the gates of the Workhouse where the 49th Foot Regiment under Captain Stack was stationed. I expected some show of interest and even allowed for opposition if all the soldiers were not Chartists, but no trouble came: even the sentry on guard stood at ease as

RFAP35

we flooded past him with loud hurrahs, and some of the lads behind me called rough banter to him, and waved.

"Queer, mind, that he didn't wave back," commented Jack Lovell.

The time was eight o'clock; we were over six hours late.

Now the tramping of our boots was echoing past the turnpike at the top of Church Road, now called Stow Hill. Little clusters of people were watching from the raised footpath, showing little fear of us as we hurried by: some, probably Chartist followers actually joined in the Charter Song that the men were shouting hoarsely.

The labourer toils and strives the more
While tyrants are carousing.
But hark! I hear the lions roar,
Our British youth is rousing.
The rich are liable to pain,
The poor man feels the smart, sir.
So let us break the despot's chain,
We soon will have the Charter!

Outside the Mayor's House, I wheeled the column about, guns to the front, pikes to the rear, as always. I could hear Benfield, Waters and their men breaking down the wicket gate at the back of the Westgate, and cried, now in the Square:

"Show yourself to the front, lads. For this will be our headquarters. Prisoners have been taken — our Chartist brothers — into the hotel and release them!" And I was nearly knocked off my feet in their mad rush for the front door of the Westgate.

Glass shattered in a breaking of windows: within the main body of the attackers, I saw the main door slam and the hatchets go splintering into the woodwork. From comparative peace there arose a clamour that grew in volume and fury, and I heard Jack Lovell's bass voice shout:

"Give up your Chartist prisoners! We are here to release the prisoners!" and for reply:

"No, never!"

This was accompanied by explosions from within the building: had Benfield, I wondered, managed to penetrate in from the stables? Meanwhile, I was crushed and hemmed in by the shoulders of furious men; swearing, cursing men struggling to rise up the Westgate steps: all was a forest of mandrels, pikes and waving swords as those behind shoved forward, and those in front shoved back for room to swing the hatchets.

"In, men, in!" Again, it was Lovell's voice, and the men carried me forward in a surge of strength that lifted me bodily off the steps.

"On, on — get into them, into them!" Now Jack Rees, the captain, not the fifer, well to the front, as always. And I saw the hotel door suddenly crash back upon its hinges as the black wedge of struggling, gasping men swept forward into the Westgate hall. David the Tinker, the fifer's friend was beside me, his face split in a grin of determination. Where is he now, I wonder, this man whom the fifer loved as a brother. "You all right, Mr Mayor?" cried he.

"If I can get forward," I shouted back.

"Then hang on to me and we'll have ye in the hall," and he bent from his great height so that I could grip his shoulders, and heaved me onward through the squabbling, fighting crush of men now infuriated by the slow progress.

He got me close to the shattered door

where our Chartists were spilling into the hall in a tangle of legs and arms. Here were spreadeagled men; men staggering along the ornate walls, muskets levelled, pikes held for the thrust. And the moment I reached the broken door, a great rush of bodies propelled us out again, tripping over the entrance steps. I lost my grip on the tinker and fell; instantly to be kicked and trodden upon in a mêlée of boots: and I saw in the moment before falling, a baton come crashing down on my friend's head. Unconscious, he lay bleeding: now lying beside him, under the hacking boots and incredible softness of bodies struggling to be free, I heard a staccato volley of musket shots come from the Westgate hall. Again, again; now shrieks; a slamming of doors, and the muskets roared anew. I was nearly upright when I was flung headlong again by retreating men who came floundering out of the Westgate hall; some were screaming, many clutching at wounds, and I covered my head with my hands, enduring the hammering boots that used me as a sack to hasten their escape.

Now, rolling sideways, I saw a new mob of men coming up behind me with pistols, swords and mandrels for the next attack. Yelling for the Charter, they came gloriously into the fire of the redcoats, for the window shutters had gone crashing back, exposing the soldiers. I saw their scarlet coats clearly; some were kneeling, others standing above them to get enfiladed point-blank fire into the ranks of the mob. As one rank exploded in flame and smoke, so fired the others while their comrades reloaded with the calm of a Sunday School outing. And my men wilted to the smack of the musket balls, flung up their arms and died, or slowly sank down to the boots of others. It was the age-old story of fanatical courage against the methodical precision of trained men under cover. Again detonated the muskets; again, again: men expired in shrieks and groans . . . some rising with bloodstained faces to bellow the Charter call, before sinking out of sight.

Twenty-two dead lay in crumpled heaps over the Westgate Square; a score more, many who would die later, were feebly moving shattered limbs. And there arose from these the mutilated groans of their iniuries. Others, who had been dragged away to safety by their comrades, told of their passage in trickles and gouts of blood: more still fled, like me, in wild disorder.

The sight of blood has never sickened me: during the blood-stained bull baitings, my sole emotion has been that of compassion; so it was now.

With my life dedicated to the succouring of the poor, I now saw these helpless ones crying piteously in the agony of their hurt . . . and could do nothing for them. And now, propelled along the cobbles of the square by a rush of retreating Chartists, I was stepping over the convulsing limbs of those whom I called comrades: seeing me, they raised hands to me; some begged, entreating help from a leader who was deserting them.

To pause for a moment would be to fall and be trampled by an army fleeing in wild confusion; and within the daze of my own shock and pain, I, too, obeyed the herd instinct, and left them where they had fallen. With the muskets of the red-coats crashing behind us, self-preservation was the first law.

I do not remember how I got into Tredegar

Park, leaving behind the main body of our defeated Chartists, who, meeting William Jones and his column on the march from Malpas — too late to serve the Cause — advised him to retreat as well; and this he did in the face of the Westgate holocaust: up to six thousand men of Pontypool and its vicinity, turned tail and fled in the face of graphic stories of massed killings of Chartists in batches, of brutal interrogation, of torture by hordes of drunken English soldiers; these rumours grew with every moment into banal ferocity.

The day was lost, and so was I: amid the lush grounds of the park, within sight of the noble pile of Tredegar, I wandered aimlessly.

There was a line of stationary trams in a siding on the Golden Mile, and I climbed into one, contemplating the astonishing purity of a now sunlit morning; the whiteness of the drifting clouds, the azure beauty of the sky. This serene loveliness, I thought, so contrasted the icy downpourings and bitter enmity of the night that it was impossible to discount the Deity's planned hostility.

So could it be, I wondered, in the

face of such proof — the mutilation of young men, the starvings of the old, the outrages against our children, the squalor, filth and diseases perpetrated by men in power . . . could it be that all I believed in must come to naught by the command of an omnipotent God, who, by dint of irreducible proof right down the ages, had condoned the acts of evil men and heated the fires below the feet of martyrs? Already the *Merlin* and a score of other gentry mouths would be trumpeting the claim of Divine Providence over the forces of evil in this conflict. Soon the churches and chapels would be crammed with ethical disbelievers singing praise and thanks to one who had set back Man's progression to a civilized society by a century and more.

I took from my pocket one of my pistols: history later recorded that I carried three, but it was only two . . . I held it before my eyes, balled and primed it, but the powder, as well, was damp in the flask.

It was a bitter realization. I could not even kill myself.

Recrimination and self-loathing for my

cowardice in the face of the enemy now swept over me in waves of increasing intensity. It was like a decomposing of the soul, a putrefying of the body.

I who had indicted Dr Price for fleeing was now a prime culprit. History, written as usual by the learned competents of the ruling classes — charlatans all — would now possess at least one truthful statement — John Frost's timidity . . . the man of poltroonery, funk and baseness who had led his thousands into death or imprison-ent; the chicken-hearted Frost; Frost the milksop; the dunghill cockerel of the spouting beak, whose arse was white feathers.

I tortured myself: never in my life, even in earlier depths of despair, have I known such a sense of debasement.

I decided to give myself up; by delivering my body to my enemies for punishment I might escape some measure of this guilt, and in doing so, expiate my crime.

To this end I began to walk back to Gold Tops, which soon I could see glowing in sunlight, the ancient trees near my home. There I would beg Mary's forgiveness and take my leave of the children.

On that walk in the direction of Newport many men passed me; tattered men; many clutching wounds, all staggering in the final stages of hurt and weariness, and I braced myself as I saw the first of them . . . for the curse or even the blow. But this did not happen. Seeing me coming, just as men meeting on a Sunday walk, they raised their arms to me in greeting.

"Hi-ho, Mayor Frost!"

"Turn about, sir, you're going the wrong way!"

"Are ye hurt, Mr Mayor?" They gathered about me, delaying their flight to assure themselves of my good health.

"But we shall rise again, eh? That's the bloody ticket!"

"They had us this time, but just them bloody wait!" I met them in groups, sometimes two arming along a wounded comrade, and from all, without exception, I received the same cheerful banter.

"Mind you, mister, my missus'll give me hell!"

"Mine played Hamlet about going on this caper with you, John Frost!"

Even their fine humour, raised for my comfort, only added to my personal degradation.

But we shall rise again, eh? I thought. *God Almighty!*

Reaching my house I prepared to enter it at the back, but then saw the figure of John Partridge in his window, so changed my mind and knocked upon his door; his property's back garden was linked with mine.

Instantly the door swung open, he gripped my arm, pulled me within the little hall and slammed shut the door.

"God in Heaven, Frosty — what you doing here?"

I said, "I've come to say goodbye to Mary — I happened to see you first."

"They're after you — you know that?"

I nodded. He added:

"They've been here twice and they'll come again, they said. These bloody special constables — just dying to break heads. Have you heard about Zeph?"

"Zephaniah? No."

"Faded clear away. You know him. He probably had the bolt-hole weeks ago. And

William Jones and his lot?"

"Going like demented lemmings for the hills!"

And he said suddenly, with fearful emphasis, "My God, when I get my hands on Old Sam ... !"

"He left the plans about, you mean?"

"More than that. He waited to see which way the wind was blowing; once it was physical force, the bugger was up on the fence."

"But he didn't purposely betray us — Sam wasn't up to that."

"Perhaps not, but I can't tolerate a man who changes his coat."

I sat down at his table with a sigh. "He won't be the last, Partridge. There'll be a few turning Queen's Evidence before this lot is sorted out. Got a drink of something?"

"Oh, Christ, Mr Mayor, I'm sorry." He put the kettle on the fire. "I'll get my missus down to make ye some breakfast — she's upstairs under the bed."

"Leave her, lad, I'm too sick to eat."

"I'll get you a hot drink then — Jesus, you look terrible."

I said, "I'm worse than I look. God help

me, in the square I counted twenty-two dead. I expect Prothero's dancing with delight."

"Thomas Phillips caught it, you know . . ."

"The Mayor?"

"Aye, the fool came out of the hotel to read the Riot Act — about five minutes before the lads came down Stow. He got it in the thigh, and they say his left arm's nearly off." He went on, "Rumour has it that there's over forty dead, but you know what they are, and not a soldier touched, they say."

"Trained men under cover. We didn't have a chance."

"God beat us, mun, not the bloody soldiers."

The kettle was in tears on the hob; the tea died to the scald, and I had just got my half-frozen hands around the heat of the cup when the door nearly went down to baton hammering.

"They're here," said Partridge, and opened the door.

The first special constable in the room was the clerk to the magistrates: he had come, he said, to search the Partridge house for papers, and was clearly astonished to see me, crying to his fellows in the garden:

"Look lively in here, men; we've come to see Partridge and found Mother Goose!" To me, he said:

"John Frost?"

I got up from the table. Resistance was useless.

Searching me, they took the two pistols, ball and powder flask. I stood silently under their hands; in some strange and grievous manner, I knew a sense of calm: the adventure might now be in the hands of Beelzebub, but at least it was ended, if the retribution was yet to come. John Partridge said, and I'll always remember it:

"I am sorry it was in my house, Mr Mayor."

The man searching me said, "Five minutes more and it would have happened in your house, anyway, Frost. We've just come from there."

"After papers, and we've got a few that'll hang you," enjoined another.

I said, "Papers are not people, constables. I make one request of you, and one only. Let me see my wife and children."

"Do you think we're daft? And me clerk

541

to the magistrates?"

"Please. I beg you. Just one minute." Another answered:

"Oh aye? Bloody listen to it! More'n his life's worth, mun."

Partridge said, his hands together, "A moment ago his wife was at the window. If there's any humanity in you . . . "

They put the manacles on my wrists and took me out the back way, so I would not even see Mary standing at the window.

It was seventeen years before I saw her again.

# 36

CHAINED to the arm of a chair in the public room of the Westgate, I looked around at the shambles of the place I knew so well; such was the activity of redcoats and constables that, after the initial surprise accorded to my arrival, few appeared to notice my presence.

The floor was littered with weapons and slippery with blood; just three yards further, I thought, and the lads would have gained the day, but this is where the soldiers had stopped them — in the confined passage to the hall from which there was no escape.

Away from me, beneath the shattered window that faced the square, lay Thomas Phillips, my old enemy, Prothero's partner in financial crime: some Mr Mayor, I thought, yet to his credit he had conducted himself bravely: now he was on his back and gasping with pain as the surgeon prodded him for the ball. He'd be lucky, I thought, to save that arm, for it was spouting blood, and Phillips turned his bloodstained face to mine, and said through gritted teeth:

"By God, Frost, you'll pay for this day!"

Shouts of pain and groans were rising in a devil's chorus from the courtyard behind me, and I rose and looked into it from the back window, which was wide open to give Phillips air, and I saw my lads lying there with terrifying clarity . . . the dead lying silently together, side by side in mute convocation and sightless eyes, the ragged horror of their wounds full testimony to the raking fire. And it seemed to me, since some propped up against the walls were facing me, that they were indicting me for the manner of their dying . . . in the full flush of youth; their eyes seemed to follow my every move.

In the middle of the cobbles two surgeons were operating, and the men under their hands, their blood-soaked clothing cut away, were shrieking like women being mutilated under the knives. Others, the walking wounded, turned their faces from the English helpers with contemptuous disregard. But one I particularly noticed — a lad of about twenty, his features constantly obliterated by the disorganized crush in the courtyard. A sergeant redcoat gripped the youngster as he passed, I noticed, and cried:

"Hey, you — your name?"

The shrieks of the men under the knives momentarily rose shrilly, but I clearly heard the reply:

"Iestyn Mortymer."

"A Chartist, eh? We'll give you Chartist. You'll dance for eighteen bloody months when we get you to Monmouth," and then he added, "You're wounded . . . ?" And turned again, bawling, "This man's arm is broken Hey you!" And it was broad, broad Lancashire. "Drop that musket and break me a pike for a splint!"

The sergeant slit the sleeve, tied the splint and bandaged it. But the young man, in thought, did not appear to be there: it was as if his body was in the yard of the Westgate, but his soul was elsewhere. Muttering gruff service to an enemy, the Englishman turned to help another, but the lad was still stood motionless, staring above the wall of the yard towards the distant hills beyond, and then he turned, and I recognized the boy I had seen on the march, he whose son had been born in the old ironworks, Cwm Crachen, the Hollow of the Scab.

Earlier, I had heard my name shouted, and came closer to the window. A man right under the sill said, "Where's John Frost in this bloody lot?"

"John Frost, John Frost — all is not lost?" And they cat-called and whistled, and I did not blame them. A man yelled:

"Goin' like a rabbit for Tredegar Park, I heard. Dodging the gentry's keepers and playing touch-me-last!"

"Thank God for such a leader!"

"No wonder he's bloody English!"

"English? Don't be daft, mun, he's as Welsh as us!"

A man sagging on the ground, cried, "And Zephaniah's Welsh an' all, ye boobs. Don't blame the nationality for we're big enough fools as it is," and an Irish voice shouted:

"To say naught of William bloody Jones — where's he this mornin'?"

The stable gates swung back and more prisoners came barging in, a few falling, thrust from behind and battered by redcoat muskets.

I saw in their gray, expressionless faces the tragedy of my pathetic leadership, and my appalling inefficiency in not considering the weather . . . Then I heard a man say, "Christ, they'll bring back the stake to tame us, these English, with burning too good for us — to put other rebellions down. They'll hit the country so hard that she won't stand straight for another thousand years. By Christ, I'd give me life to lay hands on that bloody John Frost!" And a man whose son was dying, turned his face to the sky and cried aloud, "Oh God, pity me, oh God, pity me?" And he wept.

Some dropped to their knees, their hands over their faces; some lay in attitudes of total exhaustion, instantly asleep despite the booting of the soldiers.

The wounded were calling for water; the men in the hands of the operating surgeons were still writhing to the bone-saw amputations; stretchers and hurdles came, brought by six redcoats hurrying down from the Workhouse. I'll say one thing for the English: they brutalize war with their demon-like aggression and unpitying mutilations, but they usually succour the defeated. But not this one, the commanding officer: thick and swarthy was he, hands on hips as he wandered among the wounded, and "Get these damned ruffians out of here quick!"

"Officer," cried a man with a battered face, "Officer, my son is over by there, and dying. For God's sake let me to him?"

A soldier said with furious disregard, "He pulled me off him, sir, and billocked me one," and he dismally felt his eye.

"Then he will stay where he is," said the lieutenant. "Let nobody near the wounded, understand? By God, we'll teach these bloody Welsh a lesson!" And the father of the boy said, with tears upon his face: *"O, fy mab, fy machgen, fy machgen bach dewr!"*

I bowed my head at the window, trying to obliterate the crying wounded, the blood.

Now, sitting in a farm cart of doubtful odour, with a burly special constable either side of me and a troop of four dragoons following behind, I took the road to

Monmouth, and prison.

My companions were little luckier; William Jones the Watch-maker was caught hiding in a wood near Crumlin, after brief resistance; they found upon him a copy of Hugh Williams' *Horn of Liberty*. Zephaniah fared no better: at large for three weeks, he was betrayed, and arrested aboard a ship bound for Portugal. Many, like David the Tinker, escaped, but others died who were not recorded, spirited away with their wounds to lonely places; thus the true total of the dead and wounded will never be known. Dr Price of Merthyr, dressed as a woman, took ship to Liverpool and escaped to Paris, but there was no escape for one as guilty as me.

High above me a kestrel was soaring in the vaporous blue, a harbinger of the freedom that I, and a hundred others, was soon to lose.

Here, in summer when I walked these roads with Mary, one heard the felicitous protestations of the redbreast amid the languorous blooms of convolvulous; here little streams bubbled their merriment down to snowy waterfalls, where in spring-time flowered a wilderness of blossom. But now the music of my lost summers died in the grating of iron-shod wheels and the clopping of the big shire horse.

Earlier, when leaving Newport for what might be the last time, I saw the townsfolk lining the pavements, silent; clutching the day with some unknown, inner anxiety . . . and a few raised their hands to me as I went past in my shame, head bowed, manacled.

And, by some strange chemistry of the heart, I thought I saw a girl I knew standing among the spectators in the place where Jack Lovell died: all in white was she, as had been dressed the girl so many years back on the morn of *Calan Mai*, one whose name was Mary; and by some quirk of sun and disposition, when she put her parasol back, she inclined her head, and winked. But, when I looked again, she was not there . . .

The cartwheels ground along the cobbles.

Is my country dead now? I wondered. Will Welshmen ever understand the spirit of the age that made our heroes intrepid in war and fearless? Did they know enough of ancient times to learn of Cattraeth — here our lovers were slaughtered to a man, but only under mead and the stupidities of brave Cadwallon. Will our young ones, now under England's wilful domination, find foreign princes to replace our lost tribes? For we, down the ancient years, have spawned magnificent Welshmen — a royal line of kings, from Cunedda to Iago and Rhun to Maelgwn. Is all this lost on the rush of my generation's tears and the yoke of a foreign power? Has the soul of my beloved country died in the clutch of a neighbour's greed and exploitation? In all our past centuries, from Glamorgan to Gwynedd, ours has been a rage of slaughter by our warring princes of red-stained men who have come for booty, and been driven from our shores.

Now this.

All our Welsh banners are trailing in the dust.

And as the cart ground onward to the prison walls of Monmouth I seemed to hear another voice within me, and this was Mary's.

"Make in me a little one, John . . . flesh of your flesh, heart of your heart . . . " When she was young and twenty, and I was lithe and supple and free . . . now so many years ago that I nearly forget. "Here, John, touch my breast . . . and make in me a little one?"

Faintly on the wind as we neared the gaol of Monmouth where died our forebears of rebellion, the brave Jacobeans, I heard another sound coming faintly on the wind that rippled the river under Monmouth Bridge the scene of other tragedies . . . the sound, jangled and discordant, of men singing in chorus.

In the middle of the cell I stood, listening as the door slammed behind me: and clearly heard their voices.

For ages deep wrongs have been hopelessly borne;
But despair shall no longer our spirits dismay,
Nor wither the arm when upraised for the fray;
The conflict for freedom is gathering nigh.
We live to secure it, or gloriously die!

# Epilogue

JOHN FROST was released on probation in Van Dieman's Land in November 1843. Working for several private employers in Hobart, he was granted 'ticket-of-leave' in 1846, and for the next eight years was a teacher, when he received a conditional pardon, which allowed him to leave the Convict colony, but not return to Britain. Sailing for America six months after the conditional pardon, he there lectured extensively on the horrors of convict life, with special emphasis on the unchecked spread of homosexuality, which, he claimed, the British Government of the time condoned. With a free pardon granted him in February 1857, and at the age of seventy-two, he returned to Britain, where a crowd of a thousand welcomed him in a flower-decked open carriage which it pulled through Newport's streets to the steps of the Westgate Hotel in triumph. With his revolutionary ideas apparently unchanged, John Frost, from the window of a hotel in Llanarth Street, then addressed the crowd, violently criticizing Parliament, the evils of the transportation system and the economic and social abuses still existing in Newport. A still greater demonstration of loyalty awaited him in London: *The Times* reported that more than 20,000 people followed his carriage in a procession through Cheapside to Fleet Street where it paused to burn a copy of the *Daily Telegraph* . . . and thence proceeded to Primrose Hill, where Frost publicly responded to an address by Ernest Jones, the Chartist poet.

Retiring to Stapleton, near Bristol (his wife dying but a year after his return) he died on 27th July 1877, aged ninety-three, always promising to write his autobiography, but not achieving it owing to failing eyesight.

He is buried in Horfield Parish Churchyard in Bristol, his grave being recently discovered and a stone raised upon it by members of Newport Local History Society; this was funded by Newport Borough Council.

# Further Reading

*The Last Rising* (The Newport Insurrection of 1839) D.J.V.Jones. Clarendon Press. Oxford.

*A Social and Economic History of England* (From 1700 to 1970) A.H.Stamp. Research Publishing Company.

*The Chartists* Peter Searby. Longmans.

*The Extraordinary Black Book* John Wade. Marchant.

*Two Lectures* (The Horrors of Convict Life) John Frost. British Museum

*Victorian Values* — William Lovett & Education Brian Harrison.

*The Trial of John Frost* (Shorthand by J. & T. Gurney) Saunders & Benning.

*Convicts and the Colonies* A. G. L. Shaw. Faber and Faber.

*Historic Newport* (Gwent) Newport Public Library.

*The Poor Law in Nineteenth-Century England* Anne Digby. Historical Assn.

*Port Arthur a Hundred Years Ago* (1842) David Burns; Tasmanian Journal. Oldham, Beddome & Meredith Pty Ltd

*Letter First* (A Lecture to the People of the United States) John Frost. Newport Public Library.

*A Letter to Thomas Prothero* John Frost. Samuel Etheridge, printer.

*Letter to Feargus O'Connor* John Frost (manuscript)

*Letter To Dr A. McKecknie* Zephaniah Williams (manuscript)

*Letter to Mr Morgan Williams* John Frost (manuscript)

*Handbills and Declarations* — Newport Public Library.

*Letter to His Wife* from Tasmania. Zephaniah Williams. Newport Public Library.

*Letter to his Wife* from Tasmania. John Frost. Newport Public Library.

*A Hundred Famous Australian Lives* Paul Hamlyn. State Library Service of Western Australia.

*Governor Arthur's Convict System*, Van Dieman's Land 1824–36. A study in Colonization W. D. Forsyth. Sydney University Press.

*Port Arthur Historic Site — Management Plan* National Parks and Wildlife Service 1985.

*The Irish At Port Arthur.* A commemoration. Port Arthur Conservation & Development Project. National Parks and Wildlife Service, Tasmania.

*Richmond Gaol Historic Site* (Brief history of gaol) A leaflet.

*The Welchman. No. 1* (Cheap Government; Cheap Law; Cheap Religion) John Frost 1832. Newport Public Library.

*The English Prison Hulks* W. Branch Johnson. 1897. Phillimore.

*John Frost* David Williams. Cardiff University of Wales Press Board.

*Welsh Folk Customs* Trefor M. Owen. National Museum of Wales, 1939. Welsh Folk Museum. 1959.

*Other titles in the*
*Ulverscroft Large Print Series:*

## TO FIGHT THE WILD
### Rod Ansell and Rachel Percy

Lost in uncharted Australian bush, Rod Ansell survived by hunting and trapping wild animals, improvising shelter and using all the bushman's skills he knew.

## COROMANDEL
### Pat Barr

India in the 1830s is a hot, uncomfortable place, where the East India Company still rules. Amelia and her new husband find themselves caught up in the animosities which seethe between the old order and the new.

## THE SMALL PARTY
### Lillian Beckwith

A frightening journey to safety begins for Ruth and her small party as their island is caught up in the dangers of armed insurrection.